Praise for Ag

'Agnes Owens' hallmarks have been a frank irony, a deadpan gothic quality and a down-to-earth insistence on the surreality of most people's normality.'
ALI SMITH

'I think of another literary hero, Agnes Owens. What if Agnes had been "granted" a proper chance to write when she was fighting to rear her family? . . . When she saw the squeak of a chance she grabbed it and produced those great stories we know. How much more could it have been?'
JAMES KELMAN

'Agnes Owens is the most unfairly neglected of all living Scottish authors. I don't know why.'
ALASDAIR GRAY

'Agnes Owens stuns her readers, as usual, with her good, blunt-weaponed clarity in *Bad Attitudes*.'
THE GUARDIAN

'Owens pulls no punches. her understated prose finds acerbic humour in the lives of characters hovering between farce and tragedy . . . Owens is a gift to the Scots urban world.'
OBSERVER

'Owens is a gentle writer with a slicing wit . . . honest and unaffected.'
SUNDAY TIMES

'Agnes Owens has a canny eye for tragi-comedy, a compassionate heart for the unfortunate, an acute ear for dialogue and a mind that clamps her characters like a steeltrap in the predicaments of passion, poverty and the patterns of their lives.'
FINANCIAL TIMES

'Like all Owens' fiction *Bad Attitudes* is as terse and grimly, comically deadpan as the best of Evelyn Waugh and Beryl Bainbridge.'

DAILY TELEGRAPH

'Agnes Owens has an appealingly wicked eye for familial love on the dole . . . reminiscent of Muriel Spark.'   SUNDAY HERALD

'These stories leave an echo. Their compassion lies in their honesty. Owens will not let us look away.'   THE HERALD on *People Like That*

'A remarkable book . . . funny and sinister'

BERYL BAINBRIDGE on *A Working Mother*

'Something in common with early Billy Connolly . . . in the sense that its observation and timing bring humour to a sad reality.'

NME on *Like Birds in the Wilderness*

'The best things in *Lean Tales* are the stories of Agnes Owens . . . she creates little dramas – rich gobbets of life.'   FINANCIAL TIMES

'Owens's reliance on the rhythm of ordinary speech is aggressively non-literary.'   LONDON REVIEW OF BOOKS on *Lean Tales*

'Strong, realistic and thoughtful'   MOIRA BURGESS

'A remarkable and idiosyncratic voice'   THE HERALD

'Accomplished and resonant and . . . always informed with a comic astringency'   THE SCOTSMAN on *Gentlemen of the West*

Agnes Owens

THE COMPLETE SHORT STORIES

Agnes Owens

Polygon

To all those who are interested

This collection published in Great Britain in 2008 by Polygon,
an imprint of Birlinn Ltd

West Newington House
10 Newington Road
Edinburgh
EH9 1QS

9 8 7 6 5 4 3 2

www.birlinn.co.uk

ISBN 10: 1 84697 059 8
ISBN 13: 978 1 84697 059 7

British Library Cataloguing-in-Publication Data
A catalogue record for this book is available on request from the British Library.

Typeset by Hewer Text (UK) Ltd, Edinburgh

Printed and bound by CPI Cox and Wyman, Reading

Contents

CONTENTS

Introduction

I've just read 'Arabella' again. And it had exactly the same effect on me as it did the first time I read it all those years ago. From the shift in the second sentence when it had me doing a double take, it began its work of filling me with a mounting, irresistible and exhilarating black glee. It shocked, amazed and delighted me. As it has every time I've read it – which is quite a few times, for I have never tired of it since I encountered it on the very same night I first met its author. In, oh, 1976 or maybe 1977? Here's how I remember that – which might not be exactly accurate, but is true to my memory at least.

'Get in, get out, don't linger' is Raymond Carver's famous good advice to the writer of short stories. This dictum would apply also to the tutor of the creative writing workshop – anything *in general* about writing one has to say that's of any value at all can be said in one or two classes. I don't know why Alasdair Gray and Jim Kelman and I were getting in, getting out, and sharing the job of tutoring that short course of evening classes in the late 1970s for beginning writers in Alexandria; was it run by the libraries, or, as I seem to remember, the extramural department of Glasgow University? I suspect, though we were certainly doing it for the money (we were all three more or less broke at the time), we still couldn't bear to commit to a full twelve wintry weeks of 45 minutes-plus there and 45 minutes back, going down every Tuesday or Wednesday or whatever night it was by blue train from Central to this wee back room in the exotically named Alexandria. (Vale of Leven, the place next door, sounded like something out of the Psalms and Paraphrases!) Anyway, far from being Egyptian, Alexandria was actually a pretty dreich and miserable wee rain-and-windswept town in the

West, so we agreed to four weeks each. Maybe the local writers had various skills to hone and had asked to have a poet and a short story writer and a novelist? At any rate, I did the first stint. At the end of the first evening, frankly, with the usual sinking feeling, I took away the wee pile of writings eagerly pressed upon me by most of the dozen or so men and women who had attended the class.

Among these was a single neatly typed piece of prose by Agnes Owens called 'Arabella'. (Agnes was working as a typist in a local factory at the time.) It began with what I'd soon know as her typical deadpan aplomb:

> Arabella pushed the pram up the steep path to her cottage. It was hard going since the four dogs inside were a considerable weight.

The *four dogs*. I sat up. The blue train rattled through the darkness, I read on and it was only a swift paragraph later when, taking in how Arabella had given her mother what she'd clearly meant to be a daughterly pat on the head, I learned that 'the response was a spittle which slid down her coat like a fast-moving snail'.

In case you've not read it yet – it opens this collection – I'm not about to spoil your fun by giving away what happens to Daddy, or with Murgatroyd or to the Sanitary Inspector, but Flannery O'Connor herself would, I think, have approved. (You know, the great Flannery O'Connor who deplores how 'most people seem to know what a story is till they sit down to write one', and is keen to remind us that what they forget is that it 'must be a complete dramatic action'.) That night on the train with 'Arabella', taken aback, I tried to put this terrifying, terribly funny story, so anarchic and archetypal, so short and so complete, together with the class I'd just left and that middle-aged lady in the neat coat and woolly hat with the fringe of dark blonde hair sticking out and the full mouth that turned so decisively down at the corners. A mouth she'd hardly opened except to say a couple of laconic and sensible things. (Creative writing workshops are generally very short of either sensible or brief remarks.)

I'd like to say I recognised Agnes's genius straight away but it's not quite true. In those days I didn't have very much confidence in my judgements (nowadays I have too much and tend to be far too dogmatic about what I do not like) and I remember a couple of days later showing 'Arabella' to Alasdair Gray, saying something like, 'Have I lost it altogether, or is this . . . I mean it's *wild* . . . but isn't it really rather good?' I remember him reading, very quickly and sitting very still, till he'd finished, and the gleam in his eye and the wee wince around his mouth when he looked up and said very quietly: 'Oh, yes.'

Alasdair and, a few weeks later, Jim really were the ones to help Agnes. (I remember her saying with not quite resentment but a baleful mock consternation, 'Jim has made me take out *all* my adverbs.' But I knew she knew he was right, otherwise she'd not have altered a word of it.) At the time, she was writing the stories that would eventually be published as *Gentlemen of the West*. Actually, I believe it was the class – she said later she only came to it because she was fed up – that made her *start* writing the stories about Mac and his cronies (although cronies is far too sentimental a way of putting it).

Gentlemen of the West is a kind of novel, because there is an overall progression of narrative towards a hopeful ending, the only hopeful ending – escape. I like though to enjoy these not as chapters but as discrete stories, particularly as the later ones, 'McCluskie's Oot', for instance, seem to take a quantum leap and show her coming into her own, refusing to be cute anymore. They are tough and realistic in the way all her mature work is, making you open your mouth and shut it again.

At the time, I think I read these stories, the early ones at least, as a kind of downbeat and depressed West of Scotland Damon Runyon, without the dollars or the dolls. (If you read Alasdair Gray's postscript, which is reprinted here on page 111, you'll see I was underestimating them.) I just found them very, very funny. Bleakly, blackly funny, my favourite kind. What I greatly admired was Agnes's nerve in ignoring the feminist imperative of the day to redress balances and dutifully record from the inside-out the female experience. Utterly convincingly, to my ears at least, she wrote with a throwaway bravura in the persona and from the point of view of a young male and it was thrilling you could do that. (Well, it wasn't as if Mac's voice had had much of a shot in fiction so far either.)

By the time of the publication of her first book I knew Agnes was a great and quirky original. Her sisters, if she had any at all, were . . . oh, Beryl Bainbridge, Molly Keane and Shena Mackay. But by the time I was reading 'Bus Queue', 'People Like That', 'When Shankland Comes', I was thinking Chekhov and Isaac Babel.

Every time I see Agnes – not often, not often enough – she seems utterly unchanged from my memory of the first time I saw her. She has had a hard life – see her rare autobiographical story (it'll take your breath away) 'Marching to the Highlands and into the Unknown' – and, like the not particularly sympathetically drawn Isobel Anderson in 'Meet the Author' (who 'can only write about failures'), publication for Agnes never led to her being transmuted to the ease of Artist Class. But she still looks middle-aged, not old, and her mouth still turns down humorously at the corners. Any of the quiet wee deadpan things she says are more than well worth listening to. One-to-one she is especially good company. She'd crack you up.

It is a great thing to have, at last, *The Complete Short Stories*. Opening with 'Arabella', including, hurrah, fourteen new ones in print for the first time and ending with the delicious 'The Dysfunctional Family'. Another one. But it strikes me that if Agnes Owens has a theme it's the *functioning* of families. It's never easy . . .

Liz Lochhead
February 2008

Arabella

Arabella pushed the pram up the steep path to her cottage. It was hard going since the four dogs inside were a considerable weight. She admonished one of them which was about to jump out. The dog thought better of it and sat down again. The others were sleeping, covered with her best coat, which was a mass of dog hairs; the children, as she preferred to call them, always came first with her. Most of her Social Security and the little extra she earned was spent on them. She was quite satisfied with her diet of black sweet tea and cold sliced porridge kept handy while her children dined on mince, liver and chops.

The recent call on her parents had been depressing. Loyal though she was, she had to admit they were poor company nowadays. Her bedridden father had pulled the sheet over his face when she had entered. Her mother had sat bent and tight-lipped over the fire, occasionally throwing on a lump of coal, while she tried to interest them in the latest gossip; but they never uttered a word except for the terse question 'When are you leaving?' – and the bunch of dandelions she had gathered was straightaway flung into the fire. Arabella had tried to make the best of things, giving her father a kiss on his lips before she left, but he was so cold he could have been dead. She had patted her mother on the head, but the response was a spittle which slid down her coat like a fast-moving snail.

Back inside her cottage she hung her hat on a peg and looked around with a certain amount of distaste. She had to admit the place was a mess compared to her mother's bare boards, but then her mother had no children to deal with. Attempting to tidy it up she swept a pile of bones and bits of porridge lying on the floor into a pail. Then she flung the contents on to a jungle of weeds outside her door. Good manure, she thought, and didn't she have the loveliest dandelions for miles.

'Children,' she called. 'Come and get your supper.'

The dogs jumped out of the pram, stretching and yawning nervously. One dragged itself around. It was the youngest and never felt well. Arabella's training methods were rigorous. This had been a difficult one at first, but the disobedience was soon curbed – though now it was always weak and had no appetite. The other three ate smartly with stealthy looks at Arabella. Her moods were unpredictable and often violent. However, she was tired out now from her chores and decided to rest. She lay down on top of a pile of coats on the bed, arranging her long black dress carefully – the dogs had a habit of sniffing up her clothes if given half a chance. Three dogs jumped up beside her and began to lick her face and whine. The one with no appetite abandoned its mince and crawled under the bed.

Arabella awoke with a start. Her freshened mind realised there was some matter hanging over it, to which she must give some thought. It was the letter she had received two days previously, which she could not read. Her parents had never seen the necessity for schooling and so far Arabella had managed quite well without it. Her reputation as a healer was undisputed and undiminished by the lack of education. In fact, she had a regular clientele of respectable gentlemen who called upon her from time to time to have their bodies relaxed by a special potion of cow dung, mashed snails or frogs, or whatever dead creature was handy. Strangely enough, she never had female callers. (Though once Nellie Watkins, desperate to get rid of the warts on her neck, had called on her to ask for a cure. Whatever transpired was hearsay, but the immediate outcome of it was that Nellie had poured the potion over Arabella, threatening to have her jailed. But she never did. Arabella's power was too strong.)

The councillor's son, who had been the caller on the evening after she received the letter, explained that it was from the Sanitary

Inspector and more or less stated that if she didn't get rid of her animals and clean her place up she would be put out of her home. Then he changed the subject since he knew it would be out of the question for Arabella to clean anything, that was one thing beyond her powers, saying, 'Now we have had our fun get me some water – that is if you use such a commodity. I know soap is not possible.' And while Arabella fetched the water lying handy in an empty soup tin on the sink, he took a swallow from a small bottle in his jacket pocket to pull himself together. Arabella did not like the tone of the letter. Plaintively she asked, 'What will I do, Murgatroyd?'

'That's your worry,' he replied, as he put on his trousers. 'Anyway the smell in this place makes me sick. I don't know what's worse – you or the smell.'

'Now, now, Murgatroyd,' said Arabella reprovingly, pulling a black petticoat over her flabby shoulders, 'you know you always feel better after your treatment. Don't forget the children's money box on your way out.'

Murgatroyd's final advice, before he left, was, 'Try your treatment on the Sanitary Inspector when he calls. It might work wonders.'

After giving this matter a lot of thought and getting nowhere, she decided to call on her parents again. They were rather short on advice nowadays, but she still had faith in their wisdom.

Her mother was still huddled over the fire and she noticed with vague surprise that her father did not draw the sheet over his face. Optimistically, she considered that he could be in a good mood.

'Mummy, I'm sorry I had no time to bring flowers, but be a dear and tell me the best way to get rid of Sanitary Inspectors.'

Her mother did not move a muscle, or say a word.

'Tell me what to do,' wheedled Arabella. 'Is it chopped worms with sheep's dropping or rat's liver with bog myrtles?'

Her mother merely threw a lump of coal on to the fire. Then she softened. 'See your father,' she replied.

Arabella leapt over to the bed and almost upset the stained pail lying beside it. She took hold of her father's hand, which was dangling down loosely. She clasped it to her sagging breast and was chilled by its icy touch, so she hurriedly flung the hand back on the bed saying, 'Daddy darling, what advice can you give your little girl on how to get rid of Sanitary Inspectors?'

He regarded her with a hard immovable stare then his hand slid down to dangle again. She looked at him thoughtfully and pulled the sheet over his face. 'Mummy, I think Daddy is dead.'

Her mother took out a pipe from her pocket and lit it from the fire with a long taper. After puffing for a few seconds, she said, 'Very likely.'

Arabella realised that the discussion was over. 'Tomorrow I will bring a wreath for Daddy,' she promised as she quickly headed for the door. 'I have some lovely dandelions in my garden.'

Back home again, Arabella studied her face in a cracked piece of mirror and decided to give it a wash. She moved a damp smelly cloth over it, which only made the seams of dirt show up more clearly. Then she attempted to run a comb through her tangled mass of hair, but the comb snapped. Thoroughly annoyed, she picked out a fat louse from a loose strand of hair and crushed it with her fingernails. Then she sat down on the bed and brooded. So engrossed was she in her worry she forgot to feed her children, who by this time were whining and squatting in corners to relieve themselves. She couldn't concentrate on making their food, so she took three of them outside and tied them to posts. The fourth one, under the bed, remained very still. Eventually she decided the best thing to do was to have some of her magical potion ready, though such was her state of mind that she doubted its efficiency in the case of Sanitary Inspectors. Besides, there was no guarantee he suffered from afflictions. Sighing, she went outside. Next to her door stood a large barrel where she kept the potion. She scooped a portion of the thick evil-smelling substance into a delve jar, stirred it up a bit to get the magic going, then returned indoors and laid it in readiness on the table. She was drinking a cup of black sweet tea when the knock came on the door. Smoothing down her greasy dress and taking a deep breath to calm herself, she opened it.

The small man confronting her had a white wizened face under a large bowler hat.

'Please enter,' requested Arabella regally. With head held high she turned into the room. The Sanitary Inspector tottered on the doorstep. He had not been feeling well all day. Twenty years of examining fetid drains and infested dwellings had weakened his system. He had another five years to go before he retired, but he doubted he would last that long.

'Please sit down,' said Arabella, motioning to an orange box and wondering how she could broach the subject of cures before he could speak about his business. She could see at a glance that this was a sick man, though not necessarily one who would take his clothes off. The Sanitary Inspector opened his mouth to say something but found that he was choking and everything was swimming before him. He had witnessed many an odious spectacle in his time but this fat sagging filthy woman with wild tangled hair and great staring eyes was worse than the nightmares he often had of dismembered bodies in choked drains. Equally terrible was the smell, and he was a connoisseur in smells. He managed to seat his lean trembling shanks on the orange box and found himself at eye level with a delve jar in the centre of a wooden table. Again he tried to speak, but his mouth appeared to be full of poisonous gas.

'My good man,' said Arabella, genuinely concerned when she saw his head swaying, 'I can see you are not well and it so happens I am a woman of great powers.'

She knew she had no time for niceties. Quickly she undressed and stood before him as guileless as a June bride. The small man reeled. This grotesque pallid flesh drooping sickly wherever possible was worse than anything he had ever witnessed.

'Now just take your clothes off, and you'll soon feel better,' said Arabella in her most winsome tone. 'I have a magical potion here that cures all ailments and eases troubled minds.' So saying, she turned and gave him a close-up view of her monumental buttocks. She dipped her fingers in the jar and tantalisingly held out a large dollop in front of his nose. It was too much for him. His heart gave a dreadful lurch. He hiccuped loudly, then his head sagged on to his chest.

Arabella was very much taken aback. Nothing like this had ever happened before, though it had been obvious to her when she first saw him that he was an inferior type. She rubbed the ointment on her fingers off on the jar, then dressed. The manner in which he lay, limp and dangling, reminded her of her father. This man must be dead, but, even dead he was a nuisance. She would have to get rid of him quickly if she didn't want it to get around that her powers were waning. Then she remembered the place where she had buried some of her former children and considered that he would fit into the pram – he was small enough. Yet it was all so much bother and very unpleasant and unpleasantness always wore her out.

She went outside to take a look at the pram. The dogs were whining and pulling on the fence. Feeling ashamed of her neglect, she returned to fetch their supper, when the barrel caught her eye. Inspiration came to her in a flash. The barrel was large – it was handy – and there would be an extra fillip added to the ointment. She felt humbled by the greatness of her power.

Cheerfully she approached the figure slumped like a rag doll against the table. It was easy to drag him outside, he was so fragile. Though he wasn't quite dead because she heard him whisper, 'Sweet Jesus, help me.' This only irritated her. She could have helped him if he had let her. She dragged his unresisting body towards the barrel and with no difficulty toppled him inside to join the healing ointment. With a sigh of satisfaction she replaced the lid. As usual everything had worked out well for her.

GENTLEMEN OF THE WEST

McDonald's Dug

McDonald's dog was not the type of animal that people took kindly to, or patted on the head with affection. It was more likely to receive the odd kick, along with the words 'gerr oot', which it accepted for the most part with indifference. If the kick was too well aimed it bared its teeth in a chilling manner which prevented further kicks. Large, grey and gaunt it roamed the streets, foraged the dustbins and hung around the local co-operative to the disgust of customers coming and going. The manager, who received continual complaints about it, as if it was his responsibility, would throw pails of water over it to pacify plaintive statements such as, 'Ye'd better dae somethin' aboot that dug. It's a bloody disgrace the way it hings aboot this shop.' Though he had no heart for this action, as more often than not he missed the dog, which had the sensory perception of a medium and could move like a streak of lightning, causing innocent housewives to be soaked instead. Even so, McDonald's dog was a valuable asset to its owner. With its height and leanness, plus a sharp, evil face, it might have been a greyhound on the loose, but in fact its character was determined from a lurcher ancestor, an animal talented in the art of poaching. I had an interest in McDonald's dog due to the following incident.

One particularly dreich evening I was waiting at the bus stop, soaked to the skin. My bones ached from damp clothing. All day I had been sitting in the hut at the building site waiting for the rain to stop in order to get on with the vocation of laying the brick, but it never halted. We played cards, ate soggy pieces and headed with curses for the toilet. On that site it was wherever you happened to find a convenient spot.

So I was thankful when Willie Morrison drew up with his honky-tonk motor like something out of Wacky Races.

'Jump in Mac,' he said.

I did so with alacrity, hoping the door would not fall on my feet. It was that type of motor.

'Thanks Wullie.'

We proceeded in silence since Willie had a job to see where he was going. The windscreen wipers did not work too well. I was on the point of falling asleep when suddenly we hit a large object.

'Watch where yer gaun,' I said, very much aggrieved that my head had banged against the window. A spray of liquid spurted over our vision. For a sickening minute I thought it was blood, then I realised it was water from the radiator.

'My God, that's done it,' croaked Willie. Panicking, I opened the door regardless of the danger to my feet. I was just in time to see the shadow of an animal limp towards the hedge.

'Ye've hit an animal o' some kind,' I said.

'Whit wis it – a coo?'

'Don't be daft. This motor wid have nae chance against a coo. I think it wis a dug.'

'Och a dug. It's nae right bein' on the road.'

He started up the engine and with a great amount of spluttering the car roared off at thirty miles an hour. I felt a bit gloomy at the thought of a dog maybe bleeding to death in the sodden hedgerow, but Willie was only concerned for his car.

'This motor's likely jiggered noo.'

I couldn't be bothered to point out that it was jiggered before. I was only wishing I had taken the bus. We reached our destination without saying much. Hunger had overcome my thoughts on the dog. I hoped my mother had something tasty for the dinner, which would be unlikely.

Some days later I happened to be in McDonald's company.

McDonald was like his dog, very difficult at times. But in the convivial atmosphere of the Paxton Arms we were often thrown together, and under the levelling influence of alcohol we would view each other with friendly eyes. Though you had to take your chances with him. On occasions his eyes would be more baleful than friendly. Then, if your senses were not completely gone, you discreetly moved away. McDonald labelled himself a ploughman. To prove it he lived in a ramshackle cottage close to a farm. Though the word cottage was an exaggeration. It was more like an old bothy. Some folk said he was a squatter, and some folk said he was a tinker, but never to his face. On this occasion I was not too sure about his mood. He appeared sober, but depressed.

'How's things?' I asked, testing him out to see if I should edge nearer to him.

'Could be better.'

'How's that then?' I asked.

'It's that dug o' mine.'

'Yer dug?'

'Aye. Some bastard run him ower.'

'That's terrible Paddy.' My brain was alert to danger.

'As ye know yersel,' continued McDonald, unobservant of the shifty look in my eyes, 'ma dug is no' ordinary dug. It's a good hard-working dug. In fact,' his chest heaved with emotion, 'ye could say that dug has kept me body and soul when I hudny a penny left.'

I nodded sympathetically. McDonald's dole money was often augmented by rabbits, hares and pheasants that he sold at half the butcher's price.

'An' d'ye know,' he stabbed my chest with a grimy finger, 'I've hud tae fork oot ten pounds for a vet. Think o' that man – ten pounds!'

I didn't believe him about the ten pounds, but I was relieved the dog wasn't dead.

'Where's the dug noo?' I asked.

'The poor beast's restin' in the hoose.'

I remembered his house. On one or two occasions I had

AGNES OWENS

partaken of his hospitality. A bottle of wine had been the passport.
He kept live rabbits in the oven – lucky for them it was in disuse
– pigeons in a cage in the bedroom, and a scabby cat always asleep
at the end of a lumpy sofa, with the dog at the other end. I don't
know if this menagerie lived in harmony, but they had survived
so far. I thought at this stage I had better buy him a drink to take
the edge off his bitterness before I shifted my custom. It was
obvious his mood would not improve with all this on his mind.
McDonald swallowed the beer appreciatively but he was reluctant
to change the subject.

'An' I'm tellin' ye, if I get ma haunds on the rat that done it I'll
hing him.'

'It's a right rotten thing tae happen.' To get out of it all I added,
'I wish I could stay an' keep ye company, but I huv tae gie Jimmy
Wilson a haun' wi' his fence, so see ye later.'

Swiftly I headed for the Trap Inn hoping I would see Willie
Morrison to break the bad news to him. However, it was a couple
of days before I met Willie again. He was waiting at the bus stop
motorless, and with the jaundiced look of a man who has come
down in the world. He grunted an acknowledgement.

'Huv ye no' got yer motor?' I asked.

'Naw.'

He shuffled about, then explained. 'Mind that night we hit that
dug?'

I nodded.

'Well, the motor has been aff the road ever since. And dae ye
know whit it'll cost me tae get it fixed?'

'Naw,' I said, although I was not all that much agog.

'Twenty nicker.'

He stared at me for sympathy. Dutifully I rolled my eyes around.

'That's some lolly.'

'Anyway I've pit it in the haunds of ma lawyer.' His eyes were
hard and vengeful.

Before any more was said the bus rumbled up. Justice was

12

forgotten. We kicked, jostled and punched to get on, and I was first. Before Willie managed to put his foot on the platform I turned to him saying, 'I heard it wis McDonald's dug ye run ower.'

In his agitation he sagged and was shoved to the back of the queue.

'That's enough,' shouted the hard-faced conductress. The bus drove off leaving Willie stranded.

'I hear that somebody battered Johnny Morrison last night,' said my mother conversationally as she dished out the usual indigestible hash that passed for a meal by her standards.

'Whit's this then?' I asked, ignoring the information.

'Whit dae ye mean "whit's this"? It's yer dinner.'

'I don't want it.'

'D'ye know whit I've paid for it?'

'Naw, an' I don't want tae.'

'You really sicken me. Too much money an' too many Chinese takeaways, that's your trouble.'

'Shut up, an' gies a piece o' toast.'

'Oh well, if that's all ye want then,' she said, mollified.

She was very good at toast.

Then her opening remark dawned on me. 'Whit wis that ye said aboot Johnny Morrison?'

She poured out the tea, which flowed from the spout like treacle. 'Jist as I said. He opened the door aboot eleven at night an' somebody battered him.'

'Whit for?' I asked. I would have seen the connection if it had been Willie.

'How should I know? He got the polis in but he didny recognise the man. He had a pair o' tights ower his heid.'

'Tights,' I echoed. 'Do ye no' mean nylons?'

Stranger and stranger, I thought. I could hardly see Paddy McDonald wearing either tights or nylons, just to give somebody a doing. Anyway, two odd socks were his usual concession to

style. And why batter Willie's brother? Not unless he was out to
get the whole family.

I was soon put out of my bewilderment. On Saturday night I saw
Paddy McDonald in the Paxton, swaying like a reed in the wind.
His expression was one of benignity for all mankind, but like a
bloodhound or his lurcher he spied me straightaway.

'There ye are son. Here whiddy ye want tae drink?'

Straightaway I said, 'A hauf an' a hauf-pint.' I was in a reckless
mood and heedless of hazards. It was a Saturday, and I was out
to enjoy myself. I was going to get bevvied.

He took a roll of notes from his pocket and waved one of them
in the direction of the barman like a flag of victory.

'You seem to be loaded,' I said.

'Aye.'

'Did somebody kick the bucket and leave you a fortune?'

'It's no' a' that much,' he replied modestly. 'Only twenty pounds.'

'How dae ye manage tae have that on a Saturday?'

McDonald's money was usually long gone by that time. He got
his dole money on a Friday.

He was lost in a reverie of happy fulfilment. Before he could
make any disclosures Johnny Morrison entered. Both his eyes were
a horrible shade of yellowish green and there was a bit of sticking
plaster above one of them. McDonald regarded him with concern.

'That's a terrible face ye have on ye Johnny.'

'D'ye think I don't know. Ye don't have tae tell me!' replied
Johnny with emotion.

'Have a drink John,' said McDonald. 'Wi' a face like that ye
deserve one.'

He waved another pound at the barman.

After doing his duty by Johnny he turned to me and put an
arm round my shoulder.

'I wis really sorry aboot Johnny,' he whispered.

'Wis it you that done it then?'

'Dear God naw, though I know how it happened.' Dreamily he paused.

'How?' Now I was interested and hoped he would not sag to the floor before he could tell me. He swayed a bit then came back to the subject.

'D'ye know that heid-banger Pally McComb?'

I nodded.

'Well, I heard it was Wullie Morrison that ran ower ma dug. So I gave Pally a couple o' rabbits tae gie him a doin'. I wid have done it masel but I didny want involved wi' the law.' His voice sank confidentially. 'As ye know I huvny got a dug licence. Anyway, Pally is that shortsighted that he didny know the difference between Wullie and Johnny, so he banged Johnny.'

'I see,' I said, but I didn't think it was such a great story.

'How's the dug then?'

'I selt it.'

'Ye selt it?'

'Aye, it wis gettin' past it. Matter o' fact it wis a bloody nuisance wi' a' these complaints aboot it. But dae ye know who I selt it tae?'

'Naw.'

He began to laugh then went into paroxysms of coughing. I was getting impatient. He finally calmed down.

'It wis Wullie Morrison that bought it.'

I said nothing. I couldn't make any sense out of it.

'Ye see,' McDonald wiped the tears from his eyes, 'I sent Pally up wi' a note tae Wullie this afternoon tae say he'd better buy the dug, due tae its poor condition efter bein' run ower, or else. Well, he must have seen the state o' his brother's face, so he sent the money doon right away. Mind ye, I didny think he'd gie me twenty pound. Personally I'd have settled for a fiver.'

'Wullie could never stick the thought o' pain,' I said. I began to laugh as well, and hoped Paddy would keep on his feet long enough to get me another drink.

'Right enough, Paddy,' I said, holding firmly on to him, 'ye're a great case, an' I'll personally see that when ye kick the bucket ye'll get a big stane above yer grave, me bein' in the buildin' trade an' that.'

McDonald's Mass

I was taking a slow amble along the river bank. The weather was fine, one of those spring mornings that should gladden anyone's heart. The birds were singing, the trees were budding and the fishing season had started, but I was feeling lousy. The scar in my temple and the cuts round my mouth were nipping like first-degree burns. My neck felt like a bit of hose pipe and the lump on the back of my head was so tender that even the slightest breeze lifting my hair made me wince. My mother's remark, 'You look like Frankenstein', had not been conducive to social mixing, but since I wanted someone to talk to I decided to look up my old china Paddy McDonald because at times he could be an understanding man if he was not too full of the jungle juice.

I turned with the bend in the river and there on the bank, under the old wooden bridge, was a gathering of his cronies, namely, Billy Brown, Big Mick, Baldy Patterson and Craw Young. They were huddled round a large flat stone that displayed two bottles of Eldorado wine and some cans of beer, but I could not see Paddy.

They did not hear or see me approaching. Billy Brown jumped up as startled as a March hare when I asked, 'Where's Paddy?' at the same time staring hopefully at the wine.

'Paddy's died,' he informed me.

My brain could scarcely adjust itself to this statement.

'That canny be true.' Without waiting for the offer I took a swig from the bottle.

'It's true right enough,' replied Billy, smartly grabbing it back.

'I found him masel up in the Drive as cauld as ice an' as blue as Ian Paisley.'

The Drive was a derelict building where the boys did their drinking when it was too cold for outdoors.

'Whit happened to yer face?' asked Big Mick.

'That's a long story.' I was so stunned by the news that I had forgotten about my face for the first time since I woke up. Billy wiped his mouth with the back of his hand. His eyes were like saucers and his face greyer than grey. He was a close associate of Paddy's. Not exactly a mate, more like a sparring partner, but they spent a lot of time together except when they were in jail.

'I didny know whit tae dae, so I got the polis in an' they sent for an ambulance. They carted him off while I waited ootside.'

'How dae ye know he wis deid? When Paddy wis out cauld he always looked deid,' I said.

'If ye'd seen the colour o' his face you'd hiv known he wis deid.' No one disputed this fact.

'That wis a rerr wee hoose he had,' said Baldy Patterson wistfully. He was referring to the broken-down bothy where Paddy lived. 'I think I'll go up efter an' see tae his pigeons.'

'That's great,' I said. 'The man's hardly cauld an' ye're gaun tae move in.'

'He wis cauld enough when I seen him,' said Billy. 'Onyway, somebody has tae feed his pigeons.'

The second bottle was opened and passed around with some beer, and now I was included in the company. Normally I don't care for wine and beer first thing in the morning, but this day was an exception what with my sore face and Paddy being dead. Now that I was hunkered down on eye level with them they began to study me.

'Yer face has improved a lot since I last saw ye,' said Craw Young who always fancied himself as a bit of a wit. 'Ye've got a bit o' character in it noo.'

'Better watch I don't put a bit o' character in yours,' I retorted, but I didn't put any emphasis on my words because they were all away beyond my age group and fragile with years of steady drinking and sleeping out. I thought Paddy had been the toughest despite his burst ulcers and periodical fits if he was off the drink for more than a week, but I was wrong. Mellowed by the wine and the sadness of Paddy's death, I explained how five fellows from the city had picked a fight with me and stuck broken tumblers in my face. It was really only two fellows but I had my reputation to think of.

'It's the bad company ye keep,' said Billy sagely. 'We auld chaps know the score.'

'Is that so,' I said, 'an' jist how many times have you been in jail?'

'Och, that's only for disturbin' the peace and vagrancy. Ye canny count that.'

'Anyway, Paddy must have been OK this mornin' if he was in the Drive, otherwise how wid he manage tae get there.'

'He got lifted last night wi' the polis as far as I heard, but they must have let him oot early. I didny get in tae the Drive till aboot eleven this mornin',' explained Billy.

'Where were you last night then?' asked Big Mick with suspicion.

'I don't mind much aboot last night,' said Billy sheepishly. 'Matter of fact I woke up in Meg Brannigan's.'

We all jeered. Meg Brannigan was a slattern who drank anything from Vordo to meths. Even Billy was a cut above her.

'Anyway I jist happened to pass oot on her couch.'

We jeered again.

'Here,' said Craw who had been deep in thought. 'How d'ye know it wisny murder?'

'It wid be murder bein' wi' Meg,' chortled Big Mick.

'I mean how d'ye know Paddy wisny murdered?'

'I never murdered him onyway,' said Billy vehemently.

'OK, OK,' said Baldy, 'the main thing is whether he wis murdered or no' who's gaun tae bury him?'

'Bury him?' we echoed.

'He's got tae be buried an' don't forget that'll cost money.'

We looked at each other with dismay.

'He'll jist have tae go intae a pauper's grave,' said Craw with a lack of taste.

'Terrible tae think o' poor Paddy in a pauper's grave,' said Baldy.

'It'll no' dae him ony harm. He'll have plenty company.'

'Maybe he wis insured,' said Big Mick.

'Nae chance,' said Billy. 'He discussed it wi' me once. The insurance company wid have nothin' tae dae wi' him. He's whit ye call a bad risk.'

'Maybe we could get up a collection,' said Baldy.

'Who the hell is gaun tae put tae it? Who dae we know that's got money? I mean real money.'

My face was feeling painful again and I was fed up with all this debate. Paddy had been the only one with any smattering of intelligence about him. Now he was gone.

'Anither thing,' said Big Mick. 'We'll have tae let the priest know.'

'First I heard Paddy wis a Catholic,' said Craw sharply. He turned to Baldy, 'Did you know that?'

'Naw, but I always thought there wis somethin' funny aboot him.'

'He didny tell me onyway,' said Craw bitterly, 'for he knew ma opinion aboot Catholics.'

'I never knew you had opinions aboot anything,' said Big Mick. I could see he was becoming angry. Likely he was a Catholic too with a name like Mick.

'Anyway,' Billy Brown butted in, 'you don't even know whit you are. You telt me ye wir an orphan.'

'I might've been an orphan but I wisny a Catholic.'

'Who cares?' I said.

We all glared at each other for some seconds. Then to prove how displeased he was with the subject Big Mick finished off the remainder of the wine in one swallow. We stared gloomily at the empty bottle.

'I'm off,' said Mick with the air of a man who is going to get things done. He threw the bottle into the river and marched off with as much determination as his long shaky legs would allow him.

I said, 'Me too.' Groggily I arose, wishing I had gone to work. It couldn't have been any worse.

After the evening meal of sausages and mash, one of my mother's favourite dishes, I sat staring glassily at the television. I didn't particularly wish to venture into the Paxton Arms to meet types like Willie Morrison. He would be overjoyed at the brilliance of my savage face and even more so at the news of Paddy's departure. After all, he had been so terrified of Paddy he was forced to buy his dog, and Willie hated that dog, though he was too frightened to get rid of it. And that dog, for all its mean look, had a loving nature. It trailed on Willie's heels like a shadow. Willie would dodge up closes to avoid it, but to no avail. It could always seek him out panting and slavering with joy. With Paddy gone the dog was definitely a goner too. My mother sat down to view the telly twitching about and straightening cushions. I suspected my company was a bit of a strain for her. I said, 'Did ye know that Paddy McDonald is deid?'

'Is he?' she replied in a flat voice. We both stared at the box. Finally she said, 'He'll no' be much loss anyway.'

'I suppose not.' I kept my voice neutral.

'He wis nothin' but a tinker anyway,' she added.

'There wis nae proof he wis a tinker.'

'He wis worse. He wis just a drunken auld sod that neither worked nor wanted.'

I let the remark go. I could not expect her to have any understanding of Paddy.

'By the way,' I said, 'I heard he wis a Catholic. If he just died this mornin' when wid they haud his mass?'

'Usually the same night, I think.'

'Whit time aboot?'

'Maybe seven. I mind that's when they held mass for Mrs Murphy.' Then looking aghast she added, 'Don't tell me ye're gaun tae the chapel for that auld rotter.'

'Don't be daft,' I said, but inwardly I thought I should. It would be the decent thing to do. I was feeling a bit emotional about it all, and stood up quickly before she noticed my eyes were wet.

'I'm away oot,' I said before any more remarks could be made.

I headed for the chapel with a lot of indecision. It's right next door to the boozer which is handy for the Catholic voter. I noticed there was more business going for the chapel though. You would have thought there was free beer by the manner in which everyone rushed up the stairs. I hung about until the rush was over and looked up and down the street furtively. Which was it to be, the boozer or the chapel. Then I thought, what the hell, I should pay my respects to Paddy. I took the plunge and scurried up the stairs. I didn't know what I expected to see behind these dreaded doors, but apart from a couple of statues and something that looked like a fancy washhand basin, there was nothing much to put me off.

I sneaked in through another door to be confronted with all the solemnity of the papal worship. My face was red as I squeezed into a bench at the back because all the seats were jam-packed. But not a soul bothered or even gave me a glance, so engrossed were they in the sermon. The priest's voice was a meaningless drone to me, and I wondered if the mass for Paddy had begun. After a time I felt relaxed enough to look around at the decor. I considered it quite tasteful and if anything, except for the odd statue here and there, quite plain. I liked that. It was peaceful and uplifting. Maybe Paddy's death had a meaning for me. Maybe it was to join this mob and get a bit of religion. Definitely food for thought. Though it would be fine if I could hear what the priest was saying, but whatever it was it would be appropriate and Paddy would be pleased if he could hear. Probably he could. In this place anything was possible. Then it struck me I couldn't see Paddy's coffin. Perhaps it was too early for this. I wished I knew more about these matters. To see if it was lying handy I stood up. An old woman sitting next to me whispered as loud as a shout, 'Sit doon son. It's no' time for staunin'.'

I sat down quickly. No sooner had I sat when everyone stood up. For the next half-hour we were up and down like yo-yos. Though you didn't sit all the time you were down. Sometimes you had to kneel on the long stool on the floor. I was beginning to get the hang of it but it was very sore on the knees. Still there was no sign of Paddy's coffin, nor had I heard a mention of his name. At one of the sitting parts I whispered to the old woman next to me, 'Could ye tell me missus if the priest is saying mass for Paddy McDonald?'

I don't know if the message got through but her reply made no sense.

'Look,' she said balefully, 'I don't know anything aboot Paddy McDonald, but whatever they tell you I've lived a decent life for the past ten years and atoned for everything. I'm never away from this bloody place atoning – so don't start.'

Her voice finished on a hysterical note. All eyes that had been transfixed forwards were now transfixed backwards on me. The priest, as distant as a postage-stamp picture, had stopped swinging the smoky stuff. I was so burnt up with embarrassment I felt my wounds were opening up to drip blood. I wiped my face on an ancient paper hanky but sweat only dampened it. Then the pressure was released. The eyes turned away and the priest carried on swinging the smoky stuff. I had scarcely got over all this when, out of the blue, everyone got up from their seats and began to walk down the aisle in a single file, even the old woman. I couldn't stand any more so I stood up as though I was going to join the queue but instead turned quickly to the right, out of the door, passing the fancy washhand basin and into the marvellous fresh air. It was the only sensible thing I had done all day.

*   *   *

The first person I bumped into, or rather he bumped into me, was Paddy McDonald. I wasn't all that surprised. The absence of his coffin or any mention of his name had cast doubts anyway. I didn't want to know him now. He was in one of his complicated, mindless moods. In other words, completely stoned. He clung to me as if I was a long-lost lamp-post. If he had been sober there were a million questions I could have asked him, but as it was I merely said, 'Hi Paddy.'

Stoned though he was, he was bursting with information. 'D'ye know whit I'm gaun tae tell ye?'

'Whit?' I said.

'Because o' that stupid sod Billy Broon I wis carted off tae hospital this mornin'. They widny let me oot. Telt me ma liver was a' tae hell. It took me a' day tae get ma haunds on ma clathes.' He paused to regain the drift of his conversation, still gripping me tightly. 'Noo they tell me that Billy an' the team are in ma hoose lettin' a' the pigeons away an' God knows whit else. Wait till I get ma haunds on the bastards.'

I tried to break from his vice-like grip, saying, 'Ye'd better hurry hame then before they set yer hoose on fire.'

In his agitation he released me. Facing the Catholic church, he uttered every blasphemy he knew. It seemed to me that Catholics are a very extreme lot. If they are not one way they are the other. Of course that is only my opinion. In the middle of it all I walked away. Though I hoped he had the energy to batter Billy Brown to a pulp for the bother he had caused me. And all this had to happen when I had a sore face.

Grievous Bodily Harm

'Any old rags! Toys for rags! Any old rags!'
The voice of Duds Smith, magnified through an old tin trumpet, roared up our street, penetrating the thickest eardrum.

'I wid jist as soon burn ma rags than gie them tae that auld cheat,' said my mother in her usual arrogant style.

'I thought ye usually wore them,' I muttered.

'Whit's that?'

'Nothing.' I then added the uppermost thought in my mind, 'How's about a pound till Friday?'

'Don't be daft. For a' the money you gie me I couldny afford nothing.'

She went on to explain at great length that I must be unaware of the fact the cost of living had risen in the past five years and surely I must realise the fiver I gave her every week would hardly keep a dog going. Fixedly I stared out of the window. I knew she would eventually wear herself out then begin to feel guilty at my lack of defence. At the least I might get fifty pence from her which was the entrance fee for the Paxton Arms. Her tirade petered out and she sat down breathing heavily while Duds's voice penetrated the pregnant silence. His motor was now opposite our window. Kids were running out with bundles large and small leaving a trail of scruffy articles behind them while Duds was handing out balloons and Hong Kong whistles in a benevolent style and deftly slapping to the side any of them who were returning burst balloons and soundless whistles.

'Mean auld swine,' said my mother as she joined me to survey the scene. I knew she was playing for time.

'Here, I tell ye whit,' she said suddenly excited, 'gie Duds that auld telly lyin' in the bedroom an' ye can take a pound aff the money ye get.'

'Don't make me laugh!' I allowed the flicker of a smile to crease my face which was just beginning to heal from the broken tumbler episode. 'Ye'd have tae pay him tae take that telly away. It must be the original one Baird invented.'

'It could be fixed easy. Ye can still get a picture.'

'I'll tell ye whit,' I said, not wishing to waste time on the merits of the television, 'I'll take the telly doon tae him if you gie me a pound for tryin', whether he takes it or no'.'

'OK,' she said.

Duds was not thrilled when I laid it down on the pavement. My arms were almost wrenched from their sockets with the weight.

'Look Mac, I've more televisions in ma back yard than auld lawnmowers.'

'Maybe,' I gasped for breath. 'But this one still works.'

He stared at it in disbelief.

I explained, 'Ye see, we've got a new telly, so ma mother wants rid o' this one, but if ye don't want it I'll take it doon tae auld Mrs McMurtry. She said she would gie us a fiver for it, that is if ye could oblige me wi' a lift roon tae her hoose.'

Duds was convinced. 'I'll gie ye two pounds for it.'

'It's a deal,' I said.

I told my mother, 'Duds only gave me a pound.'

'Is that all?'

'Ye were lucky even tae get that.'

'Have I tae get the pound then?' she asked hopefully.

I became indignant at the way she was trying to get out of her deal. 'C'mon, ye said ye'd gie me a pound if I got rid o' it or no', so I keep the pound an' you've saved a pound.'

'I gie up,' was her final comment.

* * *

Later on I was enjoying my pint of beer in the Paxton Arms and having a friendly chat with Flossie the barman, when in came Willie Morrison, down in the mouth as usual, and not enhanced by a piece of sticking plaster decorating his chin.

'Did ye manage oot withoot yer dug then?' I asked.

Willie looked over his shoulder nervously, 'I don't know where that animal has got tae. Took it oot for a walk the other night an' the bloody thing jist disappeared.'

'Better watch the farmer disny catch it worryin' the sheep, an' shoot it.'

'I hope no',' he said brightening slightly.

'Still, Paddy McDonald wid be terrible disappointed if it wis shot,' I pointed out.

'I'm past caring whit Paddy McDonald thinks, or any o' his damned relatives.'

I wondered what the relatives had to do with anything.

I changed the subject. 'Did ye cut yer face shavin'?'

'Naw, did you?' he replied, giving my face a keen look.

'Maybe.' My face was healing but I had to keep it poker straight or the cuts near my mouth would open up.

'Whit are ye wantin' tae drink then?'

I was surprised. Willie is not famed for these kind of impulses.

'A hauf an' a hauf-pint,' I answered quickly.

He gave the order without a blink and said, 'It's a terrible thing when a fella canny take a drink withoot somebody wantin' tae pick on him.'

'Did somebody pick a fight wi' ye?' I asked dutifully and fingered one of the fifty pences in my pocket wondering how I could avoid wasting some of it on Willie.

He replied, 'Ye know Murdo McDonald?'

'Ye mean Paddy's nephew?'

'Aye. One's as bad as the other.'

I nodded. I had gone off Paddy myself.

'Well, he gave me a punch for nothin'.'

'Did ye no' punch him back?'

'I don't believe in punch-ups. I charged him but he got aff wi' it.'

'I'm no' surprised. I've seen more damage wi' a midge bite.'

'There's jist nae justice in the world,' Willie moaned.

He was beginning to weary me. I decided to inform him about my financial position. 'I'm sorry I canny return the drink. I've only enough here for one pint.'

Willie shrugged like a man who is used to disappointments.

Just then the subject of discussion, Murdo McDonald, and another rat-faced fellow joined us. I nodded over to Murdo. I had nothing against him. He was a volatile, quick-tempered type with a strong sense of fair play. He stood close to Willie with his pitted face almost touching Willie's. Willie shrank visibly.

'Er – would ye like a drink?' he asked Murdo.

'Sure thing. Make it a double whisky an' one for ma mate.'

Hastily Willie ordered two doubles. 'That's me skint,' he mumbled after he paid. Nobody answered. He swallowed a remaining mouthful of beer and made a sheepish exit from our company. The coast was clear. With my fifty pence I ordered a whisky and beer for myself.

'That wee scunner wid make ye sick,' said Murdo inclining his head towards Willie's back disappearing through the door.

'How's that then?'

'He wis cheatin' at cards the other week, so I punched him. No' much. Jist opened up his face a wee bit. The next thing he had me charged wi' grievous bodily harm. I warned him wi' ma haunds roon' his neck I wid gie him real grievous bodily harm if he didny withdraw his statement. Well, anyway, the case came up yesterday. When the magistrate asked him tae point oot the accused, meanin' me, Willie said he didny know who punched him. I thought you said it was the accused here, said the magistrate, meanin' me. Willie said he didny know who it wis, but it definitely wasn't the accused, meanin' me. The magistrate wis that fed up wi' him he fined him a fiver for contempt o' court.'

I refrained from laughing for obvious reasons. Murdo did not laugh either because being the great avenger that he is, he has no sense of humour and the rat-faced mate likely had heard it all before. With the remainder of my two pounds I ordered a drink all round.

For the rest of the evening I was kept going in beer by Murdo and his mate who were glad of an audience. My head was swimming in a mild haze of alcohol, nothing extreme, but quite enjoyable for through the week when you don't expect much. As a further bonus, at closing time Murdo ordered a carry-out of a half-bottle of whisky and cans of beer. He then asked me if I'd like to pay Paddy a visit along with him and his mate. 'Sure,' I said without hesitation. 'I think Paddy's a great case.'

In fine spirits the three of us tramped up to Paddy's place. Over the boggy fields, skirting the farm, down the lane plastered with cows' dung, past the stinking byre, cheerfully assuring each other that the smell was good for us, until we reached the moss-covered dwelling of Paddy's. A pig might have turned up its nose at this hovel, but when our senses were blunted we enjoyed its homeliness. Without knocking we marched straight in and found Paddy lost in the magic world of television. I could hardly take my eyes off it. Paddy barely glanced in our direction.

'C'mon Paddy. Get the glasses oot. We're havin' a party,' said Murdo.

What was uppermost in my mind was that this television was the one I'd sold Duds. My mother was right. It went fine, and to think I'd only got two pounds for it. The drink was dumped on the table, which was really a wooden crate covered in flowery plastic material. The cat was knocked off the sofa by Murdo to allow us to rest on the exposed springs, but we were all feeling deflated by Paddy's lack of enthusiasm. Finally he had the decency to say, 'Jist haud on a sec till this programme's finished. It's great.'

We all stared at Kojak's hairless face. I can take Kojak or leave him, but right now I preferred to leave him. However, it finished off with the usual farewell speech to a dishy bit stuff, then thankfully we turned to the plastic bag with the drink.

'Right Paddy, get the jeely jars oot. We came tae see you, no' watch the telly.'

Reluctantly Paddy turned it off. He removed the plastic cover to reveal an impressive display of stained glasses inside the wooden crate, no doubt owned originally by the Paxton Arms.

'Help yersels lads, but jist drink the beer oot the can. It'll save me washin' up later.'

Murdo poured a big measure of whisky for Paddy. It must have shot straight into his bloodstream for he brightened up right away like a flash bulb.

'How did the case go, son?' he asked Murdo.

'Fine. I got aff.'

'I should think so. Fancy anyone accusin' Murdo o' grievous bodily harm. A nicer fella ye couldny meet,' appealed Paddy.

Rat-face and me stared sympathetically at Murdo's pitted face.

'Ye're right there Paddy,' I said. 'By the way, how did ye manage tae get a telly?'

'It wis Murdo here that got me it.'

I looked enquiringly at Murdo.

'Ach, it wis nae bother.'

'It's a fine telly. Who selt ye it?' I asked.

He laughed, which was unusual for him. 'Folk don't sell me things. They gie me them. Anyway, I'll tell ye whit happened. Ye know that twister Duds Smith, the ragman? Well, I happened tae be hingin' aboot when a wee laddie gave him a great bundle o' rags. Duds gave him a balloon that widny even blaw up. The laddie wis greetin' so I telt him tae get me a breid knife, if he had one in the hoose. He brought me a great carving knife. I showed it tae Duds. I telt him if he didny gie the boy somethin' better than a balloon I wid gie him the knife – right in the ribs. So Duds gave me this telly. I kept the telly and gave the laddie ten pence.'

'You're a decent fella Murdo,' said Paddy.

Murdo bowed his head to hide his embarrassment.

Rat-face said, 'So ye urr.'

I drained my beer from the can and said nothing.

Tolworth McGee

The other Saturday I met up with one of my old schoolmates, Toly McGee. I think his correct name was Bobby, or it might have been Rabbie, but I always knew him as Toly on account of one or two accidents he had in the classroom. In those days he had a very nervous disposition. I gave him a genuine 'how's it gaun' welcome and noticed he hadn't altered that much. The big brainy forehead wrinkled in perplexity as he peered at me with the same flickering eyes of old. They slowed down to a standstill when recognition dawned on him.

'It's yourself,' he said with such a great grin of pleasure I wondered if he really knew me. He shook my hand with hot enthusiasm and I had difficulty in ungluing it from his clammy grasp. I was beginning to regret my impulsive greeting because I could see I'd have difficulty in getting away from him and I was in a hurry to put a bet on.

'Huvny seen ye for a while,' I remarked.

'I've been in England since I left school,' he told me.

I thought that explained the posh accent. 'Did ye run away?' I asked.

'Of course not! Mum and Dad left for London with the family. You remember Dad?'

I remembered Dad. He used to be 'the auld man' to Toly. He was a shuffly, ferrety-faced wee guy who worked on the railway and, when drunk, battered Toly stupid.

'Right enough,' I said, 'I remember ye a' lit oot for the big smoke.'

Vaguely it came to me that the talk with my mother at the time was the McGees had done a moonlight after getting free passes

32

on the train. It also struck me that Toly was dressed neatly in a brown suit with tie to match, and a crew-cut which did not enhance his naked face. It wasn't my idea of style. Still, there was an air of success about him compared to the old days when he wore his father's shirts with cuffs turned up a mile, ragged trousers which barely reached his ankles, and either wellies or sandshoes regardless of weather conditions. I could sense he was about to embark on a long conversation so I cut him short.

'I'll huv tae get this bet on before the one-thirty race,' I explained and smartly headed across the road to the bookie.

'That's alright. I'll wait for you,' he called.

'Jesus,' I muttered. I hung on till after the race, but my luck was out. The horse had been lame, and Toly was waiting.

'It's really great to see you again,' he said for the umpteenth time as we walked along the road. I knew I was lumbered with him, and for his part he didn't notice my lack of interest in his life story.

'So, anyway,' he said, 'after I got the money I thought I would return and look up my old friends.'

'Whit money?' I asked, jerked out of my apathy.

Impatiently he said, 'I've already explained about the money Dad won on the pools. He gave me two hundred pounds to start me off in business, but I thought I would come back and have a holiday in my home town first. I've told you all this already.'

'Sorry,' I said, 'wi' that fancy accent o' yours I couldny follow whit ye were telling me. Anyway, I'm glad tae hear aboot yer good luck. I like tae see folk gettin' on.'

Although I'm not a grasping type I was relieved that Toly at least possessed money to splash about.

'Do ye take a bevvy?' I asked cautiously.

'Bevvy? Oh, I see. Yes, I don't mind an occasional pint. In fact,' he added with genuine pleasure, 'I would be glad to treat you.'

I breathed a sigh of relief because if Toly didn't indulge I would have dumped him there and then. Hurriedly I invited him into the Paxton Arms, since there was only an hour's drinking time left. Toly ordered the beer and with our pint tumblers before us, we stood like two clothes poles waiting for a line.

Eventually I said, 'I don't care a' that much for the taste o' beer withoot a whisky tae go wi' it.'

Toly took the hint. He ordered two whiskies. His face went a fine shade of lilac after he swallowed his, but it must have put some sense into him because after shuddering he said, 'Don't worry, I'll buy you all the whisky you want.'

'That's very decent o' ye Toly.'

He regarded me uneasily and said, 'I'd prefer if you didn't call me that name. Do you mind addressing me as Robert?'

I gave a bark of laughter, 'That's a helluva name. Toly suits ye better.'

His eyes fluttered with embarrassment. 'In Tolworth they call me Robert. No one has said it doesn't suit me.'

I felt sorry for him, so I said, 'So ye stay in Tolworth? That's the game. I'll call ye Tolworth. I'd forget tae call ye Robert, but Tolworth sounds like Toly. How's that?'

He brooded a bit then conceded, 'I suppose so.'

I slapped him on the back. 'Right Tolworth, I'll have a hauf an' a pint.'

After another couple of rounds he began to sag inside his neat suit. I thought he looked all the better for it. His tie flapping at the side of his neck gave him a touch of class and more in keeping with the Paxton Arms style.

Not having much to talk about we began to reminisce on the subject of our schooldays. Tolworth confessed that he had detested school.

'You wereny the only one,' I said.

'It wis different for you.' I noticed he was relapsing into the vernacular of his race. 'You didny seem to bother aboot beatin' ups.' Then he gave my face a long look. 'I see you still don't bother.'

'I bothered the same as everybody else,' I said. 'Ye jist had tae put on a front.'

34

'Aye, but ye didny have to put on your faither's auld shirts that made you a handy target.' His voice was bitter.

'That's true,' I admitted. I never had a father so I had better fitted shirts from the welfare.

'By the way,' I said, 'there wis one thing that puzzled me aboot you.'

'What?'

'Well, mind how we used tae come whoopin' an' shoutin' oot o' the class at playtime?'

'Aye.'

'It wisny as if I wis spyin' on ye, but it began tae dawn on me that efter ye came whoopin' an' shoutin' the same as everybody else, ye disappeared intae thin air. One day I wanted tae ask ye for the len' o' yer sandshoes for drill but I couldny find ye anywhere.'

Tolworth looked at the glass of whisky in his hand sadly. I could sense there was a big confession coming.

'I widny tell anyone else but you,' he hesitated, then continued. 'As you know I've always been very allergic to pain, on account of gettin' battered from ma auld man when he was drunk. Ma bones were always that sore that I couldny stand any shovin' or punchin', and nobody wid play wi' me anyway. So I used to run straight oot and wait inside the toilet till the bell rang.'

I looked at him with genuine compassion. Imagine standing for fifteen good playtime minutes in the toilet, waiting for the bell to ring to get back to the torture. I put my hand on his shoulder as a measure of my sympathy. 'Ye've had a terrible life,' I said when he ordered another two glasses. He began to unburden himself even further.

'Do you know, many's a time I was standing at the school gate at seven in the morning.'

I was aghast. 'I always thought ye were brainy but I didny think ye were that keen on school.'

'It wisny that,' he said with such an air of tragedy that I was dreading what he was going to say. 'You see, ma auld man sometimes sat up a' night drinkin'. He hudny a clue whit the time was. He would stagger through to ma room to get me up for school and if I didny get up he would pull the blankets aff and pour cauld water over me. It wis better to wait at the gates, even in the winter, than argue wi' him.'

I felt a lump in my throat. Tolworth blew his nose on a spotless white handkerchief, saying in a matter-of-fact way, 'Oh well, that's the way the cookie crumbles.'

At this point I ordered two whiskies, being the decent thing to do in the circumstances. After that everything became fuzzy. Whatever we discussed or how I got home I don't know, but the next apparent event was my mother shaking me hard and bawling in my ear, 'There's a fella wantin' tae speak tae ye.'

I sat up, surprised to see I was in bed. I tried to pull myself together.

'Whit's the time. Is it Sunday?'

'It's half-past four, and it's still Saturday.'

Thankfully I lay back. The evening was still ahead of me untouched.

'D'ye hear whit I'm sayin'? There's a fella wantin' tae speak tae ye. Strikes me as bein' one o' these queers.'

My mother had queers on the brain due to a recent television play. Even I was under suspicion.

I said, 'Tell him tae beat it.'

'Tell him yersel. He's waitin' in the living room.'

In a stinking mood I stumbled out of bed. It was Tolworth awaiting. There wasn't much resemblance to the neatly dressed fellow I had first met. There were more creases in his suit than a concertina. His shirt hung outside his trousers and there was no sign of a tie. He clutched me by the vest and said in a sickening whine, 'You'll have to help me. There's a mob after me. I don't know what to do.'

My mother viewed the scene with arms folded and nodding her head as if her worst expectations had been confirmed. 'Who's this then?' she challenged.

I explained that he was Tolworth McGee alias Toly. Surprise and recognition softened her. She asked, 'How're ye keepin' and how's yer mither an' faither?'

In between the snivelling Toly replied, 'Fine,' then returned to the snivelling. My mother became bored with the lack of information and said, 'I'll pit on the tea.'

'For God's sake, pull yersel the gither,' I said when she had gone into the kitchenette. 'Whit happened?'

'I don't know whit happened. After you left I think somebody picked an argument wi' me. I threw a glass o' beer in his face. The next thing I was ootside and a gang was chasin' me. I managed to get away.' He added with a touch of pride, 'I wis always good at runnin'.'

'Whit dae ye want me tae dae?' I asked.

'Can you no' help me?'

'Listen chum, I'm no' gaun tae spoil a good Saturday protectin' you.'

My mother entered with two cups of tea and a plate of banana sandwiches.

'Ye've excelled yersel,' I said looking darkly at the meal.

Ignoring the comment she addressed Toly, 'Mind an' tell yer folks I wis askin' for them.'

'Sure, I can hardly wait,' he mumbled, drawing the cup shakily up to his mouth.

The tea must have revived Toly a bit for he said, 'If only I could get to the railway station I would be OK but these guys might be waitin' for me.'

'I'll tell ye whit,' I said with inspiration, 'we'll wrap yer haund in bandages then we'll put yer arm in a sling. Nobody will touch ye then, an' I'll take ye tae the station.'

Toly was doubtful, but I had the feeling if I didn't get him out of the house right now he would stay forever, like a refugee in hiding, and my mother would be glad to keep him as company for her old age.

My mother was annoyed at the sight of one of her sheets being torn up for bandages, but as she must have felt sorry for Toly she assisted in making him appear a pathetic casualty. She waved a cheerful hand out the window as I prodded him along the road. Sure enough, further on the way, two of the Hoodlum Gang were leaning against the fence. I gripped Toly's arm hard to keep him from running away.

'Whit a horrible sight,' sneered one of the gang.

'Look,' I explained, 'he's already had a doin' an' broke his wrist. So there's nae need tae gie him anither one.'

'That's right,' said Toly with a ghastly ingratiating grin. With wooden faces they stared at him. One stabbed a knife into the fence. Toly gasped. Hurriedly we moved on. When I looked back the knife was still being stabbed. But anyway we reached the station and I left Toly on the platform, ignoring his plea to wait with him. I had done my duty and the Paxton Arms would be open. I was in the pub for only half an hour when my mother marched right up to the bar beside me. I was surprised. She wouldn't enter a lounge let alone a public bar. She explained, with a face like flint-stone, that Toly was back in the house with a genuine broken wrist waiting on the ambulance.

Sure enough, when we got back Toly was lying on the couch at the end of a trail of bandages beginning from the outside door, and bellowing like a bull.

'Whit's happened noo?' I asked, tempted to damage him further.

He stopped his noise long enough to tell me that the two Hood-lums had followed him to the station. 'I showed them my wrist, telling them it was broken.'

'We already telt them that,' I said with irritation, adding, 'so, whit did they dae?'

Toly sobbed. 'They must be monsters. They kicked it six times.'

He carried on sobbing until the ambulance came.

*   *   *

38

During the next few days my mother visited him in hospital, taking in grapes and bananas. Then she told me she was thinking of giving him a holiday when he came out because the McGees had been awful nice folk. She asked me if I would mind giving Toly my bed and I could sleep on the couch, assuring me it was quite comfortable. This morning they let Toly out and I was waiting at the hospital gates in a taxi. I reminded him that the Hoodlum Gang never forget, so in order to make a quick getaway before they got on his trail again he could take the taxi to the railway station. He was very grateful, and we parted the best of mates.

The Auld Wife's Fancy Man

I could scarcely believe my eyes when I came home early the other day from work to see Proctor Mallion drinking tea with my mother. His round, shiny face was unusually benign, though tinged with embarrassment, when he said to me, 'Hullo son.' My mother glared at me as she said, 'You're hame early.'

I shook my wet tammy over the table. 'I got rained aff,' I said, and snapped, 'Hurry up wi' the dinner.'

I turned on the telly and sat with my eyes glued to Bugs Bunny in order to avoid looking at Proctor. Drunk, he was a psycho case, sober he appeared a smarmy greaseball. He finished his tea off with a noisy slosh, 'I'm jist away.'

'Aye, ye'd better hurry. The pubs have been open for a full five minutes,' I shouted after him.

The sausages and mash were dumped with a bang before me.

'When's the wedding?' I asked.

'Don't be so bloody sarcastic. Just because I gave the man a drap o' tea ye needny try tae make something o' it.'

'I don't want tae see that man in this hoose,' I said.

'So, it's your hoose now.'

I tried being reasonable. 'Look, that man's a nut case. He'll come back here when he's drunk an' smash the place.'

'As far as I'm concerned it's a case of the pot calling the kettle black,' said my mother coldly.

I could see it was useless. 'I'm away tae bed for a rest.'

'Aye, only till the pub gets busy.'

*   *   *

Later on I ran into Paddy McDonald in the Paxton, quite sober. I told him about Proctor Mallion drinking tea with my mother.

'Tea?' he echoed.

'That's beside the point. I got the impression he was courtin' the auld wife.'

Paddy shook his head. 'Never,' he said. Paddy is very courteous as far as women are concerned. I don't think he ever had much to do with them. He told me, 'Yon's a bad one, and no' the type any woman should take up wi'. His first wife ran away wi' the insurance man and his second wife left him efter he pushed her oot the windae. Lucky for her it wis on the ground floor.'

'The worst o' it is,' I continued, 'I canny lay a finger on him or she'll turn against me.'

'D'ye want me tae lay into him?' asked Paddy.

If Paddy had been a hard man there were not many signs left. Years of steady drinking had worn him away nearly to skin and bone.

'Thanks Paddy, but better leave it.'

'You could always slip Pally McComb a fiver tae dae him. Pally's a good hatchet-man,' said Paddy.

'I widny waste ma money on Pally. Proctor would floor him wi' a glare. It's no' Willie Morrison ye're dealing wi'. Naw,' I added thoughtfully, 'it's got tae be something subtle.'

'Look,' said Paddy, 'there's Proctor comin' in.'

I looked to see him staggering up to the bar, staring with unfocused eyes around him, likely looking for someone to latch on to. He zig-zagged towards us, then crashed into a chair. Flossie, the barman, emerged from his hideaway and glared at Proctor with hands on hips. Ineffectually he had barred Proctor on a number of occasions, but Proctor either ignored or never remembered them. Flossie, a peace lover at heart, usually forgot he had barred Proctor until he got the current bouncer to throw him out again. Bouncers in the Paxton Arms ran the same hazards as deputy sheriffs so it was never the same guy twice that dealt with Proctor. I could see that Flossie was trying to make his mind up whether to call on the latest bouncer who was happily playing darts, impervious to the disturbance. I was trying to make my mind up whether to leave. Proctor was slowed up by the chair, but he headed towards us with drunken determination. Then he did some intricate steps as one foot tripped over the other and fell flat on his face. Flossie's mind was made up, 'Benny!' he shrieked in the direction of the dartboard, 'Get this pest out.'

Benny threw a dart wildly at the board and approached Proctor. He hauled him up to a standing position, gave him a kick on the legs, then threw him backwards through the swinging door.

'To think,' I said despairingly to Paddy, 'that's the auld wife's fancy man. Maybe my future stepfaither.'

'Ran into yer boyfriend,' I informed my mother when I returned home at the early hour of nine o'clock.

'Who's that then?' she asked, keeping her eyes on the telly.

'That lovable bundle of fun, Proctor Mallion.'

'Ye've got a nasty tongue on ye.'

'It's nothin' compared tae yer boyfriend's. When I last seen him he wis gettin' flung through the doors o' the Paxton. Still, he might take a look in later, provided he husny got picked up wi' the police.'

Her answer was to turn up the telly very loud.

'Get the tea on!' I commanded, thoroughly incensed by everything.

'Get it on yersel! Ye're big an' ugly enough.'

I regarded her with distaste. With her frizzy hair and torn tights Proctor might be the best she could get. I supposed it wasn't much of a life watching the telly and the occasional bit of gossip for entertainment. Pity moved me into the kitchenette wherein I prepared a pot of tea and some slices of toast. She wasn't impressed when I handed her my offering.

'Wonders will never cease,' she uttered, pointedly breaking off a black bit crust.

I tried again, 'Whit's for tomorrow's pieces, an' I'll make them masel. It'll save ye gettin' up in the mornin'.'

'Spam,' she said, then, 'are ye sure ye're feelin' alright?'

As I buttered my eight slices of bread I reflected it was going to be hard wakening myself. Still, if this soft soap was applied long enough she might consider it better to have me than Proctor in the house, because it would have to be one or the other.

'Goodnight,' I said to her before I retired. I tried to add the word 'mother' but since we seldom addressed each other by our names it was difficult. She didn't even answer, so engrossed was she in the telly.

Everything went wrong in the morning. First of all I slept in. I had to leave without tea. On the site I discovered the bread I had buttered was minus the spam. The wall I built collapsed because the ganger insisted I use wet brick. 'Get ma books ready, I'm packing it in!' I told the foreman.

'Away hame an' tell me tomorrow,' he said. I returned home about three in the afternoon to find Proctor drinking tea and eating cheese sandwiches. I grabbed him by his greasy collar and ran him out the door. 'Come back here an' ye're oot the windae the same as yer last wife!' was my message.

My mother's mouth was still open from shock when I came back into the living room. 'And don't think I don't mean it!' I said.

I entered my bedroom and lay down feeling exhausted but unable to sleep because of the rage that tore at my head. But I must have dozed off because I woke with a start at the sound of a tray being dumped on the coffee table. I knew I had to begin again. I didn't feel like it, but I must get rid of Proctor once and for all.

'Sorry about the carry on,' I mumbled as she wiped spilled tea off the table with one of my nearly new vests.

'Think nothing of it,' she sneered, throwing the vest violently onto the bed.

'Tell ye what,' I said, 'how's aboot comin' wi' me into the Paxton lounge for a wee break? I'll buy ye a sherry.'

'I don't drink,' she replied through clenched teeth. But somewhere I must have struck a chord for she added, 'Anyway, I might gie ye a showin' up. I've nothin' much tae put on.'

Inwardly I conceded that could be true. I said, 'Put on that nice fur coat ye got frae the Oxfam an' ye'll be lovely. In fact I'll introduce ye tae a real gentleman compared tae which Proctor Mallion looks like a bit shit on the pavement.'

I didn't add that the gentleman was Paddy McDonald. She must have been impressed for she said, 'Anything tae keep ye happy.'

We sat in an obscure seat at the back of the public bar, although my mother was under the impression she was in the lounge, and I did not disillusion her. Self-consciously she patted her frizzy hair fresh from the curling tongs. I hoped no one would mistake her for a girlfriend. Doubtfully she informed me she would have a sherry. As I ordered the bevvy Paddy entered. I was glad to see that he was miserably sober.

'Do me a favour,' I asked him, 'I want ye tae meet the auld wife. She's sittin' back there.'

He looked round furtively, but said courteously, 'An' a fine lookin' woman tae. I'm surprised ye don't bring her here mair often.'

'Are ye kiddin'? Listen, I'm trying tae get rid o' Proctor Mallion, an' this is all part o' the set-up. Have a word wi' her an' prove there's better fish in the sea.'

He was aghast. 'Ye're no' suggestin' I should start courtin' her?'

Actually I hadn't considered this. Paddy would have been as unwelcome a stepfather as Proctor. 'Nothin' like that,' I assured him, 'jist come an' sit at the table for a while tae take the bad look aff us.' Reluctantly Paddy brought over his beer.

'Meet Paddy McDonald,' I said in the way of introduction.

My mother turned pink. I was surprised considering the

contempt she had for him. Stiffly Paddy seated himself, also looking flushed. I thought this was going to be great. The two of them acting like teenagers.

'Very pleased to meet you,' he said.

Her face lit up. 'It's a pleasure I'm sure.'

After the second sherry my mother relaxed and addressed herself exclusively to Paddy. He was listening avidly to her every word. I gave up all pretence at listening because, apart from the fact that I was bored to tears, I spied Proctor Mallion at the bar arguing with Flossie. The upshot was that Flossie conveyed the message to him loudly, 'Listen sonny boy, you are barred!' Proctor's answer was to hurl a glass through the mirror behind the bar. Flossie screamed and ran for cover. My mother gave a moan of fear. This excited Paddy's chivalrous instincts. He hurried up to Proctor and smashed a lemonade bottle on the counter over his head. Immediately my mother gathered up her coat and ran out the bar shouting, 'That's the last time I come oot wi' you.'

As it was too early for a bouncer to be on the scene, impulsively I took on the job myself. I'm not all that keen on a fight but if there's one set out handy before me I have no alternative but to take part. Besides, Paddy was about to be executed any minute. Proctor, whose skull must have been as thick as concrete, was rising to his feet with bared teeth. Neatly I tripped him up, at the same time instructing Paddy to beat it quick. After I put the boot in on Proctor once or twice he was out for the count, and it was easy to deposit him on the pavement. The police van, which is as regular as a good taxi service, cleaned him off and all was quiet again. Flossie was grateful. He asked if I would like a job as a bouncer. 'Naw, but I'll have a double whisky.'

When I returned home my mother was watching the telly as usual.

'Some carry on that wis,' she said. 'Ye'll no' catch me in one o' these lounges again.'

'It was a' your fault anyway.'

She was amazed, 'My fault!'

'If it hudny been for the fact that ye were encouragin' Proctor Mallion I wouldny have taken ye to the Paxton. I thought ye must be havin' a right dreary time when ye took up wi' a character like him.'

She appeared to be so stunned that she became breathless. Finally she said, 'Me, takin' up wi' Proctor! The only reason he was in the hoose wis because I wis sellin' him that set o' tools lyin' under yer bed. They've been lyin' there for ages an' I could never get cleanin' the room right because o' them. I only got a fiver but it was well worth it tae get rid o' them.'

'Wait a minute,' I said, scarcely able to credit my ears. 'You didny gie him ma set o' tools that took me two years tae pay up when I wis an apprentice brickie?'

'Well, ye never had them oot the box as far as I can remember.'

'Ye don't understand,' I said slowly, my head beginning to ache. 'Ye never use yer own tools if ye can help it. Ye always nick somebody else's. If ye took yer own tools they wid jist get nicked.'

She was unperturbed. 'How should I know that?' Then she had the cheek to add, 'How's aboot makin' a cup o' tea?'

'Get lost!' I replied.

Up Country

Come this particular Saturday, a day I normally look forward to with great enthusiasm, I lost interest in the usual programme. Maybe I was becoming too aware of increasing pressures. All Friday night's talk had seemed loaded to me. Usually discussions go above my head unless I'm personally involved, but phrases like 'Are ye lookin' for trouble', 'Stick the heid on him' or 'He's only a Tim' pierced through my ears and stuck in my brain until, for no apparent reason to anyone, I threw a glass at the mirror behind the bar.

'Bouncer!' shrieked Flossie.

I walked out voluntarily to save any bother. So here I was on Saturday morning heading for a bus to take me to the splendours of the west away from alcoholic fumes and unreliable moods.

Collie Lumsden and a mate were sitting on the wall at the bus stance. Collie used to work beside me on the building sites until he gave it all up to be a full-time alcoholic.

'Where are ye gaun?' he called.

I replied, 'Up country.' At present I was not on the same wavelength as him and did not fancy his company. To cover up I asked civilly, 'Waitin' for the boozer tae open?'

He nodded then offered me a can of lager. Collie always took it for granted everyone was gasping for a drink. Usually he was right. Reluctantly I took the can, wishing the bus would hurry before I was sucked back into my familar social life.

'That's an idea,' he said with inspiration. He turned to his mate, 'We'll get the bus up tae the Clansman. It should be open by the

47

time we get there.' I was fed up. I could see how things were going.

Luckily his mate replied, 'Don't be daft. You are barred in the Clansman.'

Collie was incredulous. 'For Christ's sake, when wis I barred?'

'Dae ye no' mind dancin' on tap o' the table when ye wir last there? Then they pit ye oot.'

'Christ,' repeated Collie, dismayed, 'I don't mind that. Maybe ye're right.'

The bus moved into the stance. Thankfully I got on, and bumped into a big fella who was getting on at the same time. He stood back apologetically but not before I nearly choked on a mouthful of his long hair. I don't mind long hair but this was ridiculous. It almost reached his waist. I gave him a cool stare as I quickly scrambled aboard. Then with a wave to Collie and his mate I settled down to view the fresh pastures flying past.

By the time I reached my destination I was squeamish. The bus had been stuffy and the road had possessed the structure of a scenic railway. I tottered off wondering whether to head for the Clansman, but I forced myself to give it a miss. Instead I purchased a bottle of lemonade and a pie then headed for the pier and a boat alongside. A chalked board informed me that the mailboat was due to leave any minute for passengers wishing a trip round the islands for fifty pence. This was worth a try, so I climbed aboard. There were some sightseers on deck with the loud English patter. I hunched into a corner and the wooden rails dug uncomfortably into my shoulder blades. Seconds before the boat moved off the big fella with the long hair climbed on. Our eyes met with the awareness that one lonely type has for another in closed company. But I turned my head to convey the message that if I was alone I liked it that way. I made up my mind there and then I was getting off at the first island. I had no intention of being trapped on this boat for any length of time with these foreigners.

'Going off already?' asked the highland boatman, pocketing my fifty pence and no suggestion of change when I conveyed my wish to him.

'Aye, if ye don't mind.'

'Not at all son, we'll catch you on the way back,' he said as though I was a fish.

Ignoring his helping hand, I leapt onto the jetty of an unknown island. I nearly fell in the drink, but desperation saved me. Like a fugitive I scurried up the first path which led me away from the shore. I sensed contemplative stares following me, but when I turned round the moon faces on the boat were becoming harmless dots. Only the big fella stood out like a well-drawn sketch. I retreated into the undergrowth.

The path carried on through woods, ferns and streams. I was feeling great now, like Chief Chingachgook. The path began to lead upwards over the top of the island. It was hard going hauling myself up over bits of rock and slippery earth, but it was worth it when I reached the top. Panting and sweating, I lay down on the bracken to get my breath back. The view was terrific, all lochs and mountains. I felt contempt for my mates who would be firmly established in the boozer by now, slugging away at whisky and beer, unaware that there were better ways of passing the time. Yes, this was the life. I brought out my pie and lemonade. The pie was squashed and the lemonade lukewarm, but it was the most enjoyable meal I had eaten for a long time. I took off my jacket to make a pillow. With the droning of the bees and the heat of the sun on me like an electric blanket, I fell sound asleep on my bracken bed.

I don't know how long I slept but the heat had faded and I was stiff and thirsty. I shivered as I took the last swig of lemonade. Shakily I arose and followed the path downwards into a wood. But it was still great, I assured myself. I started to sing, 'I love to go awandering', but the sound of my voice was so unnatural I changed it to a whistle. I wished I could see a wee furry animal, or even a deer. That would be something, but I appeared to be the only animal that was moving. Or was I – I wondered. I could hear the noise of branches breaking now and then, and there were rustlings in the bushes. I hoped it was one of these wee furry animals, or likely it was a bird.

'Come oot, come oot, whoever ye are,' I shouted recklessly. No one answered right enough, which made it worse. I began to walk quickly, then ended up running. I don't know why, but once you start running it makes it a certainty that somebody's following you. Then I saw the loch looming through the trees. I reached the open space of the shore. I slowed down. The panic was over. The sun switched on again and a speedboat streaking along the horizon was reassuring. I sat on a bit of rock and looked over the water. Now I thought it was a pity there was no one to talk to. But it was even more of a pity I hadn't brought a half-bottle of something to calm the nerves. Still, I wasn't used to walking about islands and staring at lochs. I must concentrate on how great it all was. I looked hard at the loch for ten minutes until I had to admit that I was just fed up. I began to get a thirst and it wasn't for water, so I started moving again.

I followed the path deeper into the wood fighting through ferns which were as tall as myself. It was getting harder to follow the path and I was beginning to think I would never get out of this jungle when I emerged at last into a clear grassy bit where the trail led upwards again. I could be heading back to the jetty, the escape route to civilisation and the Clansman. Then I spied the top of a building on another path to the left. I thought I might as well investigate this while I was here.

The building turned out to be merely a hut, neatly boarded up and of no earthly interest, but beyond that was the entrance to a graveyard. It was a very wee graveyard and very old. The gravestones were a dirty dark grey and standing at all angles. A perfect background for Dracula. I studied one big stone closely and could make out a fancy design with words written underneath, 'Here Lies the Corpse of Jessie Buchanan'. On another there was a cheerful verse which I managed to decipher after peering at it for five minutes:

> Here Lies Tom,
> His Life was Squandered,
> His Days are Done,
> But Yours are Numbered.

In the middle of all this creepiness was a wooden seat twisted and gnarled as a corpse itself. I could picture Tom of an evening coming out of his grave and sitting there peacefully with arms folded and legs crossed. So I sat down too. It was strange but I couldn't hear any birds singing now. The only sound was my breathing and I tried to quieten this down a bit. I sat as still as the vision I had of old Tom because I didn't think I could move even if I tried. I had the crazy feeling I was part of the seat. Then from the wood there was a crack as if someone or something had stood on a branch while he or it was watching me. I could bear it no longer. I wrenched myself off the seat and ran past the hut down the path then up over the top of the island like a mountain goat. I didn't stop until I reached the jetty, just in time to be caught by the mailboat returning.

Once I got my breath back I noticed everybody had loosened up since I last saw them. They gave me broad, forgiving smiles for leaving. I smiled back gratefully because at least they were human, if English. 'I'll take the High Road and you'll take the Low,' they sang to me with big winks. 'An' I'll be in the pub afore ye,' I rendered back as quick as a flash. This caused a laugh all round. The big fella still stood apart looking at me calmly as if he had planned it all. Anyway all this did not matter because the boat was chugging towards the mainland and the Clansman.

* * *

Beneath the plastic beams and cross swords of the Clansman I downed my beer in one gulp. In the bar there was only myself, the barman and a tweedy type in the corner, of no consequence. The barman wasn't much cop either. Pointedly he wiped a spot of beer on the counter, spilled from my glass. 'Lively,' I thought. Then I became aware of a looming presence behind me. I turned to encounter the gentle blue eyes of the big fella.

'Could you tell me, pleaze,' he asked in the exact English of the educated foreigner, 'how I ask for some beer and spirits?'

'Sure. Ye jist say a hauf an' a hauf-pint.'

'Zank you.' He turned to the barman, 'A hoff and hoff pint.'

The barman was puzzled. 'What's that?'

'A hauf an' a hauf-pint,' I explained.

'That is what I say,' said the big fella.

'Aye, but it's no' whit ye say, it's the way that ye say it.'

'Beg pardon.' His voice was uncomplaining.

I sighed. I become bored when I have problems in making myself understood.

As if he knew what I was thinking he said, 'I hope you shall speak with me. All this day I have been alone and now I think it would be pleasant to speak with someone.'

I looked steadily at my beer so he could not read the annoyance in my eyes.

'Speak away chum.'

'Chum?' he questioned.

'Mate then.'

'Mate?'

I sighed, 'Friend then. Savvy – friend?'

His big face creased into a beautiful big smile.

'Friend – that is good. You will be my friend.'

I could see it was going to be hard to shake this guy off. Maybe he was a nut case. It was hard to tell with foreigners. For them and us there would always be something lost in the translation. I looked him over. His gear was casual but expensive, down to the open sandals. Leather, definitely not plastic. Probably a foreign hippy. One of the flower people. All love and marijuana. Though he looked familiar, as if I had met him before. But I wasn't happy with his company. He was not my style. He swallowed his whisky with the ease of a professional drinker. Then I thought maybe he wasn't so bad.

'Whit's yer name?' I asked.

He understood this. 'Max.' He held out his hand. His grip was warm and firm.

'Call me Mac. Everybody does,' I told him, with no hope of understanding.

He laughed. 'Mac and Max. It is the same. Perhaps we are the same.'

Privately I didn't think so, but I agreed. 'Sure,' then, 'you're a Gerry, I mean a German?'

His face straightened. 'Yes, but I would prefer to be Scottish.'

'How's that then? I mean why do you prefer to be Scottish?'

'In Scotland everyone is kind. In Germany they are not kind. All they wish to do is work and make money. They do not care about people. In Scotland people do not have this wish to work and make money all the time. If they have enough they are satisfied. Here people have helped me and many times buy me whisky. Sometimes they speak loud and violent but I think they have kind hearts.'

It did cross my mind that he might be a con man, but still I did not wish to disillusion him about our kind hearts, so I ordered two whiskies.

'Pleaze,' he protested, 'I will buy you a whisky.' He carefully extracted a fifty pence piece from a leather purse.

The barman frowned. 'Another ten pence,' he snapped.

To save time I quickly slapped down the ten pence. At this point the big fella brought out a parcel from his stylish anorak and laid it on the counter. Fascinated, the barman and I watched as he unfolded it to reveal sandwiches and a hard-boiled egg. He offered us both a sandwich and then started to unshell the egg.

I accepted mine gratefully but the barman refused his. He seemed to be searching for words. Unpleasant ones, I suspected.

'Do you have castles in this place?' the big fella asked him.

The barman was defeated. Without answering he walked away. Maybe to look up a rule book, consult his union or 'phone the police.

'Whit dae ye want wi' castles?' I asked.

'I have come here to study Scottish castles,' he explained as though it was as normal as cleaning windows. 'Then I shall write my book. I shall send you a copy since you are my friend. I shall have it specially translated.'

'Whit dae ye want tae dae that for?' I asked, returning to my original opinion that he was a nut case.

'Because you are my friend.'

This guy definitely had the knack of making a fella feel self-conscious. To change the subject I said, 'You remind me o' somebody.'

He considered then replied, 'I understand. I remind you of Jesus Christ,' without as much as a smile. I was convinced, definitely a nut case.

He went on, 'In Germany many people say I look like Christ. I have been asked to take this part in the Passion Play, but I refused because I do not like to pretend.'

He offered me his last sandwich. I declined. My appetite was gone. I was not certain, but the sandwich could be a test. He shrugged and ate it.

'My friend,' he said, 'I would willingly buy another whisky, but I have only a little money, just enough to buy a ticket on a ship to return home.'

That figures, I thought. 'Don't worry, I'm gaun for the bus anyway.'

'Good, I must get the bus also.'

It all loomed up. Back home to the auld wife with Max. She would love him. He would have my bed and I would have the couch. Quickly I ordered a carry-out, leaving the barman wiping crumbs off the counter with a pained expression on his face. When we were seated on the bus I handed him a can of beer. The old dames in front gave us cold stares. He didn't notice. I didn't care. For me it was always the done thing. The booze had no effect on him. My head was feeling swimmy but I was resigned. The big fella was coming home. I was not going to be the one who turned him away.

Again he read me for he said, 'I have a room to go to this evening. As you call it, a bed breakfast place.'

With relief I said, 'That will cost you plenty. Ye can always get a kip, I mean a bed, in ma hoose. Ma mother is a great person. She will put anybody up for the night.' I took care to look away as I said this.

'This woman is also good. She does not charge much money, because she explained I must stay in the kitchen since I might upset the guests.'

I was indignant. 'Jesus Christ!' I blushed at the expression. 'That's terrible. How could ye upset the guests?'

'My hair is very long as you see. Sometimes it is upsetting to others. In Germany when people drink too much they wish to cut my hair off. For this reason I did not go out at night.'

I was disappointed at this gutless attitude so I forgot to look away.

'You may think,' he explained as though I had said so, 'that I was afraid, but I do not believe in violence. Many times in the past I gave my parents much sorrow. Once I was a drug addict.' At least I had guessed that correctly. 'But with their love they helped to cure me so I keep my hair long that I will remember my disgrace. It is my penance.'

He looked at me intently. 'In your face I see the scars of violence. Perhaps that is your penance.'

I said nothing. He was wrong. I liked my scars. They were status for me. The bus drew in at the terminus. We got off. Everybody rushed away, maybe glad to escape from his loud, open conversation, and we were left alone. In a last attempt to do the right thing I said, 'Are ye sure ye'll not meet me later? We could have a drink the gither.'

He placed a hand on my shoulder, 'This would not be wise. For you my presence would cause violence because you are my friend, but give me your address so that I can send you my book.'

I wrote my address down on the back of my bus ticket. He placed it carefully in a wee book.

'How can ye be so sure of everything?' I asked. 'I mean that ye'll even get it published.'

'I am sure,' he replied with his awful certainty. He tucked his hair neatly inside his polo-neck jumper, shook my hand then walked away.

I looked after him wishing I could be as sure of everything. I turned the corner to head for home, kip, then tea and the boozer. Outside my close two lassies were skipping to the chant of

> *Old King Billy has a ten foot willie,*
> *He gave it to the lady next door,*
> *She thought it was a snake*
> *And hit it with a rake,*
> *Now it's only nine feet four.*

Trust the papes to know all the good ones. 'D'ye want a kick in the backside?' I asked them.

'King Billy! King Billy!' they shouted, then ran away laughing.

They are a right ignorant lot round here, but some day I will get away from this place. Some day I might go and see castles myself.

The Group

The modern trend was catching up with the clientele of the Paxton Arms. For the first time in living memory we were going to have entertainment. Behind the bar, sellotaped to the mirror, was a poster informing us in bold black print that a group called the Basket Weavers were, at great expense to the management, making a personal appearance every Friday at 8 p.m. We, the regulars, were suspicious of this development because, being creatures of habit, we always expected to have the same conversations and the same arguments with the same faces.

'Once they start bringin' groups in here it'll never be the same,' pronounced Paddy McDonald. 'A' these microphones an' amplifiers will only deafen us an' droon oot the conversation.'

'Too bloody true,' agreed Splash Healey, spraying Paddy with beer as he spoke.

Paddy wiped his face and considered, 'Still, it might serve a purpose. Some folks are better keepin' their face shut.'

Now though Splash was one of the most affable and generous of fellas nobody could stick his company too long. He was usually left alone at the end of an evening swaying about the bar talking to himself or his dog. Even the dog didn't pay too much attention to him. It was always sprawled sound asleep in front of the bar, causing folk to trip over it every time they went up for a glass of something. Not that he was excluded completely from our company, because as I said he was generous when he had the cash. Many a time he kept me going in drink through the week when I was stuck for the ready, though my discussions with him were limited and usually confined to pats on the back to both he and his dog. Speaking of his dog, I knew it well. It had been Paddy McDonald's before it became Willie Morrison's, and it had taken a lot of effort on Willie's part to convince it that it was not wanted – like trying to brain it with boulders. Splash had came across it one night in a dazed condition. Being a kind-hearted fella he had adopted it on the spot. It turned out to be a suitable arrangement since the two of them had a lot in common.

However, to get back to the subject of the group, when Friday came we were all in the Paxton as usual. Despite our prejudice about entertainers we were curious about them. It must have been about half-past eight before they appeared, and by then we had forgotten about them and were getting involved in deep discussions. Twice Paddy had tripped over Splash's dog and what was worse he had spilled his drink the second time.

'That bloody dug wants drooned,' he said, giving it a kick. The dog opened one eye. If it remembered Paddy from away back it gave no sign. It just growled and shut its eye again.

'Sorry aboot that Paddy,' spluttered Splash. 'I'll get ye anither drink.'

'Aye, well watch it then,' said Paddy. He added, 'I never thought tae see the day when an animal wid put a man aff his drink – here, whit the hell is that?'

A noise like a balloon letting out air exploded in our ears.

'It's only the group testing,' explained Flossie nervously.

We turned to see what was going on and there was the group testing their gear and tossing their hair about.

'Whit a racket,' groaned Paddy, 'if that's whit it's gaun tae be like I'll be givin' this place the go-bye.'

'That we should be so lucky,' gushed Flossie.

'Gie the fellas a chance. They're only testin',' I said.

'Aye, they're only testin',' repeated Splash.

'Sounds mair like they're testin' their arses,' said Paddy tersely. However, sensing that opinion was against him he kept quiet.

After coughing and repeating the word 'testing' for ten minutes the group finally got going. They gave us 'A Boy Named Sue' and 'A Girl Called Lou' which went down great and got loud cheers from everybody except Paddy who was staring moodily at his empty glass. He had been trying to attract Flossie's eye for a while, without success, since Flossie was giving all his rapturous attention to the group. He was recalled to reality when Paddy threw a box of matches, hitting him on the nose. But Paddy's views had lost their impact. By now we were all livened by the beat and thought the group were great. Eventually they stopped to refresh themselves and we were plunged into comparative silence.

'That wis rerr,' said Splash with enthusiasm and straightaway ordered three points for the group to show his appreciation.

'Ma heid is fair nippin' me,' said Paddy, 'I think ma eardrums are burst.'

'Gie us a break an' stop yer moanin',' I said, and moved away to have a word with Joe Duffy, a workmate on the site. If Paddy did not appreciate good music that was his hard luck. Big Joe and I spoke for a time about the work in general and the ganger in particular. Suddenly Joe broke off his discussion to say, 'Will ye look at that eejit?'

I turned to see Splash gripping the mike and prancing up and down in a silent mime of Al Jolson.

'Put that mike down!' yelled Flossie. 'Ye'll break it.'

'He's doin' a lot better than the other bampots anyway,' Paddy declared. 'At least he disny make as much noise.'

This triggered off fellow feeling for Splash. 'C'mon Splash – sing up! Gie us A Four-Legged Friend,' someone shouted. This was the song Splash usually sang outside the pub at closing time as his four-legged friend walked away in disgust. Splash did not need much encouragement. He never had it so good. He began in a screechy tone, 'A four-legged friend, a four-legged friend –' He broke off. 'Naw, wait a minute, that's too high,' and began again, 'A four-legged friend, a four-legged friend,' in a deep bass. 'Naw, wait a minute, that's too low.'

The audience was enchanted and falling all over the place with laughter. Then someone shouted, 'Get aff!' Another one shouted, 'Gie the fella a chance!'

Splash tried again, 'He'll never let you dow-en,' in the right pitch for shouting 'coal'. Being satisfied he carried on. The microphone must have been saturated. Apart from the cracking of Splash's voice it was making cracking sounds of its own.

All this did not pass unnoticed by the group. They tried to laugh it off at first. Then they quickly finished their beer.

'OK, that's enough. You've had your fun,' said one of them. He tried to disentangle Splash from the mike, but Splash was glued, and he carried on like the true trouper, 'He's honest and faithful right up to the end –'. The group member relinquished his hold. Likely he thought it was the last verse. When Splash started on another he lost his head.

'Gie's a haund wi' this nut,' he called to his mates, and they all began struggling with Splash. Bravely he held out, encouraged by the audience shouting, 'Let the fella alone!', 'Ya big cowards!', 'Pit the heid in Splash!' Even the dog, awakened by his master's voice, gave threatening snarls. I was surprised when Big Joe, normally a level-headed fella, rushed up with great fire to pull two of them away and grab the third by his psychedelic tie, almost throttling him. After a temporary surprise the group pulled itself together and made a combined onslaught on Joe, knocking him to the ground and putting the boot in with a lot of determination. Pandemonium broke out. Glasses were hurtled indiscriminately in the direction of the group and anyone near at hand. Beer was poured over Splash to quieten him down as he still continued to belt out the four-legged friend, and Flossie beat a hasty retreat into the back premises. I noticed one or two old scores which were nothing to do with the present matter being settled. My loyalties were divided. I thought Splash had it coming, but at the same time I felt bound to give Joe a hand. Just as I reached out to grab a chunk of hair there was a restraining grip on my arm. It was Paddy's. 'I telt ye groups wir nae use in a bar. Leave it. The polis will sort oot this lot. They'll sort ye oot as well if ye interfere.'

Paddy was usually right in a lot of things so we retreated into a corner to await the final crunch. It didn't happen because three regular bouncers with three volunteer bouncers took care of the situation. The group, defeated by sheer numbers, were pushed out into the world beyond with their equipment crashing behind them. Everyone simmered down except Splash, who burst into tears.

The night wore on. Drinks were set up. I seemed to be losing the power of speech and movement. This happens to me once in a while. I fell asleep over the table. When I woke up my back felt as curved as a hoola-hoop. Where is everybody I wondered. I lifted my head and tried to get everything into focus. I swivelled my eyes and managed to contact Splash slumped over a table to the left and Paddy drinking beer sitting at a table to the right. Ahead of me Flossie was listlessly moving a cloth over pools of liquid on the counter. The Indians must have attacked again for the mirror behind the bar was smashed for the umpteenth time.

'Whit happened?' I croaked. 'Where is everybody?'

'Away hame,' answered Paddy, 'an' it's time we wir as well.'

'Get us a drink.' I knew if I could even get a short one I would feel better.

'Bar's closed!' Flossie informed me with relish.

'Listen bum-boy,' said Paddy, 'get the lad a drink afore I beat ye to a pulp.'

I sensed Paddy had undergone a lot of pressure while I was sleeping it off. Flossie shrugged his shoulders. Insults hardly touched him. He put two whiskies on the counter and I noticed no money was passed. I gulped my whisky and felt a fraction better. Splash's dog sat up alert and ready for anything now that everyone was gone. It padded around, sniffing here and there then finally peed up against a chair. Flossie ventured the message, 'Do ye no' think it's time ye were away.'

'I'll go when I'm good an' ready,' said Paddy.

Splash was beginning to surface. He lifted his face to the ceiling and began on the four-legged friend again.

'Gie Splash a drink as well,' demanded Paddy.

Flossie banged another whisky on the counter. 'I canny take much more o' this,' he said.

'Look Paddy,' I said, 'Flossie is right. Ye'll only get the polis in.'

'Don't worry,' said Flossie, 'the polis will no' touch *him*.' He put a lot of emphasis on the word 'him'.

'Whit dae ye mean by that?' I asked.

Flossie's face twitched. Paddy said nothing.

When Splash began to sing again after swallowing his drink Flossie's control ran out. 'The polis don't touch Paddy these days. He's an informer.'

'Is that right?' I asked Paddy.

'Maybe.' He changed the subject as if it was of no consequence. 'Dae ye want anither drink?'

'There's no chance of that,' said Flossie, and continued with abandon, 'he thinks because he's in wi' the polis he can dae whit he likes. See when you wir sleepin' the group came back, but they wir hardly in the door when they were lifted. I saw Paddy gie one o' the polis a wee nod. He thought I never noticed.'

'Let's hope naebody notices this,' said Paddy. He drew the back of his hand off Flossie's cheek, causing a trickle of blood to ooze from the barman's nose. Flossie began to whimper.

'Is that true,' I asked, 'that ye're an informer?'

Paddy shrugged. 'Think whit ye like. That's a good word "informer"? but I'll gie ye better ones. How aboot "psychiatry treatment"? How wid ye like these words thrown at ye every time ye come up in dock? They say, "Just once mair Paddy – or else".'

'Or else whit?'

'Christ's sake, dae I have tae draw ye a diagram?' He went into a brooding world of his own and finally muttered, 'I want tae die in my ain hoose. No' in jail or hospital.'

'Ye mean yer ain midden,' I sneered.

'Call it that if ye like.'

It appeared as if he had answered my question. I regarded Splash who had returned to the senseless stage. I shook him viciously.

'C'mon, get up,' I said, 'ye're gaun hame. You and yer dug.'

He yelled as I hauled him up by the skin of his shoulder. 'Where are we gaun?'

'Hame – wi' me.'

Splash was the last person I wanted to take home, but I was filled with a twistedness that wanted to do the awkward thing.

'How's that?' he asked, spitting over me as usual.

There was nothing better to say than, 'Because ye're a better man than he is Gunga Din,' jerking my head in Paddy's direction.

Flossie had dried his eyes by this time and was handing Paddy another whisky. I walked past them both without a word. Splash lurched behind me with his dog following. The night air must have nipped my eyes because they were wet, and I had the cheek to talk about Splash being a wet guy, but then if ever I had liked a fella it had been Paddy and him an informer.

Paid Aff

'Whit's happened tae that wee layabout Rab Tunnock?' the ganger asked me in an aggrieved tone.

'How should I know,' I replied as I wiped the mortar off my trowel.

'Well, ye might know if he has been in the pub recently.'

'Never seen him.' I turned my back and placed a brick with marked concentration.

'If ye dae – tell him he's paid aff.'

I carefully evened off the mortar and said nothing. I wasn't going to be the one to do the ganger's dirty work. I had seen Rab the night before lying stupefied on the grass outside the Paxton Arms, but what had happened to him since was anybody's guess. Besides, at the moment I didn't give a damn about anything. My hands were stiff and my feet were numb. It was a damp, freezing morning. My jacket, bought in the height of the summer, was as warm as a piece of net and my year-old boots were as sturdy as a pair of sandshoes. In the summer you completely forgot about the winter so when it came you were never prepared. You just wondered how you could wangle a sick line. But if you did go on the sick you hated every minute of it, being exposed to the heavy breathing of the auld wife bitter about money prospects. Who would work on a building site, the worst trade in the world in the winter? Talk about the miners. At least they had Mick McGahey. The nearest we ever got to a strike was one from a winey's spade. Anyway who could protect us from the sleet and the frost? Then we had to put up with gangers like Harry McCafferty who must have served his apprenticeship in Siberia, intolerant of anything

64

above a twenty-five-watt bulb in the workmen's hut and a nip of alcohol to put a bit of heat in you.

McCafferty walked away. 'Whit's the time?' I asked the apprentice.

He looked at his digital watch. 'Half-past eleven.'

'Dear Christ, another hauf 'oor tae go. Ma fingers will have fell aff by then.'

'Mine as well.'

'How's that? Ye've had them in your pockets a' mornin'. Look lively, we'll never make oor bonus at this rate.'

He glared at me then picked up his trowel. Right enough he was a knockout. The first wall he had built collapsed as he was admiring it. Luckily the wind blew it away from him instead of on top of him.

'Always lock yer hut before ye leave in case the tools get stolen,' I had told him. He had done that, never bothering about who was in it. After shouting themselves hoarse McCafferty and the foreman had managed to unpick the lock to free themselves. However, he was now McCafferty's blue-eyed boy because he never drank, never took a day off and never answered back. He never did much work either.

Eventually the whistle blew. We all stamped into the hut.

'It's bloody freezin' in here,' we complained.

'Whit aboot gettin' us a heater? We're fed up strikin' matches,' said Fitty Peters to McCafferty who was munching away on his sandwiches.

'You lot don't work hard enough to get the circulation going,' said McCafferty. We ignored this statement and chewed on our pieces.

'Another thing,' he said, 'ye don't eat the right grub. Whit's that muck ye've got?' he asked me.

'Spam,' I replied.

'Ye're lucky,' said Fitty, 'I've got jam.'

'I've got roast pork and pickles,' said the apprentice.

'It's a' rubbish,' pronounced McCafferty. 'The best thing for keepin' oot the cauld is a flask o' soup followed by broon breid an' peanut butter sandwiches.'

'Imagine that,' said Randy Smith, 'a flask. We couldny afford one.'

'Naw,' said McCafferty, 'but ye can afford tae staun in the pub a' weekend.'

'That's how we canny afford a flask,' I said. 'It's a vicious circle.'

'Anyway,' said Big Joe to McCafferty, 'if I lived like you I'd hang masel, but we're no' interested in yer diet. We want a heater or else we don't work.'

'Is that whit ye call it – work?' said McCafferty. 'Well, if ye don't work ye're paid aff, so please yersels.' He gave a righteous belch then marched out.

'Maybe he's away for a heater,' said Randy wiping the drips from his nose.

'Mair likely away for a shit,' said Fitty.

'He hasny a good one in him.'

The apprentice turned red. 'Don't talk dirty in front o' the boy,' laughed Randy.

I stepped out of the hut to throw away a tea bag. 'Will you credit that,' I shouted, 'it's rainin'!'

'Good, we canny work then. Get the cards oot.'

We put ten pence each in the kitty. I dealt the cards. We played in silence, apart from the odd curse. After losing two games the apprentice said he was fed up and threw in his hand. We played some more. Then Fitty said, 'I've nae money left, unless somebody wid like tae pay me in.'

'No thanks,' we all said.

So far I had won fifty pence when McCafferty returned. 'OK boys, time's up – oot!'

'Whit do ye mean?' we asked. 'It's rainin'. We don't work in the rain.'

McCafferty exploded. 'It's only drizzlin'. Ye don't work in the cauld! Ye don't work in the rain! Who dae ye think ye are – a bunch o' bloody civil servants!'

66

'We don't work in the rain,' Big Joe repeated and proceeded to deal out the cards.

McCafferty swore. 'You mollycoddled bastards! This job is away behind schedule as it is. Every day somethin' happens wi' you lot.'

'Like last week when auld Jimmy broke his leg fallin' through a hole that wis covered up wi' sackin',' I said.

'It wisny covered wi' sackin',' growled McCafferty. 'He wis half blind wi' booze.'

'Ye needny worry aboot bein' behind wi' the schedule,' said Big Joe, 'because ye've saved this firm a lot o' money in compensation wi' a' these accidents ye swore were pure carelessness.'

'I'm no' gaun tae bandy words wi' you lot. Just get back tae work or ye're a' paid aff.'

The apprentice stood up and placed himself beside McCafferty.

'Right!' said McCafferty when he saw we were unmoved, 'Ye're a' paid aff except the apprentice here.'

The apprentice was now outside the hut. We carried on with the cards.

'That's it then,' said McCafferty, and banged the door behind him.

At this point we threw our hands in. Randy put the cards in his pocket. 'Might as well take them hame.'

'Oh well,' said Big Joe stretching himself, 'I could dae wi' a week or two in front o' the fire.'

'Aye, but it's no' so good when ye've nae money,' said Fitty.

'We're OK for the weekend anway. Who's worrying aboot the future?' I said with bravado.

'There's always the supplementary,' Big Joe reminded us.

'Aye, efter six weeks.'

I was beginning to get depressed. 'How aboot runnin' doon tae the licensed for a bottle of wine?' I asked Fitty. 'I'll pay for it. I've just got enough.'

'That's a good idea,' said Randy. 'I'm no' that keen on gaun hame. The wife'll no' be exactly overjoyed.'

There was a general agreement. Fitty returned with the wine

and we poured out a measure into our mugs. We started to play cards again. This time it was for matches – not much of an incentive. Now a bottle of wine might be an average drink for one but between four it does not last long, and finally we were pouring it out in minute measures. The talk ran out and the game became boring. The bottle was drained and flung in the bucket. Then the door opened and McCafferty said, 'I telt ye all. Ye're sacked! There's nae point in hingin' on.'

'Get stuffed!' said Big Joe.

McCafferty turned away. 'Well, ye'll have tae go hame sometime.'

We sat in silence for about three minutes. 'This place is as cheerful as a mortuary,' said Big Joe. 'I'm away hame.'

'I'll have a drag before I go,' said Randy. He brought out his shag and handed us each a roll-up. My eyes were nipping. I closed them to ease the tiredness. When I opened them I was alone. I lit the roll-up and lifted the bottle from the bucket to drain the dregs, feeling cold and hopeless but reluctant to move. The aftermath of being paid off was always the same. I tried to recall how many times this had happened. Perhaps I never should have been a brickie. I had always fancied myself as a joiner. Once I spent a fortnight converting a set of drawers into a bookcase. It hadn't been a success, but I always had the yearning. When the Youth Employment sent me to Smeddon's Building Contractors, the foreman had said, 'We don't need apprentice joiners, but a big lad like you would do well as a brickie.'

'No thanks,' I had said.

'You might change your mind. You've got a great build for a brickie. Come back tomorrow if you do.'

My mother had told me to get back up the road to Smeddon's. 'Ye'll no' get another chance,' she said.

'I don't want tae be a brickie,' I had shouted as I banged my fist on the wall, but the next day I returned to Smeddon's and become an apprentice brickie. I carried the hod, laid common brick, facing brick and coping stones. I laid brick down manholes and laid brick up ten storeys, but I never had a pound in my pocket beyond a Monday unless I won it at cards. I was twenty-two. My arms were knotted like a man of forty-two, and sometimes my back ached as if I was fifty-two. And it all added up to being paid off once again. Oh well, there was no point in feeling sorry for myself. I might as well get a bit of shut-eye before I returned home to break the glad tidings. I eased myself up onto the bench and tried to forget it all.

I woke up freezing, and had to stamp up and down in the hut to get the circulation going. I opened the door. It was grey fog, so I shut it quick. There was nothing to hang around for, but it was funny to think I would never see these four wooden walls again, or that naked pin-up above the kettle, or that Carlsberg Special ashtray stolen from the boozer. I was getting that feeling of foreboding which strikes me now and again like a clammy hand on the shoulder. For Christ's sake, I thought, I'm only twenty-two with no real problems, but sometimes I could see myself winding up on the river bank like the wineys, with all my possessions in a plastic bag. Let me kick the bucket before I reach that stage was the nearest I ever got to a prayer.

'Are you there McCafferty?' a voice roared in relief to my thoughts.

The door burst open and there was Rab Tunnock stoned out of his mind brandishing a brick hammer. He aimed it at the side of the hut.

'Calm doon,' I said.

'Calm doon! That bastard McCafferty has paid me aff!'

'We're a' paid aff, so forget it.'

'Bastards!' he said.

He lurched over to the wall and pulled the brick hammer out and swung it round his head. He was a terrible spectacle. Oaths spewed from him like the bile as his eyeballs swung in harmony with the hammer. If my sympathies were not for McCafferty, at that moment they were not for Rab.

'I'm gaun tae smash in this hut,' was his ultimate recognisable statement. I thought it was time to get going. 'Please yersel,' I said and hastily left.

I met McCafferty further along the site. 'Rab Tunnock is smashing up the hut,' I informed him. 'Better look out. He's pure mental.'

'Don't worry I'll take care o' that nut.' He added, 'Ye'd better get hame. There's nae point in hingin' aboot on a day like this. I'll put yer time in tae five, but be sure tae be in sharp tomorrow and tell the rest o' the layabouts tae be in sharp as well.'

'Sure Harry, we'll a' be in sharp.'

'That'll be the day,' he jeered.

I walked on shivering. I put my hands in my pockets and passed the apprentice laying brick in slow motion like a phantom in the fog.

'Mind!' McCafferty shouted, 'Be in sharp!'

'Get stuffed!' I said, but not too loud, and thanked God I wasn't paid off yet.

McCluskie's Oot

'Did ye hear that McCluskie's oot!' declared my mother when I was just in from work and not in a great mood.

'Who?'

'Ye know fine. Him from along the road. Him that did auld Muncie in.'

'Oh him. Whit's for dinner?'

'Ye'll see when it's ready!' she snapped and charged through to the kitchenette, adding, 'The trouble wi' you is that you're interested in nothin' but yersel.'

'How should I be interested in McCluskie? He's nothin' but a heid-banger.'

'He's no' the only one.'

'Don't gie me that fork,' I instructed when she placed some chips and egg on the table. 'It's a' rust.'

She studied the fork. 'Nothin' wrang wi' it. It must be great tae have servants.'

'It must be great tae have cutlery.'

'Anyway, I think it's terrible,' she said.

'Ye mean this fork?'

'I mean it's terrible that McCluskie's oot.'

'I thought ye were pally wi' his auld wife.'

'I feel sorry for her right enough havin' a son like that, but I've nae time for him.'

'I'm sure he's worried.'

'Well, worried or no', I hear folks are gettin' up a petition tae put the McCluskies oot their hoose.'

'The trouble wi' folk,' I informed her, 'is that they should mind their ain business, including yersel.'

'Oh sure, everybody should mind their ain business, then we could a' get murdered in oor beds.'

'As far as I can remember the verdict was manslaughter.'

'It was murder. The poor auld soul had his heid caved in.'

'Well, if your heid banged aff the pavement it might cave in. Anyway, shut up. I want tae read the paper.'

I propped the paper up against the milk bottle, but I was really thinking fancy McCluskie getting out. I was sure he would have been put away for eight years. In fact I was hoping he would have been put away for eight years. Not that I gave a damn about Muncie.

At one time McCluskie had been my one and only pal – a long time ago – when we were at school. In those days we had very fine ideas about our future. He was going to be a fireman and I was going to be a veterinary surgeon. I liked the sound of that. But things didn't work out. He got a job in the distillery and I got started as an apprentice brickie. There had been nothing sensational about him then. He was a short, beefy, fair-haired lad with the scrubbed look that blond folk have. 'A nice boy,' was my mother's comment. 'I wish you looked half as tidy as him. That hair o' yours is always hingin' ower yer eyes.' Our main pastime had been to go to the pictures as often as we could afford it and throw apple stumps at the heads in front of us. In the fine weather we would read dirty magazines whilst sunning ourselves on top of the bin lids. But we became fed up with the pictures and dirty magazines and took to drinking. This was mainly because of McCluskie's easy access to the stuff. On Fridays he would come along for me carrying a lemonade bottle filled with undiluted spirits sneaked from the distillery. We would drink this in an old washhouse, and finish up rolling about the floor and being violently sick more often than not. We stayed out as late as possible so I could stagger to bed undetected while my mother was involved in the television, as she was even in these days. We enjoyed the excitement of this illicit drinking even if we never felt well. My mother would remark on how puky I looked but she was never suspicious. Maybe she thought it was a stage I was going through.

It all came to a head one Friday night when my mother was gossiping outside the close with a neighbour. Being drunker earlier than usual we had misjudged the time. The two of us were hitting off the fence as we rolled along the road. I must have been getting to the chronic stage because I couldn't see very well.

'Stop that stupid carry on,' she said abstractedly in the middle of her discussion. McCluskie rolled on by heedlessly but I collapsed over the fence.

'The boy looks right bad,' the neighbour said.

'In the name o' God whit's up wi' ye?' said my mother.

'I canny see!' I gasped out, then sank to the pavement.

'Looks like he's got meningitis,' said the neighbour.

'Get me a doctor, quick!' I pleaded.

This statement struck a false note with my mother. She pulled my head up by the hair and smelled my breath.

'He's bloody well drunk. 'Phone the doctor, Aggie, an' I'll get him aff the pavement.'

I wasn't well for a fortnight. During that time my mother kept up a tirade of abuse between plates of tinned tomato soup. I never knew what happened to McCluskie but for the time being I had had enough of booze. Gradually I came out of my misery and returned to work. I lost touch with him and my mother had altered her opinion.

'I never want tae see that fella near this hoose again,' was her command.

In those days she did have some jurisdiction over me, but it was a lonely business going to the pictures on your own or watching the telly with mother. I longed for a bit of excitement. Once or twice I went to the washhouse on a Friday hoping McCluskie would show up even without the lemonade bottle. Once in desperation I went straight from the site to the distillery in the chance I would bump into him. Sure enough I got there in time to see him sauntering along the road with another fella. Happiness surged through me at the sight of his moon face. Great, I thought, I was going to live again. I couldn't reach him quick enough.

'How's it gaun John?' I said.

The laughter faded from his face. 'Tolerable son, tolerable,' he said coolly. He walked on without as much as a slowdown. My face flushed as if the skin had been stripped off. I had to keep going. I walked straight on, as if I was wound up, right through the distillery gate.

'Where do you think you're goin'? asked the gateman.

'Jist waitin' for somebody,' I mumbled.

'Well wait back doon the road.'

I hung around for a minute outside the distillery for appearance's sake and to keep me from catching up with McCluskie, then slowly I returned home.

I went through a bad period at that time. I stayed in at nights. Then I would pace up and down staring out of the window wondering if I could risk going out for a walk without folk taking a note of my loneliness. I could have become a recluse without any bother. Finally, one Friday I was adventurous enough to buy a half-bottle of cheap wine from the licensed grocer. I drank it in the seclusion of my bedroom. Courage hardened in my nerve cells enough to make me move outwards. I moved along to the first pub I came to, which was the Paxton Arms. Everybody was standing about in casual attitudes talking and laughing, but I was stiff with embarrassment. I knew the lonely sign was written all over me. Desperately I ordered a pint of beer and found it gassy and hard to swallow. A grizzled-looking guy came over and stood beside me. His eyes were wise and searching. The heat rose within me.

'Does yer mither know ye're oot?' he asked. I stood rigid and scarlet.

'Relax son. I'm no' gaun tae report ye for bein' under age if the barman canny see that himsel.'

'I'm auld enough.'

'Sure – auld enough tae drink shandy.'

'Look mister,' I said, 'shut yer face or I'll shut it for ye!'

He laughed. 'Ach, ye widny hit an auld man. Here I'll buy ye a decent drink.'

He ordered two whiskies and placed one before me, saying solemnly, 'My name is Patrick Grant McDonald, but you can call me Paddy.'

From then my social life began.

I saw McCluskie once or twice in the Paxton after that, but I looked through him. He didn't bother me. He looked through me. I told Paddy McDonald that McCluskie was in the habit of stealing money from his mother. After that I never saw him in the Paxton again. Maybe Paddy had influence. Anyway I became one of the regulars and forgot about McCluskie. Then last year he hit the headlines. Apparently he was running round with some crazy gang out of the district and he was selling Muncie, the nightwatchman of Paterson's Sawmills, bottles of undiluted whisky. Muncie watered this down and sold the stuff at a nice profit. The gang always drank in his hut before they went out on the rampage. One night a fight broke out. Muncie must have interfered. He finished up with his skull smashed on a paving stone. McCluskie was charged. It could have happened to anyone but I was glad because I figured he had it coming. Now he was out it seemed a bit of an anti-climax. Then I thought, why bother about McCluskie? He was nothing to me now one way or another.

At least that was what I thought until I got Big Joe along the road to the site on Monday morning.

'I hear there's gaun tae be a new start,' he informed me. That wasn't worth a reply. There were always new starts on a Monday.

'Did ye hear whit I said?' he repeated.

'Aye – so what?'

'I'll tell ye so what. It's McCluskie that's the new start. Him that did auld Muncie in.'

'How did he manage that?' I asked. 'He's never worked on the sites.'

'Well, ye know McCafferty always has a soft spot for jailbirds since his son-in-law did time for ripping copper off an electric cable and putting the lights oot all over oor world. He was a pushover for McCluskie.'

'Whit can he dae on the buildin'?' My mind was trying to cope with this set of circumstances.

'Anybody can dae general labourin'. It's better than hard labourin'.' He went into convulsions at his joke.

'Ye're no' funny. I don't want tae work beside that murderin' bastard.'

'I didny know ye were carryin' a cross for Muncie. I heard he was very fond o' wee lassies.'

'In this place everybody gets a name for somethin',' I said angrily.

As I said before I didn't give a damn about Muncie but it had taken me seven years to get over McCluskie. Now I might be back to where I started. I retreated into silence as we pushed on.

Sure enough, when we got into the hut there was McCluskie sitting in the corner. I looked him over furtively. He had changed a lot. He used to be beefy and red-faced. Now he was lean and pale. He gave me no sign of recognition. His eyes were on his feet. The squad were doing the usual Monday morning routine of grumbles about hangovers and giving highly coloured versions of their week-end, and kicking empty cans from Friday afternoon's booze-up. I took no part in this. I was too busy watching McCluskie. He rose to his feet and said, 'I'm new at this game fellas,' then laughed – a pitiful attempt at a laugh anyway. 'I don't know whit I'm supposed tae dae, so if ye could gie me a clue like –'

For a minute nobody said anything. Then Fitty Peters, who is always on the ball, started to sing 'Jailer Bring Me Water'.

As everybody is always ready for a laugh, especially on a Monday which is a very nervous day; we all joined in. McCluskie turned pink.

He sat down, scratched his head and joined in as well. Then everybody went silent. He was left singing 'My throat is kind of dry' on his own. In an offhand way I noticed that his gear was worse than mine. He had been charged in the summer and still had the open season gear. The thin stylish jacket, the coffee-coloured strides, the suede shoes, topped off with a yellow tee-shirt. All great for the beach but weird on a building site. I didn't feel like laughing any more, but he wasn't going to get any sympathy from me so I hurriedly gathered up my tools and left for the weary load ahead. Some folk had it coming to them and that was all there was to it.

'Is that the fella that murdered auld Muncie?' the apprentice asked me in a reverent tone.

'It wis manslaughter – no' murder.'

The apprentice sickened me. He had seen nothing, done nothing and was always a goody.

'Whit's the difference?' he asked.

'Well, the difference is, if I take this brick hammer an' smash it ower yer heid, that would be murder. On the other haun', if I accidently push ye aff the scaffolding when we get up, that's manslaughter.'

'Oh,' he replied.

'But there's nae point in tellin' ye anything. Ye're too thick.'

'I'm learnin',' he said and added quickly, 'so if I accidently pushed you aff it wid still be manslaughter.'

I gave him a long look. You can never trust anyone. 'That wid be a bloody miracle.'

Eventually the whistle blew. I was dying for the break, but I wasn't keen to see McCluskie again.

*   *   *

He wasn't in the hut when I came in and I was hopeful he had chucked it. Then he arrived along with McCafferty. Conversation ceased. McCafferty brought out his flask of soup unaware of the silence. McCluskie brought out a paper bag from his pocket and produced a flattened pie. He looked as miserable as hell. Joe Duffy unfolded the newspaper and said straightaway, 'Fancy, here's a chap that got eight years for murderin' his wife. Ye'd have thought he wid have got aff. Just shows some folks are lucky and some folks are no'.'

McCafferty munched on oblivious to the nudges and winks. He said to McCluskie, 'Are ye gettin' the hing o' things noo?'

'I suppose so,' answered McCluskie. His eyes were bleak.

'That's the game,' said McCafferty. He looked around us trustingly.

'The lads here will show ye the ropes. They're no' a bad lot. That right Fitty?'

Fitty looked in the other direction. 'Depends,' he said.

'On whit?' said McCafferty. It was beginning to dawn on him that all was not light and happiness.

'Depends if we feel like it,' said Big Joe.

McCafferty's face went sour. 'Listen you lot. I don't want any trouble. McCluskie has had a bad break.'

'So did Muncie, if ye ask me,' said Randy Smith.

Suddenly McCluskie arose and stood stiff with fists clenched.

'Ye can stick yer job, Harry. There's a lot better men in the stir than whit's in here, and as for *you* –' I looked up startled to see that he was addressing me. 'I can see ye don't want tae know me, though I wis good enough for ye when I wis gettin' ye free drink at one time.'

His point of view left me speechless. Then I said, 'For years ye widny even say hullo to me, an' as for yer free drink. It wis lethal. Ye nearly killed me wi' it.'

'Naw, it wis Muncie he killed,' interrupted Fitty. 'You were lucky. You got away.' There was unroarious laughter.

'Harry,' pleaded McCluskie, 'pay me aff and let me oot o' here. If ye pay me aff the auld wife will get broo money. Dae us that favour.'

McCafferty shrugged. 'Away hame and I'll send yer cards on. I'll say ye wereny fit for the buildin'.'

McCluskie nodded. He gave us a long stare. Now we looked at our feet. He looked around as if he had forgotten something. There was only his empty paper bag. He crumpled it and put it in the bucket as though he was obliged to leave the place tidy. Then he left.

Somebody said, 'That's got rid o' that bugger anyway. He should never have started.'

McCafferty said, 'Ye canny tell wi' folk. Some are no' cut oot for the buildin'.'

'That's true,' said Big Joe, 'he wis mair suited for a distillery.'

'Mind ye,' said McCafferty, 'I never held Muncie against him.'

'Muncie wis nae loss tae onybody,' said Fitty Peters. 'He deserved it.'

I looked out of the hut door. I could still see McCluskie in the distance and I couldn't help thinking we never gave him much of a chance. After all it was only manslaughter, not murder, and nobody had given a damn about Muncie anyway.

Christmas Day in the Paxton

It was Christmas Day, a Saturday. The streets were covered in ice and nothing was moving except me. There was not a soul, a dog or even a bus in sight and worst of all I suspected the pubs would be closed. I headed in the direction of the Paxton with my mother's Christmas message ringing in my ears.

'Where's yer Christmas present ye ask? Well, where's mine? Every year it's the same. Not a sausage dae I get aff ye. No' even an extra pound an' a' the neighbours showin' aff their presents. Well, I'm sick o' it –'

'And a merry Christmas to you!' I had shouted as I walked out.

I stood outside the Paxton. My pessimism was justified. It was shuttered and bare, but there was a drone of voices from somewhere. I went round the back and there was Baldy Patterson and Big Mick swaying over a prone figure on the gravel. Baldy was waving an open bottle of wine about as he studied the object. It was Paddy McDonald. He was blue, but breathing.

'Better get him aff the ice. He'll die o' exposure,' I said.

'That's jist whit I wis sayin',' replied Baldy as he splashed me with the wine.

'I'd rather have that doon ma throat,' I told him.

He handed me the bottle. It was great how they managed this so early. But when it came to the wine they could always work the miracle.

'How long has he been lyin' here?' I asked.

'Maybe a' night. We jist came alang tae see if the place wis open.'

'There's nothin' open the day except the hotels.'

'We don't fancy the hotels,' said Big Mick.

I wasn't surprised. Unshaven, bloodshot and filthy, they were not exactly the hotel type.

'Anyway,' said Baldy, 'the Paxton is supposed tae open at twelve.'

I took heart at the words but I knew he wouldn't have a clue about anything, even that it was Christmas Day. Paddy twitched in his sleep.

'Whit are ye gaun tae dae aboot him? He'll get pneumonia.'

'He's no' ma responsibility,' said Big Mick.

'Nor mine,' said Baldy, but to prove he had Paddy's welfare at heart he gave him a kick saying, 'Get up ya stupid bastard!'

Paddy merely turned on his side. I was dying to get away but it was difficult to leave a potential corpse, especially at this time of the year.

'Can ye no' drag him up tae his hoose?' though I knew this was beyond their capabilities.

'Better leave him for the polis,' said Big Mick. 'They'll take care o' him.'

'The polis will never see him roon' here.' I tried to haul him up but he was as limp as a bundle of rags. They both watched me with indifference.

'Ye're wastin' yer time. When the Paxton opens we'll drag him in an' let Flossie take care o' him.'

I let Paddy go and he slithered down the wall. Baldy handed round the bottle and we studied the problem. Mick finished the wine and rolled the bottle along the ground.

'Keep the place tidy,' said Baldy. He flung it in the bushes.

Conversation petered out. Sullenly we regarded Paddy. For the sake of doing something I took his pulse. It was faint but flickering. Anyway his breath steamed the air. What bloody luck to walk into this set-up. I leaned against the wall and folded my arms. I was beginning to freeze.

Finally Mick said, 'Whit's the time?'

'Time we wir away. Ye might as well face facts. The Paxton is no' gaun tae open the day. It's Christmas.'

Baldy was amazed. 'Is it?'

'Aye. Good King Wenceslas an' a' that.'

'An' whit did ye get frae Santa then?' asked Mick with a bronchial laugh.

'A bottle o' wine,' said Baldy promptly, 'an' guess who Santa is?'

'Who?' asked Mick.

I said nothing. They were getting on my nerves.

'Paddy here. He wis lyin' on the ground wi' a bottle stickin' oot his pocket for his auld mate.'

'Christ, ye'd rob the deid,' I said.

'He bloody well looks deid,' said Baldy giving Paddy another kick.

'Listen!' said Mick. 'There's somebody in there.'

We listened. We could hear the noise of dishes being clattered.

'An' look,' said Baldy, 'the light's on.'

Sure enough there was a beam of light from the back window.

We all ran round to the front. The door was still shut. We banged it with our feet. Eventually the door opened and Flossie peered out. His face was all screwed up.

'For God's sake, can ye no' wait?'

'How much longer?' I asked. 'Paddy McDonald is lyin' roon' the back an' he looks as if he's gaun tae kick the bucket any minute.'

'Well he can kick it ootside. He's no' gaun tae mess up things in here.' He slammed the door in our faces.

'That's fuckin' marvellous,' said Big Mick.

'Ach, I'm away,' said Baldy. 'I think I've got a bottle planked somewhere in the Drive.'

'For Christ's sake! How did ye no' mention that sooner?' said Big Mick.

They stumbled off without a backward glance.

I thought I had better see to Paddy. It was a surprise to find he had managed an upright position. His arms were stretched against the wall as if he was holding it up. He began to thump it.

'Haud on Paddy. It's gaun tae open soon.'

He tried to speak, but his teeth just chattered. I led him round to the front.

'Ma feet,' he moaned. 'I canny feel them.'

'Maybe ye've been up in the Yukon an' got the frostbite. C'mon, ye'll be a' right once we get inside. It's gaun tae open soon.'

By the time we reached the entrance Flossie was unlocking the door. Paddy tried hard to resurrect himself but Flossie said, 'He's no' gettin' in here in that condition.'

I pushed past him, dragging Paddy along with me, and placed him on a chair.

'Get us two haufs quick, before I have tae call an ambulance.'

The word 'ambulance' knocked the argument out of Flossie. He served us rapidly.

'Get this hauf doon ye!' I ordered Paddy. He did as he was told then gave a long quiver and relaxed.

'Thanks son,' he said.

I didn't like the look of him. His eyelids and lips were purple. I looked around for a bit of distraction but the bar was empty. Doubtless folk would be celebrating in the comfort of their homes with the turkey and plumduff. My mother didn't go in for that sort of thing. Though maybe she would stretch a point when I got back and produce a steak pie and jelly. This effort would be rounded off with a box of five cigars. To hell with Christmas.

Paddy began to fumble in his pocket but he gave it up and fell asleep with his head on the table. I shook him to make sure he was only sleeping. He looked at me with a blind stare. Then the sight returned. He said, 'I don't feel sae good. The worst I've ever felt.'

The blind stare came on again. He slumped forward. Flossie

looked over with suspicion. I straightened Paddy against the chair but he lolled about like a rag doll. I approached the bar. 'Right Flossie, get an ambulance.'

Flossie was outraged. 'Whit dae ye think this is – a surgery?'

'If ye don't get one ye might have tae attend an inquest.'

Flossie was convinced. He darted through to the 'phone. I checked with Paddy again. He had gone back to the fumbling stage.

'Whit are ye lookin' for?'

He gestured for me to be quiet. Finally he produced two crumpled pound notes.

'Buy yersel a drink.'

The notes were greasy and torn. I pushed them back. 'Haud on tae them Paddy.'

'Naw, naw. I want ye tae have a drink.'

To save any argument I shoved them in my pocket and got two whiskies with my own respectable pound note. Gradually Paddy began to look a bit better. His face was now pallid instead of ashen.

'How long were ye lyin' ootside anyway?'

'I don't know. Maybe since last night.'

'Good God man, it's a miracle you're no' deid!'

'I'm a hard man tae kill, but I think –'

Whatever he thought I don't know for his eyes went glassy again.

'Did ye 'phone the ambulance?' I shouted to Flossie. He was talking to a couple of fellas who had just arrived.

'Aye,' Flossie hissed over, 'but keep yer voice doon. We don't want customers tae think they're in a morgue. We want tae keep the place a bit cheery like.'

'Somethin' wrang wi' Paddy?' asked one of the fellas, 'Or is he jist stoned?'

'Stoned cold is mair like it. Actually he's a sick man.'

I said to Flossie, 'Maybe ye could show a bit o' Christmas spirit an' gie Paddy a drink before he withdraws his custom.'

The fellas nodded in agreement. Flossie looked pained but put two small glasses on the counter. I swallowed mine and placed the other one before Paddy. He tried to lift it to his mouth but it smashed on to the floor. I wished the ambulance would hurry. Then he spoke as if we had just met. 'Pleased tae see ye Mac. I thought we had fell oot.'

'I widny fall oot wi' you.'

'Aye ye did. Mind ye thought I wis a polis informer?' He attempted a laugh. 'I widny even inform them the time o' day.'

He went quiet again. I could hear the distant whine of an ambulance. Again he came out of his reverie. 'I don't want it tae get around, but I hivny been feelin' well lately. Ye see, ma hoose wis burnt doon the other night. A' ma pigeons are deid. Maybe the cat as well.'

I looked away in case he was going to cry, but he carried on dry-eyed. 'Ye don't happen tae know o' anybody who takes in ludgers? I widny be any bother.'

I had to smile. 'Afraid not Paddy.'

'Of course,' he took a deep breath, 'I can always go tae the Drive wi' Baldy an' the team. Though they're no' really ma type.'

He lost the thread of things and closed his eyes. The ambulance men entered. 'Did somebody send for us?'

Paddy heard this. Painfully he stood up and said with a touch of his old wrath, 'It wisny for me I hope!'

I nodded to them and jerked my head towards Paddy. Flossie stopped polishing his glasses and looked over, no doubt sensing a commotion, but there was very little for at that point Paddy crashed back on to the floor and lay like a log. An ambulance man knelt down beside him and felt his pulse. He didn't have to say anything. It was plain he was gone. The other one asked me, 'Are you a relative?'

'Jist an acquaintance.'

'Bloody shame,' said a fella at the bar.

'He wisny actually a regular,' Flossie explained as though anyone gave a damn, 'only a derelict that came in noo an' again –'

'Shut up!' I said.

The ambulance men ignored all this and placed Paddy on a stretcher, then carried him away.

'Did ye know him well?' asked the fella at the bar.

'Well enough.'

'Here, have a hauf,' said the other one.

'No thanks, but thanks all the same, I'm away hame.'

'Back already?' asked my mother.

'Aye, everything is deid this morning.' This was unintentional.

'By the way, I tried tae get ye somethin' for yer Christmas believe it or no', but everythin' wis shut, so here's two pounds. Buy yersel a present.'

Her face went red. 'Thanks,' she said stiffly, then 'I didny mean whit I said earlier on. I know ye didny have much money.' She looked at the notes. 'They're awfy dirty right enough. Did ye find them?'

'Naw, they're mine. Very legitimate, but I'll take them back if ye don't want them.'

She laughed. 'I wis only jokin'.' Then she kissed me timidly on the cheek.

'Nane o' that stuff,' I said. 'Away an' get the dinner ready.'

She went into the kitchenette. 'Happy Christmas!' I called after her. Then I thought of Paddy lying in the morgue, and his burnt-out bothy, his dead pigeons and possibly the cat. I was lucky. I still had five cigars.

The Aftermath

I suppose it was bound to happen some time. The Arabs say 'it is written' and for me it was written.

All the week after Christmas I was in a foul mood. It was a long holiday for the building-site worker. My money was gone by Boxing Day. I faced the New Year without a penny in my pocket and Paddy McDonald's death lay heavy like a lump of indigestion. I never went to his funeral or knew of any who did and I never saw the team from the Drive, nor wanted to. Anyway, the dead are taken care of. I have my problems.

After being out of circulation for three days I tapped my mother for a pound. This would lessen my chances for a loan at Hogmanay but I had given up caring about the future. With the money I headed for the Paxton and ran into Paddy's hard-boiled nephew, Murdo.

'How's it gaun?' I asked, noting he had a fair bevvy in him. He looked at me with the speculation of the boozer who wonders whether to pick a fight or be friendly. He chose the latter.

'Terrible aboot Paddy,' he said.

'Aye,' I thought I had better not say too much in case I got the rap for Paddy's death. Murdo's temperament was inclined to blame folk for events. It could be society in general or anybody who was handy. He was a great one for causes and Paddy's would be the latest. Still, I felt bound to add something. 'Big funeral wis it?'

'Naebody there except me an' the undertaker.'

Quickly I said, 'I couldny manage masel. I've been in bed a' week wi' the flu.'

He thought over this remark, and accepted it.

'I know ye wid have come if ye could. Paddy wis fond o' ye.' He laid his arm, weighing like a ton, on my shoulders.

'Gie that man a double,' he said to Flossie. 'He's one o' the best.'

'Here's tae Paddy, an' wha's like him!' was the toast. Solemnly we clinked our glasses.

'That reminds me,' said Flossie, 'there's three pound chalked against him on the board. I don't suppose ye want to keep his memory pure an' pay it?'

I admired Flossie's guts, though maybe it was just stupidity.

Murdo glowered. 'Of all the mean bastards –'

'That's OK,' said Flossie hurriedly, 'I wis jist sayin'.'

I changed the subject. 'Wis there enough money tae bury him then?'

'Oh sure. A man like Paddy doesny need a fancy grave wi' a heidstane. He had as good a coffin as anybody. It wid jist be a wee bit hard tae find the exact spot he wis buried.'

'Who wid want tae visit a grave anyway?' I said. 'We'll always remember him the way he wis.'

'That's true,' said Murdo. 'Every time I come intae this bar I'll always mind Paddy staunin' at the end o' the counter wi' his glass.'

'Always crackin' a joke,' I said.

'Aye, always the cheery one.'

We stared sadly into space.

'D'ye know,' said Murdo breaking the spell, 'I'm gaun tae be stony broke this New Year. I've hardly a tosser left whit wi' a' the arrangements. I'm due twenty-five pounds aff the Social Security for Paddy's funeral, but I'll no' lay ma haunds on it for a week or two. You know whit the social is like.'

Straightaway I said, 'I'm stony masel.' There was another silence. 'I'll get ye a hauf though,' I added in the way of consolation.

Murdo in a bad mood was a grim prospect. He accepted a glass of whisky gratefully. I looked around to see who I could join. Before I could move he said, 'Did ye ever consider doin' a job?'

'Whiddy ye mean?' I knew what he meant.

'There's a hoose alang the road jist askin' tae be done. Plenty o' good gear an' maybe money lyin' aboot.'

'A hoose? Do ye mean a mansion o' some kind?'

'Naw. It's a tap flat up a close. We could get in through the loft, but I need somebody tae gie me a punt up.'

'That's a mug's game. For a start how do we get rid o' the gear?'

'Dead easy. I've got connections.'

I wasn't interested. Not that I'm averse to a bit of pauchling. For me the building site was fair game for easy pickings. Many a time I sold Sanny Hamilton, a private contractor, cheap bags of cement and such like. But I didn't fancy house-breaking.

'Mind ye,' said Murdo, 'I only dae this kind o' thing when I'm stuck. I don't make a livin' at it. But things are gettin' right hard these days. Imagine, nae drink for the New Year.'

I agreed. 'It hardly stauns thinkin' aboot.'

'Well, whit aboot it then?'

'Naw.'

His eyes hardened. 'Maybe ye're jist yellow.'

'Maybe, but if ye come ootside ye'll find oot.'

I picked up an empty tumbler. I wasn't going to be unarmed. Murdo always carried a knife. We stared at each other in deadlock.

Finally he said, 'Don't get yer back up. It wis only a chance I wis gie'n ye. There's plenty others will take it.'

He ordered two pints. I accepted mine without any thanks. Time to get going and leave Murdo to his project. There was no point in getting into a drinking mood. I had about twenty pence in my pocket so I might as well go home. I couldn't even sell anything off the site. Nobody was in business this week. But Murdo's proposition, unacceptable though it was, had set the wheels in motion. How was I going to lay my hands on the ready? There was nothing to pawn in the house except the telly and I might as well go in for armed robbery as attempt that. It would be a sick business scrounging off my mates at the New Year. I would never live it down. Then I began to figure, if Murdo had decided to do a job the house would be robbed anyway. If it wasn't me that got the share it would be somebody else. It would make no difference to the folk in the house, but it would make a difference to my financial standing. I gave Murdo a sidelong glance. He was leaning against the counter, shoulders hunched in the get lost sign. The shutters were down, but I took a chance.

'Anyway,' I said as if the subject hadn't been dropped, 'these folks might be mates o' mine.'

He said coldly, 'It's no' likely. The daughter is a Sunday school teacher and her faither is Kilty Cauld Bum McFadjan, the Scottish Nationalist. I don't know aboot the mother, but she must be another bampot. They say she leaves her door open a' the time tae let the cat in and oot.'

I was surprised. 'Surely no' Cauld Bum! He's no' worth much.'

'Don't you believe it. He goes aboot fixing bagpipes. His hoose is stacked oot wi' them. These bagpipes are worth a fortune. Tinker Geordie that plays ootside the Clansman wid gie us at least a fiver for a decent set.'

This was different. Kilty Cauld Bum was a joke with most people. Especially us of the socialist class. He cycled about, delivering his pamphlets with his kilt flying in the wind like a bad imitation of Rob Roy. I never had much regard for the highland gentry, but he wasn't even a real one.

'How dae ye know when they'll be oot?'

'Dae ye want a guarantee wi' the job?'

'Forget it then.'

'Right.'

I noticed his glass was empty. So was mine.

'I might have enough for two half-pints,' I said.

'That's more than whit I've got.'

I slammed the money on the counter. 'Two half-pints Flossie, and chalk the difference up.' Flossie complied with tight lips.

Murdo softened. He said, 'I know they're oot the night. They're gaun tae a ceilidh up the bay. I know this for a fact because Kilty selt a ticket to one o' ma mates. He said he wid be playin' the bagpipes, an' his wife an' daughter wid be gaun.'

There was a pause. 'Are ye on then?' asked Murdo.

'I suppose so, but it's only because it's McFadjan. I widny rob any other hoose.'

'Don't gie me the sermon. Are ye on or no'?'

'Right.'

We shook hands on the matter.

At ten o'clock the same night we were standing on the top floor of a tenement and facing McFadjan's door. We took the precaution of trying it just in case it wasn't locked, but of course it was. We peered through the letter-box, and all was black. We peered through the letter-box of the flat opposite, and all was black, which was an added bit of luck.

'Right,' said Murdo, taking out a torch from his pocket. 'Gie's a punt up.'

'Whit are ye gaun tae dae anyway?' I asked.

'I jist go alang the rafters for a wee while, bash a hole in the ceiling, then in.'

I placed my arms on the wall, at the same time stooping a bit.

He managed to get his feet on my shoulders but the weight was terrible. I straightened myself as best as I could manage, to allow him to reach the trapdoor of the loft.

'It's helluva stiff,' he said to my dismay.

He banged on it for ages. The sweat was blinding me.

'For God's sake, hurry! I canny take yer weight much longer.'

Finally he eased it open and the weight lifted from me. I could hardly take my arms from the wall to straighten myself, but when I did he had disappeared into the loft.

*   *   *

Nervously I paced about peering over the three flights of stairs. I was supposed to bang on the trapdoor if anyone came. It occurred to me I couldn't reach it, so I prayed no one would come. Then I heard footsteps. Skliff, skliff, they came up on the first landing. Skliff, skliff, up to the second landing. Skliff off into a flat I prayed, but they skliffed right on up to the third. Trying to look casual I knocked on McFadjan's door as if I was a legitimate caller. From the corner of my eye I saw a man and woman approaching. At first they didn't see me.

'Don't think I never seen you winkin' tae that piece behind the bar,' the woman was saying.

'I wisny winkin'. There was somethin' in ma eye.'

He stopped short when he saw me. I knocked again with a show of impatience.

'The McFadjans are no' in. They're away tae a ceilidh,' said the woman.

'Oh dear,' I said.

'Have I seen you somewhere afore?' asked the man.

Nervously I shuffled. Then there was a crash from above and a muffled roar.

'They must be in, Tommy. I hear somethin',' the woman said.

'Maybe he's burst his bagpipes an' blew hissel up,' said the man with a laugh and a wink to me.

The woman banged the door and shouted through the letterbox, 'Are ye in?' She looked at me puzzled. 'That's funny, they're no' answerin' an' they left the key wi' me tae let the cat in.'

'Don't worry,' I said, trying to look normal, 'if they're in they'll come oot eventually. But there's nae point in yous two hingin' aboot. It's too cauld.'

'Hmm,' was her doubtful reply.

The man was losing interest, God bless him.

'Get intae the hoose,' he said, 'an' mind yer ain business.' He put his key in the door. Reluctantly his wife turned away. I knocked on McFadjan's door again. As soon as they disappeared I was getting to hell out of it. The woman closed her door slowly, staring at me all the while. Just then a skinny black cat flew up the stairs. Quickly she opened the door. 'Tommy!' she shrieked, 'There's somethin' funny goin' on. The cat's still oot, an' there's somebody in there, an' they're no' answerin'.'

The cat rubbed itself against my leg in ecstasy. I could have kicked it to death.

'And bring McFadjan's key aff the sideboard,' she added.

The man came out in a temper. 'Whit the hell's up noo?' he shouted.

She snatched the key from his hand and opened McFadjan's door in a flash. I would have ran off, but I was transfixed with indecision. Anyway there might be a chance to bluff it out. If Murdo kept quiet we might still get away with it.

'Follow me,' she commanded. 'I don't like the look o' things,' and marched up the lobby. I daresay she had guts, but I hated them.

The man muttered, 'She canny keep her nose oot o' things.'

We followed her into the living room. I noticed it was even worse than ours. A tattered three-piece suite, a carpet nowhere near fitting wall to wall and leaving large surrounds of floorboards, plus an ancient piano adorned by stale photographs and tinny candlesticks. Then she investigated the bedroom while we trailed behind her, shouting, 'Is onybody there?' At this point she gave a shriek.

My nerves were cracking. 'Whit is it?' said the man, 'Are they a' deid?'

'Look!' she screamed. We looked. A leg was dangling from the ceiling.

'Who's up there?' she demanded. 'Answer me!'

At last came the answer, 'Fuckin' Kilroy!'

Murdo might be trapped, but I wasn't. I took to my heels and ran.

*   *   *

I didn't have to worry about drink for Hogmanay. That particular night I was in the police cells. So was Murdo, after the law prised him from the beams where he had been jammed. There was no bones broken, otherwise he would have had the comfort of a hospital bed. My mother bailed me out the next morning and we passed New Year's day in silence watching the television. Murdo and I are putting forward the plea that we were drunk and breaking into lofts for a bet. After all, who in their right mind would break into McFadjan's if they were intending robbery? I think this is a good point. Murdo said we will only get a fine at the most and he promised to pay it off Paddy's funeral money from the social, but whatever happens I knew I had it coming. As the Arabs say, 'It is written'.

The Ghost Seeker

I t wasn't the usual thing for me to be heading over the hills on a frosty morning instead of lying in bed until midday, then afterwards swilling a couple of inches of beer in my glass in the Paxton. It wasn't usual either being unemployed for a month, but this had happened at the beginning of February. Redundancy was the order of the times for the building-site worker, who was in as much demand as a pig at a palace.

I decided to take a saunter through the old Douglas Estate. I hadn't set foot in it since my schooldays. The old lodge cottage was gone, only a bit of broken wall remained to mark the garden where we used to pinch hard green apples which gave you the dreaded diarrhoea and the trees were black and gaunt like monuments to the passing of the cottage and my youth. I reached the stable quarters, deserted, but not quite a ruin yet. It had been the last place to be inhabited when the gentry had abandoned it after a fire had burned the big house to the ground. The loyal workers had hung on here, hopeful that the master would rebuild the place to allow them to return to their happy serfdom. He never did. So the workers left for council houses and factory jobs, leaving the estate to marauding poachers, lovers and vagabonds like myself.

I studied the many desecrated doors facing me, splintered and barely hanging on by their hinges. Which one was it that another boy and myself had pushed open with great effort to explore its secrets? It had been solid and in good condition then. Steep, wooden stairs had confronted us. The boy had climbed up recklessly, but

95

I had hung back. I remembered having a foreboding about those stairs.

'C'mon fearty,' the boy had shouted.

'I canny.' I couldn't explain, but my legs were paralysed when I placed them on the stairs.

'It's great up here. There's furniture an' everythin'.'

I had forced myself up, fighting against an invisible weight pressing on me. When I reached the top I had been blinded by the sun shining through the skylight. Except for the boy's gaping grin I couldn't see anything clearly other than a vague impression of rafters above me and a bed in the corner.

'This is a great wee den,' the boy had said. 'We could play here every day and naebody wid know.'

He was full of enthusiasm and probably right. But all I could feel was iciness – a dreadful iciness on that warm summer day. My teeth had chattered.

'It's c-cauld in here,' I had mumbled.

'Cauld! Ye must be jokin'.'

I hadn't waited. I rushed down the stairs, ignoring the boy's taunts.

We had returned home together without saying much and he never played with me again. Maybe that's why I don't remember his name. I never found out what had created that icy sensation and I never heard of any sinister tale about the stables. Maybe I just imagined it.

Now I wondered where the door was. I kicked the one facing me wide open, but there were no stairs, just a tangled mass of rubble, and felt only the normal iciness of a February day without any past impression: I also felt cheated, because then it had all been so important. We scruffy kids had been so worthless compared to the grandeur of the nobleman's wonderland. Even after he had gone the 'Trespassers Will Be Prosecuted' notice had remained to warn us not to enjoy what once had been his. But now the bluff was called. The estate was finished. Even the bushes intruding over the estate road in order to establish their position were wasting their effort. It was down on the redevelopment plan that in one year's time everything would be levelled to the ground in order to build a school for the increasing number of undisciplined and unappreciative council-house kids.

A few yards onwards I came across the 'hut wi' the hooks' as we called it, reduced to a pile of black rotting planks of wood. Once the hut had been used to hang game or venison until it was decayed enough to eat but when we took it over it was merely used as a base for hide and seek or whatever. At the worst it was a good shelter. Yet I was never too sure of it except when there was a gang of us around. When you were alone and looked at it back over your shoulder as you were leaving you got this funny feeling. At least I did. I remember sitting on its wooden steps with a black dog for company – one of those nameless animals that walked with anyone at all when it took the notion. The dog had shivered, whined and raised the hairs on its back. For me that was proof that the place was haunted. Of course condemning places as being haunted was a vocation with the kids in my day. It ranged from the outgoing community centre to Faroni's chip shop if you had to pass them in the dark and they were closed. Even your own back green wasn't above suspicion if you were ordered to bring in a shirt from the line in the dark and it was stiff with frost, waiting for you with outstretched arms. Wee Peter Ratchitt swore blind that he had peered in through our classroom window at ten o'clock one night and saw the ghost of a long-dead janitor cleaning the other side of the pane. He was a notorious liar, wee Peter, but on that subject we believed him. We had 'being haunted' on the brain.

One late summer evening twelve years ago I had sat on the steps of this hut with two pals. We were tired out playing cowboys and Indians or Tarzan or corpses hanging from the hooks. Strewn all around us were trampled bushes and bits of branches, so we sat in brooding silence for a while scratching our midge bites. Then it began to dawn on us it was dark. Everything looked different. Bushes and trees were assuming the shapes of hunchbacks and Draculas. One of the pals, Bobby Smith, said, 'It's in a place like this ye see Frankenstein crashing through the trees.'

We peered about us and had to admit by the look of things any kind of weird character could show up.

'I think I'll go hame,' said the other pal. 'My ma will kill me for bein' oot sae late.'

'So will mine,' I said.

'Couple o' cowardy custards,' said Bobby Smith.

'I'm no' a coward!' I shouted.

'Ye are so! Ye're feart o' yer mother, an ye're feart o' this place in the dark.'

I was stung into a show of bravado. 'I'll prove I'm no' as feart as yous two.'

'How?' asked Smith.

I tried to think of something impressive. Then I got an idea that would let me head home at the same time.

'I'll go a hundred paces in front. Then I'll wait for the two o' ye at the lodge.'

'Ye mean ye'll walk through this place yersel!' said the other one in a tone of awe.

'Aye.' Inwardly I was aghast at the prospect. But it was too late now. I had flung down the gauntlet.

Smith said, 'I'll bet ye'll no' dae it.'

'Whit are ye bettin'?'

This was a difficult question. We didn't own much. Smith searched about his pockets and brought out a pocket-knife.

'This is one o' the sharpest knives ye can get. I'll bet this against yon cricket bat ye were playin' wi' yesterday.'

He flicked the knife open. I couldn't see its qualifications in the dusk. Anyway I didn't care how sharp it was. I didn't care about the cricket bat. I had found it in the council dump and I could get another one any time. What bothered me was the journey down to the lodge. I stared into the grey void ahead and said, 'Right then, start counting up to a hundred, an' follow.'

Without a backward glance I began running down the estate road looking neither to the right or left lest I spied some horrific creature waiting for me. I could hear Smith's voice counting, 'Forty-eight, Forty-nine –', while I kept running until I could no longer hear him, at the same time willing my brain to remain blank from the memory of some awful scene from a film that might creep in. Then an idea occurred which almost made me forget my terror. I almost wet myself thinking about it. It was this. I would hide behind a tree near the road and when the other two passed I would give out loud panting noises or even mad fiendish laughter, terrifying them out of their wits. Then I would take a short-cut through the woods to the lodge and be there in bags of time before them. I scrambled up the grassy verge and took up my post behind a tree. Even in the dusk I had a good view of the road – so I waited. I waited and waited but they didn't come. I became colder and colder as the panic rose again. Something must have happened to them. I figured whatever it was could happen to me so I'd better get back to that lodge pronto.

I didn't even try to find the short-cut. Blindly I waded through tall weeds and bumped into trees. Then I plunged into a bog camou-flaged with thistledown. Keep going, I told myself. I must come out somewhere, and I did. One second I was squelching through bog and the next I was hurtling downwards. I rolled over bits of wire, broken bottles and bundles of smelly stuff, and just managed to grab on to a thick bush to stop myself landing at the bottom of this pit, which I recalled was an illegal rubbish dump. With difficulty but determination I scrambled upwards, bruised, bleeding and stinking horribly. When I finally crawled into the house my mother went mad at the sight of me. She only refrained from battering me because of the blood dripping over the linoleum. I was ordered to divest myself of all clothing while she bathed my cuts, nagging at me all the time, but I was comforted if humiliated, for God knows what had happened to the other two. Next day I was sent to school as usual. Even if my face and legs were a mass of criss-cross cuts I could still walk and that was good enough for my mother. There were no sensational developments because the other two were in the playground as large as life.

'Whit happened tae ye last night?' I asked Smith's companion. 'I waited at the lodge for ages.'

'We didny come doon the estate road. Smith knew a short-cut ower the wall on tae the main road.'

He stared into my face. 'Whit happened tae you?'

'Mind yer ain business, ya cheatin' wee coward.'

The bell cut short any further discussions. I made a beeline for Smith at playtime. He let forth loud guffaws of laughter at the sight of me, but he didn't laugh long. I knocked him to the ground and pummelled into him.

'Where's ma knife?' I said as I kicked him.

Blubbering like a first-class infant he gabbled, 'Leave me alane an ye'll get it.'

So for a day I was a hero and kept Smith's knife in a drawer for a long time as a souvenir. It was no use for anything else for it could hardly cut paper. Eventually my mother threw it in the bin.

Yes, these were the days of real adventure, real heroes and real villains. Now it was all grind, booze or trying to get by on the dole.

The damp, cold air cut through my reveries and I decided it was time to get going. As a gesture I patted the clammy wet wood of the remains of the hut a farewell. It had been once a refuge to the ghost seekers and at heart I was still one. Any old ghost would have pleased me. Even the faintest suggestion of one. Anything, just anything to give me a hint of something beyond.

* * *

Quickly I walked back through the estate where the trees were still hopeful and came over the hill. I passed a heap of charred ash and blackened stone which had been Paddy McDonald's home. Scattered around this debacle was an ancient cooker, a bit of table and a half-burned sofa, the same one that I had sat on along with Paddy's cat. It would be something to see that cat sitting there right now. It would give a bit of justification to everything. You could think then, if you were that way inclined, that Paddy's spirit was inside the cat. But the fact was that there was no cat, no spirit, and not even a bit of singed fur. To hell with it all; I would make my own ghost. I picked up a piece of blackened char and marked on a bit of wall that remained 'PADDY WILL RETURN' then left quickly before anyone saw me.

Goodbye Everybody

The queue at the unemployment exchange had slowed down to a standstill.

'Whit's the hold-up?' asked the wee fellow in front of me.

'Sounds as if somebody's no' pleased.'

'Who wid be in this place an' nae work.'

'Ye'd be surprised,' said another. 'Work wid kill some folk.'

I suspected he was referring to Big Mick sprawled comfortably along the bench behind us, swigging a bottle of wine.

'Are ye lookin' for a job?' I asked him.

'Naw – jist waitin' on Baldy.'

'Great innit,' said the wee fella. 'All the home comforts. Drink while you wait.'

'An' why no'?' said Mick. 'There's nae law against it. Here, d'ye want a gargle?' He offered me the bottle. To be sociable I took a mouthful.

'Ye're no' frightened,' said the wee fella, 'ye could get typhoid drinkin' efter him.'

'Who's worryin'. Ye could get it it anyway. The niggers tramp doon the grapes for the wine wi' their feet,' I said.

I suspected the wee fella was peeved because he hadn't been offered any.

Somebody said, 'I mind ma faither tellin' me that in his day ye wereny allowed tae smoke in the broo, never mind drink.'

'That wis in the dark ages afore Keir Hardie.'

'Never heard o' him. Here, whit's the racket aboot?'

'Ye might guess. It's Baldy Patterson.'

We stopped talking to hear all the better.

'You've already had your money sent out,' the clerk was saying.

'Indeed and I have not!' replied Baldy with heat. 'Big Mick back there will tell you.' He shouted, 'That right Mick?'

'Aye, that's the God's truth,' Mick shouted back waving his bottle about.

'Are you here on business?' asked the clerk.

'Naw, I'm jist waitin' on Baldy.'

'Then wait outside.'

Big Mick leaned back all the more complacently and took another swig from the bottle.

'Where did ye say ye sent it?' Baldy was asking. 'Ye know I've got nae fixed address.' He made this sound like a reference.

'I'm aware of that,' the clerk replied with an exasperated sigh. 'I sent it where I always send it, care of William Brown, twelve Mid Street. I suggest you make your enquiries there.'

I remembered the situation. Billy now had a legitimate address. He had moved from the derelict Drive to the slightly less derelict Mid Street through a lucky break. His uncle had died and Billy fell heir to his room and kitchen.

'So,' the clerk continued, 'the matter is out of our hands, and if you are looking for work I'm afraid there is nothing.'

'Work ma arse!' said Baldy, 'I'm lookin' for money.'

'Next please,' said the clerk.

The wee fella pushed Baldy aside and took the position over.

'Anythin' in the scaffoldin' line?'

'Nothing,' said the clerk, picking up a pad and pencil.

The wee fella persisted. 'Can ye no' gie me a card for Cumlocktown then? There might be work there.'

'There is nothing there. We have enquired,' said the clerk writing on the pad to show he had better things to do.

'Too bad,' I said to the wee fella as he turned away. I knew it would be the same for me.

'Bloody hopeless,' he said. 'I'm thinkin' o' gaun up tae the oil rigs.'

'Don't fancy it.'

'Well it's the money –'

'Next please!' said the clerk loudly.

'Be seein' ye,' I mumbled.

'Anything for brickies?' I enquired. This request was a matter of formality. There had been nothing for the past six weeks.

'Nothing,' was the reply.

'Whit aboot labourin' then? Any kind o' labourin' on the sites?'

'Nothing.'

On an impulse I asked, though I had no notion of it, 'Whit aboot up north near the oil rigs? Is there nae buildin' gaun on up there?'

He looked at me irritated. It was clear he did not wish any deviation from the word 'nothing'. 'I'm afraid you will have to enquire about that yourself.' He began to write on his pad again.

I walked away in time to see an empty wine bottle hurtle through the door. It was in keeping with my sentiments exactly.

I caught up with the wee fella.

'Nothin' doin'?' he asked.

'Nothin'.'

'Ye're daft. Go up north. That's where the work an' money is.'

'I don't fancy it.'

I didn't know why. There wasn't much to stay for. I couldn't think of anybody who would give a damn whether I left or not. I often felt my mother was relieved when I went out. Anyway I knew I irritated her more than usual hanging around the house. I had even lost the guts to complain about the meals or kid her on about anything.

'I'll gie ye the name o' a firm up north that's desperate for brickies,' said the wee fella. 'Try it.'

'I might at that.'

Back home I thought I had better mention the subject to my mother – although we had been silent for so long it was difficult to begin.

'Have ye got a cuppa tea ready?' I began, more for the sake of testing out my voice.

'Tea?' she said, as though she had never heard of it.

'Aye, ye know. These wee leaves ye pit in a teapot.'

'Put it on yersel,' she said.

'Dae ye want one?' I asked, ignoring her coolness.

'Whit's the snag? Ye might as well know I canny lend ye anythin'.'

I clenched my teeth. I could get nowhere with this woman.

'I'm no' wantin' the lend o' anythin'.' I made the tea and poured her cup out with a grudge.

'Whit I was wonderin',' I said as I handed it to her, 'was if I should go up north tae look for work. It's hopeless here.'

She was startled. 'An' leave me here masel!'

That surprised me. I never considered myself great company for her.

'I wid send ye money.'

'I wisny thinkin' aboot the money.'

She stared at her cup and blinked her eyes. I could hardly credit there were tears in them. I hoped not. Now that I was talking myself into leaving I was going to be resentful of any opposition.

'Whit aboot yer pals?' she asked. 'An' Mrs Smith doonstairs thinks ye're an awfy nice big fella.'

'Whit's that got tae dae wi' it?'

'Nothin',' she said, 'but ye might no' like it away from hame.'

I didn't like to point out that 'hame' for me was only a place to sleep and eat. 'Besides I can always get other pals,' I said.

'Whit aboot Paddy McDonald? He'll miss ye.'

Patiently I explained, 'Paddy is deid. Dae ye no' remember?'

'Oh aye,' she said absently. 'Well it's up tae you.'

She disappeared into the kitchenette. Apparently she didn't want to discuss it. Next thing she was back. 'Here's a lend o' a pound until ye get yer broo money.'

I didn't particularly want it, but I just said 'Thanks' and walked out.

*   *   *

I didn't go to the pub. I walked along by the river. Under the bridge in the usual place sat Baldy and Big Mick. There it was, all set out, my future. The wine bottle bulged in Mick's pocket.

'Where are ye gaun?' he asked.

'Naewhere.'

He pulled the bottle out and handed it to me. I took a mouthful.

'Did ye get yer money then?' I asked Baldy, handing the bottle over to him.

'Aye, Billy found it on a shelf. He wis that drunk this mornin' he forgot it had came – stupid wee sod!'

'Still no' workin'?' asked Mick.

'Naw. Have ye no' heard? There's a depression on.'

He laughed. 'It's no' affectin' us.' Then he became serious. 'I know times are bad. Dae ye want a len' o' a fiver?'

I could have laughed myself. I was better off than they would ever be. I was on the point of refusing, then it struck me a fiver would come in handy. Come to think of it, it was necessary.

'Thanks Baldy. I'll pay ye back when I get ma broo money.'

He brought out crumpled notes rolled into a ball. It was two fivers. He separated one and handed it to me in the manner of a true philanthropist.

'Tae think,' said Mick, 'that the bastard has been drinkin' ma money a' mornin'.'

'Keep yer hair on. I've got a fiver for us tae spend the night an' still one left for the morra when the boy here gets his broo money.'

Mick looked sheepish. 'I wis only jokin'. Sit doon on that plastic mac an' I'll gie ye a dram.'

They thought I had nothing and they were bending backwards to give me what they could.

'Whisky?' I asked hopefully.

'Naw, wine. A wee dram o' the wine.'

I sat down beside them on the stone. I might as well join them. It was the least I could do. They handed me the bottle while Mick rolled a fag. He studied it to make sure it was a good one then handed it to me with a flourish. I had the feeling I was being initiated. Maybe I could do worse than join them, because at least they had the communal outlook. The booze was usually shared. You might lack comfort but not company. You might be an outcast but you were free. It was tempting.

'Too bad Paddy's no' here,' I said.

'Aye.' They were suitably silent for a minute but I sensed they were not too concerned. Folk come, folk go. It could be their turn any time. After another swallow I felt talkative. 'I wis thinkin' o' gaun up north,' I told them. I knew they wouldn't take the statement seriously.

'Whit for?'

'Work.'

'Work never done onyone ony good,' said Baldy spitting in contempt. 'That's for mugs. Look at us, we can drink withoot workin' for it, an' plenty tae eat. A fish supper noo an' again, breid, cheese or a tin o' soup. Eatin' is a fallacy onyway. We're perfectly healthy.'

They could have fooled me, but I nodded in agreement.

'So long as ye've enough tae drink, that's the main thing,' said Mick wisely. 'Onyway, folk up north are no' like us. Especially in the north-east where the work is. You could be dyin' in the street and they wid walk ower ye.'

'They don't care,' confirmed Baldy. 'They widny gie ye a match tae light yer fag.'

'Ye've been up north then?' I asked.

'Naw,' said Mick, 'but I've got a brither that has. He couldny get back here quick enough. They're as mean as fuck.'

'I think it's the weather that does it,' said Baldy.

'They don't get the rain the same as us, but there's an icy wind blawin' a' the time that wid shrivel yer balls.'

'If ye had ony,' Mick interrupted.

'And that's whit makes them sae mean an' dour. Forget it son. Stay wi' yer ain kind. They're aye the best. That right Mick?'

'It's the very truth.'

Maybe they were right. You could say Mick and Baldy were the true gentlemen of the west. Generous, treacherous, vicious and kindly with no admiration for the rich and successful. Yet the difference between them and me was that I liked working. My body was used to it. I preferred to earn my drink and hand in a few pounds to my mother. Their philosophy was all right for them, but not for me, not yet.

'Ye're very likely right,' I said.

I decided it was time to go and leave them while there was still some wine in the bottle. They had given me enough.

'I'll have tae get back hame. Ma mother will have the dinner ready.'

They looked sad as I arose from the stone. 'Cheerio son, be seein' ye.'

'Come roon tae the Drive later,' Baldy shouted after me. 'We'll gie ye a good drink.'

'I might at that. Keep a place warm for me.'

As I gave them a last glance I wondered if I would ever see them again.

'Have ye got a case or a bag o' some kind?' I asked my mother. 'I've made up ma mind. I'm gaun up north tomorrow.'

She looked confused and rubbed her cheek. 'Dae ye think ye should?'

'I'll have tae gie it a try. This hingin' aboot the hoose is nae use. I'll end up doin' somethin' stupid.' I thought I'd better lay it on a bit. 'Look how I got intae bother at Hogmanay. Ye know how it is. When ye've nothin' tae dae ye get intae trouble, even if ye're no' lookin' for it. Ye widny like that.'

She became indignant. 'I got a right showin' up that time the polis came tae the door, an' then yer name in the paper and everythin'. I didny go oot for a week.'

'Well, if I'm aff much longer it might get intae the *News of the World*. It's better that I go an' get work somewhere.'

'I suppose so,' she conceded. 'I'll see if Mrs Smith has somethin' tae put yer clathes in. But how will ye manage the fare? I've hardly any money.'

'Jist lend me two pounds and ye can keep the broo money.'

She brightened and said, 'That's too much.'

I waved this aside. 'I'll manage. As soon as I get a wage I'll send ye somethin'. An' when I make the big money I'll send ye enough tae get a coloured telly.'

Her eyes moistened. To prevent any sentiment I said, 'Hurry up wi' the dinner, I'm starvin'.'

Afterwards I went to my room to collect my gear. It wasn't impressive. Surprising how little you own when you are faced with the total sum. I wouldn't even have got a balloon from Duds the ragman for the lot. I packed a pullover, two tee-shirts, a pair of pants, two pair of socks, a pair of denims and a pair of boots into Mrs Smith's shabby holdall, and was all set. I looked at my watch. It was only six o'clock. The pubs would be open. A tempting thought to get a couple of pints, but I decided against it, because I might blow the lot and that would be easy. Tonight I would keep my mother company with the telly viewing and please her for once. I counted my notes. Eight in all. Hardly a fortune but folk had set out with less – and starved to death.

I was up early next morning and made myself a cup of tea. No sense in wakening my mother any sooner than necessary. Everything was ready all too quickly. I hung around a bit playing for time. Then I went into her room. She sat up wide awake. 'Ye should have got me up,' she accused, 'I would have made ye somethin' tae eat.'

'That's OK. I've had somethin'.'

She faced me in her dowdy petticoat, or whatever it's called. She was shaking and seemed to be searching for words. 'I'll miss you,' was all she said.

'I'll miss you as well.' It was the truth. Right then I felt I would genuinely miss her. After all we had been together for twenty-two years. I put my arm round her cold shoulder, 'Don't worry, I'll be OK.'

I kissed her then left before it got any worse. She knocked on the window as I passed. God, what now. She opened the window. 'Mind and write.'

'I will,' I assured her. I didn't look back but I knew she would stay there watching until I was out of sight.

As I headed for the bus-stop I began to feel better. It was a bright cold morning with a hint of spring in the air, just enough to make me feel optimistic – and even happy. As I waited at the stop I could pick out the landmarks of my life. Facing me – the Paxton Arms. On the hill behind – the building site. Over the river in front – the derelict Drive. Behind the Drive – the cemetery wherein lay the nameless grave of Paddy McDonald. But that was all finished. It was, goodbye everybody. I was on my way to better things. I was on my way to adventure.

Postscript by Alasdair Gray to
Agnes Owen's *Gentlemen of the West*

You will not have read as far as this unless you enjoyed the foregoing tale, so you are probably relieved that Mac has had the sense and energy to step out of the trap his world had become, and leave us with a convincingly hopeful end. This may be the place for someone who has read the novel more than once to explain why he values it, and I will approach my explanation through some remarks about other writing. Readers who dislike windy summaries should read only the last three paragraphs.

There are many reasons why there are few good fictions about folk with low incomes. Great poverty is so disgusting that even the poor hate to be reminded of it, and modest incomes which allow some spare-time pleasure and independence – the incomes which Burns called 'honest poverty' – are usually earned by work which feels like slavery. It is a horribly ordinary truth that our imaginations reject most of the living we do, so from the earliest days of recorded wealth we have lifted up our eyes to the wealthy. Wealth is enchanting, even at a distance. It bestows freedom, or a convincing illusion of it. Love, friendship, loss and pain are the materials of every life, but the rich wear their materials with distinction. Lord Marchmain can choose to die in a Queen Anne four-poster set up in the Chinese drawing room by the estate carpenters. Getting and spending has not laid waste *his* powers. Which is why (says D. H. Lawrence in his study of Thomas Hardy) artists have an inborn taste for aristocrats. Other classes exist by making things and making money, but unearned wealth allows people to make *themselves*, to develop their distinct individualities. This is what every flower that grows does, and what we all ought to do, says D. H. Lawrence. Maybe Lawrence was influenced by his marriage to the daughter of a German baron, but he was also pointing to a fact. Not just writers but the mass of the public like to imagine they are Gods, owners of great lands and houses, highly paid man-killers, monarchs, priests, politicians and gifted youngsters Making It to the Top. This cast list contains the main characters in fairy stories, the Old Testament, Homer, Shakespeare, all history books until recently, and most of today's newspapers.

But heroes and heroines need servants to help them, buffoons to amuse them, criminals and rabbles to bring out, by contrast, their distinct individualities. Folk with low incomes are not wholly excluded from history and the daily news, and in nearly all the world's great fictions – yes, even in that Homer who most celebrates the courage and cunning of the mighty – a truculent commonsense voice declares that heroic grandeur is not worth the cost of its upkeep, that all but some selfish winners are degraded by it. And a Shakespearian prince tells a band of artists the aim of their profession in language which must have inspired Brecht. 'Your job,' he says, 'is to hold, as 'twere, the mirror up to nature; to show virtue her own feature, scorn her own image, and the very age and body of the time his form and pressure.' The nature mentioned here is human nature, of course, with whatever in land and climate influences it; but to show the whole age and body of a time *to* a time – to reflect the constitution and abuses of a whole commonwealth – is an enormous undertaking. Langland, Chaucer and Sir David Lindsay tackled it. Shakespeare partly tackled it in the history plays. His princes of the church and state, rustic squires and horde of normally unemployable ruffians are drawn into social union by an imperial plundering raid on France. Fluellen and the Archbishop of Canterbury, Prince Hal and Falstaff are of equal dramatic and historical weight. That war needed all of them.

But not until the nineteenth century did a lot of geniuses deliberately describe, with an attempt at equal sympathy, most of the sorts of people who made their nations: Scott first, then at least twelve others in France, England, Russia and America. The French and industrial revolutions had shown that history was what everyone did. A Clydeside engineer, a Corsican corporal, a club of Marseilles republicans, the Lancashire stocking-weavers had changed the world faster than any king or house of lords. In Britain *shake-up* would have been a better word than revolution. None of the mighty had been brought low, but it was now possible to sell books without flattering the aristocracy. It had been joined by whole classes of newly prosperous people with intense curiosity about how wealth and status were acquired and how the less lucky were living. The less lucky had also become literate. Of the three best English authors after 1850 one had been a child-labourer in a blacking factory, one the kept woman of a London editor, one had earned money as a fiddler in country pubs. Through journalism, translating and a builder's drawing-office they had become popular novelists. They were qualified to show the struggles by which self-respect and money were gained, or barely kept, or wholly lost. While Karl Marx in the British Museum investigated the matter statistically, Dickens, George Eliot and Hardy described dependencies between makers of wealth in workshop, colony and farm, and users of it in the bit of society which called itself Society.

In 1895 *Jude the Obscure* was published. The critics condemned it, and Hardy decided to devote himself to poetry. After that, with few exceptions, there were no writers with the talent and experience to create lowly paid people with considerable viewpoints. Lawrence is the great exception, but in the twenties he deliberately 'washed his hands of England'. In the mining town where he grew up he had known a community: people who accepted each other for what they had in common as workmates, neighbours, chapelgoers. His mother wanted her children *not* to be common, but professional and moneyed. By his talents he became these things,

AGNES OWENS

and found that the professional, talented, wealthy folk he now mixed with, though good friends who recognised his uniqueness, had no community beyond cliques based on love-affairs and conversations about art and ideas. So he went searching through Australia, New Mexico and Italy for a working community like the Eastwood of his childhood, but not based on wage-slavery, and with room for a free spirit like his own.

He left behind a literature almost completely class-bound, and bound to the propertied classes. Galsworthy, Forster, Virginia Woolf, Wyndham Lewis, Aldous Huxley, Elizabeth Bowen are dissimilar writers, yet all describe people so detached from their source of wealth in land, trade or industry that they can ignore it, because it is handled by their bankers. The sensitive among them think this unjust. Forster's Miss Schlegels feel that they stand on an island of golden coins in a wide ocean. Their finely tuned existence consumes the coins, but the sea-waves keep casting more at their feet. The ocean is *people*. The hydraulic pressure which howks the money up from the human depths and casts it on the lucky island is depicted in *The Ragged-Trousered Philanthropists* and *A Scots Quair*, exceptional novels which show the pressures being resisted by working men's defiance and organisation. In other fiction, highbrow or popular, the lowly paid have become what they were in Homer's fictions: servants, helpful or truculent eccentrics, a rabble jostling in the street. When authors attempt a larger view of them the usual angle of vision presents something like beetles crawling on each other at the bottom of a tank. There is no suggestion that such people can initiate anything of value, or *be* much, even to themselves.

When I spoke of people looking like beetles crawling in a tank I was not thinking of Greenwood's *Love on the Dole* but of a shallower book called *No Mean City* set in depression Glasgow. Then the image reminded me of some stage plays by Pinter, Orton and Bond. Why did the war with Hitler not change Britain's literary sense of itself? 'The only good government' (says Gulley Jimson in *The Horse's Mouth*) 'is a bad government in a fright.' Perhaps. The National Coalition which saw Britain through the war was a right-wing body, but it would have been destroyed if it had not mobilised the nation. It froze profits, took control of industry, imposed rationing, fixed wages and prices. It got the unions on its side and ensured that nobody starved or was unduly exploited. It had spokesmen who said the post-war Britain would *not* return to the poverty and unemployment of the inter-war years. To some extent that promise was honoured. Attlee's government set up a welfare state. Macmillan's government did not propose to dismantle it. Butler enlarged the education grants, and in 1954 Somerset Maugham was regretting, C. P. Snow applauding, what they agreed was the first literary fruit of the newly educated proletariat: *Lucky Jim* by Kingsley Amis. Then came *Room at the Top* by Braine, *Look Back in Anger* by Osborne, and reviewers said that a social revolution had discovered its voice. Yet these authors had depicted no working-class experiences whatsoever! Jim Dixon's bumbling irreverence toward authority is not different in kind from Bertie Wooster's. Jimmy Porter's contempt for Britain where 'all the good old causes have been won' (he means full employment and some welfare services) was voiced at that time by many aristocratic people, frequently in the press. Joe Lampton thoroughly enjoyed the lives of the affluent who accepted him. The most working-class thing about these men is the sound of their names. They and their authors are examples of a very commonplace shake-up. Like Lawrence they entered an affluent part of England through the educational system. Unlike Lawrence they enjoyed it and stayed. Nor, in getting there, did they feel they left anything worthwhile behind. Their reputation as messengers of social change came from a temporary failure of nerve by a rich conservative (Maugham) followed by a rich socialist's premature faith that a just nation had at last been founded (Snow). Not the book but the critics showed the state of society, but nobody noticed this.

The first post-war stories to make good use of low-income experience came out of the English north in the sixties and are firmly set there, but tell truths about the whole country. *This Sporting Life* shows a gifted youngster Making It to the Top, and also a love-affair. The hero's talent is rugby football. The machinations by which he pushes his career estrange him from the woman he loves, but as a well-paid sportsman he tries at the end to reclaim her: he has so much to offer! Himself, money, etc. He stands in the street before a burdened aging woman with a shopping bag, and pursues her home, and cannot get her to see him, hear him or acknowledge his existence. He has become that part of the nation which is no use to her. If she were to submit to him and become his mistress or wife it could only be as his property, his appendage. She would feel, look and *be* out of place. If we seek the flaw which cracks the couple apart we can point, if we like, to his ambition, but the flaw is in *Britain*. The comic novel *Billy Liar* is equally desperate. Billy's mother thinks of her family as 'just ordinary people'. His father says, 'I may be just an uneducated working man, but . . .' They take wage-slavery as a norm, and treat their son's imagination as a disease: which it is, even to him, because all he makes with it are fantasies and comic dialogue. He is part of a community which wants to keep him. His boss is so disconcerted by the thought of Billy trying to be a script-writer in London that he refuses to accept his resignation. And at the end Billy skulks away from the London train and the adventurous girl who shared his daydreams. He returns to his parents' council house, cheered by an imaginary army marching at his heels. His imagination will be used not to free but to keep him as he is. Billy loses his lover by crushing his imagination in order to stay in the community. The rugby star loses his lover by developing the skill which takes him out of it. In *Kes* the picture is yet harsher. A victimised schoolboy learns a falconer's skills by nursing a wounded hawk – he is healing his own spirit and teaching it to soar. The community barely tolerates this, and his working brother kills the hawk out of spite. And in *The Loneliness of the Long Distance Runner* the talented sportsman deliberately loses the race, to stop his victory being used by a highly paid headmaster to glorify a kind of boys' prison.

These stories demonstrate the Great British assumption, which is also the Great British lie, that any special talent, initiative or knowledge not advertised as *popular* is a property of the affluent, a luxury of the posh. This particular lie is the unwritten British constitution. It lets Royalty, the government and most professional people raise their wages and keep themselves employed without drawing much attention, and ensures that coalminers who try to do the same are treated like greedy unpatriotic scoundrels and enemies of the state. When a lie is acted upon by most of the highly and lowly paid parts of a nation it must be treated as a fact. Unluckily for the truth, therefore, stories which show how the lie works can be read as mere matters of fact. Many kindly conservatives who enjoyed the books I mention above will have thought: 'Yes, that is how they must live down there. How sad!' The moral then drawn is not that the nation's wealth should be used to create productive jobs with high wages and pleasant conditions for everyone, but that talented people of lowly birth should have easier admission to the society of those who can make use of them.

It's a pity that storytellers cannot be moralists. They may invent people who pass moral judgements, when these are convincing and appropriate, but if they make their inventions the text of a sermon then a sermon is all they will write, no matter how well they have reflected their time. Readers must be enticed to their own conclusions, which cannot be predicted. In his study of the novel in the west of Scotland, Douglas Gifford notes that the commonest theme is the crushing of imagination by poverty, and that Archie Hind and I have both written stories about artists of lowly paid origin who, after tough struggles, despair of producing anything good. Douglas regrets that neither novel indicates what he, a lecturer and critic, lives by indicating: these books are in a Scottish tradition which has made several good things. But we were trying to write tragedies about makers whose work is not wanted by their own kind. A sense of elevated tradition would only give them hope of being 'taken up' by people of a different kind.

But perhaps all parables of the talent are fundamentally ambiguous. A talent is a measure of silver as well as an inborn capacity or well-learned skill, and when we sit down to write what *we* want to read and which nobody else has written, we enjoy a rich privilege. At that moment we are self-employed and self-sufficient. Nothing need dominate us but our sense of the good, exciting or true. Then we put words on paper, notice these are not very good or exciting or true, and the work begins. But what keeps us writing is an occasional heady feeling of being above the world, above everything but a dim, supportive excitement. Wordsworth thought this sense of freedom, power and possibility was an intimation of immortality. It is well known to children whose growth is not pressed down by labour and responsibility; and stories which revive the sense in adults are likely to be read. Working-class novelists usually incarnate it in someone like themselves who has left or will leave his community, or is suffering because he can't or won't. I say *he* because women are less likely than men to seek satisfactions which detach them from their community. Working-class women are usually too busy holding the community together.

So who will tell good stories about the people in Britain who still labour with their hands? Who can write a whole novel about (for example) an unambitious bricklayer? Someone whose culture and education have made him a manual worker, and who likes manual work, but finds there is less and less of it to be had? Someone who lives in a housing estate which was thought a great gift to the lowly paid in 1950 because each flat had an inside lavatory, but which otherwise has fewer amenities than an army barrack? I fear that no talented male author could embody himself in such a man for 127 pages without feeling stifled or wanting to rave or do something violently nasty. It is true that Mac, at the start of the 'Up Country' chapter, flings a glass across a pub out of rage at the dull bigotry of the surrounding conversation, but despite his scars he is conventional in his judgements and kindly in his actions, though his judgements and actions tug in opposite directions. His feelings towards the hippy German tourist and poor Tolworth McGee are as dismissive as those of anyone else in his community, yet the hippy and McGee get all the companionship and assistance he can offer them. Like his companions in that part of the community which is no longer employable, he is a *gentle* man. I cannot imagine the social pressures which would drive him to riot. He is a socialist, living in a labour-voting area, but has no expectations that the Labour Party or trade union action will do anything to help him. If, to the three million unemployed Britons at the time of writing (October 1985) we add twice as many casual labourers whose work is part-time or threatened, then Mac is typical of a huge piece of Britain. Conservatives can draw soothing morals from his existence. I hope they will not.

Why read about this man? Is *Gentlemen* a dod of social reality we should dutifully rub our noses on because so many folk are sunk down in it? Yes, if you like reading for that reason, but I read it first because I found it funny. Indeed, I thought the first two chapters too funny by half, the characters a mere grotesque bunch of comic proles. Many popular tales about the poorer classes exploit that sort of condescension in the reader. Had the other chapters been equally facetious, *Gentlemen* would have been as enjoyable in small doses, and as disappointing on the whole, as any book by O. Henry or Damon Runyon. But I think Agnes Owens writes better than those good Americans. As her hero's stories accumulate they become a real novel, a moving picture of a hard, surprising world which is forcing a young man to understand both it and himself. The fun is not in the casual violence of oaths, black eyes and falling down drunk. The narrator takes these for granted but does not dwell on them, for he usually wants to avoid them. The fun is in the comedy of mainly decent people misunderstanding themselves and each other. This is the social essence of all comedy from *A Midsummer Night's Dream* to *What Ho, Jeeves!* The council flat, the Paxton Arms, the building site and the wino squat are not grotesque anarchies but societies maintained, like all societies, by affection and by codes. The affection is usually invisible, because the codes regard it as a dangerous weakness. The codes promote much misunderstanding because nobody knows all of them. The mother sells a box of tools her son has kept under her bed for years. She cannot grasp that, like crown jewels in the Tower of London, they are not for use but for status:

> 'Wait a minute,' I said, scarcely able to credit my ears. 'You didny gie him ma set o' tools that took me two years tae pay up when I was an apprentice brickie?'
> 'Well, ye never had them oot the box far as I can remember.'
> 'Ye don't understand,' I said slowly, my head beginning to ache. 'Ye never use your own tools if ye can help it. Ye always nick someone else's. If ye took your own tools they wid just get nicked.'
> She was unperturbed. 'How should I know that?'

By the last chapter our man has been unemployed for several months, his only close friend has died of drink and exposure, and he has been arrested as accessory to an unusually futile crime. Heavy drinking has so washed out his chances of a sex-life that he has never considered one, and this is lucky. In his community sex leads to children and marriage, and who would gladly bring children into such a community? It is collapsing. The only choice is, collapse with it or clear out. If he had children his decent instincts would lead him to collapse with it. So his worst habit allows him a hopeful ending.

I began the last paragraph but two with an extended rhetorical question which I had better answer. *Gentlemen of the West* could only be written by someone who knew and liked building-workers and, without approving the harsh parts of their lives, found release, not confinement, in imagining them. It had to be written by a mother.

LEAN TALES

Bus Queue

The boy was out of breath. He had been running hard. He reached the bus stop with a sinking heart. There was only a solitary woman waiting – the bus must have gone.

'Is the bus away missus?' he gasped out.

The woman regarded him coldly. 'I really couldn't say,' then drew the collar of her well-cut coat up round her face to protect herself against the cold wind blowing through the broken panes of the bus shelter. The boy rested against the wire fence of the adjacent garden taking in long gulps of air to ease the harshness in his lungs. Anxiously he glanced around when two middle-aged females approached and stood within the shelter.

'My it's awfy cauld the night,' said one. The well-dressed woman nodded slightly, then turned her head away.

'Ah hope that bus comes soon,' said the other woman to her companion, who replied, 'The time you have to wait would sicken ye if you've jist missed one.'

'I wonder something is not done about it,' said the well-dressed woman sharply, turning back to them.

'Folks hiv been complainin' for years,' was the cheerful reply, 'but naebody cares. Sometimes they don't come this way at all, but go straight through by the main road. It's always the same for folk like us. If it was wan o' these high-class districts like Milngavie or Bearsden they wid soon smarten their ideas.'

At this point a shivering middle-aged man joined them. He stamped about impatiently with hands in pockets. 'Bus no' due yet Maggie?' he asked one of the women.

'Probably overdue.'

Her friend chipped in, 'These buses would ruin your life. We very near missed the snowball in the bingo last week through the bloody bus no' comin'.' The man nodded with sympathy.

'Gaun to the bingo yersel' Wullie?'

'Naw. Ah'm away to meet ma son. He's comin' hame on leave and is due in at the Central Station. Ah hope this bus comes on time or Ah might miss him.'

'Oh aye – young Spud's in the army ower in Belfast. It must be terrible there.'

'Better that than bein' on the dole.'

'Still Ah widny like bein' in Belfast wi' all that bombin' and murder.'

'Oor Spud's got guts,' said the man proudly.

The boy leaning on the fence began to sway back and forth as if he was in some private agony.

The well-dressed woman said loudly, 'I shouldn't wonder if that fence collapses.'

The other three looked over at the boy. The man said, 'Here son, you'll loosen that fence if you don't stop yer swingin'.'

The boy looked back in surprise at being addressed. He gradually stopped swaying, but after a short time he began to kick the fence with the backs of his heels as if he was obliged to keep moving in some way.

'You wid think the young wans nooadays all had St Vitus dance,' remarked the man.

The well-dressed woman muttered, 'Hooligans.'

It was now becoming dark and two or three more people emerged from the shadows to join the queue. The general question was asked if the bus was away, and answered with various pessimistic speculations.

'Hi son,' someone called, 'you'd better join the queue.' The boy shook his head in the negative, and a moody silence enveloped the gathering. Finally it was broken by a raucous female voice saying, 'Did you hear aboot Bella's man? Wan night he nivver came hame. When he got in at eight in the morning she asked him where hud he been. Waitin' for a bus, said he.'

Everyone laughed except the well-dressed woman and the boy, who had not been listening.

'Look, there's a bus comin' up,' spoke a hopeful voice. 'Maybe there will be wan doon soon.'

'Don't believe it,' said another, 'Ah've seen five buses go up at times and nothin' come doon. In this place they vanish into thin air.'

'Bring back the Pakkies,' someone shouted.

'They're all away hame. They couldny staun the pace.'

'Don't believe it. They're all licensed grocers noo.'

'You didny get ony cheap fares aff the Pakkies, but at least their buses were regular.'

Conversation faded away as despondency set in. The boy's neck was painful from looking up the street. Suddenly he stiffened and drew himself off the fence when two youths came into view. They walked straight towards him and stood close, one at each side.

'You're no' feart,' said one with long hair held in place with a bandeau.

'How?' the boy answered hoarsely.

'The Rock mob know whit to expect if they come oot here.'

'Ah wis jist visitin' ma bird.'

'Wan of oor team is in hospital because of the Rock. Twenty-four stitches he's got in his face – hit wi' a bottle.'

'Ah had nothin' to dae wi' that.'

'You were there, weren't ye?'

'Ah didny know big Jake wis gaun tae put a bottle on him.'

'Neither did oor mate.'

All this was said in whispers.

'Hey yous,' said an irate woman, 'Ah hope you don't think you're gaun tae jump the queue when the bus comes.'

'That's all right,' said the one with the bandeau. 'We're jist talkin' tae oor mate. We'll get to the end when the bus comes.'

The crowd regarded them with disapproval. On the other side of the fence where the youths were leaning, a dog which was running about the garden began to bark frantically at the bus queue.

'Shut yer noise,' someone shouted, which incensed the dog further. One of the youths aimed a stone at its back. The bark changed to a pained howl and the dog retreated to a doorstep to whimper pitifully for some minutes.

'Nae need for that,' said the man, as murmurs of sympathy were taken up for the dog.

'This generation has nae consideration for anyone nooadays,' a voice declared boldly.

'Aye, they wid belt you as soon as look at you.'

Everyone stared hard at the youths as if daring them to start belting, but the youths looked back with blank expressions.

'They want to join the army like ma son,' the man said in a loud voice. 'He disny have it easy. Discipline is what he gets and it's done him the world of good.'

'Ower in Ireland, that's where Wullie's son is,' declared one of the women who had joined the queue early.

'Poor lad,' said the woman with the raucous voice, 'havin' to deal wi' the murderin' swine in that place. They should send some o' these young thugs here tae Ireland. They'd soon change their tune.'

'They wid be too feart to go,' the man replied. 'They've nae guts for that sort of thing.'

At this point the youth in the middle of the trio on the fence was reflecting on the possibility of asking the people in the queue for help. He considered that he was safe for the moment but when the bus came he would be forced to enter and from then on he would be trapped with his escorts. But he didn't know how to ask for help. He suspected they wouldn't listen to him, judging by their comments. Even if the bizzies were to pass by at this moment, what could he say. Unless he got the boot or the knife they would only laugh.

Then someone shouted, 'Here's the bus,' and the queue cheered. The blood drained from the youth's face.

'Mind yous two,' said a warning voice as the bus moved up to the stop, 'the end of the queue.'

'That lad in the middle can get to the front. He was wan o' the first here,' a kindly voice spoke. The well-dressed woman was the first to climb aboard, saying, 'Thank goodness.'

'That's OK,' said the youth with the bandeau, 'we're all gettin' on together,' as both he and his mate moved in front of the other youth to prevent any attempt on his part to break into the queue.

'Help me mister!' he shouted, now desperate. 'These guys will not let me on.' But even as he said this he knew it sounded feeble.

The man glanced over but only momentarily. He had waited too long for the bus to be interested. 'Away and fight like ma son,' was his response. In a hopeless attempt the youth began punching and kicking at his guards when everyone was on. The faces of those who were seated peered out at the commotion. The driver started up the engine in an effort to get away quickly. One of the youths shouted to his mate as he tried to ward off the blows. 'Quick, get on. We're no' hingin aboot here all night.' He had already received a painful kick which took the breath from him. The one with the bandeau had a split second to make up his mind, but he was reluctant to let his victim go without some kind of vengeance for his mate in hospital. Whilst dodging wild punches from the enemy he managed to get his hand into his pocket. It fastened on a knife. In a flash he had it out and open. He stuck it straight into the stomach of the youth. His companion who had not noticed this action pulled him on to the platform of the bus just as it was moving away.

'Get aff,' shouted the driver, angry but unable to do anything about it. The other youth, bleeding, staggered against the fence, immersed in a sea of pain. The last words he heard when the bus moved away were, 'Ah wis jist waitin' on wan number –' Then he heard no more. Someone peering out of the back window said, 'There's a boy hingin ower the fence. Looks as if he's hurt bad.'

'Och they canny fight for nuts nooadays. They should be in Belfast wi' ma son.'

'True enough.' The boy was dismissed from their thoughts. They were glad to be out of the cold and on their way.

Getting Sent For

Mrs Sharp knocked timidly on the door marked 'Head-mistress'.

'Come in,' a cool voice commanded.

She shuffled in, slightly hunched, clutching a black plastic shopping bag and stood waiting for the headmistress to raise her eyes from the notebook she was engrossed in.

'Do sit down,' said the headmistress when Mrs Sharp coughed apologetically.

Mrs Sharp collapsed into a chair and placed her bag between her feet. The headmistress relinquished the notebook with a sigh and began.

'I'm sorry to bring you here, but recently George has become quite uncontrollable in class. Something will have to be done.'

Mrs Sharp shifted about in the chair and assumed a placating smile.

'Oh dear – I thought he was doing fine. I didn't know –'

'It's been six months since I spoke to you,' interrupted the headmistress, 'and I'm sorry to say he has not improved one bit. In fact he's getting steadily worse.'

Mrs Sharp met the impact of the gold-framed spectacles nervously as she said, 'It's not as if he gets away with anything at home. His Da and me are always on at him; but he pays no attention.'

The headmistress's mouth tightened. 'He will just have to pay attention.'

'What's he done this time?' Mrs Sharp asked with a surly edge to her voice.

'He runs in and out of class when the teacher's back is turned and distracts the other children.'

Mrs Sharp eased out her breath. 'Is that all?'

The headmistress was incredulous. 'Is that all? With twenty-five pupils in a class, one disruptive element can ruin everything. It's difficult enough to push things into their heads as it is –' She broke off.

'Seems to me they're easily distracted,' said Mrs Sharp.

'Well children are, you know.' The headmistress allowed a frosty smile to crease her lips.

'Maybe he's not the only one who runs about,' observed Mrs Sharp mildly.

'Mrs Sharp, I assure you George is the main troublemaker, otherwise I would not have sent for you.'

The light from the headmistress's spectacles was as blinding as a torch.

Mrs Sharp shrank back. 'I'm not meaning to be cheeky, but George isn't a bad boy. I can hardly credit he's the worst in the class.'

The headmistress conceded. 'No, I wouldn't say he's the worst. There are some pupils I've washed my hands of. As yet there's still hope for George. That's why I sent for you. If he puts his mind to it he can work quite well, but let's face it, if he's going to continue the way he's doing, he'll end up in a harsher place than this school.'

Mrs Sharp beamed as if she was hearing fulsome praise. 'You mean he's clever?'

'I wouldn't say he's clever,' said the headmistress cautiously, 'but he's got potential. But really,' she snapped, 'it's more his behaviour than his potential that worries us.'

Mrs Sharp tugged her wispy hair dreamily. 'I always knew George had it in him. He was such a bright baby. Do you know he opened his eyes and stared straight at me when he was a day old. Sharp by name, and sharp by nature – that's what his Da always said.'

132

'That may be,' said the headmistress, taking off her spectacles and rubbing her eyes, 'but sharp is not what I'm looking for.'

Then, aware of Mrs Sharp's intent inspection of her naked face, she quickly replaced them, adding, 'Another thing. He never does his homework.'

'I never knew he got any,' said Mrs Sharp, surprised. 'Mind you we've often asked him, "Don't you get any homework?" and straight-away he answers, "We don't get any" –'

The headmistress broke in. 'He's an incorrigible liar.'

'Liar?' Mrs Sharp clutched the collar of her bottle-green coat.

'Last week he was late for school. He said it was because you made him stay and tidy his room.'

Mrs Sharp's eyes flickered. 'What day was that?'

'Last Tuesday.' The headmistress leaned over her desk. 'Did you?'

'I don't know what made him say that,' said Mrs Sharp in wonderment.

'Because he's an incorrigible liar.'

Mrs Sharp strove to be reasonable. 'Most kids tell lies now and again to get out of a spot of bother.'

'George tells more lies than most – mind you,' the headmistress's lips twisted with humour, 'we were all amused at the idea of George tidying, considering he's the untidiest boy in the class.'

Mrs Sharp reared up. 'Oh, is he? Well let me tell you he's tidy when he leaves the house. I make him wash his face and comb his hair every day. How the devil should I know what he gets up to when he leaves?'

'Keep calm, Mrs Sharp. I'm sure you do your best under the circumstances.'

'What circumstances?'

'Don't you work?' the headmistress asked pleasantly.

Mrs Sharp sagged. She had a presentiment of doom. Her husband had never liked her working. 'A woman's place is in the home,' he always said when any crisis arose – despite the fact that her income was a necessity.

'Yes,' she said.

'Of course,' said the headmistress, her spectacles directed towards the top of Mrs Sharp's head, 'I understand that many mothers work nowadays, but unfortunately they are producing a generation of latch-key children running wild. Far be it for me to judge the parents' circumstances, but I think a child's welfare comes first.' She smiled toothily. 'Perhaps I'm old-fashioned, but –'

'I suppose you're going to tell me a woman's place is in the home?' asked Mrs Sharp, through tight lips.

'If she has children, I would say so.'

Mrs Sharp threw caution to the wind. 'If I didn't work George wouldn't have any uniform to go to school with –'

She broke off at the entrance of an agitated tangle-haired young woman.

'I'm sorry Miss McHare,' said the young woman, 'I didn't know you were with someone –'

'That's all right,' said the headmistress. 'What is it?'

'It's George Sharp again.'

'Dear, dear!' The headmistress braced herself while Mrs Sharp slumped.

'He was fighting, in the playground. Ken Wilson has a whopper of an eye. Sharp is outside. I was going to send him in, but if you're engaged –'

The headmistress addressed Mrs Sharp. 'You see what I mean. It just had to be George again.'

She turned to the young teacher. 'This is George's mother.'

'Good morning,' said the young teacher, without enthusiasm.

'How do you know George started it?' asked Mrs Sharp, thrusting her pale face upwards. The headmistress stiffened. She stood up and towered above Mrs Sharp like a female Gulliver. Mrs Sharp pointed her chin at a right angle in an effort to focus properly.

The headmistress ordered, 'Bring the boy in.'

George Sharp shuffled in, tall and gangling, in contrast to his hunched mother, who gave him a weak smile when he looked at her blankly.

'Now,' said the headmistress, 'I hear you've been fighting.'

George nodded.

'You know fighting is forbidden within these grounds.'

'Ken Wilson was fighting as well,' he replied hoarsely, squinting through strands of dank hair.

'Ken Wilson is a delicate boy who does not fight.'

'He kicked me,' George mumbled, his eyes swivelling down to his sandshoes.

The headmistress explained to no one in particular, 'Of course George is not above telling lies.'

Mrs Sharp rose from her chair like a startled bird. 'Listen son, did that boy kick you?'

'Yes Ma,' George said eagerly.

'Where?'

He pointed vaguely to his leg.

'Pull up your trouser.'

George did so.

'Look,' said Mrs Sharp triumphantly, 'that's a black and blue mark.'

'Looks more like dirt,' tittered the young teacher.

'Dirt is it?' Mrs Sharp rubbed the mark. George winced.

'That's sore.'

'It's a kick mark. Deny it if you can.'

'Come now,' said the headmistress, 'we're not in a courtroom. Besides, whether it's a kick mark or not doesn't prove a thing. Possibly it was done in retaliation. Frankly I don't see Ken Wilson starting it. He hasn't got the stamina.'

'Is that so?' said Mrs Sharp. 'I know Ken Wilson better than you, and he's no better than any other kid when it comes to starting fights. He's well known for throwing stones and kicking cats –'

The headmistress intervened. 'In any case this is beside the point. I brought you here to discuss George's behaviour in general, and not this matter in particular.'

'And bloody well wasted my time,' retorted Mrs Sharp.

The headmistress's mouth fell open at the effrontery. She turned to the young teacher.

'You may go now, Miss Tilly,' adding ominously to George, 'You too, Sharp. I'll deal with you later.'

George gave his mother an anguished look as he was led out. 'Don't worry,' she called to him.

The headmistress said, 'I don't know what you mean by that, because I think your son has plenty to worry about.'

Mrs Sharp stood up placing her hands on her hips. Her cheeks were now flushed.

'You know what I think – I think this is a case of persecution. I mean the way you carried on about George fighting just proves it. And all this guff about him distracting the class – well if that flibbery gibbery miss is an example of a teacher then no wonder the class is easily distracted. Furthermore,' she continued wildly before the headmistress could draw her breath, 'I'll be writing to the authorities to let them know how my son is treated. Don't think they won't be interested because all this bullying in school is getting a big write-up nowadays.'

'How dare you talk to me like that,' said the headmistress, visibly white round the nose. 'It's your son who is the bully.'

Mrs Sharp jeered, 'So now he's a bully. While you're at it is there anything else? I suppose if you had your way he'd be off to a remand home.'

'No doubt he'll get there of his own accord.'

The remark was lost on Mrs Sharp, now launched into a tirade of reprisal for all injustices perpetrated against working-class children and her George in particular. The headmistress froze in the face of such eloquence, which was eventually summed up by the final denunciation:

'So if I was you I'd hand in my notice before all this happens.

Anyway you're getting too old for the job. It stands to reason your nerves are all shook up. It's a well-known fact that spinster teachers usually end cracking up and being carted off.'

The change in their complexions was remarkable. The headmistress was flushed purple with rage and Mrs Sharp was pallid with conviction.

There was a space of silence. Then the headmistress managed to say, 'Get out – before I call the janitor.'

Mrs Sharp gave a hard laugh. 'Threats is it now? Still I'm not bothered, for it seems to me you've got all the signs of cracking up right now. By the way if you lay one finger on George I'll put you on a charge.'

She flounced out of the room when the headmistress picked up the telephone, and banged the door behind her. The headmistress replaced the receiver without dialling, then sat down at the desk with her head in her hands, staring at the open notebook.

Outside Mrs Sharp joined a woman waiting against the school railings, eating crisps.

'How did you get on?' the woman asked.

Mrs Sharp rummaged in her plastic bag and brought out a packet of cigarettes. Before she shoved one into her mouth she said, 'Tried to put me in my place she did – well I soon showed her she wasn't dealing with some kind of underling –'

The woman threw the empty crisp packet on to the grass.

'What about George?'

Mrs Sharp looked bitter. 'See that boy – he's a proper devil. Wait till I get him home and I'll beat the daylights out of him. I'll teach him to get me sent for.'

Commemoration Day

Molly strolled through the gates of the big city park possessed by a mild sense of adventure after she had cashed her giro and purchased twenty cigarettes instead of her usual ten. She walked over the grass to the pond and watched children throw bread at the ducks but the wind blowing over the water was too keen for comfort. She moved onwards, tightening the belt of her skimpy yellow raincoat that clung to her lumpy hips like orange peel. A stone thrown by one of the children skimmed close to her fat legs. When she reached the protective shrubbery of the gardens she allowed herself the luxury of a few puffs. She studied tags tied to foreign-looking plants and was none the wiser. When she pulled on a bud about to bloom into some mysterious flower, the stem broke. Guiltily she threw it down. Following a side path in the hope of finding someone to chat with, even if only about the weather, she almost collided with a young man running hard towards her. As they stood, nearly eye to eye, she saw he looked as startled as she felt, but when she stepped aside to let him pass he asked harshly, 'What's the time missus?'

'Half-past two,' she said, glancing at her watch and not liking the word 'missus' or anything else about him.

'Is that all?'

'My watch keeps good time,' said Molly coldly.

'Got a match on you?'

'I have not.' A right ignorant one, she thought, with his spiky hair and hollow-cheeked face. He stroked his chin nervously and she noticed a jagged cut on the back of his hand. She said, 'You've a bad gash there.'

He looked at it. 'Must have caught it on barbed wire.' He stared behind him.

She said, 'Better get it seen to,' and added, 'Where does this path lead?'

He put his damaged hand in the pocket of his crumpled jacket. 'I wouldn't go up there if I was you.' His voice was threatening.

Molly retorted, 'I can go wherever I like. It's no business of yours.'

'Please yourself, but the north lodge is closed to the public. One of the upper crust, Sir Peter Carlin himself, is exercising his horses, as if the old bastard didn't have anything else to do.'

'Perhaps he hasn't. Anyway,' she added suspiciously, 'how come you were up there?'

'I wasn't. They chased me.'

She softened at the information. 'Oh well,' she laughed, 'no doubt the rich have got their troubles, like the poor.'

'Not quite the same though.'

'Trouble is trouble, no matter who you are.' She looked him over considering he was a poor-looking specimen, but that was the style of them nowadays, seedy and ill-mannered.

'True.' He nodded his head.

'And I've had mine, I can tell you.'

'How's that,' he asked, twisting his head backwards.

'When you've lost a husband and a son in the space of a year, there's not much left to worry about.' She was aware this fellow wasn't all that interested by the jerky look of him, but she was glad of the casual way she could say this now.

'Hmm,' he muttered, then, 'God, I wish I had a match.'

She searched in her bag and threw him a box. He lit a half-smoked cigarette and returned the box, grunting something which could have been thanks.

'Better get that seen to.' She touched his hand.

'It's only a scratch.'

Fumbling again in her bag, she brought out a neatly ironed

handkerchief. 'Tie that round your hand anyway. It will keep it clean.'

'It doesn't matter,' he said, backing away.

Molly shrugged and shifted about to ease her aching legs. The young man drew fiercely on the butt end of the cigarette then stamped it into the ground and shivered violently. 'Do you feel all right?' she said.

'I feel fine.'

'You look cold. I just wondered –'

'I had a dose of the flu recently. It's left me dizzy. Is that OK with you?'

'It's no concern of mine,' she said coolly and made to move onwards.

He tugged at the sleeve of her coat. 'Sorry missus. No offence meant. It's just that I've had a rotten day.'

She studied his thin hard face. If Tommy had lived he would have been about this fellow's age, otherwise there was no comparison. Tommy had been fresh-faced and handsome, though not at the end.

'That's all right. We all have our off days,' but she kept on walking.

'You haven't a fag on you?' he asked, catching up.

She stopped and gave him one. He accepted it without any kind of thanks. His hand shook.

'Not in trouble are you?' she asked.

'Trouble?' he repeated.

'It's not unusual nowadays.'

He regarded her with a blank expression, then smiled crookedly. He put the cigarette in his pocket.

'Aren't you going to smoke that?'

'Later.'

Like a mother and son on an enforced outing they continued to walk together back along the path leading out to the open park.

'Working, are you?' Molly asked by way of conversation.

'No.'

'That's the style of things nowadays –'

'I expect I'll get something soon,' he said. 'I hate all this hanging about. It stinks.' He mumbled this as if he was speaking to himself rather than her.

'I can understand.'

'Can you?' he said bitterly.

Molly wished she was back home with a pot of tea on the boil. This young man's presence was worse than none at all. She'd be better off listening to the news on the radio, and that was bad enough.

'I don't think you do,' he added.

'Listen,' she said, stopping short, 'don't talk to me about understanding. I've had enough of that. My husband and my son used to say, "Keep out of our affairs – you just don't understand." Well they're both gone. One died for nothing and the other from drink, and here I am, still not understanding.' She quickened her footsteps out of anger but he kept pace with her easily.

'Sorry missus,' he said.

'It wasn't only the drink though,' she said, turning to her companion, 'I've no doubt his heart was broken, my husband's I mean, after Tommy was gone.'

'Tommy?'

She sighed. 'I don't want to talk about it any more.'

They walked on in silence. Molly judged that in another ten minutes she would be out of the park and on her way home – a pity the excursion had done nothing for her at all, and by the look of it, this one at her side was no happier than she was – poor sod, at his age too.

'I suppose you young ones have a lot to be bitter about – no work, no future, nothing to do,' she said giving him a sidelong glance.

He shrugged, looked behind him, then asked again, 'What's the time now?'

'Twenty to,' she informed him, adding, 'Meeting someone?'

141

'Maybe.'

She thought possibly he wasn't all there in the head. People like that sometimes had a passion for wanting to know the time as if there was nothing else to care about.

'They might be looking for someone in Maloney's bar. If you like I'll put in a word for you. I used to work there. Maloney would listen to me.' After a pause she added, 'He liked my Tommy.'

'I've heard of Maloney,' he said, without enthusiasm.

'It's good money and free drink, within reason.'

'I don't drink.'

'It's not a qualification.' Molly considered with the face he had, as sour as piss, he'd as much chance as a snowball in hell with Maloney, then she tripped over a stone embedded in the grass.

'Watch out!' he said catching her elbow.

She laughed to cover her distaste at the touch of him saying, 'Swollen feet, that's my problem.'

'Hold on to my arm,' he offered.

Amazed at his decency she complied, but when she discovered she was being led towards the duck pond she said, 'I'd rather go home now, if you don't mind. I can manage fine.'

'Wait a minute. I've a fancy to see the ducks,' but he looked backwards as if he'd more of a fancy to see what was behind him. They reached the pond before she could think of the right words to allow her to head for the gate. It was deserted except for the ducks bobbing up and down in the water like plastic toys. Straightaway the young man turned his back on them and looked over to the park gate, breaking her hold. 'What's the time?' he asked.

'Nearly ten to.' There was definitely something wrong. He was either mad or – her mind swivelled away from other possibilities as she knelt down and dipped her handkerchief in the edge of the water. Avoiding his face she stood up. 'Wipe that cut. It's starting to bleed.' He wiped his hand carelessly and threw the cloth into the water as if its crisp whiteness offended him.

'Did you have to do that?' Molly said, angered by the sight of the spreading piece of linen with the blue initial T embroidered on the corner attracting the ducks, which turned away fastidiously on closer investigation. His face remained pointing towards the gate like a dog that smells wind of a rabbit.

'I really must go,' she snapped.

'No, don't.'

'Why shouldn't I?'

'You're Tommy's ma, aren't you?'

Molly held her breath. Her head swam and she felt sick, a sure sign of blood pressure. She closed her eyes until the nausea passed. 'My son is dead.'

'I know.' His thin face appeared less harsh, almost sympathetic.

'What has he to do with you?' She wanted to strike the insinuating look from him.

'I never knew him really,' he explained with his half-smile, 'but we are keeping faith with him. You might say this is his commemoration day.'

A spasm of fury shook her. 'Commemoration day?' she shouted. 'Dear Christ, will it never end!' She looked upwards for a second then faced him steadily. 'I'll tell you something. I don't want no commemoration for Tommy from you or those others. As far as I'm concerned he wasn't my son at the end, dying the way he did – poisoned with hatred and half mad, just like you.'

His face was hard again. 'I'm sorry you think that way missus, but it's nothing to do with you.'

'Nothing to do with me? You knew who I was didn't you, else why have you clung to me like a limpet, talking about commemoration day.'

The young man's eyes swivelled to the gate then back to her. 'I hadn't a clue who you were. I only needed you for the time on your watch. I lost mine climbing over the barbed wire and I have

143

to be at the gate on the hour to get picked up, otherwise I'm done for.' His voice harshened. 'So, what's the time now missus?'

In an exaggerated fashion Molly lifted up her arm and studied the watch.

'The time missus – the time.' He stepped forward as if to grab her.

She laughed. 'The time is it? I'm afraid I can't tell you that exactly, because you see my watch is always slow, I should think by quarter of an hour roughly. I should have got it fixed long ago but I'm never too concerned about what the exact minute is. It suits me, especially now Tommy and his Da have gone. Why should I care about the time?'

There was a space of silence during which Molly could observe the whites of the young man's eyes enlarge around the green and yellow flecked irises. She had always admired green eyes, yet Tommy's had been deep blue with long eyelashes. Probably this young man with the green eyes was going to choke the life out of her since he was done for anyway, but he just sighed then sat down on the wet grass, reclining on one elbow, staring over at the ducks still bobbing up and down like plastic toys. He looked exhausted. It was time to get going, thought Molly. There was nothing to be done, but she couldn't resist asking, 'I suppose old Carlin won't be exercising his horses any more?'

'I reckon not,' he said with his lop-sided smile. He sat up and searched in his pocket and brought out the cigarette she had given him earlier. It was crushed and bent. He threw it in the water. The ducks swam over. Before she left Molly handed him her cigarettes and matches. It was the least she could do. Now she dreaded going out into the street to hear the fearful whispers, the jubilant shouts and see the gloating eyes. It was all going to begin again.

The Silver Cup

I f you glanced in at Sammy's room when the door was open it seemed to be on fire. This was the effect of the flame orange paint which he had stolen from a garage. The room was really as damp and fetid as an old shed and contained a sagging bed, a set of drawers riddled with small holes caused by darts (not woodworm) and a carpet tramped free of its original pattern. Sammy liked his room. It was his territory and a haven to his friends who shared it with him most evenings from five to ten o'clock. The message on the outer panel of the door, 'KNOCK BEFORE ENTERING', was directed at his parents. Sammy's Ma did her best to comply with it. His da was inclined to kick the door open if enraged by the noise coming from within, but usually ordered his wife to 'see what that bugger's up to' rather than risk raising his blood pressure to dangerous heights. Sammy's Da was not a happy man. He was banned from smoking and alcohol, was on an invalidity pension due to a poor heart condition from over-indulgence on both counts, and saw little in his son to give him pleasure. Yet pinned above the mantelpiece, the faded photo of himself when a youth was the spitting image of Sammy.

'Why don't you take your dinner beside us?' asked Sammy's Ma, entering his room with a tray of food after knocking.

'His face wastes my appetite,' said Sammy sitting on the edge of his bed, wrapped in a multi-coloured sleeping bag, twanging his guitar. Sammy's Ma sighed.

'What a sight you look. If the cruelty man could see you –'

'Close the door behind you,' said Sammy, his face invisible behind a fringe of hair.

* * *

Back in the living room she lifted her husband's plate the second he had mopped up the final trace of gravy with a chunk of bread.

'Going somewhere?' he asked, with a touch of sarcasm.

'I think I've left a pot on the gas,' she explained, dashing through to the kitchenette where she felt safe amongst the unwashed dishes. She focused her thoughts on the evening ahead. The western film on the television was not to her taste but it should keep her husband quiet. He always maintained he liked a bit of action, but none of that lovey dovey stuff, nor plays that were all gab, nor anything which related to female predicaments. Sammy's Ma had learned to keep her mouth shut about what she liked. After the film he was certain to go to bed with, as he described it, brain fatigue, prompted by 'certain persons', whom she took to mean herself. Then, alone, she would sit through the remainder of the viewing, her eyes flickering between the clock and the set, marking time until twenty-past eleven when she would make herself a cup of tea. By half-past eleven she was back at her post, cup in hand, leaning towards the screen, all attention to the preacher on 'Late Call'. She considered his sermon as good as a tonic. If she closed her eyes she could imagine she was in church. Not that she ever attended church. Her husband viewed darkly any mission which necessitated her being gone from the house for more than an hour. Besides, her wardrobe was lacking in the formality required for such an occasion. 'Late Call', brief though it was, gave her an impression of being part of a congregation listening and nodding in unison. Sometimes, in a more fanciful mood, she imagined she was sailing down the Mississippi in a steamboat while an invisible choir sang 'We shall gather by the river', which was strange, since she had never been further than the townhead in all her fifteen years of marriage.

'Have you seen my good ball-point pen?'

Her husband's voice broke into her thoughts, causing her to drop into the sink a plate, which immediately cracked.

'Not recently.'

She turned on the water forcefully to hide the ruined plate.

'I've looked everywhere!' he shouted.

Sammy's Ma shook her head in despair. His pen, his screwdriver, his socks, his heart pills, were just a few of the articles which he lost daily.

'Have you tried behind the clock?'

'Everywhere, I told you,' then he added, 'except that bugger's room.'

'I don't think Sammy's in his room.'

She had been dimly aware of a door slamming a while back, which could have meant anything.

'All the better,' said her husband, and strode off.

Sammy's Ma suspected the pen was an excuse for him to search her son's room. Once he had found a heap of empty beer cans and a half-full box of potato crisps under the bed. 'Thieving – that's what he's up to,' had been his cry at the time. Sammy's staunch denials and assertion that one of his pals' uncle owned a licensed grocer's had not impressed her husband. She was placing the cracked plate in the bin when the roar came. When she entered Sammy's room her husband was holding aloft a large trophy in the shape of a silver cup. Senselessly she asked, 'What is it?'

'What does it look like?' he thundered, pointing to an inscription on the base which said 'PRESENTED TO THE PENSION CLUB BY COUNCILLOR HOOD'. Sammy's Ma placed her fingers on her lips, unable to speak.

'He'll not get away with this,' said her husband.

She sat down on the bed feeling giddy. To rob a pension club was unforgivable. A football club was more acceptable, when one considered the risks.

'He'll do time,' her husband stated with satisfaction.

In a feeble manner Sammy's Ma said, 'But he's not old enough.'

'He'll go to an approved school then.'

'Oh no,' she whispered, while her husband peered inside the cup, saying, 'This must be worth a few bob.'

Blinking rapidly Sammy's Ma chanced the suggestion, 'Maybe if you returned it there might be a reward.'

His eyes bulged. 'Me – return it?'

'You could say you found it in a field when you were out for a walk.'

'The only place I'm returning it to is the police station,' he replied, banging down the trophy on the chest of drawers.

Sammy's Ma almost bit through her lip. She could picture the neighbours in the street watching Sammy being led into a police van. They would snigger, and look up at her window, and shake their heads as if it was only to be expected. She knew they talked about her. Once from her kitchenette window she heard a woman in the back green say to another, 'That one upstairs is a proper misery. Never has a word to say and runs along the road on her shopping errands as if she hasn't a minute to spare.' She also knew they nicknamed her the road runner. Desperately she blurted out, 'If Sammy gets lifted they'll only say we're to blame, and you most of all because you're his Da. They'll say –'

She broke off when her husband punched the wall in anger.

'Who'll say?' he demanded.

Sammy's Ma shrugged her shoulders and closed her eyes for a second. She had a great wish to stretch out and sleep on this sagging but quite comfortable bed of Sammy's and forget it all, but a groan from her husband snapped her to attention. He was rubbing the knuckles of his right hand.

'Are you all right?' she asked dutifully.

He sat down beside her breathing heavily. 'I'm never all right in this bloody house.'

Surreptitiously Sammy's Ma moved away from the proximity of her husband's body. She stared at the cup on top of the drawers. To her it had the look of a memorial urn on a grave. Moved by the association she suggested sullenly, 'Perhaps we should bury it.'

'Bury him is more like it,' said her husband lifting the cup from the drawers now with a proprietary air, and polishing it lightly with the cuff of his sleeve. He appeared calm and breathed normally. 'Could be worth a few bob,' he said again.

'I shouldn't wonder,' agreed Sammy's Ma without enthusiasm.

For some moments her husband continued to polish the cup with one cuff then the other. Finally he cleared his throat and said, 'Our Perry could do something with this.'

'You don't mean he could sell it?'

'I'm not saying he could, but,' he looked furtively towards his wife, 'he knows all the fences.'

'Fences?'

'Somebody who handles stolen goods.'

'It wouldn't be right.'

Her husband shouted, 'God dammit woman we didn't lift it in the first place, but it's one way of getting rid of it with some money to the good!'

'I'm not bothering about money,' said Sammy's Ma primly. 'Besides, it will be traced with that writing on it.'

Her husband wiped beads of sweat from his forehead. 'Silver can be melted down,' he said through clenched teeth.

To placate his mounting wrath she said dubiously, 'I suppose it's not the same as stealing a purse, but all the same they'll miss it.'

'It will be insured. They can get another one.' Her husband jumped violently to his feet. The rebound from the sagging mattress threw Sammy's Ma across the bed.

'I don't care what you say!' he said. 'I'm getting rid of this cup the best way I can, even if it's only to see the look on that bugger's face when he discovers it's gone.'

He slammed the door hard as he left as if to shut her in.

Back in the living room Sammy's Ma looked down from her window to the street opposite where a group of women sat on the steps outside their flat, chatting and laughing and carelessly exposing their legs beyond the limits of decency. She clutched her husband's small bottle of heart pills, which she had found behind the curtains. She was thinking that for once she would have them ready on his command, when Sammy suddenly appeared.

'Who's been in my room?' he asked vehemently.

'If you must know it was your Da,' she replied, placing the pills in her apron pocket.

'What? Why?' he queried in a high-pitched tone. She regarded him sadly, standing with arms folded.

'B-but,' Sammy spluttered, 'you know my room is private.'

'Better tell him that.'

'Where is he?' said Sammy, jerking his head about.

'Out.' She added, 'Seems he found a big silver cup in your room. Thought he'd better get rid of it. Thinks it's worth money, so he took it to your Uncle Perry. Appears he can get in touch with a fence.'

When Sammy remained open-mouthed, eyes as usual concealed behind his fringe, unresponsive to the statement, she said, 'Imagine anyone being called a fence.'

'It's not his cup to get rid of,' Sammy finally gasped.

Sammy's Ma sniffed. 'It's not yours either. Donated to the pension club it read.'

Sammy punched the air and shouted. 'It was a pal who left it here! He was taking it to the jeweller's to get the inscription fixed! He just left it while we went out for a gang bang with the guys up the lane.'

Sammy's Ma wrinkled her forehead. 'Gang bang?' she repeated.

'What am I going to tell him?' demanded Sammy.

'Tell him it's probably being melted down,' said Sammy's Ma with a nervous snigger.

For a second her son stood as if turned to stone, then he was out of the room in one long stride shouting, 'He'll go to jail for this.'

Two minutes later the sound of raucous laughter came from his room. Apparently Sammy's pals had a sense of humour.

*　*　*

She checked the time on the clock on the mantelpiece. It would be a long wait for her tea before 'Late Call'. She decided to waive the rules and make it now. In any case the prospect of the religious programme had lost its appeal after all this stimulation. She longed to speak rather than listen. At the window again she sipped the tea and noticed only three women remained on the steps. They no longer laughed. One yawned as if bored. The other two stared in opposite directions in an estranged manner. Clearly they sought diversion. Sammy's Ma became quite giddy with the notion that seized her, which was to join them on their steps. The story of the silver cup was too good to keep to herself. They would appreciate the humour and the irony of it. The difficulty lay in the approach, since a bare 'good morning' or 'good afternoon' was the most she had ventured to any of them. Then she conceived a great idea. She dashed into the kitchenette and quickly brewed three cups of tea, which she placed on a tray and carried down the stairs of her flat. She was crossing the street towards the women, flushed and smiling, when her foot caught on the grating of a drain close to the pavement. The cups shattered on the ground, followed by the tray. As she bent down to retrieve the one unbroken cup the pills fell from her pocket through the bars of the drain. Peals of laughter resounded in her ears like the bells of hell going tingalingaling as described in the song. But the mocking women were not unkind. Two of them arose from the steps and led her back across the street. They escorted her up the stairs to her flat saying, 'You'll be all right.'

'It's about this silver cup,' she began when they pushed her gently inside the door.

'I must tell you about this silver cup,' she said again.

'Yes, yes,' they soothed, placing her down on a chair inside the living room, while they looked around furtively.

'I really must tell you about the silver cup,' Sammy's Ma insisted.

'Do you think we should phone for a doctor?' one woman asked the other.

'Is your husband around, dear?' said the other to Sammy's Ma.

They decided to leave when Sammy's Ma began to laugh hysterically. On their way out they heard the discordant strum of a guitar from Sammy's room. One of the women tapped the side of her head significantly while she gave her companion a meaningful glance. Softly they closed the door behind them to create no disturbance, and tiptoed down the stairs.

Fellow Travellers

Jean boarded the train standing at the station and pulled at the top of the sliding door to the empty compartment. It was stiff and hard to move but she wanted a few moments' privacy to assemble her thoughts. She settled down in a corner and opened her bag to take out cigarettes, then changed her mind. Her throat was as rough as sandpaper with the concentrated smoking of the morning. She peered through the smeared window. By the platform clock there were still five minutes before the train left. Now she was undecided. Should she go back? Perhaps she had acted hastily. She rose and hauled upon the compartment door again. As she stood wondering, the electrically controlled outer doors of the train slid shut. She pressed the button, but they held fast. It was disgraceful. How were people to get in or out? She banged on the window, but the platform was deserted. The doors opened and she was confused again. To return now was to admit defeat. She went back to her corner. To her chagrin a man and woman of advanced years got on. They dithered in the doorway of the compartment. The woman smiled at Jean. Jean's eyes dropped. Subdued, the couple settled for the seat adjacent, and spoke to each other in whispers. Then the whistle blew like a sigh of relief.

Just before the outer doors closed a man hurtled through the compartment and threw himself at the seat opposite Jean, breathless and unpleasantly close. He bumped her knee. 'Sorry,' he leered. She had a quick impression of dark hair and brown eyes. Before she could draw her breath he had thrust a packet of cigarettes towards her. Hypnotised by his forcefulness she took one. With similar speed he produced a lighter and held it under her nose.

'Damned cold,' he stated with a cigarette dangling from his lips. He leaned back and crossed his legs. The tip of his shoe prodded her calf.

She nodded and withdrew her leg. His gaze veered over to the couple then back.

'I'm bloody frozen,' he said confidentially.

He shivered in an exaggerated way and blew his free hand. She took an instant dislike to him, but what was worse she suspected he had been drinking. The prospect of being confined with this person for the half-hour's journey was daunting, but to move away seemed drastic. Besides, she was smoking his cigarette.

'The weather's bloody awful,' he complained.

She grunted something unintelligible. Her throat was dry and her tongue fired with smoke.

'Going to the city?' he asked.

'Not exactly.' She considered getting off at the next stop, but then she would be landed in a village with nothing to offer except the Railway Hotel.

'I'm going to see my brothers,' he confided. 'City lads.'

'I don't care for the city,' she said, hoping to discourage him.

'City folk are the best.' His eyes were bold and disturbing. The old couple were staring openly at them.

She backed down. 'I've nothing against city people.'

He leaned forward. 'My family come from the city – great people.' He added, 'And my father was born in the city. He's been dead for ten years.'

He sighed. Jean's eyes were glazed with apathy.

'Do you know,' he said pointing his finger, 'they had to hold me back in the hospital when they told me he'd snuffed it. One of the best, he was.'

'Hmm,' said Jean.

'He gave us everything. It wasn't easy, mind you.' He shook his head sadly, and ground his cigarette end into the floor creating a black smear near her shoe. The train sped through the start of the built-up area. Jean tried to calculate the stops ahead of her.

Unthinkingly she took out her cigarettes, then felt obliged to offer him one. He took it without saying thanks.

'I could get off at any stop and I would be sure to meet a relative.' He smirked and added, 'Where are we anyway?'

They gazed through the window to multi-storey blocks of flats flashing by.

'My uncle lives up there somewhere,' he said.

'Fancy,' she said, looking out to a field of cows.

'Do you remember Dickie Dado, the footballer?'

She lied. 'Uh huh.'

'He was my nephew – great player wasn't he?'

'Er – yes. I don't know much about football though.' She gave a depreciating giggle.

He glared at her. 'He died two years ago. Surely you knew that.'

'I'm sorry. I didn't know.' Jean's face reddened.

'The team was never the same.'

He looked over at the old couple and raised his voice.

'To think he died at twenty-three and some of these old fogeys go on for ever.'

Jean pulled hard on her cigarette. The old man stiffened. She concentrated on the view but she could feel her companion's eyes probing through her skin.

'You wouldn't think I've got a great family of my own – would you?'

She was forced to confront his sly smile.

'No. I mean, have you?'

'Two girls and a boy. Marvellous kids.'

The information angered her. So what? she wanted to scream. Then to add to her misery the train increased its speed and caused them to bump up and down together in a ridiculous fashion. She pressed herself back against the compartment wall as he lurched about slackly, giving off a sour smell of alcohol. Her cigarette fell from her fingers and rolled about the floor. Mercifully the bumping stopped. Jean wiped the sweat from her forehead.

He began again. 'The wife says I shouldn't show any favouritism. She thinks because I bought the boy a fishing rod he's my favourite. It's not true you know.' His eyes pleaded for justice.

To stop his flow of words she began in desperation, 'I've got a headache, would you mind –'

He appeared not to have heard her.

'I bought the girls a teaset,' he went on. 'You should see them with it. They make me drink tea out of the wee cups – simply marvellous.' He shook his head, overcome at the image.

'I see,' said Jean letting her breath out slowly. Her eyes wavered towards the couple, who were whispering intently. She pulled herself together and stated in a loud voice, 'I find families a complete bore.'

'Never,' he said, taken aback for the first time. 'The trouble with people nowadays is they don't care enough about their families. Pure selfishness, that's what's wrong with everyone.'

He looked over to the old couple for support but they were staring ahead with blank expressions.

He continued, 'Take my girls, they're just great, and the boy as well. Mind you I don't show any favouritism – the wife's wrong, but she can be a bitch at times.' His lips curled and he repeated, 'A pure bitch.'

'If your kids are so wonderful, why didn't you bring them with you?' Jean snapped and looked upwards to check the position of the communication cord.

He spread his hands out and whined, 'The wife wouldn't let me. I told you she's a pure bitch.'

Jean felt worn out. The train was slowing down for the next stop.

'I think this must be Duntrochen,' she mumbled, toying with the idea of getting off.

'Not this place,' he said with authority.

As the train pulled out she spied the signboard.

'It was Duntrochen,' she accused, and closed her eyes to avoid any further involvement. Her eyelids flickered as his leg brushed against hers. She was obliged to move. Her companion was staring over the top of her head when she faced him with fury. To sever all contact she turned to the woman sitting beyond.

'Very tiring these train journeys,' she gabbled. The woman looked startled.

'Yes, they are,' she stammered.

'I was really intending to get off at Duntrochen,' Jean added, hoping to establish a safe relationship with the dreary pair.

'It's a one-eyed hole anyway,' her brown-eyed companion stated.

Jean was trapped into answering. 'That's a matter of opinion.'

'My mother died in Duntrochen hospital.'

Jean was prepared to sneer at this disclosure, but the couple were looking at him with concern.

'That's enough to put you off any place,' the woman replied.

'She was a wonderful person. Brought up ten of us without any complaint.'

The couple nodded with compassion. Jean pictured with contempt a family album portraying a white-haired woman with ten leering faces looking over her shoulder.

'She couldn't do enough for us,' his voice jarred on.

Jean coughed and began searching in her handbag. Anything to distract her from the creeping weight of his words.

'Mind you, she liked her drink now and then.'

The couple were definitely attracted by this news. Their eyes blinked rapidly as the image of the saintly mother changed to one of a boozy hag.

'It was her only pleasure.'

'Amen,' said Jean under her breath.

But the subject was not finished. He touched her knee and said, 'He was never off her back, my old man.'

AGNES OWENS

For a hideous moment she thought he was making a sexual innuendo.

'Gave her a life of hell,' he added.

'Oh you mean,' Jean spoke in relief, 'a kind of persecution –'

The woman tutted. Her husband looked ill at ease. Jean rejoiced at their discomfort.

'Not surprising,' she said, addressing the couple.

Her companion gave her a hard look, but he let the remark pass, and stated, 'She was one of the best.'

'But,' said Jean, determined now to expose his inanity, 'you told me your father died ten years ago, and he was one of the best.'

'That's right,' he replied, defiant.

'Now you say he gave your mother a life of hell and she was one of the best. I don't follow you.' She bestowed a knowing smile on the old couple, but they looked at her uncomprehendingly.

'She never complained,' he said with the quiet triumph of one who holds the ace card.

Jean wiped her clammy hands on her skirt. She judged she could be on the verge of a nervous breakdown. The word Valium came into her head. Her friend Wilma took Valium pills regularly and she was in charge of a typing pool. They must work wonders. She decided to get off at the next stop, no matter where it was, and head for the nearest chemist. She stood up and tugged at the compartment door.

'What's the hurry?' he called, but she was transfixed by the thought that she might have to get a doctor's prescription for Valium. As the train pulled up she was flung back almost on top of the woman.

'Are you all right?' the woman asked with concern.

'Yes,' said Jean, pulling down her skirt. To justify her erratic behaviour she explained, 'I thought I was going to be sick. I haven't felt well all morning.'

'I see,' said the woman darting a considerate glance in the direction of Jean's stomach. Jean shot up like a jack-in-the-box. A tic beat on her cheek and her mouth twitched.

158

'I must get out of here,' she gabbled.

'Don't upset yourself.' The woman pulled on her arm. Her grip was surprisingly strong.

Jean fell back on the seat. She explained in a heightened manner, 'Not morning sickness – just ordinary average sick.'

The woman patted her hand. Jean rounded on her with venom. 'I'm not even married.'

The couple regarded each other with dismay. The brown-eyed man blew smoke through his nostrils.

'Of course,' said Jean, forcing herself to be calm, 'I think you are all of your rockers.'

'Really,' said the old man. His wife shook her head as if in warning. The other man continued to blow smoke like steams of fury.

'I thought it was bad enough listening to that loony,' she gestured towards the other man, 'but you two appear to be in your dotage.'

The couple cowered close to the window. The man tapped his head significantly.

'Thank goodness I'm getting off here,' Jean uttered wildly and charged out of the compartment. She alighted from the train without a clue to where she was.

'Ticket please,' said the collector when she scuttled through the barrier. 'Always have your ticket ready,' he reproved as she fumbled in her bag.

She moved out of the station in a distraught manner. She hesitated, torn between the beckoning brightness of Woolworth's and a telephone box on the opposite pavement. She braced herself and headed for the box. She dialled a number and held the receiver to her ear. Almost immediately the voice spoke. She cut through the querulous preamble.

'It's me – Jean. I'm sorry I rushed out like that –' She paused to listen as the voice gained strength. 'I know, mother,' she replied wearily, 'but you must understand I have to get out sometimes for a bit of relaxation. I won't be doing anything desperate. After all I'm not a teenager.'

Her reflection in the stained mirror on a level with her eyes verified the statement, showing the marks of the crow's feet.

The voice began again like the trickle of a tap. Jean interrupted.

'Yes mother I'm fine. I won't be gone for ever you know. I'll be back around tea-time.'

She replaced the telephone and stood for a moment within the box feeling she had placed herself beyond mercy. In retrospect the man with the brown eyes became desirable. He had spoken to her and touched her knee. In his inept way he had offered her an association. She should have been flattered if not actually grateful, and really he had not been all that bad-looking. It would have been something to boast about to her friend Wilma, who according to herself was continually exposed to such encounters. When she stepped out of the telephone box she was shamed by the memory of her neurotic outburst. She walked along the pavement, head downwards, hunched against the cold – going nowhere.

McIntyre

After fifteen years I could scarcely credit my eyes when I saw McIntyre again. I had come to the meeting because I was lonely. It would pass a little time and I would at least be warm. The issue would be boring, but members were always welcome. McIntyre looked older than the fifteen years warranted. I hoped the same did not apply to me. I thought I did not look my age though in the mirror the sight of criss-cross lines round my eyes made me wonder. His hair was now sparse and his once ruddy complexion had a jaded look, but his gaze was as direct as ever.

'How are you keeping?' he asked.

Tonelessly I replied, 'Fine – and you?' but inwardly I felt an upsurge of pleasure at this chance encounter, wishing at the same time I had applied my make-up more carefully. After an awkward pause we drifted into the hall along with the others. It was the usual number of desultory figures waiting for the curtain to rise on the evening's business. He sat down at the table beside another shabby, younger man, and the six from our branch, including myself, sat opposite. The branch secretary spoke at some length on the matter of pay rises. I dreaded the moment for questions because I never had the courage to ask any, but I wanted to prove to McIntyre that I was still the same political enthusiast of old, though why, I don't know. We had gone our separate ways long since. Before any questions could be asked he had taken over.

'Five years ago,' he informed us in his slightly nasal voice, 'we were as poorly paid as yourselves, but we fought the management tooth and nail. We resisted their threats. We stuck together, and while I'm not boasting I am pleased to say we are one of the highest paid factories in the district. Don't give up. Don't be swayed and don't be intimidated. You will win in the long run. Yours is the power. Yours is the glory.' He continued in this vein. I had heard it all before, but it still sounded authentic. Often it held good. Often, but not always. Fifteen years before he had been saying much the same.

'Let there be no increase in the rents. It is up to us, the people. We shall fight. We shall resist. We shall harass.' And so we had.

My sister and I along with seven hundred or so council tenants had marched with McIntyre at our head to the Town Hall. We chanted 'No increase in rents' until we were hoarse. It must have been difficult for the councillors inside to carry on with their business, which, McIntyre informed us, was the implementation of the new Rent Act. To us at that time it seemed the thin end of the wedge, calling for drastic measures.

The faces of the councillors peered anxiously out of the Town Hall windows while we all booed loudly. McIntyre turned to us, holding up his hands for silence. We quietened down, but not before Walter Johnson, normally an inoffensive simpleton, in the heat of the moment flung a full can of beer at Colonel Martin's car. This caused a large dent and some of the crowd were splashed. The Colonel was one of the few able councillors, but had no time for the tenant, so irrespective of the Rent Act we couldn't stand him. Still, we thought it was going a bit far flinging cans of beer around.

McIntyre looked angry. 'I suggest the person who threw that can return home or I will call an end to this demonstration. There must be no violence.'

He took it for granted that outside his commands we had no will of our own – which we hadn't, so we moved away from Walter, leaving him in a lonely circle. He shuffled about with a downcast face then finally slouched away from our midst.

A messenger emerged from the building in the shape of Daniel Smith, the town's well-known benefactor, who was always getting mentioned in the papers for his donations to natives in Moly Pololy or Chitinbanana. This charity cut no ice with us. We believed it should begin at home. McIntyre and Smith withdrew from our earshot. You could have heard a pin drop as we tried to listen, but apart from the nodding and shaking of their heads nothing could be gleaned. Then Smith retreated hurriedly and McIntyre conveyed the message. 'I think we've got them worried. I am informed they are going to discuss all the implications of the Rent Act and will tell me first thing in the morning what the result is. I am confident they are impressed by the wishes of you, the people. So my friends, I would ask you to return home and await the verdict, which I think will be favourable.'

We all cheered and broke up in good spirits.

In the morning the headlines of the local paper read, 'RENT ACT GOES THROUGH, DESPITE DEMONSTRATION BY TENANTS'. My sister, one of our revolutionary committee, was very angry.

'Who does that McIntyre think he is, trying to fool us last night that there would be no increases?' Though McIntyre was the leader of our movement she had never liked him. I was disappointed too, but more on his behalf, rather than because we would have to pay a few shillings extra on the rent.

'Well, he tried,' I said. 'It's no reflection on him. He did his best.'

'Thanks to him my husband is not speaking to me. He is fed up with my gallivanting to all those tenant meetings.'

'That's not McIntyre's fault.'

'You are infatuated with the man, and always have been.'

I didn't answer. Infatuated was not the correct word, though I had never met anyone like him before. He spoke of little else but how to change the world for the benefit of the people – when his eyes would light up with a passion which would probably never be inspired by me or any other woman.

The first time I had had any contact with him was at a meeting my sister and I attended more out of boredom than anything else. He spoke against the council and the careless manner in which they spent the ratepayers' money. I admired his style and thought he had guts. Previously I had assumed the councillors were a bunch of well-meaning citizens, but he opened my eyes. On the way out I was close behind him wondering if I dare make any kind of an approach. Suddenly I was pushed against him with the surge of the crowd. He placed his hand on my shoulder to steady me and smiled. I wanted to say something intelligent, but before I could, he looked beyond me to someone he recognised. It seemed he was always looking beyond me.

'You won't get me to come to any more of his stupid meetings,' my sister stated. She was wrong. Curiosity always got the better of her. Our next meeting was very much reduced in numbers, but the hardy few of us left apparently had another part to play. It was then I got the impression that McIntyre had forgotten that the Rent Act had gone through, because he ignored this point and carried on to tell us of the next stage of his campaign.

'As you know,' he said, 'Saturday is the opening of the new Town Hall. We must be there to demonstrate how we feel about this colossal waste of money and get as many people as we can to turn up. I'll do some organising and you can do the same – get banners and slogans ready. We will meet outside the cinema. Maybe', he added dreamily, 'I could get a band going – I've got contacts.'

My sister was doubtful. 'We haven't much time. It's a lot of work. There's hardly any of us left –'

McIntyre smiled at her sweetly, 'Of course you can do it.'

'We'll try,' I said.

'That's right my dear,' he said, patting my hand. 'I know you both will try.'

On Saturday at the proposed time my sister and I along with her kids set off, giggling nervously, and carrying our banners self-consciously. But when we reached the busiest part of the town without meeting any other demonstrators, our faces became frozen with doubt, and we let the kids carry the banners. Eventually they were trailed along the ground until the brave slogan of 'No Rent Increases' became unrecognisable with dirt. Outside the new Town Hall, as perfect as a doll's house, we spied another committee member, Curly MacFadyen, the worse for drink, but no sign of McIntyre or any kind of band. We peered through the glass door and saw that the official opening had begun. My sister looked at me bitterly. Always a woman of quick decisions, though, she opened the door. We barged in, right in the middle of a speech by an elegant lady in a floppy hat. She broke off immediately she saw us. The kids rushed in ahead of us perhaps thinking they were going to the Saturday film matinee, and Curly, bringing up the rear, fell on his back on the slippery polished floor. This should have been funny but no one laughed. The local bigwigs and officials were transfixed in horror behind draped tables. Then an official came to life and moved in front of the floppy-hat lady perhaps anticipating violence but we merely chanted in quavering voices, 'Justice for the tenants – down with the rent increase.' For good measure the kids aimed their banners at the table and upset an arrangement of flowers. With crimson faces we caught hold of them and marched them out by the scruff of the neck. Then we had to go back and get Curly who was punching soundlessly at the glass door. And still there was no sign of McIntyre.

'Don't ever mention that man's name to me again,' said my sister through clenched teeth.

She never forgave him. He explained to me later he had come to the Town Hall, but we were gone. Apparently we had been too early. Whether it was true or not I still admired and loved him, but it was like banging my head against a brick wall. It was only the cause he loved – any kind of cause, or excuse for one. No matter how often I accompanied him to drab halls where dedicated men and women gathered together to fight against injustice, or supposed injustice, I could sense he just tolerated me. Eventually I gave up and drifted out of town. I had affairs with other men but they always came to nothing. I think McIntyre had ruined me. He gave me an inferiority complex from which I never recovered.

The meeting finished inconclusively, as usual, with an optimistic call from McIntyre to keep going. He was hurrying out of the hall with the shabby young man, the latest disciple no doubt, when I caught up with him like a body that runs on when the head has been chopped off. I touched his arm. He turned – expressionless.

'Still carrying on with the good fight?' I questioned foolishly.

He looked at me as if I was a troublesome heckler then, after a moment's pause, asked, 'Would you like a drink?'

I had not the will-power to refuse. 'All right.'

He turned to the shabby young man. 'I'll see you later John,' he said with such contrasting warmth I could have wept. The young man shrugged and nodded towards me with a flickering glance of calculated understanding. Inside the lounge I clutched my glass of gin while McIntyre sipped his beer. He stared at me encouragingly. 'You were saying?'

'Saying?' I strove to remember. 'Oh yes – I asked you if you were still carrying on with the battle.'

'What else is there?'

That was true. He had that at least. I had nothing. Spitefully I said, 'Some people are betrayed in the battle.'

He raised his eyebrows. 'I never betrayed you. You betrayed yourself.'

'It may have seemed like that to you, but you didn't really care what I did.' My face flushed. I knew I was talking out of turn. I laughed to prove it didn't matter. 'It's all in the past anyway. I was definitely one cause you lost.'

'Sometimes I lose, sometimes I win, but I must keep trying,' he said loftily, as if he was God.

'And old man river he just keeps rolling along,' I replied.

He looked at me with dislike. I knew I had to get away.

'I really must be going. I've made arrangements –'

'I understand,' he said. He finished his beer. I swallowed my gin, and we walked out together. It was ironic but before he left me he said, 'Don't blame yourself too much.'

I wanted to shout after him, 'Your feet still smell.' I had noticed that. McIntyre might be a great man but he never understood that from many people's point of view smelly feet are worse than capitalism. Only to me had it been a comforting fault.

I returned to my shabby flat which was not very presentable, but then there was no one to see it but myself. After fetching a bottle of cheap wine from the cupboard, I settled down as comfortably as I could in front of the one-bar electric fire, holding my glass high as though drinking a toast.

We Don't Shoot Prisoners
on a Sunday

'We don't shoot prisoners on a Sunday.'

I looked at César, suspecting a joke, but his face was straight.

'Only horses then?' My remark was flippant, under the circumstances, but I was tired of his arguments, his excuses, and most of all, his smell.

'Not even horses.' He added 'Señor' within a bubble of laughter. I stared at the floor of the cell and wished he would vanish, like the cockroach I saw slide into a crack in the stone, but I was obliged to respect his last wish to talk to me. In a flash he became serious.

'Here, we recognise Sunday as God's day.'

'And how many have you killed, even if not on Sundays, including the priests?'

'How many have you?' He clasped me by the shoulder. I flinched. It was just like him to try to establish old bonds. 'Besides,' he added, 'it was them or us.'

'And the priests, was it them or us?'

'Before the treaty it was them, now after the treaty it is us.' He added, 'Or at least me.'

He angered me, even now, with his one-track mind.

'Besides,' he said, 'priests are only men, and they must learn to die quickly too, otherwise they lose sight of God.'

'A Sunday is as good a day as any to learn to die quickly.' My voice shook with strain and exhaustion. I hoped he wouldn't mistake it for weakness. 'I don't give a damn about the day or the time, so long as the sentence is carried out in the name of retribution and justice for the village. Understand?'

'Yes – Señor.'

'Don't start calling me Señor at this late date.'

'Yes, Josetti.'

'My gringo name is Joseph.' There was a stench of sweat between us which could not be solely attributed to César.

'But you are wrong about Sundays,' he said.

I shut my eyes for a second to banish the sight of him picking his teeth.

He continued, 'It is a day to rest and reflect on our sins, and why if actions were right in the past they are wrong in the present, and we might consider that possibly today's decisions could be wrong in the future.' Then he wiped his finger on his jacket and faced me with black eyes, his lips stretched to expose the decay caused by a poor diet. As always he looked happy.

'Why plead so hard for yourself?' I asked.

He squinted at me dangerously. 'I do not plead. I only ask for this day so that you may consider your decisions. I have no cares or worries for myself, but I worry for you, because you are my friend, who may live a long time with a bad taste in his mouth.'

I had no answer. His cunning was too deep to be defeated by words. I sat at the rough table and flicked through a greasy bible to distract myself from his pressure. The pages were scored and mutilated, perhaps by César himself, but I suspected they were older marks.

'A worthy book for those clever enough to read?' he questioned.

'It is badly written.' I thought I should leave.

'Perhaps the priest can help us to understand it,' said César quickly when I stood up.

'You are expecting one?'

'For me he will happily come.'

I was forced to laugh. It was either that or strike him. We both laughed. The noise within the sombre stone walls was indecent, but I felt much better for it. Finally César slumped over the table and I collapsed into the chair. He fetched out a pouch and rolled me some tobacco which smelled nostalgically of old blankets.

I inhaled deeply. 'So already they are creeping back for you?'

'Who, Josetti?' He spoke my name as tenderly as he would have done a whore's.

'The priests.'

'Like the vultures they wait for death – even for yours.'

'Not for me. I'm not one of the genuflectors.' I looked at my watch. There was plenty of time yet – in fact, too much.

'You will have no choice – unless,' his eyes narrowed, 'you think to get away from here.'

I crushed the tobacco stub into the stone floor. 'One can hope.'

He put his face close to mine, stinging my eyes with his peppery breath. 'Josetti, if we become good friends again, I could arrange for you to leave here with much money.'

'Where would you get it?'

He gripped my arm hard, as always when he was carried away with a stupid plan. He whispered, unnecessarily I thought, within the thick walls. 'When the priest arrives we could hold him to ransom.'

'Who would pay it? The village rots in hunger.'

'The church. It stinks of gold.'

'The churches are burned. Every bit of gold was taken.'

He laughed, tightening his grip cruelly. 'In the city there is plenty more: stored in the earth; in the walls; in the tombstones; in the graves with the dead. Anywhere they can think of to hide, and they will get it for a brave priest who has survived to give the last rites for a last peseta.'

His grip loosened. I pushed him away and stared at the wall, the bars on the window, then finally at César who was breathing hard.

'Think of it Josetti – you could leave this place you hate and live the rest of your life at peace with yourself – eh?'

I considered his plan desperate, though not impossible, but I suspected one way or another I would never be at peace with myself.

'I can never understand you,' I answered to avoid commitment.

'So,' he continued, 'normally we don't shoot prisoners on a Sunday to give everyone time to think matters over.'

'Normally,' I echoed, then, 'Does it ever occur to you I could be tired of the gold, the tears, the killings? That's why we are in this situation.'

'There will be no killing this time. The gold will be enough,' but his tongue passed over his lips as if he could taste blood.

'I don't think you could resist it, the killing, I mean.'

'I swear on that bible I will resist it.' He reached for it but I shook my head and laid my hands over it.

'I will swear on my life.'

'Your life?'

He saw the joke and laughed.

'Besides, who would keep law in the village afterwards?'

He shrugged. 'Who cares – let them stew.' A mosquito crawled up my arm and I brushed it off. It fastened on César's hand apparently unnoticed. 'But someone must give the order to hold the priest,' he shouted, as if the plan had been approved.

'I wonder who?'

He threw up his hands, disturbing the mosquito. 'Should we ask that insect who sucks my blood without any great considerations?' His voice was menacing now. I knew he would become violent if he was not humoured. To play for time I crossed the room and peered through the small barred window. The view of the stains on the bleached wall outside was accusing.

'César,' I asked, 'why do you make it hard for both of us?'

Now he looked more sullen than dangerous. 'Forget it then.'

I tapped the bar of the window with my nail, goaded by images of green fields, wet streets and blonde women. 'And how could you be sure of the gold?'

'I am sure of nothing.' He blew a smoke ring into the air and it hovered above his head like a halo.

'Then the plan is not foolproof?'

'Who knows?' He was becoming more remote by the second, despite the sweat on his forehead.

'There is a place', he began, as if the subject oppressed him now, 'where, for not too much money, you can buy a passage.'

'It's too late,' I started to say, but he had slid down the wall, falling asleep with his mouth open, grunting in a drunken fashion, because the tequila never quite left his system. I was reminded of a clown who, defeated for the umpteenth time, will leap up to be defeated again. His excuses for the cause were lost. I never had any, and the cause itself was a blood-stained memory better forgotten. To be fair, he had saved my life on a number of occasions, but then I had saved his on a similar number. The score meant nothing to me any more.

Now I was hungry and alert, but it was too early to call upon the guards. Doubtless they would rush in thinking it was time to carry out the sentence, and if this happened before the priest arrived the village would see it as a gross injustice, only to be expected from a gringo. César had a point when he said let them stew. Apathetically I fingered through the bible. The only state-ment worth reading was the name of the owner and the comment under it. 'To Sancho, on his tenth birthday, in the hope he will follow the teaching of our Lord.' I looked at this for a time, then closed my eyes in an effort to induce sleep and remained still within the sound of César's piggish grunts. Eventually the door opened and the guards slithered in on their bare feet. They seized César, who writhed and protested like a small boy called to face school. He struggled for a second then apologized. Carefully he arranged his hat and had actually turned to go with them, when he paused and looked at me saying, 'About the plan. You have decided?'

'I have decided,' I stated with deliberation, 'to shoot prisoners on a Sunday if I am required to.'

His jaw slackened. The pupils of his eyes dilated for a second, then shrank. He threw back his head and laughed, too loud, even for him. 'So, you shall remain here?' he asked.

'Yes.' Just then I wanted to kick the guards out and tell him it was all a bad joke, but a name held me – Sancho, whom I didn't know and who was likely dead, when someone had scored and mutilated his book. Someone, if not César, like César.

'Why?'

I wanted to give convincing reasons without appearing pompous, but failed. 'Because there must be no more killings in the village.'

He regarded me with distaste, then shrugged. 'Goodbye Josetti,' he said with one final flash of his bad teeth. The guards straightened and saluted me crazily. 'Watch out for the priest,' I warned them. 'See he is not harmed.'

A short time afterwards there were shots – too many for my liking, but you couldn't expect the guards, who were the poorest of dirt farmers, to be good marksmen. Some day they might learn.

A Change of Face

I was five pounds short of the two hundred I needed by Thursday, and I had only two days to make it up.

'Why do you need two hundred pounds?' asked Ingrid, my room-mate.

'Let's say I promised myself that amount.'

'That explains everything,' she said. 'I once promised myself a holiday in Majorca, but things don't always work out.'

'In your case things never work out.'

'I think you're crazy,' said Ingrid. 'What good is money to you anyway?' Her fatuity was maddening, but I kept calm.

'Lend me a fiver. You won't regret it.'

Her tinny laugh pierced my ear. 'What, me – with scarcely a bean!'

'Get out,' I said, 'before I cripple you.'

She folded down her tartan skirt and walked out the door with a hoity-toity air, ludicrous, I thought, in a down and out whore. I waited a good five minutes to make sure she was gone before I fetched the briefcase from under my bed. I never failed to be impressed by the look of it. Good quality leather was more in my line than the trash Ingrid flaunted. The briefcase had originally belonged to one of her clients. I remembered his piggish stamp of respectability. Mind you that was ten years before when Ingrid was in better condition. He had left it by the side of the bed, complete with lock and key and containing two stale sandwiches, while Ingrid slept off her labours. I explained later I had found it in a dustbin. Once again I counted the money acquired in pounds and pence but it still totalled only one hundred and ninety-five.

In Joe's Eats Café I leaned over the counter. 'Joe,' I asked, 'how's about lending me a couple of quid – five to be exact. Until the giro comes on Saturday.'

Joe kept his eyes on the trickle of heavy tea he was pouring. He breathed hard. 'What for?'

'Oh I don't know. Who needs money?'

'It don't pay to lend money. I should know.'

'Of course, never a borrower or a lender be,' I said, fishing for ten pence.

'I've been done before. No reflection on you.'

I looked round, then leaned over and whispered. 'You can have a free shot and I'll still owe you the fiver.'

He recoiled then hooted with laughter. 'You must be joking – not even with a bag over your head.'

I shrugged and put on what passed for a smile. 'It's your loss. I know some new tricks.'

Joe patted my shoulder. 'I know you mean well, Lolly, but you're not my taste – nothing personal.'

We brooded together for a bit. Finally Joe said, 'Ingrid might lend it to you.'

'Not her.'

'Oh well . . .' He turned to pour water into the pot.

'I've got one hundred and ninety-five pounds,' I threw at him. His back stiffened.

'What's the problem then?'

I knew I was wasting my time but I explained. 'I need two hundred by Thursday. It would alter my whole life.'

He chortled. 'You paying for a face lift or something?'

'Better than that.'

He shook his head. 'Sorry kid, you see –'

I took my cup of tea over to the table without listening. Ten minutes later I was strolling along a quiet part of the city occupied mainly by decaying mansions.

'I'm short of a fiver,' I explained to the tall man in the black suit.

His eyes glowed with regret. 'I'm sorry. Two hundred is the price. I can't accept less.'

'Will it be too late after Thursday?'

'I'm afraid so.' He could not have been more sympathetic.

'What should I do – steal?'

'I can give you no advice.'

He closed the door gently in my face and left me staring at the peeling paint. A cat leapt on to the step and wound itself round my legs. I picked it up and forced it to look at my face. 'Stupid animal,' I said as it purred its pleasure. I threw it away from me and returned home.

I walked into the bedroom and grabbed Ingrid by her sparse hair as she lay splayed over Jimmy Font, identifiable by his dirty boots.

'Out!' I shouted.

She pulled on her grey vest screaming, 'I'll kill you!'

Jimmy thrashed about like a tortoise on its back clutching his privates as if they were gold.

I towered above him. 'Hurry!' He gained his feet, made the sign of the cross, grabbed his trousers and ran.

'May you burn in hell,' moaned Ingrid, rubbing a bald patch on her head.

I tossed over a handful of hair. 'Before you go, take that filth with you.'

'Where can I go?' she sobbed.

'The gutter, the river, the madhouse. Take your choice.'

She pulled on her dress. 'I don't feel well.' I didn't answer. 'Anyway,' she added, 'if you had let Jimmy stay I might have earned a fiver to lend you.'

I was not swayed by her logic. A drink from Jimmy's bottle would have been the price. I walked out of the room to escape from her staleness.

At one time they had told me in the hospital plastic surgery could eventually work wonders. I did not like the word 'eventually'. Civilly I had requested that they terminate my breath, but they merely pointed out how lucky I was to be given the opportunity. Suspecting they would only transform me into a different kind of monster I had left them studying diagrams. That happened a long time ago, but I still had my dreams of strolling along an avenue of trees holding up a perfect profile to the sun.

'Are you listening?' said Ingrid, breaking through my thoughts with some outrageous arrangement she would fix for me to get five pounds. She backed away when I headed towards her. As she ran through the door and down the stairs I threw out her flea-ridden fur coat, which landed on her shoulders like the mottled skin of a hyena.

The Salvation Army Band on the street corner blared out its brassy music of hope. I settled down on the bench beside Teddy the tramp and spun thoughts of fine wire in my head.

'Nice?' commented Teddy from the depths of an abandoned army coat. He offered me a pale-green sandwich from a bread paper, which I declined.

'We have much to be thankful for,' he said as he bit into the piece.

A body of people gathered on the far side. The music stopped. Everyone applauded. I joined the group, who courteously stood their ground when I brushed close. My eyes were on the Sally Ann coming towards us with trusting goodwill and the collection box in her hand. I slipped my hand beneath the other hands holding out donations, then tugged the string loosely held by the good lady, and ran.

Six pounds and forty-seven pence lay strewn over my bed in pence and silver. I blessed the kindness of the common people and the compassion of the Salvation Army who would never persecute or prosecute a sorry person like me. Tomorrow was Thursday and I had the two hundred pounds, with one pound forty-seven to the good. With a mixture of joy and fear I poured five pounds into the briefcase. Then I studied a single sheet of parchment, the words on which I knew by heart. The message was direct and unfanciful, and unaccountably I believed it, perhaps because of its simplicity, and

AGNES OWENS

also the power which emanated from the black handwriting. Even the mercenary demand for two hundred pounds strengthened my belief in a force much deeper than plastic surgery. I calculated there must always be a price to pay, which for effort's sake should go beyond one's means, to accomplish results.

All evening Ingrid did not return. I wasn't surprised or sorry. In my mind's eye I could see her tossing against dank alley walls in drunken confusion – her wispy hair falling like damp thistledown over her forehead, her eyes rolling around like those of an old mare about to be serviced. Not that I wished her to be any different. Her degradation had afforded me stature, though after tomorrow I hoped never to see her again. Fancying a bout of self-torture to pass the time, I began searching for a mirror, suspecting it would be useless since I had forbidden them in the flat. I peered at my reflection in the window. Like a creature from outer space it stared back without pity. Satisfactorily sickened I raised two fingers, then turned away.

'See your pal Ingrid,' declared Maidy Storr when I passed her stall of old hats, shoes and rusty brooches.

'Not recently.'

'She stole a bundle of money from Dan Riley when he dozed off in Maitland's bar last night.'

'Never.'

'Well she did. I sat on one side of him and she was on the other. I remember she left quickly without finishing her drink. Next thing he woke up shouting he'd been robbed.'

'How much?' I asked.

'Fifty quid, he said. Mind you I was surprised he had that much.' She added winking, 'You'll be all right for a tap.'

'Haven't seen her since yesterday morning.'

'Done a bunk has she?'

'Couldn't say.'

'Well she would, wouldn't she. The law will be out for her.'

'For stealing from a pickpocket. I don't see Dan complaining.'

Maidy frowned. 'I see what you mean. It makes you sick to think she'll get away with it.'

'Couldn't care less whether she gets away with it or not.' I picked up a single earring. 'Have you many one-eared customers?'

'Leave that stuff and get going.'

I walked away quickly when Maidy threw a shoe at me, and headed towards Joe's for breakfast.

'I think I'd like something special today,' I informed him.

'How about some weedkiller?' he suggested.

'I said something special, not the usual.' I considered his confined choices.

'Be quick and move to your seat before the joint gets busy.' Being a liberal-minded fellow Joe allowed me in his place when it was quiet, provided I sat in the alcove behind the huge spider plant. I chose a pizza and a glass of tomato juice.

'Living it up,' he sneered.

'Might as well. Anyway I'm tired of the little creatures in your meat pies.'

I could see Joe looking anxiously at a neatly dressed old lady approaching. Hastily I moved to the alcove with my pizza and tomato juice. The old lady was having an intense conversation with Joe. I suspected she was complaining about me. I finished my pizza and deliberately took my tomato juice over to a centre table. At a table nearby a couple with a child looked at me, aghast. The child wailed. I smiled at them, or in my case, grimaced. The child's wails increased in volume. Joe charged over and signalled for me to get out. The neat old lady appeared out of the steam.

'Don't you know this is a friend of mine,' she said, looking hard at Joe then bestowing a loving smile on me. Joe looked unconvinced, but he was stumped.

'If you say so.' He moved the couple and the child behind the spider plant.

AGNES OWENS

The old lady sat down beside me and said, 'I'm sorry you have to put up with this sort of thing.'

I shrugged. 'That's all right.'

'Such a lack of kindness is terrible,' she continued.

'I suppose so.'

'Can I get you something?' she asked.

'A pizza, if you don't mind.'

She attended to me smartly. I could feel her eyes boring through me as I ate. She cleared her throat and asked, 'Are you often exposed to such er – abuse?'

'Don't worry about it,' I said. 'You'll only upset yourself.' Her eyes were brimming over by this time and I couldn't concentrate on eating.

'Is there nothing that can be done?' she asked just as I had the fork halfway up to my mouth.

'About what?' I was really fed up with her. I find it impossible to talk and eat at the same time.

'I mean, my dear – what about plastic surgery – or something.'

I threw down my fork. 'Listen, if you don't like the way I look, bugger off.' I paid her no further attention when she left.

'That's another customer you've lost me,' Joe called over. I told him to bugger off too, then hastily departed.

For the remainder of the day I kept checking on the time, which meant I had to keep searching for the odd clock in shop windows. I half expected to bump into Ingrid. In a way I would have been glad to see her, because even if she was completely uninteresting, in her vapid manner she used to converse with me. She was still out when I returned home, no doubt holed up somewhere, frightened to stir in case she met Riley. I washed my face, combed my hair, put on a fresh jumper, and looked no better than before, but at least it was a gesture. Then I checked the money in the briefcase and left without a backward glance. I headed slowly to my destination so that I would arrive on the exact minute of the hour of my appointment. Normally I don't get excited easily, for seldom

180

is there anything to get excited about, but I must admit my heart was pounding when I stood on the steps of the shabby mansion. The tall man in the black suit received my briefcase solemnly. He bowed, then beckoned me to follow him.

'Are you not going to count the money?' I asked.

His sepulchral voice resounded down the corridor. 'If you have faith in me I know the money will be correct.'

I wanted to ask questions but I could scarcely keep pace as he passed smoothly ahead of me. Abruptly he stopped outside a door and turned. The questions died on my lips as I met his opaque glance. It was too late to have doubts so I allowed him to usher me into the room. I can give no explanation for what followed because once inside I was dazzled by a translucent orange glow so powerful that all my senses ceased to function. I knew nothing until I woke up outside the corridor holding on to the tall man. Even in that state of mesmerism I knew I was different. My lips felt rubbery and my eyes larger. Tears were running down my cheeks, which in itself was a strange thing, since I had not cried for years. The man carefully escorted me into another room and placed me before a mirror, saying, 'Don't be afraid. You will be pleased.'

I breathed deep, and looked. I didn't say anything for a time because the image that faced me was that of Ingrid. I leaned forward to touch her, but it was only the glass of a mirror.

'You are much nicer now?' the man asked in an ingratiating manner.

What could I say? I didn't want to complain, but I had been definitely altered to be the double of Ingrid. Certainly the face was the same, and we had been of similar build anyway.

'Very nice,' I croaked. 'Thank you very much.'

His lips curled into what could have been a smile, then he tapped me on the shoulder to get going. I shook hands with him when I stood on the step outside, clutching my empty briefcase.

'It's a funny thing –' I began to say, but he had vanished behind the closed door.

It might have been a coincidence but Ingrid never showed up. This was convenient because everyone assumed I was Ingrid, so I settled into her way of life and discovered it wasn't too bad. Certainly it has its ups and downs but I get a lot of laughs with her clients and its doesn't hurt my face either. The only snag is, now and again I worry about bumping into Dan Riley. Sometimes I consider saving up for a different face, but that might be tempting fate. Who knows what face I would get. Besides, I have acquired a taste for the good things in life, like cigarettes and vodka. So I take my chances and confront the world professionally equipped in a fur jacket and high black boots, trailing my boa feathers behind me.

PEOPLE LIKE THAT

The Lighthouse

'Let's go somewhere else,' said Megan to her brother Bobby playing on the beach with his pail and spade. 'Let's go to the lighthouse.'

'I don't want to,' he said, without looking up. At three and a half years he had the face of an angel, but his appearance belied a strong determination to have everything his own way. So thought Megan, aged ten.

'You can stay if you like,' she said, 'but I'm going and I just hope a monster doesn't get you.'

At the mention of the word 'monster' he began to look over his shoulder. It was only recently she'd been telling him about monsters and how they ate children. She'd even shown him a picture of one in an animal book, which was actually that of a gorilla, but it had been enough to make him refuse to sleep with the light off and even with it on he would waken up screaming.

'I don't want to go to the lighthouse,' he said, running over and butting her in the stomach with his head.

'But I do,' she said, skipping off lightly over the sand.

'Wait for me,' he called, picking up his pail and spade and trailing after her.

Together they walked along in a friendly way, going at a pace that suited them both. The day was warm but with a bit of wind. Megan almost felt happy. They came to a part of the shore that was deserted except for a woman walking her dog in the distance. Bobby stopped to gather shells.

'Throw them away,' said Megan. 'You'll get better ones at the lighthouse.'

He emptied his pail then asked if the lighthouse was over there, pointing to the sea wall.

'Don't be stupid. The lighthouse is miles away.'

He said emphatically, 'Then I don't want to go.'

Megan lost her temper. 'If you don't start moving I'll slap your face.'

At that moment the woman with the dog passed by. 'Is that big girl hitting you?' she asked him.

Before he could speak, Megan had burst out, 'He's my brother and I'll hit him if I want.'

The woman studied them through thoughtful, narrowed eyes. 'Do your parents know you're out here in this lonely place?'

When Megan said they did the woman walked on with the dog, muttering something under her breath which Megan suspected was some kind of threat aimed at her. She hissed to Bobby, 'See what you've done. For all we know she could be going to report us to the police and you know what that means?'

'What?'

'Mummy and Daddy will be put in jail for neglecting us and I'll have to watch you for ever.'

At that he let out a howl so loud she was forced to put her hand over his mouth.

'Be quiet, you fool. Do you want that woman back?' He quietened down when she promised to get him an ice-cream.

'Where's the van?' he asked, looking around.

'Over there,' she said, pointing in the direction of the lighthouse. At first he believed this, running beside her eagerly, but when they went on for a considerable length without any signs of an ice-cream van he began to lag behind.

'Come on,' she said, 'or we'll miss it.'

'Where is it?'

'Don't ask me stupid questions,' she snapped, thinking how it wasn't fair that she had to be saddled with him all the time. 'You're a silly bugger anyway.'

'I'm telling you swore.'

'Tell if you want,' said Megan, thinking her parents couldn't say much considering the way they swore.

'If you don't come –' she began, when he started walking again, and just when she thought he was going to act reasonably for once he stopped in front of a rock.

'Look! There are fish in there,' he said.

Grumbling, she went back to investigate. It was true. There were tiny fish darting about a pool of water within a crevice in the rock.

'Aren't they pretty?' she said, just as he threw a stone into the pool causing them to disappear. She shook him by the shoulders.

'You have to spoil everything, don't you?' she said, letting him go suddenly so that he sat down with a thud. But he was up on his feet quick enough when she said, walking backwards, 'A monster's going to get you one of these days, the way you carry on.'

After a good deal of tramping over dry sand that got into their shoes and made their feet sore, Megan suggested they climb up over the dunes on their right-hand side to see if there was a better and quicker path that would take them to the lighthouse. He didn't answer. She suspected he was still brooding about the ice-cream, but he followed her, which was the main thing.

Climbing the sand dunes wasn't easy. They kept sliding back down. Bobby did it deliberately thinking it was funny. Megan was glad to see him in a better mood. When they got to the top they found they were on a golf course stretching for miles with nobody on it but a man in a grey track suit. He saw them, came over and said, 'Better watch out you don't get hit with a golf ball. It's not safe up here.'

Megan asked him if he was a golfer – she noticed he wasn't carrying any clubs. When he told her he was just out for the day collecting golf balls, she began to wonder if he might be one of those strangers they'd been warned not to speak to.

'Bobby,' she said loudly, 'we'd better go back. Mummy and Daddy will be looking for us.'

'But I thought –' he began and was cut off by Megan pulling him back down the sandy slope. When he got to the bottom he said that he'd wanted to stay up there.

'It's not safe,' she said.

'Why not?' Then, as if it had nothing to do with anything, he let out a tremendous wail.

'In the name of God, what is it now?' she said, in the same tone her mother used when totally exasperated.

'I've left my pail and spade,' he said, pointing up at the sand dunes.

She felt like strangling him. 'Well, I'm not going for them,' but when he began to wail loud enough to split the rocks, she said she would go if he came with her to the lighthouse.

'I don't want to,' he said, stamping his feet in temper. 'I want to go back to that other beach where Mummy left us.'

It was then she decided she'd had enough of his tantrums. 'Go then,' she said, giving him a shove so that he tottered on blindly for a few steps. 'I don't want to ever see you again.'

When he turned round she was racing along the beach at a fair speed. He called on her to come back, though it was doubtful she heard him above the cries of the seagulls, but even if she had, she probably wouldn't have stopped anyway.

On arriving at the lighthouse, she saw there was no way to get close to it as it was surrounded by water, not unless she waited until the tide went out, and that would take hours. Sullenly, she looked up at its round turreted shape thinking it was much more boring from this angle than it had seemed from a distance. She wished she'd never come. The sea was stormy now with the waves lashing over the rocks. The whole venture had been a complete waste of time and energy, she decided. Suddenly her attention was riveted to what looked like a body in the water. For a split second she thought it was Bobby, which would have been quite impossible considering the distance she'd come. Nevertheless, it was a great relief to discover this was only a mooring buoy. She laughed at her mistake then began to feel uneasy. She could picture him stumbling into the sea for a paddle thinking it was all shallow water. It was the kind of stupid thing he was liable to do. Panic swept over her. What if something terrible happened to him? She should never have left him like that. Without another thought for the lighthouse or anything but Bobby, she began running back to where she'd left him, praying that he'd be all right.

From a distance she saw him hunkered down, digging in the sand. He must have gone up the sand dunes to get his pail and spade after all, she thought. She slowed down, her legs tired and aching, then to her dismay she saw the man they'd met on the golf course. He was hovering a few yards behind Bobby poking some debris on the shore with a stick.

'Bobby!' she called out sharply. 'Come over to me at once.'

He either didn't hear this or pretended not to, but the man did. He looked up at her and began to walk smartly in their direction. Galvanised into taking some kind of action, she ran forward to reach Bobby first. In fact she'd almost got to him when she slipped on a stone covered in seaweed and went down, the back of her head hitting off its sharp edge.

Her eyes were staring up at the sky as the man and Bobby crouched beside her. Bobby said, 'You shouldn't have left me. I'm telling Mummy.'

The man pulled him back. 'Leave her alone. She's in bad enough shape.' Then he put his lips close to her ear. 'Can you hear me?'

When her eyes flickered he put his hand over her mouth and nose and held it there for a considerable time. After that he turned to Bobby saying, 'We'll have to get an ambulance. You can come with me.'

Bobby said he didn't want to get an ambulance. He wanted to go back to the other beach.

'All right,' said the man, taking him by the hand and dragging him towards the sand dunes with Bobby protesting all the way. His cries died down when they vanished over the top.

Later that afternoon, a strong breeze sprang up along the shore, lifting clouds of sand into the air as well as the strands of Megan's hair drifting across her race. Seagulls came down to stand on her and poke her with their beaks, then, as if not liking what they found, they flew off to the horizon whilst imperceptibly and gradually her body sank into the sand, making a groove for itself. A passer-by might have thought she was asleep, she looked so peaceful. But no one came by that day, and in the evening when the sun went down she was gone with the tide.

The Collectors

Davey came up over the steep, stony track that would lead him to the golf course once he had climbed a fence and crossed a burn. Sometimes he stopped to catch his breath. He was coming up for sixty and a hard life had taken its toll. When he reached the fence he became uneasy. Tam Duggan sat on a tree stump, arms folded as if patiently waiting on him.

'Saw ye comin' in the distance,' said Tam with a jovial smile. 'I thought I might as well go along wi' ye.'

'Aye,' said Davey with a nod. He could hardly refuse the offer for Tam was a big strong-looking fellow in his early twenties with a police record as long as his arm, mainly for assault.

He climbed stiffly over the fence then jumped the narrow burn with Tam following more easily.

'Up collectin' your golf ba's?' said Tam. 'I hear you dae quite well.'

'No' bad,' mumbled Davey, his voice lost in the wind that had sprung up carrying a drizzle of rain with it.

He gave his companion a sidelong glance, wondering if he was as bad as folk said – it was easy to be in trouble nowadays, especially if you were young and had nothing to take up your time.

Tam faced him and said humbly, 'I hope you don't mind me comin' along wi' ye. I thought I might try some collectin' masel'.'

His coarse, handsome face was marred by a scar running the length of the left cheek.

'Why no'?' said Davey. 'It's a free country,' though his heart sank. He didn't want anyone else poaching, at least not alongside him. Others who collected golf balls were usually solitary figures in the distance, acting as if they were out for a stroll and keeping well clear of each other.

'It's right cauld up here,' said Tam, ducking his head from the wind and sticking his hands in the pockets of his flimsy black anorak.

'The higher you climb, the caulder it gets,' said Davey, himself warm enough under the thick cloth of a donkey jacket purchased from an ex-Youth Training Scheme employee.

He paused to pick up a golf ball a few inches off the path. Tam looked round and said with surprise, 'You've got wan already and we're naewhere near the course?'

'Ye can get the odd wan as far doon as the fermer's field but up the tap beside the golf course is the best place.' The words were hardly out of Davey's mouth when Tam was bounding on ahead. 'I hope he stays oot ma road,' said Davey under his breath. Without hurrying he found two more golf balls on the way up. When he reached the top Tam was standing not far from the path, his face a picture of misery.

'Ma feet are soakin,' he said. 'It's a bog here.'

'Ah well,' said Davey, regarding his own heavy wellingtons complacently, 'you've got to put on the right gear for this business.'

'How was I tae know?' said Tam, staring ahead in a sullen manner at the long stretch of grass, moss and whin bushes parallel to the golf course.

'You can always go back,' said Davey.

'I might as well stay noo that I'm up here,' said Tam, walking on slowly. Then his long arm swooped down on the rough grass. 'A golf ba',' he shouted, 'a pure yellow wan tae. It's a beauty.'

Davey came up to join him.

'Very nice. A good make as well. You've done no' bad.'

'No' bad! I've done better than you. This is pure yellow and you've only got a white wan.'

'I've got three,' said Davey, tapping his pocket.

'Ye never telt me that,' said Tam, looking put out. 'How no'?'

'Dae I have tae tell ye everythin'?' said Davey, suddenly feeling fed up and wishing he had turned back when he first clapped eyes on this big pest. Abruptly he veered off through the moss down towards a drainage ditch where he immediately found two balls under the water. His pleasure was lost when Tam called, 'Don't tell me you've got anither wan.'

'Naw, two,' Davey called back, deciding that he was going to try and ignore Tam's attitude as best he could for there was no point in getting worked up about it. The guy was worse than bad – he was mentally retarded. At the same time he was almost glad when five minutes later Tam found a ball within a clump of gorse, cursing the needles pricking his hand as he pulled it out.

'Anither wan,' he shouted, holding it up for Davey's inspection.

Thank God for that, thought Davey to himself. Being forced to study it he noticed it was chipped but said, 'Aye, very good,' with a false encouraging nod.

The wind died down and the rain became heavier. The view of the town below was blanked out with mist. Tam said to Davey, 'This weather would sicken ye.'

'Aye,' replied Davey, thinking it wasn't the only thing. He added, 'At least it keeps the golfers away.' So far he had seen only three on the other side of the course and they appeared to be hurrying in the direction of the clubhouse.

'Them!' said Tam contemptuously. 'They want their heids examined.'

By the time they were halfway along the edge of the course, Davey had found another three and Tam another one, which Davey had kicked in his direction when Tam wasn't looking, simply to keep his mouth shut. For a minute or two it did the trick, then he began to complain again.

'I'm soaked through.'

'There's a hut no' far away,' Davey told him. 'We'll take a bit shelter and see whit happens.'

Before they reached the hut Tam said in an urgent tone, 'Listen – how much dae ye get for golf ba's?'

'How much?' said Davey, frowning thoughtfully. 'Oh well, at the maist three for a pound.'

'Is that a'?' said Tam, looking offended. 'I heard ye got a pound each.'

'I don't know where ye heard that, but I've only ever got three for a pound.'

'So you're tellin' me,' said Tam, his voice heavy with sarcasm.

'As ye know yersel',' said Davey, trying to keep his temper, 'stolen property loses hauf its value by the time it reaches a buyer.'

'I bet I could get two quid for that yellow golf ba' any day,' said Tam. He snapped his fingers in the air. 'Jist like that.'

'You try it then,' said Davey, thankful to be nearing the hut. He would take a rest, drink the can of super lager he had in the back pocket of his trousers, then return home. He'd had enough of this fellow. They entered the hut and sat on a bench against the back wall – Tam gingerly on the edge of it, as it was exceedingly damp, and Davey leaning back carelessly with his legs stretched out.

'It's as cauld and wet in here than whit it is ootside,' said Tam.

Davey brought out his can of super lager. He offered it to Tam.

'Here, take a wee drap o' this. It might heat ye up.'

'No thanks,' said Tam, with a look of disgust. 'I cannae go that stuff. It tastes like gnats' piss.'

'Maybe so,' said Davey, 'but ye get accustomed tae the taste. Besides, it's the effect I'm efter.'

'Whit effect?' sneered Tam, staring moodily through the wide-open doorway of the hut. 'I'd rather have a hauf bottle o' Bell's, or even a joint. Dae you know there's mair effect wi' a joint than that stuff?'

'I widnae know,' said Davey, putting the can to his mouth and wishing he had another two to go with it, for there really wasn't much effect from one can when he came to think of it.

'How many golf ba's did ye say ye had?' Tam suddenly asked.

'Er – eh, five,' said Davey vaguely.

'So, I've got three and that makes eight. If we got anither two that would be ten. I know where I could sell them for a pound each and that would be a fiver tae you and a fiver tae me.'

Davey took another pull at his can. Definitely there was no effect from it at all and there wouldn't likely to be with this blowhard rabbiting on in his ear.

'I'm gaun hame shortly,' he said. 'I don't feel sae good.'

'Haw – flyman,' jibed Tam.

This angered Davey. 'Whit dae ye mean – flyman? I'm gaun hame, and that's that.'

'Aye, because you've got the maist ba's, that's how.'

'So whit, if I have,' said Davey, beginning to feel a slight hit off the lager, which increased his anger. 'I found them, didn't I?'

'That's only because you were lucky. I wis lookin' every bit as hard as you and soaked tae the skin intae the bargain. Look at ma trainers. They're ruined.'

Davey continued to drink his lager while Tam paced up and down the mud floor of the hut, his face grim and determined. He stopped suddenly to point his forefinger at Davey's face.

'OK, if you're no' collectin' I want yer golf ba's.'

'You're no gettin' them,' said Davey, his voice less strong than he had intended as Tam leaned over him and growled, 'Haund them ower, pal.'

Davey's patience was broken. He flung the contents of his can straight at Tam's face, blinding him with lager.

'Ye auld bastard,' roared Tam, wiping his eyes with the back of his hands, then unzipping the top of his anorak to wipe his neck as he wriggled about to ease his discomfort. 'That lager's fuckin' frozen,' he added in an anguished tone. 'As if I'm no' wet enough.'

Eventually he calmed down and glared at Davey as though wondering how best to deal with him. At that point Davey said, 'Ye can have the golf ba's then.'

He took the golf balls out from his pocket and flung them on the mud floor one by one, but only five of them. Tam looked down at the golf balls like a dog distracted by a bone. Then he glared back at Davey, clenching his fists.

'Listen, you,' he began to say when a voice from the doorway spoke.

'I say, you fellows, have either of you seen a red golf ball? I hit it in this direction and I'm damned if I can see it anywhere.'

The speaker wore a short yellow oilskin with its hood tied tightly under his chin. What could be seen of his face was fat and ruddy-cheeked. He could have been any age between thirty and forty, and he was holding a golf-club. Tam turned and snarled, 'Naw, we huvnae,' the rage still plain on his face. The golfer's eyes narrowed when he saw the golf balls lying on the mud.

'You've been stealing our golf balls, I see.'

'We never stole them,' said Tam. 'We found them and they're oors.'

The golfer laughed unpleasantly. 'You can tell that to the manager for I'm going to report you as soon as I get back to the club.'

'Report away,' said Tam with an equally unpleasant laugh.

'In the meantime,' said the golfer, 'you can give me up those golf balls and I might let you away with it this time. That is,' he wagged an admonishing finger at Tam, 'if I don't ever see either of you up here again.'

He then addressed Davey, who had never moved off the bench, sitting with his empty can of lager in his hand and his legs crossed like a disinterested onlooker.

'As for you, you're always up here pinching our golf balls. You definitely should be reported.'

He was about to say a lot more, when Tam tapped him on the shoulder with a look of disbelief on his face and said, 'Dae you mean to say ye want me tae bend doon and pick up these ba's and personally haund them ower tae you?'

'Exactly.'

'That'll be right,' said Tam as he began to kick them one by one under the bench. 'If you want them get them yersel'.'

'Right,' said the golfer, his cheeks turning purple. 'I will and you'll definitely be reported.'

As he bent down to retrieve them Tam gave him a shove. The golfer landed flat on the mud, his nose barely missing the bench. Tam let out a guffaw of laughter.

'There wis nae need for that,' said Davey helping the golfer to his feet and making feeble attempts to wipe the mud off his chin. The golfer backed off outside the doorway shaking his fist.

'Just wait,' he shouted, 'I'll be back with my mates. You've both had it, I can tell you.' His voice became fainter as he vanished round the side of the hut.

'I soon got rid o' him,' said Tam to Davey as if nothing amiss had happened between them. Then he froze and pointed outwards. 'Christ, he's left his golf-club.' He picked it up and went outside to hit great chunks of moss into the air, calling to Davey, 'This is a' right. I think I'll have a go roon the park wi' this club.'

Davey placed his empty can under the bench and came out into the open.

'We'd best get crackin' afore these golfers come back.'

They were a good bit down the path when Tam said, 'Christ, the golf ba's. I forgot them,' and ran back towards the hut.

Davey kept walking, hoping the golfers would meet up with Tam and beat him to a pulp. It didn't happen. Tam came back five minutes later, his pockets bulging.

'Fancy forgetting them,' he said, laughing.

Davey looked behind. When he saw there was no one following, he said to Tam, 'You walk on. I cannae keep up wi' ye.'

'I'll walk slow,' said Tam. 'I came oot wi' ye. I might as well go back wi' ye.' Then after a pause he reached into his pocket, adding, 'You can take four ba's back and that'll be four each. That's fair enough, isn't it?'

'Very fair,' said Davey, just wanting to get rid of Tam at all costs.

Tam went on, 'Dae ye know whit I've been thinkin'?'

'Naw – whit?'

'I've been thinkin' I'll gie ma golf ba's and the club to the young yins that hit ba's roon the park. It's a bloody shame they cannae afford tae play on a real course. Dae ye no' think it would be a nice gesture?'

'Very nice indeed,' said Davey after picking up a red golf ball halfway down the path. Tam didn't notice, being bemused with his thoughts.

They reached the fence, climbed over it and were crossing the fields when Tam said, 'Dae ye know, I enjoyed masel' the day. It's a great wee hobby collectin' golf ba's. But the next time we go we should try that private course up at Lynmoor. We can always get the bus up. It's no that dear –'

He broke off as Davey began to run – not very fast though because of his wellingtons for one thing and his age for another. Tam caught up with him easily. He said, 'Whit's wrang wi' you? Are you in a huff or somethin'?'

The Warehouse

The middle-aged couple sat with their backs against the wall. Some drunks against the opposite wall shouted on them to come over.

'Ignore them. They'll only be wanting some of our drink. I thought that fellow with the mouth-organ would have come back this evening. Still, it's early yet.'

'What fellow?' asked the man.

'The one who was here last Friday. Remember he played some good, old-fashioned tunes. There was one I liked in particular. It was kind of Mexican –'

'I don't remember.'

'At the time, you said you knew it. You were even singing the words –'

'I don't remember,' said the man emphatically. 'What's more important is this bottle's nearly empty. We'll have to get another.'

The woman pursed her lips. 'There's plenty left in that bottle. Don't be so desperate –' She broke off when she saw the warehouse door slide open and a young woman stand within the gap.

'Come in and close the door. There's a draught!' she shouted.

The young woman closed the door behind her then called out that she couldn't see a thing.

'You will when you get used to it. How do you think we manage?'

The young woman made her way across the floor, sat beside them and explained that she'd only looked in because she'd heard voices. The older woman said, 'That's all right. It's a free country. So what's your name?'

'Jessica.'

'That's a pretty name.'

The woman thought that seen close up this Jessica looked much more mature than from a distance, with her dyed-blonde hair and heavily pencilled eyebrows.

'My name's Mavis and this is my friend Albert,' she said, gesturing towards the man. He had glanced briefly at the young woman when she came in but now sat staring at the floor. Mavis offered Jessica the bottle.

'Thanks all the same but I'd rather have a temazepam or a fag if you've got one to spare.'

'We've no temazepam but it so happens I've got fags,' said Mavis, bringing a packet of Embassy Regal from her coat pocket. She offered it to Jessica then Albert before taking one herself. After the initial puff she began to cough.

'These fags will be the death of me.'

'Don't get my hopes built up,' said Albert suddenly, winking at Jessica. She gave him a polite smile back. Mavis asked him why he looked so pleased all of a sudden when he hadn't had a civil word to say all day.

'Me pleased?' he said, surprised. 'What makes you think I'm pleased?'

'Never mind,' she said, becoming downcast for no reason she could think of, then suddenly furious because Jessica had turned to the drunks on the opposite side of the warehouse and was actually smiling at them.

'Here, don't you be giving them alckies the eye or they'll be over like a shot and we definitely don't want that. At least I don't.'

'Are you talking to me?' said Jessica, her eyes glittering narrowly.

'Who else?'

Jessica made to rise. 'I'm not stopping to be insulted by the likes of you.'

'Don't then.'

By this time Mavis had taken a strong dislike to this young

woman, who she thought looked more and more like a tart with every minute that passed. She turned to Albert.

'You can see she's only out to cause trouble.'

'Leave her alone and mind your own bloody business,' he said.

Rage boiled up inside her. She lifted the bottle and smashed it against the wall, splashing it with wine. Some dribbled to the floor. There was a silence in which the three of them stared at the small, dark-red puddle.

Finally Albert said, 'There must have been at least a good third left in that bottle.' He stood up and Mavis thought he was going to strike her. Instead he went over to Jessica and asked if she would like to come outside.

'If you want,' she said jumping up and taking his arm.

Open-mouthed, in a state of shock, Mavis watched them leave. By the time she'd pulled herself together and hurried out after them they had vanished. She hung about for a good while in the hope Albert would regret what he'd done and come back. Perhaps the whole thing had been his idea of a joke or even a punishment. Albert could be very devious. No one knew better than she how devious, but when time passed without any sign of him, she was forced to move away, unsure of everything.

Fifteen minutes later she entered the licensed grocer to buy another bottle. It was all she could think to do although she hadn't intended drinking again so soon.

'Your friend, he is not with you this evening?' asked Abdul, who took a personal interest in the affairs of his customers.

Mavis explained that it appeared he'd left her for another woman.

'But that is terrible. What has come over him?'

She then went on to say that it must be because of his age for according to what she'd heard, lots of men leave their wives or partners for younger women when they reach a certain age: the male menopause, it's called, and as the woman he'd gone off with appeared young enough to be his daughter, that's all she could put it down to.

'Perhaps he will regret it later on,' said Abdul, shaking his head in dismay, then wrapping up the bottle in brown paper and giving it an extra twist at the top. Mavis always felt like telling him not to bother with the paper as it only got thrown away but she never did in case she hurt his feelings. She went out the door, promising to let him know of any further developments. Outside she threw away the paper, unscrewed the top of the bottle and took a long gulp of the wine. It immediately put new heart into her. She began to see the affair from a different angle. If Albert never came back she would be better off without him in many ways. She wouldn't have to put up with his foul moods when he had drunk too much, nor would she have to keep him going in it when she'd hardly enough for herself. Nor would she be obliged to have sex when she didn't feel like it. She hadn't felt like it for years, come to think of it. There were hundreds of things she wouldn't feel obliged to do in order to shut his mouth. Why, life without Albert might not be so bad after all. Instead of spending half her next giro on him, she would get something decent to wear from the Oxfam shop, then have her hair done – nothing fancy, a cut and blow dry would do her fine. Then after that (her heart pounded at the idea) she would go to the local housing department and ask for her name to be put down on the list for a council flat. It was time she got in off the streets and started having a decent life for a change.

As she walked along the pavement, her head quite dizzy with thinking about the great possibilities that lay ahead, she bumped into a woman who told her to watch where she was going then tried to push her off the pavement. Mavis's mood quickly changed.

'Who do you think you're shoving?'

'Scum,' said the woman over her shoulder, which depressed Mavis. She recognised the truth of the statement but if Albert had been with her the situation would never have arisen. Coming to a row of tenements, she paused outside an entrance wondering whether to have a drink inside rather than risk taking it in the open, when a young man came from the building and told her to beat it.

'I was only looking for an address,' she said as he brushed past. He exuded an air of violence which left her dithering and too frightened to move. Her previous confidence vanished. The truth of the matter, she told herself sadly, was that on her own she could scarcely walk two steps without somebody picking on her. What a fool she'd been! She'd just have to throw her pride to the wind and go and find Albert then persuade him to come back to her. She'd buy him all the drink he needed and he could bring Jessica with him if that's what he wanted. Anything was better than being on her own. He couldn't be far away. She'd try the old warehouse first. The chances were he might be there already, waiting for her to bring along the bottle.

'Albert,' she called, entering the warehouse and leaving the door open so that she could see her way. There was no answer but it was still early, perhaps not eight o'clock yet. She reached the spot where they usually sat, and took a small sip of wine, assuring herself she would make it last until Albert arrived. Otherwise he wouldn't be pleased. To pass the time she smoked three cigarettes. After finishing the third she'd become so jumpy that without thinking she put the bottle to her mouth and took a long swig and became so fuddled that she forgot all about Albert and Jessica. The only thing in her mind now was the Mexican tune the man with the mouth-organ had played the previous Friday. The words that had eluded her before came into her head quite easily.

> *Ah, the mission bells told me that I must not stay,*
> *South of the border, down Mexico way.*

In her cracked voice she sang the whole verse and continued singing it over and over again. She stopped once when she thought she heard footsteps outside.

'Is that you, Albert?' she called, but when there was no reply she simply carried on singing, enjoying the sound of her voice and only breaking off now and again to put the bottle to her mouth. She finally stopped when it grew so dark that she couldn't see a thing. This gave her a creepy feeling. She picked up the bottle and discovered it was empty. Immediately she felt horrifyingly sober. The only thing to do was to try and sleep if she could.

'Dear God,' she prayed as she sometimes did when desperate enough, 'just let me sleep through this night and I'll not touch another drop. Or at least,' she amended, not wanting to commit herself entirely, 'I'll cut it down a bit.'

After that she lit a cigarette, inhaled deeply, and as if in answer to her prayer her eyelids began to droop. She settled back against the wall and fell asleep, the cigarette dangling from her lips. It dropped onto her coat. The smouldering tip touched particles of fluff which eventually burst into flames.

When Shankland Comes

It was a raw March morning when Ivy came into the village hotel where she was employed as a cleaner. Sometimes she served in the public bar, but at present she wasn't needed there, for trade was always poor after the New Year. In summer, though, the hotel did well. It stood on the main road and was a good stopping point for tourists on their way to the mountains and lochs beyond. The village itself could be described as sleepy. Some folks said it was merely dull. On the side of the road near the hotel was a long stretch of mansions; on the other, a grocery store and a small scheme of neat, one-storey council houses. Behind the scheme stood a church dated 1894 and refaced with pink modern brick. There was no school in the village. The kids, big and small, travelled by bus to the small town of Blairmaddie five miles away.

There were only two customers in the public bar: Geordie Forsyth, the builder, and Sam Ferguson, who was elderly and toothless. Geordie Forsyth watched Ivy wipe the bar counter. She was tall and angular-faced with an abundance of dark curling hair and a slim figure under a green nylon overall. Though almost forty, older men – including Geordie Forsyth – found her attractive.

'Ye look fair scunnered,' Geordie said.

'That's no crime,' said Ivy, tossing her head. Her mind was on Dennett, her seventeen-year-old son. He had refused to get out of bed when she called him up for work and he'd only started the job on the farm two days before. Admittedly, it was on the side and the wage was poor, but added to his social security money, she thought he would be doing fine. When she called him a lazy bastard, he'd said, well, it wasn't his fault if he was a bastard, was it? The remark had rankled. It still rankled.

'Gie us a smile,' said Geordie, when she lifted his glass to wipe under it. 'Ye're braw when ye smile.'

'I'm no' in the mood for smilin',' said Ivy; nevertheless, her mouth softened. She liked Geordie well enough. He wasn't bad-looking, in a coarse way, and he had a steady job, which said a lot in his favour, but she didn't trust him. He was a hard drinker. Everybody knew that was why his wife had left him. Anyway, she'd never had any time for men since Dennett was born.

'Whit she needs is a man,' said old Sam, wheezing with laughter.

'That I don't need,' said Ivy, rubbing away furiously. 'Besides there's no men in this place, at least no' what I'd call one.'

'Come roon the back and I'll soon show ye,' said Geordie.

Sam laughed again. Ivy tutted and said to Geordie, 'You should be at your buildin' instead of standin' here drinking. I don't know how you get away wi' it.'

'Because I'm ma ain boss,' said Geordie complacently, just as Jim Carr, the barman, came in.

'Hurry up wi' that counter so as I can get servin',' he told Ivy. Geordie put down his empty tumbler on the counter and walked out. Old Sam faded into the background, holding a glass which still contained an inch of beer.

'Who is there to serve?' snapped Ivy, and headed for the kitchen. It was almost ten o'clock and time for her cup of tea. Going down the hallway she met Walter Sproul, the manager. Although he barely glanced at her, she noted the bags under his eyes. Likely been on the bottle last night, she thought, and fighting with his wife. They could be heard first thing in the morning, either brawling at each other or thumping on their bed in a frenzy of lovemaking. Ivy despised Sproul and also that wife of his. She did absolutely nothing in the hotel except come down the stairs in the afternoon, her hair all frizzed up and her make-up thick, and drive off somewhere in her blue Mercedes. Of course when

Shankland came it was a different story. Then you'd see her hovering behind Sproul as he spoke to Shankland with a smarmy smile on his face. Albert Shankland had been manager when Ivy first started work twenty years ago. She had been taken on part time as a waitress, then full time when he'd asked her to clean. The hotel had done well in those days. It had always been a pleasure to work for Shankland. Eventually he had bought the hotel and then another one farther south. Soon after, he'd moved south himself, appointing a new manager in his place. It had been a bitter blow, but that was a long time ago. Many managers had come and gone before Sproul took over. Sproul, though, was the worst. She wished Shankland would pay the hotel one of his flying visits to study the books and give a pep talk to the staff. He always took her aside and spoke to her in a warm and friendly way. Once he even enquired about Dennett. 'He's fine,' she'd answered, not knowing what else to say.

In the big kitchen, Babs, the cook, was pouring out two cups of tea. Ivy began to spread butter thickly on a roll.

'That Sproul gets on ma goat,' Babs said.

'What's he done this time?' said Ivy.

'He says we'll have tae put less meat in the sandwiches.' Staring hard at Ivy's roll, she added, 'He'll go mad if he sees that.'

'I'm no' takin' any meat,' Ivy pointed out.

'I've got tae account for the butter as well,' said Babs, her voice aggrieved.

Ivy shrugged then sat up on a high stool with her back facing the table and her legs crossed. Babs frowned at the sight of Ivy's slim legs. Her own were short and fat. In fact she was fat all over, with a stomach that bulged out under her white overall. Her broad face was red from the heat of the kitchen.

'By the way,' she said, 'are you goin' tae the dance in the church hall on Saturday?'

Ivy wrinkled her nose slightly. 'I don't know. They're gettin' awful stale nowadays.'

'Ye always get a laugh at somethin', and the punch is free.'

'I'm no' that desperate for a drink,' said Ivy.

'There's nothin' much else happenin' in this dump,' said Babs bitterly.

'If I go, it means that Dennett's in the house by himsel' until dead late.'

'Surely Dennett's auld enough to stay in by hissel'?'

'I'll have to think about it,' said Ivy, picturing Dennett bringing his pals in and drinking cans of lager.

Ivy was washing her cup when Jim burst into the kitchen and asked her to take the bar while he had some tea, since Betty, the lounge bar waitress, hadn't come in yet.

'I don't know how she's kept on,' said Ivy. 'She's always late.'

'And she's that bloody cheeky wi' it tae,' said Babs.

'Yous two are just jealous because she's sexy lookin',' Jim said.

Ivy and Babs laughed simultaneously. 'She's as sexy lookin' as a coo lookin' ower a dyke,' said Ivy.

There was nobody in the bar except old Sam, still holding his tumbler with its inch of beer.

'Finish that pint and get anither one,' said Ivy. 'This is no' a bus shelter you're staunin' in.'

'I cannae afford anither one,' said Sam. 'I've only got ma pension tae keep me.'

'Aye, I know,' said Ivy sighing. She was about to give him a free half-pint when Betty came in, her blonde hair spiked at the top and long and flat at the back.

'I slept in,' she explained, as old Sam gave her a startled look. He finished his beer and walked stiffly away.

'I'm sure that hair-do must have taken a good hour to fix,' said Ivy.

'No' really,' said Betty. 'It's quite easy when ye know how.'

Sensing that Betty was about to launch into a long explanation about why she'd slept in, Ivy said quickly, 'Now that you're in, I'm away to clean the toilets.'

208

The day passed slowly for Ivy. Business was still poor in the afternoon, apart from a few young lads from the community programme who came in to order coffee. She looked at them enviously as they came through the hotel door wearing their donkey jackets. She wished Dennett could have been one of them. Of course he was too young for the community programme which mainly consisted of doing old folks' gardens. In bad weather they hung around the hotel entrance, laughing loud and inanely, but at least they were obliged to get up in the morning. Dennett had still been in bed when she went home at lunch-time.

Sproul's wife left as usual in her Mercedes and Sproul went prowling about the hotel like a pregnant cat, his face sullen and brooding as if looking for someone to lash out at. Ivy affected to look busy by polishing the hallway twice before she went through to the kitchen to scrub the big table. Babs had gone off duty at four o'clock and the room was empty. Ivy stared up through the kitchen window at the tormented-looking sky, thinking that it wouldn't be long till summer when the place would be packed out.

On her way home she stopped at the grocery which sold everything from a packet of pins to a jar of boiled mussels. The freezer near the door was filled with all sorts of frozen packets and half the counter was taken up with rolls, pies and doughnuts, all in separate cardboard boxes. Scarcely four people could stand inside the shop comfortably.

'My, it's a right cauld day,' said Mrs Braithwaite, the owner, from behind the counter. She was a small, stout, elderly woman who always wore a hairnet over her blue perm.

'I'm fair roastin',' said Ivy, and went on to ask for two pies and a tin of beans.

'It'll be a' that hard work ye dae in the hotel,' said Mrs Braithwaite. She put two pies in a poke, then without turning round, lifted a tin of beans from the shelf behind her. The shop was so cramped that she scarcely needed to move an inch to put her hand on any item, except those in the freezer to which folk helped themselves. 'I've heard the manager's no' very easy tae work for,' she added.

'He's no' bad,' said Ivy, reluctant to say anything that could get to Sproul's ears.

'They tell me the wages are no' very good,' said Mrs Braithwaite, when Ivy handed over a pound note for the purchases.

'They're a lot better than what ye get off the social,' said Ivy promptly.

'That's true,' said Mrs Braithwaite, opening the till, 'though I've heard there's plenty on the social and workin' forbye.' She looked directly at Ivy. 'I don't think that's fair, dae you?'

'I don't suppose it is,' said Ivy, wondering if the storekeeper knew that Dennett had worked two days on the farm. She asked for ten king-size Regal before Mrs Braithwaite could pursue the subject any further and headed for the door.

Outside the wind blew cold but invigorating in her face. Old autumn leaves stirred at the side of the pavement and in the distance she saw the peaks of the mountains covered in snow. She walked up the neat path of her council house noting the snowdrops under her window and reflecting that the village would be a nice enough place to stay in if it wasn't for some of the folk.

When she came into the living room Dennett was sitting in the armchair facing the television with the gas fire turned up full.

'So, you've managed to get up then,' she said, turning the fire low. He stretched his legs and kept his sharp profile fixed ahead. She noticed with distaste that his hair was uncombed. It lay on his shoulders, light brown and straggly. 'You might have washed yersel' at least,' she muttered, as she went through to the kitchenette to put on the kettle. A minute later she was startled to see him towering above her, looking anxious.

'Did ye get my fags?' he asked.

'They're in my bag,' she said, exasperated. 'Do ye no' think it's terrible I should have to buy you fags and you'll no' even make an attempt to earn money to buy them yersel'?'

'I wisnae feelin' well this mornin',' he said, ripping the Cellophane from the packet. 'I'll go tae work the morra.'

'Well, ye'd better,' she said, a bit mollified by this statement. 'But mind,' she added, 'don't go near the store on your way to the farm. If auld Braithwaite thinks you're workin' she could report ye. She's that type.'

'Aye,' he said, then, 'Are ye makin' chips?'

'No,' she shouted, thinking that Dennett never seemed to give a damn about anything that really mattered.

'Did ye hear that Shankland's comin'?' Babs said to Ivy when she came into the hotel kitchen next morning.

'When?' said Ivy, trying not to look excited.

'Either Friday or Saturday,' said Babs. She added morosely, 'I hate when he comes.'

'He's OK – a lot better than Sproul,' said Ivy. 'If Shankland has anythin' to say he tells ye fair and square, no' like Sproul wi' his snidy remarks for no good reason. Shankland doesnae bother me.'

'It's a' right for you,' said Babs. 'You're mair familiar wi' him than me.'

'Whit dae ye mean "familiar"?' said Ivy, her voice sharp.

'I only mean that you've known him longer than any of us, that's a',' said Babs, her eyes wide and innocent. She poured out the tea while Ivy buttered her roll heavily. 'Anyway,' she went on, 'business is that bad I wouldnae be surprised if he's up tae close the hotel. It's happenin' a' ower the place. I heard the hotel outside Blairmaddie's tae close and it only opened three years ago.'

Ivy made no comment on this, inwardly seething at the use of the word 'familiar'. It looked as though Babs was jealous of her long acquaintanceship with Shankland. She'd have to be careful of what she said to her in future. When she was washing her cup at the sink Babs said, 'Are ye still no' goin' tae the dance?'

'Definitely no',' snapped Ivy, marching off to dust and hoover the lounge, although she didn't think it would need much cleaning since it hadn't been opened since Monday.

Thursday was cold, but bright. The hotel was surprisingly busy with families tempted out for the day by the early spring sun, and some of the wealthy retired locals from the big houses. The lounge was opened and there were six men standing in the public bar, including Geordie Forsyth who came in every day anyway. Ivy was asked to serve in the bar while Betty did the lounge. All this and the fact that Dennett had got out of his bed and gone to his job at the farm put Ivy in a good mood. Jim hummed tunes under his breath as he pulled the pints and Sproul walked between the lounge and the bar with his face less haunted-looking than usual. Only Babs in the kitchen was grumbling when Ivy dashed in for a quick cup of tea; she hadn't time for a roll.

'If it's goin' tae be as busy as this,' she said, 'I'll need extra help.'

'I thought you said the hotel might be closin' down,' Ivy laughed.

'If it's no' one way it's another,' Babs shouted as Ivy dashed off. 'Don't forget one swallow doesnae make a summer.'

Ivy didn't go home for lunch as she had a lot of cleaning to do. She took a snack in the kitchen then carried on with the washing, the hoovering and dusting, the polishing. It was hard going, she thought, but worth it with the place so busy. From now on maybe business would pick up and everyone would be in a better mood. She got home at half-past five after stopping at the store to buy milk, bread and cheese. Her face fell. Dennett sat in the chair facing the television with the gas fire turned up full.

'I thought ye didnae stop until six,' she said, blinking nervously.

'I've been sacked,' he said.

'Sacked?' she said, throwing her message bag on the couch and sinking down beside it.

'Aye, sacked,' he said defiantly. 'It wis because I never came in yesterday. I've been in here since nine in the mornin'.'

'I knew this would happen,' she said bitterly.

Dennett's voice was equally bitter. 'I'm glad I wis sacked. You don't know whit it's like tae muck out dung all day, and then havin' tae eat your piece wi' yer haunds all smelly, and no' even a drap o' tea to wash it down. Anyway it wisnae a real job, I'd only have got paid in washers.'

'Did you get yer two days' money then?'

'Naw, he said I wis tae come back on Saturday.'

'And I bet like hell you bloody well won't,' said Ivy, her temper rising. 'And here's me workin' my pan in to keep you in meals and fags and put a good face on everythin' and tryin' to keep decent and there you are tellin' me you're above muckin' out byres . . . Well, I don't particularly like bein' a cleaner and gettin' paid in washers either, but I have to do it to keep a roof above our heids.'

Dennett sneered, 'That's up tae you.'

Enraged, Ivy jumped up from the couch and slapped him on the cheek. Dennett confronted her with eyes blazing. For a second she thought he was going to slap her back, but he only stared at her madly for a moment before he rushed out of the room. She heard his bedroom door slam hard, then silence. She sat down on the couch again, drained, vowing to herself that she would tell Dennett to get out. He was old enough to take care of himself, after all; why should she put up with his laziness and cheek? He could get himself a room or a bed-and-breakfast somewhere in Blairmaddie, and come to think of it, Blairmaddie would suit him better, being full of licensed grocers and pubs.

Knowing him, he'd likely just drift around spending his social money on booze or even dope: she'd heard there were junkies galore there. At least, she thought angrily, if he's out of the way he can't give me a showing-up in the village. She sat for a while thinking of what could happen to Dennett in Blairmaddie or some other bigger place beyond. But she could never do it, of course. He was too feckless. It was quite beyond her to put him out at seventeen. Besides, he wouldn't go easily, and after all he might get a job with the community programme next September when he was eighteen. Sighing, she stood up and went through to the kitchenette to make some tea and toasted cheese. It was all she felt fit to cook. Ten minutes later she shouted from the living room, 'Dennett, come and get your supper.' When he came through he peered at the plate on the worktop, saying in a perplexed manner, 'Toasted cheese? How did ye no' make chips for a change?'

On Friday it snowed and again there was hardly anybody in the bar except Geordie Forsyth, who was at one of the tables in the small room, deep in discussion with two of the brickies he employed. He hardly glanced at Ivy when she came in to clean, which annoyed her in a way, especially when she had taken extra pains with her hair, brushing it hard so that it fell smoothly round her face, as well as putting on a touch of eye-shadow and lipstick. Although all this was for Shankland's benefit, she'd expected a compliment or two from Geordie. Betty came in right on time for once, and Ivy didn't doubt that it was because she too expected Shankland at any minute. Jim stood behind Betty, polishing the glasses intently.

The morning passed and Shankland did not show up, nor was there any sign of Sproul in the hotel. This seemed strange to Ivy but she didn't remark on it, not even to Babs. In fact, they had scarcely a word to say to each other during the tea break. It was as if they had mutually decided to fall out.

Ivy came back home at lunch feeling thoroughly disgruntled. She was taken aback to see Dennett up and fully clothed, eating toast and scrambled egg. Then she remembered that this was his giro day.

'There's some egg left in the pot,' he said obligingly.

'Thanks,' she said curtly, thinking he'd have done better to make a slice of toast to go with it. Before she left she reminded him to leave his money on the sideboard after he had cashed the giro at Braithwaite's store.

'I always dae,' he answered with a touch of indignation.

In the afternoon when she took the Hoover into the lounge, she was surprised to see Sproul's wife standing behind the small lounge bar.

'Don't bother hoovering,' she told Ivy. 'The carpet's clean enough. Just separate the tables. They're far too close together.'

'I always hoover the carpet whether it's clean or no',' Ivy said hotly. 'That's how it's in such good condition.'

'Nonsense,' said Sproul's wife. 'Just do as I say.'

'Wait a minute,' said Ivy, her eyes blazing. 'Since when have you taken charge?'

Sproul's wife said tartly, 'As from today, I'm in charge of the lounge.' As Ivy stared at her in disbelief, Sproul's wife, her lips cyclamen pink and smiling, added, 'If you don't believe me, ask my husband when he comes in.'

'I'll no' bother seein' your husband,' Ivy retorted, 'I'll wait tae Shankland comes in. It seems to me he's the main one to see.'

'Do you think so?' said Sproul's wife, assuming an astonished expression. 'I'd hardly credit that, when my husband is paid to manage the hotel. However, if you want to see Mr Shankland you'll have to wait until tomorrow. He's down at Blairmaddie at the moment discussing business with my husband in the Riverbank Hotel. He thought it better to stay there for the night on account of the roads being so bad up here with the snow.'

Ivy gave Sproul's wife one black look, then turned on her heels, trailing the Hoover behind her.

'What about separating the tables,' Sproul's wife called, but Ivy was off into the toilet to try and calm herself down.

On a Friday at teatime the store was always busy, mainly with women rushing in at the last minute after collecting their husbands' wages. Although there was less rushing in nowadays than there used to be, it was still busy enough to make Ivy fume with impatience as she waited at the end of the queue. She wanted to get home quickly to make sure that her share of Dennett's giro was lying on the sideboard, but beside that, she had been thrown into confusion by her encounter with Sproul's wife. It seemed as she waited that Mrs Braithwaite was chatting longer than ever with the customers. When finally her turn came she asked in a clipped voice for bread, potatoes and half a pound of sausages. This didn't prevent the storekeeper informing her that Dennett had just been in to cash his giro. As Ivy nodded and opened her purse, Mrs Braithwaite added, 'It's a pity he cannae get work, a big strong fella like that.'

Ivy was stung into saying, 'There's no work to be had, is there?'

'I don't know,' said Mrs Braithwaite deliberately. 'There's some that widnae take a job if it was under their very nose.'

Ivy grabbed her change from Mrs Braithwaite's fat fingers and marched out past the queue that had formed behind her.

When she went in through the front door she heard Dennett running the tap in the bathroom. He usually celebrated his giro day with a bath and a hair wash before going out with his pals for a night in Blairmaddie. She put the kettle on then checked to see if her money was on the sideboard. It was – the whole twenty-five pounds of it. His dinner was on the plate when he came into the kitchen, rubbing his hair with a towel, his face pink and shiny.

'Good,' he said. 'Chips.'

'I'm glad somethin' pleases you,' she said drily, following him into the living room. Dennett stuffed chips into his mouth, gazing dreamily at the television. Ivy picked at her meal half-heartedly. Before she lifted the dishes to wash them, she told Dennett to mind and go up to the farm on Saturday and get the money owed to him.

'Aye – so I wull,' he said reluctantly, frowning as if he had no intention of going at all. Then he stood up and went into his bedroom. Within seconds the insistent beat of some pop group pounded on her ear-drums. She debated whether to go through and tell him to turn the sound down. Instead, she took a pair of ear-plugs from a drawer in the kitchen cabinet and sat down on the couch, staring blankly at a television she couldn't hear. An hour later he peeped into the living room to tell her that he was away. She took the ear-plugs out and told him not to be late.

'Aye – so I wull,' he said. She knew she was wasting her breath.

On Saturday, rain turned the snow on the pavements to slush. Ivy came into the public bar wearing a blue woollen dress minus her nylon apron. She had decided to look good for Shankland, but when Jim turned to her and said, 'For a second I thought you wir Sproul's wife,' she began to wonder if the dress was a mistake.

'I should hope no',' she muttered, dying to ask him if Shankland had come in last night. Pride kept her silent. She asked if Sproul was around.

'No' yit,' he answered, pulling a face as if something was happening that only he knew about. When she began to wipe the shelves he said in a low voice, 'Sproul's wife is takin' over the lounge.'

'So I heard,' said Ivy. 'Well, maybe it's time she did something for her keep.'

'Looks as if there's gaun to be a lot mair changes,' said Jim darkly.

Curtly, Ivy replied, 'It's all one tae me, I'm only the cleaner, thank God.'

Jim turned away to serve one of the men who had come forward from a youngish crowd sitting at a table. Every Saturday morning they came in, deafening the place with their loud aggressive talk. Ivy was glad to get out of the bar whenever they arrived.

'Would ye like to gie us a hand?' Jim asked her when another two came forward to the counter.

'I've got a lot to do,' said Ivy, hurrying away: Betty would be in any minute and she'd be overjoyed to serve that boisterous lot.

'That's a nice dress ye've on,' Babs said to her in the kitchen, evidently prepared to be friendly.

'Actually, it's quite an old one,' said Ivy.

'It doesnae look it,' said Babs. 'How have ye no' got yer apron on? It'll get a' dirty.'

'I forgot to bring it. Anyway, it doesnae matter if it gets dirty,' said Ivy impatiently.

'Here, d'ye know that Sproul's wife's in the lounge?' said Babs, handing Ivy a cup of tea and a roll which she explained was already buttered.

'Thanks,' said Ivy, suspecting the roll would be buttered thin. 'She telt me herself yesterday.'

'Did she?' said Babs, her eyes wide. 'You must be well in. Naebody tells me anythin' except when it's history.'

'I wouldn't worry about it,' said Ivy. 'There's always bound to be changes at some time.'

'Aye, but changes are never for the best nowadays,' said Babs.

'Let's look on the bright side for once,' said Ivy, feeling anything but bright. She suddenly had a premonition: either Shankland wasn't going to come in at all, or maybe he had been in last night and gone away again. So if Sproul's wife was going to take over the lounge where did that leave her? If Betty had only the public bar to do, it meant that they wouldn't need her to serve at all and there definitely wasn't enough cleaning to justify her hours from nine to five. And if they cut her hours, she might as well be on the dole. She'd have to talk to Sproul about it immediately.

Suddenly Babs said, 'Are you still no' goin' tae the dance?'

'I've already told you I'm no',' said Ivy sharply.

'Then I don't think I'll go either,' said Babs. 'I hate goin' in the door masel'.'

'Don't then,' said Ivy. She felt like screaming.

Later, when she was coming out of the toilet, Betty told her in a casual way that she'd heard Shankland was coming in the afternoon. Ivy brightened up at that. She decided that there was no need to see Sproul. Shankland would allay her fears. So what if Sproul's wife was managing the lounge? She could come to terms with that as long as they didn't cut her hours.

When she got home at lunch-time she looked in at Dennett's room to see if he was all right. Heaven knows what time he'd come home last night, and in what condition. When she'd left this morning she had been so preoccupied by the affairs of the hotel that she'd forgotten all about him. She found him lying on his back, snoring his head off, his long legs sticking out from under the blankets. 'Dennett,' she called, but he continued to snore. When she called again, 'Do ye want something to eat?' he grunted, 'Naw,' and turned on his side. She studied him for a while, almost envying his complete disregard for anyone but himself. He had no talent, no ambition and no pride, yet he looked so happy lying there with that slight smile on his lips.

The afternoon wore on and still there was no sign of Shankland. Sproul passed her once or twice as she was polishing the woodwork in the corridor, and ducked his head in an embarrassed way which made her wonder. But when Jim handed over her pay-packet at half-past four, she found out why. Inside was two weeks' money and a letter saying that due to increased overheads and poor trade, the management regretted that they no longer required her services. However, as soon as trade picked up they would send for her again.

Ivy scanned the letter twice to make sure she had read correctly. Then chalk-faced, she went off in search of Sproul. She found him behind the lounge bar, standing close to his wife. They were studying a ledger and they looked conspiratorial. Ivy thrust the letter under Sproul's nose and said, 'You cannae do this to me.'

Sproul and his wife looked up at her with pained expressions. Sproul said, 'I'm very sorry about this, but . . .'

'Never mind bein' sorry,' Ivy interrupted. 'I'm goin' to see Shankland. When will he be in?'

Sproul's wife shoved her face forward. 'He won't be in,' she said spitefully. 'He's already spoken to us about everything. Isn't that right, Walter?'

'Yes,' Sproul said heavily.

Ivy's head swam. She said faintly, 'He cannae know about this. Shankland would never sack me.'

'It was his instructions,' said Sproul.

'You're lyin',' said Ivy. 'Give me his address and I'll get in touch wi' him masel'.'

Sproul and his wife exchanged weary glances.

'Look Ivy,' said Sproul, 'if you want to see him, try the church hall round about ten o'clock. He and his wife have been invited to the dance as special guests, but I can assure you that letter was written on his instructions.'

'I still don't believe you,' said Ivy, turning away to hide the tears in her eyes. A minute later she put on her coat and walked out of the hotel without saying a word to anyone.

Prompt at ten, Ivy was inside the church hall, still wearing her blue woollen dress and fortified by two glasses of port from the bottle which had been in her sideboard since the New Year. She was dismayed to see hardly anyone but the minister and some church elders waiting by the door. On a platform in a corner near the entrance sat the band wearing maroon shirts and dark suits, the same band that played every year, its members middle-aged and bespectacled. The minister's wife and her cronies stood at the far end of the hall beside a table spread with food. Hesitantly, Ivy went over to the table and, for want of anything better to do, helped herself to a sandwich and a glass of punch from the big fruit bowl in the centre.

'How nice to see you, Ivy,' said the minister's wife, smiling horsily.

'Likewise, I'm sure,' said Ivy. She took a gulp of the punch and shuddered.

'Strong, isn't it?' said the minister's wife. 'There's a bottle of brandy in it. I made it myself.'

'It's very good,' said Ivy, forcing a smile. She added brightly, 'There's no' many turned up though.'

'They'll be fortifyin' themselves in the hotel,' said Mrs Braithwaite, who wore pink gingham and for once had no hairnet on.

'Do you mind if I sit down?' said Ivy. She was beginning to feel dizzy from drinking the strong punch on top of the port. She went over to the bench against the wall and sat there sipping from her glass until she calmed down a bit. A crowd of men and women thrust through the door like cattle from a stockade and the band began to play a slow foxtrot. The minister and his wife were the first on the floor, dancing awkwardly, their faces strained. Ivy decided to have just one more glass of punch. It would while away the time until Shankland arrived, although by now her head was so foggy that quite honestly she didn't really care whether he came or not. When she turned round from the table she saw Babs sailing towards her like a gigantic balloon in her wide orange dress.

'I thought you werenae comin',' said Babs indignantly, helping herself to a sausage roll. With crumbs falling from her mouth, she added, 'Is it true ye've got the sack?'

'Is that what you heard?' said Ivy, taking a gulp of punch.

'Well, is it true?' Babs persisted.

'Nothing that's ever said in this place is true.' Ivy pointed to the bowl of punch. 'Try some of that. It's strong stuff. There's a whole bottle of brandy in it.' She heard herself laugh foolishly.

'It seems tae be,' said Babs, staring hard at Ivy. Then she walked off to talk to the minister's wife, leaving Ivy on her own.

Geordie Forsyth came up from behind and asked her for a dance. She was vaguely surprised to see him so smart in a grey pin-striped suit. 'Right,' she said, grateful for the rescue. As they waltzed round the hall she tripped over his feet, feeling quite giddy.

'Steady on,' said Geordie. He pulled her close, his hand pressing her waist. If it hadn't been for the half-bottle in Geordie's pocket jamming hard into her hip, she would happily have floated around the hall for the rest of the night. When the dance ended Geordie asked her if she'd like to come outside for a wee nip of whisky.

'I don't know . . .' she began. And then she saw Shankland standing in the doorway. With him was a small, plump, matronly woman in a black lace dress. Shankland was shaking hands with the minister, his heavy-jowled face lit by a smile. He was a big man with a thick waist. He had never been handsome, exactly, but he attracted attention wherever he went.

Without thinking, Ivy rushed forward. 'Mr Shankland,' she said, tugging at his sleeve, 'can I have a word with you? It's very important.'

Shankland turned round, frowning. 'Later, Ivy. Can't you see my wife and I are talking to the minister?' His wife, who as far as Ivy could see hadn't been talking at all, looked her up and down with suspicion.

'I'm sorry,' said Ivy, 'but Sproul's sacked me from the hotel and I've been waitin' for you to come in.' The words came out slurred. She broke off, sick at heart at Shankland's expression.

'Yes, I'm sorry it had to happen,' he said guardedly. 'But you see, it was either that or closing down the hotel altogether. However, if the place does better in the summer we'll send for you again, don't worry on that score.' And with that he turned back to the minister, who had been listening anxiously.

Suddenly Ivy's rage erupted. 'You mean to say,' she said, her voice rising, 'that you were the one who sacked me, after all these years? All these years I've been loyal and kept my mouth shut?'

Shankland scarcely looked at her. 'Go away, Ivy,' he said wearily. 'You're drunk.'

'Yes, do go and sit down, Ivy,' the minister pleaded. 'You're not your usual self. Perhaps it's the punch. I told my wife not to put in so much brandy.'

'What do you mean – "kept your mouth shut"?' asked Shankland's wife, her face puckering.

'Don't listen to her,' Shankland said. 'She's just upset and a bit drunk. That's all there is to it.' He led his wife towards the table, bending over her slightly, while the minister followed close behind.

Ivy stood for a moment, dazed, her mind fuddled by the slow, monotonous rhythm of the band. She noticed Geordie Forsyth dancing with Babs and looking genteel. A taste of bile was in her mouth and her head was in a turmoil. She saw Shankland turn his back on her and offer his wife a sandwich from a plate. Then all at once her mind was made up. She rushed across to the table.

'That's no' all there is to it!' she said in a voice loud and clear. 'What about Dennett, my son and yours, whom I've kept for seventeen years without a penny off ye? I took the blame on myself, aye, they say it's always the woman to blame, don't they? But since you think so little of me I might as well admit in front of everybody here that you're Dennett's father. I think ye owe me something for that.'

'You're crazy!' said Shankland, with a furtive look at his wife. Her face had turned white as a sheet. All around the table a hush had fallen, and people were staring. He grabbed his wife's elbow. 'Let's get out of here,' he whispered.

The small woman stood her ground, trembling. 'Leave me alone,' she said.

Shankland tugged at her urgently. 'Come on.'

And then his wife's arm jerked up and her eyes went blank and she threw the glass of punch straight into Shankland's face.

'Oh dear,' said the minister, his hands fluttering in the air, and someone laughed. There were a few more titters. Then Shankland turned and marched towards the door, his wife following a yard or two behind.

Ivy clutched at the table for support.

'Go ower and sit down,' Mrs Braithwaite said in a surprisingly kind voice. 'I'll see if I can get a cup of tea from somewhere.' She glared at the minister's wife. 'That punch bowl's been a bloody curse!'

'I'm OK,' said Ivy, smiling wanly.

'I'm awful sorry,' said the minister's wife with an apologetic look at Ivy. 'I shouldn't have put so much brandy in.'

'Don't worry yoursel', I quite enjoyed it.'

Ivy walked over to the bench by the wall and sat down. Geordie Forsyth and Babs came off the dance floor, red-faced and dripping with sweat.

'Have you been sittin' here a' night?' Babs sounded concerned.

'No' really,' said Ivy.

'I thought I saw Shankland come in.'

'So he did,' said Ivy. 'He's away now.'

'Did he say anythin'? I mean, about you gettin' the sack?'

'No' as much as I said to him.'

Geordie took the half-bottle from his pocket. 'Do any of yous ladies want a wee nip?'

'No' straight frae the bottle,' said Babs, aghast.

'I'll take one,' said Ivy, putting the bottle to her mouth.

'Will ye look at her!' Babs said. 'To think she's aye sae proud and ladylike.'

'No' any more,' said Ivy. The rough whisky trickled down her throat. She was about to tilt the bottle again when a sudden thought stopped her. Dennett. It wasn't as if she only had herself to consider, after all. Likely he'd be in on his own, watching the television, since he never had any money left on a Saturday to go anywhere. Aye, Dennett. Somebody had to set him an example, didn't they, and she'd been doing it for years so she wasn't about to stop now. She handed the bottle back to Geordie and struggled to her feet. 'I think I'll go home now.'

'Away, it's still early,' said Geordie, looking at his watch.

'I must get home,' Ivy said firmly. 'I've left Dennett in himsel' and he's no' to be trusted.'

'There goes an awfy determined woman,' said Geordie, as he and Babs watched her leave.

'The trouble wi' Ivy,' said Babs, 'is that she's aye been too big for her boots, and now she's been sacked she cannae take it.' She sniffed loudly. 'If you ask me, it serves her right.'

A Bad Influence

'I don't like you going up to Donald's room,' my mother would say if we were visiting Granny's. 'He's a bad influence and I want you to stay away from him.'

The minute I got there I was upstairs like a shot. Uncle Donald, although only four years older than myself, was the leader of a bunch of guys who came along to play cards and smoke hash. Once they gave me a joint to try and I nearly passed out. The next time I took one I was fine. I had the feeling I was being tested for future membership.

Then there was this dame called Marian who sometimes accompanied them. I noticed she always sat right next to Donald. I'm sure he couldn't have fancied her for she wasn't the least bit attractive. Once she kissed me in front of everybody. I think this was to make Donald jealous but all he said was, 'Leave the kid alone. He's too young for you,' and I hated her for that.

Donald was extra good on the guitar. Apart from playing the stuff everybody played he made up tunes of his own. They were a bit weird, right enough, like something you hear on Radio 2, but we always acted as though we enjoyed it, except Marian who said she preferred country and western. I expect she thought she was being clever but Donald just shrugged as if he didn't care.

'I hope you're not smoking dope up in that room,' said my mother when I was going back along the road one day.

'Of course not. Only the odd fag or two.'

'For if I ever catch you –'

I walked on ahead so that I couldn't hear her. I wasn't worried though. It would be the usual empty threat.

One evening I went up to the room and no one was there. I dashed down into the living room.

'Where is everybody?'

Granny looked up at me pitifully and shook her head. My mother said she didn't know about everybody but she'd just been told that Donald had run off because he owed the drug-dealer. My heart sank. The dealer was a guy called Fat Harry, who did his business on the street corner without caring who saw. He knew nobody would have the guts to report him and even if they did the cops would turn a blind eye.

'He's in a lot of trouble,' I said.

'That's obvious,' said my mother.

'His pals owe money as well,' spoke Granny. 'I don't know why he's to take the blame.'

'Because he's the leader.'

'Then leader must be another name for mug,' declared my mother.

After that, life was so lonely and boring I wanted to cry but I didn't dare in case my mother noticed and sent me to the dentist. She had this theory that toothache was the only thing that made me cry and I'd never given her much cause to think otherwise. I became so desperate for company I took up with a guy in my class called Morton McEwan, another lonely type. Not that I'd always been a loner. It was just a stage I was going through. Anyway, Morton had good reason for being lonely. He wore thick spectacles which gave him an owlish appearance. He also had a bad case of acne. I didn't like being seen with him though I didn't mind going round to his house. He always had plenty of fags and dirty magazines.

I'd been going with Morton for a few days when my mother informed me that Donald was back.

'Back?' I said, wondering whether to be glad or not. I'd actually given up thinking about him.

'Seems he was hiding out in an old shed and his arm's broken. I reckon it was that Fat Harry done it.'

I immediately felt a strong surge of sympathy for Donald. I thought I'd go round and see him. Then my mother, who must have read my thoughts, said, 'In case you're thinking of going round, Granny says he doesn't want to see anybody.'

My sympathy vanished. 'I wasn't even considering it,' I said.

'Ever think of joining a gang?' I asked Morton as we were leafing through some magazines.

'Not really,' he said.

'I think we should. We can't go on like this for ever.'

'Like what?'

'Like drifting along without any purpose. Before you know it we'll be drawing our old-age pension.'

He took off his specs and wiped them on his sleeve.

'My mother wouldn't like it,' he said.

'Your mother wouldn't need to know.'

He put his specs on again, stared into the distance and finally said, 'I'll have to think about it.'

On an impulse I jumped up and said, 'Well, you think about it, but I'm not going to hang around here all day while you do.'

I banged the door behind me feeling an unjustifiable anger for him. Surely I could do better than that.

Outside, the street was empty, apart from an old guy hobbling along with the aid of a stick, and a woman nagging at a kid to hurry up. All the shops were closed except a pub on the corner which I was too young for, even if I had the money to drink. How are folk like me supposed to make anything of ourselves in a place like this, I thought balefully. Of course, the plain fact was that folk like me were supposed to stay in and watch the telly, if they're lucky enough to have one.

'Back already?' said my mother, who was getting dressed for the bingo.

'Why shouldn't I be back? There's nothing for young folk to do here. No wonder they take dope.'

She gave me a sharp look. 'Are you referring to yourself, by any chance?'

'No. Just to young folk in general,' I said.

'If it's something to do you're looking for, there's a pile of dishes in the sink,' she said.

'Forget it,' I said, stamping off to my room. Talking to my mother was like banging my head off a brick wall, painful and without purpose. As soon as she'd gone I washed my face and went round to Granny's.

'I heard Donald's back,' I said when she opened the door.

'Yes, and in some state too. He says his arm's broken. I told him to go to a doctor but –'

'Will it be all right if I go up and see him?' I asked. 'Do you think he'd mind?'

'Oh, I'm sure he wouldn't,' she said. 'You go up anyway. I know he's fond of you.'

'Is he?' I said, wondering what made her think that when he'd never given me any hint of it. I ran up the stairs joyfully.

Donald sat on the edge of his bed strumming the guitar, with no sign of a bandage even.

'I thought you had a broken arm,' I said. He stopped strumming and sighed as if I had interrupted him in the middle of some composing.

'No, but it felt like it. I got kicked, you know.' He put his guitar down and asked what I wanted.

'I only came to see if you were OK but if you want me to go –'

He sighed again. 'Actually, I was thinking of topping myself.'

'You were?' I said, not really surprised.

'I might as well do it and save Fat Harry the bother.'

'What about Granny?' I said. 'Wouldn't she lend you something?'

'How could she? She's only got her pension.'

'True,' I said.

We sat for a while, thinking. Then I got an idea so good I couldn't believe it.

'Listen,' I said. 'I know for a fact she's paying up an insurance policy for her funeral. Why don't you ask her to cash it in and tell her if she doesn't it could be your funeral.'

He stared at me thoughtfully through narrowed eyes.

'That's a great idea. I'll ask her as soon as she comes up with the tea. But maybe it's best you should go. She might not want to discuss it in front of anybody. You know what women are like, very secretive.'

The following evening the gang were all there, including Marian. She gave me a hostile glance which I returned with an equally hostile one. Donald told me to hurry up and close the door: did I want the whole world to know his business? I didn't like the way he spoke but before I could dwell on it he was calling for everyone's attention. I waited, thinking he was going to explain how he'd soon be able to pay Fat Harry. Instead, he was saying that Fat Harry was willing to reduce the debt if they all did a bit of collecting for him. Apparently there were so many people owing him money he couldn't keep up with it. There was a silence until Marian declared it was OK with her. I thought that was pretty stupid, considering nobody would expect her to collect. However, that seemed to do the trick. They all agreed that it was OK by them. When I asked Donald later on if this was a wise move he said maybe not but it was the only way he could pay off the debt.

'What about Granny's insurance policy? I thought you were going to ask her –'

'I was, but then I thought she'll need it for her funeral so I didn't bother.'

He turned away then began to talk to Marian as if he'd suddenly found her totally interesting. I thought it was time to leave. No one was speaking to me anyway.

A few days later my mother told me Granny had cashed in her insurance policy to pay for Donald's debt. I was eating cornflakes at the time and I could feel my face flushing, but she didn't seem to notice for she went on, 'To think she's been paying it up all these years and now she'll have nothing for her funeral. I don't know who's going to pay.'

'Maybe the social will pay,' I said, with my head bent low over the plate.

'Maybe they will and maybe they won't,' she snapped. 'All I know is that I can't.'

After that she became so angry about the whole affair that she stopped visiting Granny. She said she was liable to do something drastic to Donald if she ever ran into him.

'So where have you been lately?' asked Morton as we were about to watch *Ghostbusters* on video once again.

'Nowhere special. Just hanging around.'

He offered me a cigarette from a silver case containing five. I was quite impressed with it, then he said, 'Watch out for my ma coming in. She always likes to check up on me every so often.'

I smoked the cigarette hurriedly though I suspected it wasn't the smoking that bothered her. It was likely me. She'd a habit of staring at me very suspiciously as if I was up to something. Perhaps she thought I was gay, or we were both gay. I wouldn't have been surprised if Morton was gay by the way he carried on.

'Anyway,' he said, 'I'm glad you came.'

Then a good thing happened to us for a change. We joined up with a bunch of boys a year or so younger than us. They were right into breaking windows and wrecking fences, things like that, nothing drastic except may be for the time we set the bins alight and all the old folk were out in their shirt-tails. Not that I'd call that drastic. Nobody was burned and anyway some of these old folk had it coming, the way they went on about us playing ball in the street. Though sometimes I felt all this vandalising was a bit beneath us. I told this to Morton and he said at least we weren't into mugging anybody.

'Not yet,' I said with a laugh.

'I hope you're not in with that lot that's pestering all the neighbours,' my mother was saying when I was on my way out the door. I turned to her indignantly.

'You know I only go round to Morton's to watch videos, but if you like, I'll bring him round here and then you'll know where I am.'

I knew my mother couldn't be bothered having anyone in the house. The effort of trying to put on a pleasant face in front of strangers was always too much for her.

'Don't bother,' she said. 'This place is too big a mess to bring anyone into.'

Then Donald was the main topic with my mother once again. She'd heard in the Co-operative that he'd been arrested for being in possession of drugs.

'I knew it would come to this,' she moaned. 'It was the company he kept. They were a bad influence.'

When I reminded her how she'd once said Donald was the bad influence, she replied that she didn't remember saying anything of the kind but anyway I'd better not turn out like him or she'd put me out.

'Give us break. I've not done anything.'

'Not yet,' she said darkly, then she went on, 'Why don't you go round to see Granny? She's bound to be taking this badly.'

'Why don't you?' I said, for I didn't fancy listening to all that moaning and groaning that would go on about Donald. I could see myself slipping up to his room and strumming his guitar just to get away from it all, and that would be quite a depressing thing to do under the circumstances.

Donald did two months in jail. He came home one day and told Granny he was going to get a job down south as there was nothing doing up here and he would only get into more trouble if he stayed. Granny was quite upset at that. She said she would rather he got into trouble up here because if he got into trouble down south she wouldn't know anything about it. I was sorry to see him go. Having been in jail, he'd become something of a hero to the young lads in the street and I'd hoped some of the glory would rub onto me if we were seen together. Only my mother was pleased. Out of sight, out of mind, she said to Granny, who'd never stopped crying about him for days. It turned out that he never went south after all. We discovered he was living in another part of town with a guy who had a character as bad as Fat Harry's, if not worse.

'I might have known,' said my mother. 'We should be seeing him back any day now to upset us all.'

But he never came and things were altering for me again. It started with the weather becoming colder and some of the young guys not showing up in the evenings. They said they were staying in to study for their exams, which I could hardly believe. Then Morton said he was going to stay in for a spell as his mother didn't want him going out in the fog in case he got done in. What fog, I wondered.

Aloud I said, 'Maybe she's got a point there. I might as well stay in myself and do a bit of studying. It's the only way to get on, I'm thinking.'

I stayed in but I didn't do any studying. Mainly I sat in front of the television hoping to see something of a sexual nature. I liked when my mother went out to the bingo so that I could watch whatever I wanted to without her switching it off.

'You're a funny one,' she would say. 'First you're never in and then you're never out. There's no happy medium with you.'

When I told her that I'd go out in the summer, she said we could all be dead and buried by that time and I said I hoped so.

It's April now and the nights are much clearer, which gives me this feeling that I want to go out and kick a ball straight through somebody's window. Still, I've heard some good news today. My mother told me that Donald was seen in the street driving a car. She thinks it's stolen. I asked her if he'd been to see Granny yet and she said she wouldn't be surprised as he's got the cheek for anything.

'And I don't want you going round there,' she added. 'He's a bad influence. I've always maintained that.'

'Don't worry. I wouldn't dream of it,' I said.

As soon as she leaves for the bingo I'm going round to Granny's. Who knows, Donald might be up in his room strumming his guitar. And if he's not there I'll check on the street corner. He's bound to be somewhere near at hand and he might even be glad to see me now I'm a lot older.

People Like That

Mary sat on a bench at the top end of the central station, panicking. Her mind had gone blank again. She knew this was part of her problem, but it was a horrible feeling, as if a brick wall had shut out half her brain. For a minute she couldn't think why she was here then thankfully it came back to her. She was waiting for her son Brian to arrive on the Manchester train due in at platform 10, according to the chap in the ticket-office. It was terrible the way her memory kept going. She was not old enough to have senile dementia. She was only forty-six and it had been like that for two years now. A woman joined her on the seat, keeping to the farther end of it. Mary thought she would ask her about the train in case the chap in the ticket-office had got it wrong.

'Do you happen to know if the Manchester train is running on time? I didnae see it up on the board.'

The woman looked around. 'I'm sure I don't know,' she said, her fat face quite petulant. She had on a pale-blue shiny coat, the kind that Mary associated with those worn by older women at weddings. She didn't like the look of this woman at all but being so nervous and jumpy and alone, she felt compelled to tell the woman that she was meeting her son off the Manchester train and though he had a good job down there, he always liked to come up for a holiday whenever he got the chance because, she added appealingly, 'There's no place like home, is there?'

'Really,' said the woman, looking straight ahead. Mary coughed and settled back on the bench, staring at her wrist and surprised to see no watch on it. She must have left it behind in her hurry to get away. It had been a present from one of the staff too. Well, they could keep it for all she cared, and anyway there was a clock hanging from a pole facing platform 10, so there was no need to worry about the time. All the same, she began to get a bit uptight when she noticed the woman put on a pair of grey kid gloves then begin stroking the backs of them, one hand with another, as though they were pet mice.

'Do you mind not doing that,' said Mary.

'What do you mean?' said the woman, her eyes bulging with indignation as she stared hard at Mary.

'Well, you see it reminds me of the time Brian had his gerbils. He used to stroke them like the way you're doing. Then one day he squashed them, accidentally, mind you. He wouldn't do it deliberately. My Brian was always good with animals –'

The woman broke in. 'If you don't mind, I don't want to hear any more about your Brian.' Then she looked behind her as if expecting to see someone she knew.

'I'm sorry if I've offended you,' said Mary. 'It's just that Brian cried so hard about his gerbils.'

'This is too much,' said the woman. She stood up and stamped off down the terrazzo-tiled floor of the station, her heels clicking like castanets. Perplexed, Mary watched her go, wondering what she'd said to annoy this woman with a face like a pig and legs as thick as tree trunks. Likely she was off her head. You were bound to meet people like that in a railway station. That pale-blue coat she had was a ridiculous colour for a woman of her age. Thinking about clothes made Mary wonder if Brian would be ashamed when he saw how she was dressed. Her coat was warm and comfortable but she'd had it for ages, and as for her boots (she reflected, stretching her legs out), the tops were as wrinkled as concertinas, even though she had bought them only two years ago. She frowned. Something else had happened two years ago – something of importance. She was sure it would come to her sometime. She asked a passing porter if the Manchester train was due soon. 'Any minute now,' he said, giving her a suspicious glance. When the train arrived at platform 10 she was standing in front of it, calm and smiling. People came spilling out through the doors but no one who looked like Brian. On the other hand he might have altered a lot since he'd left home, grown taller or fatter, maybe. Her heart leapt when she noticed one young man coming towards her who might possibly be him. He had the same longish chin and colour of hair, though his was worn shorter than Brian's but it was quite possible he'd had it cut by now.

'Excuse me,' she said, standing in front of him. 'Are you Brian McGuire?'

'Shove off,' he said, his face red and indignant.

She stared after him, humiliated. It was terrible the way she got everything wrong nowadays. Come to think of it, that fellow had been nothing near as good-looking as Brian, even allowing for slight changes. Within minutes the people had dispersed and she was left standing on the empty platform. The driver pulled down his window to look at her curiously.

'Can you tell me when the next train arrives in from Manchester?' she asked him. 'You see, I expected my son to be on the one that just came in, but he must have missed it.'

'It's not due for another three hours,' said the driver, 'and it won't come into this platform. As a matter of fact, this one is now going to Greenock.'

'Greenock,' said Mary, her face brightening. 'I believe I've been there once. It's rather a nice place as far as I can remember.'

'Is it?' said the driver, pulling his window back up while she suddenly remembered it was Ayr that she was thinking of. She'd taken Brian there on his twelfth birthday. She remembered how he'd sat tight-lipped and sullen on the journey because she'd snatched the packet of cigarettes out of his hand before they'd stepped onto the train.

'It doesn't look right smoking in front of your mother at your age,' she'd told him. 'You'll get them back when we get there.'

'Aye, and that's a whole two fuckin' hours away,' he'd said.

On looking back she saw it as a good day. Brian had spent all his time in the amusements when he wasn't lighting up fags, while she had sat on a seat on the esplanade looking out on a stormy sea. After that she'd taken a walk along the beach where the sand blew into her eyes. Still, it had been May, so what could she expect. Anyway, the cold wind had made her all the more appreciative of the warm café where she ordered tea and scones. Brian had stood outside eating a fish supper. He wouldn't be seen dead in a dump like that, he'd explained. She sighed with regret that he was too old to take anywhere now and even apart from that she knew he preferred being with his pals. She began to wonder what she could do to pass the time. Perhaps she should go for a cup of tea if Wimpy's was still open. Her hand searched inside her coat pocket for the pound coin she had amongst some change. She might even manage to buy herself a cake. It was such a nuisance that she had lost track of what things cost nowadays. She was walking in what she hoped was the right direction for Wimpy's when she saw in the distance the woman in the pale-blue coat talking to a porter and pointing in her direction. Mary panicked. Was the woman complaining about something, saying she'd been sworn at, or worse still, assaulted? This had happened to her before on a chance encounter with another crazy bitch who'd said Mary had tried to steal her purse, which was a downright lie; nevertheless she had ended up in court charged with attempted theft, and fined. Don't let it happen again, she prayed. Luckily the Ladies was only a few yards away. She nipped into it quickly down a few stairs then through a turnstile marked OUT OF ORDER.

'Ten pence, please,' called the attendant.

Mary turned back and threw a few coins on the counter which she was sure was more than enough but she had no time to count them in case the woman in the blue coat was following her. Inside the cubicle she waited for at least ten minutes. By the time she came back up into the station there was no sign of the woman.

The place was strangely deserted except for a few people sitting or standing here and there. Perhaps they'd nowhere else to go, thought Mary. At least she had a reason to be here. She began to wander down past the shops on the left-hand side of the station, all closed but their windows displaying articles which Mary considered were trash. Imagine paying five pounds for a tie and worse, forty pounds for a thick, ugly string of beads no better than the ones her mother used to keep in a chest. The coffee house, still open, was more interesting in its own way with its delicious smell of coffee wafting through the door. But she would never have gone in there even if she could have afforded it. It was much too snobbish-looking. She would have been very much out of place. The Wimpy bar was closed when she came to it so she went back up to the kiosk that sold newspapers and chocolate, thinking a Milky Way would do her fine, and discovering it was closed too. She saw a man standing at the side of the kiosk wearing a long fawn raincoat and drinking out of a dark bottle. She glanced at him without meaning to as she walked past but something about him made her stop and turn back. The man took the bottle away from his mouth.

'Hey, whit are ye lookin' at?'

Bleary-eyed and unshaven though he was, Mary thought she recognised him. The more she looked at him, the angrier he became.

'You want a punch on the face or somethin'?'

It dawned on her who it could be. Of course she mustn't jump to conclusions.

'Pardon me,' she said, 'but do you happen to be Brian McGuire who used to live with his wife Mary along in Young Street twenty years ago, though I expect the place is not there now and –'

'What the fuck are you on about?' he said, wiping the side of his mouth.

She could have slapped his face at the rotten way he spoke to her, but then even in those early days he had been a foul-mouthed drunkard.

'I'm Mary, your wife.'

'Mary,' he repeated, as if this information was no surprise. He held out the bottle. 'Dae ye want some of this?'

'No thanks, I only usually have a port and lemon.'

The last time she had a port and lemon was on Christmas Day with two of the staff. It was funny how she could remember that. Yet she couldn't remember the important things, like what the thing was that had happened two years ago.

'Don't be so bloody sarcastic when I'm only tryin' to be civil,' said the drunk whose name she was convinced was Brian McGuire.

'Do you know,' she told him, 'you've got a son who's coming up in the Manchester train. Don't you think you should go and meet him?'

Even as she said this she couldn't see Brian pleased to find this man was his father. The drunk man puffed his cheeks and shook his head as if all this information was getting him down. He thrust the bottle in front of her face.

'Better take some o' that. You need it mair than I dae.'

This time Mary accepted the bottle, wiping it first with the rim of her coat sleeve before she put it to her mouth.

'Anyway,' said the drunk, 'my wife's name wis Nan and she's been deid a long time so it's no' possible.'

'Would you like to see Brian's photo?' asked Mary, fumbling inside her dress. The drunk held up a hand in warning.

'Don't try pinnin' anything on me. I've nae son.'

Mary didn't answer. Her attention was taken up by the sight of a policeman heading in their direction. The drunk must have seen him too for he shoved the bottle in his coat pocket and moved hastily towards the taxi rank. Blindly, she followed him, and the next thing she was out on the busy street, but not for long. When he veered without warning to his left, she discovered she was in a dark alley enclosed on each side by tall buildings. Unable to see very well, she groped her way along the wall thinking that the drunk man, who might not be her husband after all, would be gone by now, but when she touched his face as he stood inside a doorway, she realised he'd been waiting for her all along. He grabbed her wrist.

'Right, whit's your game?'

'I've no game. I only wanted to get away from that policeman.'

He laughed. 'You're a hoor then. Is that it?'

'I told you already, I was waiting on my son coming off the Manchester train.'

The drunk swore under his breath then asked her if she had any money. She told him that she'd only a few coins but when he pulled her towards him and began to put his hands all over her body, she gave him the pound coin she'd been clutching ever since she left the station.

'Christ, that'll no' get much,' he said savagely, peering at it in the palm of his hand. 'And you'd the bloody cheek to take some o' ma drink.'

He took the bottle out of his pocket, emptied what was in it down his throat then smashed it against the wall. Mary was frightened to move in case the glass went through the sole of her boot but that consideration was soon forgotten when she was slammed back against the wall.

'Scream and I'll throttle ye,' said the drunk as he wrenched her coat open. Mary heard the buttons she had newly sewn on that morning rattling along the cobblestones as a flaccid penis was thrust in her hand. 'Pull it,' he demanded. Mary did her best to comply in the hope he would let her go all the sooner but nothing happened. It was like flogging a dead horse, she thought. Her arm was getting tired.

'See you,' he said, thrusting it off, 'you're nae fuckin' use. Try gi'en it the kiss o' life.'

When Mary refused absolutely he pulled up her dress and said, 'Is this whit ye want?'

Then he began to pump away at her as though his life depended on it. Mary's head hit the wall and as if this jolt had done the trick she remembered suddenly that Brian had died of an overdose two years ago when he'd gone down to Manchester with his junkie friends. 'There's nothin' to dae up here,' had been his excuse.

'Oh, my poor Brian,' she said aloud, wanting to cry but unable to do so with the man's weight crushing against her.

'Never mind poor Brian. Think o' me for a change,' said the drunk. After what seemed like an eternity, he gave a shudder and became still. It seemed to be over. He must have had some success yet she expected a blow on the mouth. Her husband had always done that. However, the drunk, who was fumbling with the zip on his trousers, only said, 'Another thing. Ma name's Ronnie, no' Brian, so ye can rest assured I'm definitely no' the man yer lookin' for,' then he walked away into the dark.

Mary made sure he was gone before she went back to the station, with the smell of him in her nostrils, which she suspected might never go away. A man and woman came forward to meet her as she headed for platform 10.

'Right, Mary,' said the woman taking a hold of her arm, 'there's no need to go any farther. You're coming back with us.'

The man took her other arm. Both their grips were gentle but firm.

'You're a bad girl giving us such a hard time trying to find you. Where have you been?'

'I was waiting for the Manchester train.'

'One of these days you're going to come to real harm, you know,' said the woman, now putting her own arm through Mary's like a close friend would.

As they passed the ticket-office the chap behind the window called out, 'I see you've found her.'

'Yes,' said the man. 'I hope we haven't put you to any bother. She's a sad case really.'

'No bother at all,' said the railway clerk. 'We have them in here all the time – people like that.'

The Marigold Field

After telling me she was going to take a holiday in the Bahamas, my sister Celia thrust a black and white snapshot under my nose.

'Do you remember this?' she said.

I glanced at it. 'Not really.' Then I asked her if she could afford it.

'You mean the holiday? Of course I can.' She stared back at the photo. 'You must remember. It's the one Father took of us in the marigold field.'

I glanced at it again. 'So it is. Don't we look awful?'

Celia considered it, frowning. 'I think we look OK. That was the style, in those days. You can't compare them with now.'

'It wasn't the style. We wore cast-offs even at school. I was always ashamed.'

'I don't remember. I'm sure Mother did her best.'

'I'm not blaming Mother,' I said. 'Father never gave her enough for clothes.'

I took back the photo and studied it. Celia and I had dresses with frills round the hems that hung well below our knees while Hughie, our four-year-old brother, wore a jumper with a polo-neck covering his chin.

I pointed this out to Celia. 'A jumper in the summer? It's ridiculous.'

'That's because he always caught colds summer and winter.' She added grudgingly, 'How is he by the way?'

'Fine.' I wasn't going to elaborate on Hughie's lifestyle. Celia was bound to blame Mother for it. She always had.

243

'I can't imagine him being fine.'

'Well, he manages like everybody else.'

'Surely not like everybody else?' she said laughingly and then became serious. 'Why did we call it the marigold field? There wasn't a single marigold in it. I looked often enough.'

'It was Mother who called it that. She got the name out of a book.'

To change the subject I asked if she was going on holiday alone.

'God, no. I'm going with Dickie.'

She explained that Dickie was old enough to be her father but had plenty of money and that was the main thing. I said I was glad to hear at least one of the family was doing well. She looked hard at me, perhaps for a sign of irony, then said I could come with them if I liked. Dickie had always wanted to meet me. I thanked her and said I'd rather not. I wouldn't like to spoil their holiday.

'Whatever you think,' she said with a tight smile which I suspected was one of relief. Looking at the photo over my shoulder, she added, 'I wonder if the dam Father made is still there?'

'Dam?' I said, then after a pause, 'You mean the one where he tried to drown Hughie?'

She gave me a sharp look. 'Surely you still don't believe that after all this time?'

'Oh, yes, I believe it. I saw him, didn't I?'

It had been exceptionally warm that day in the marigold field. Celia had said she wished the stream was deep enough to swim in. Father, who always liked being busy, began to dam it up with stones and mud until a wide pool appeared. Celia flung off her clothes and jumped in with her knickers on. 'Come on,' she called out. 'This is terrific.' With one eye on Father, who stood on the bank close to Hughie, I undid my sandals. Suddenly my brother was floundering in the water like a drowning pup. I screamed when I saw his head go under. I didn't know what to do and apparently neither did Father. He simply stood there looking down. It was

Celia who pulled Hughie up, spluttering and choking and purple in the face. I'm sure if it hadn't been for her he would have drowned. Undoubtedly I was relieved that Hughie was safe. What nagged my brain was that a second before he fell I had seen Father's hand on his shoulder. I told Celia this when nobody else was listening. She said, 'What is that supposed to mean?' I said it meant Father had pushed him.

Mother, who had been sitting under a tree, came running up to ask what had happened. 'The sun was so hot I must have fallen asleep,' she explained. When it dawned on her Hughie had nearly drowned she shrieked and clasped him to her, stifling his sobs so that he appeared to be smothering. Later, I plucked up courage to tell her I'd seen Father push Hughie into the pool but she said I had imagined it and I had read too many trashy books.

And now Celia was saying, 'I don't know how many times I've asked this before but why on earth would Father want to drown his only son, for God's sake?'

I felt my temper rising. 'You don't seem to understand. A father can be as jealous of his son as he can be of a lover. Gorillas are known to kill their sons from jealousy and they are as near human as you'll get.'

'You can't compare Father to a gorilla,' said Celia. 'And what was there to be jealous of? Hughie was always a weakling. How could anybody be jealous of him?'

'Weakling or not,' I shouted, 'Mother loved Hughie best. That's why Father was jealous! I don't think you ever knew what Father was like.'

'And you did,' she sneered. I could see she was upset.

'Let's forget it,' I said. 'I shouldn't have brought it up.'

At the same time I blamed Celia. If she hadn't shown me the photo I would never have opened my mouth. To hide my rancour I asked her if she was considering getting married.

'I might,' she said. 'I wouldn't like to end up an old maid.'

When I said that perhaps marriage wasn't everything, she replied that maybe it wasn't but it was better to find that out for oneself. As we parted on the doorstep I had the feeling we might not see each other again.

'I hope everything goes well for you,' I called out as she was going down the path. She turned round.

'You too, and give my regards to Hughie.'

'I will,' I shouted back with all the sincerity I could muster, though I hadn't seen Hughie for weeks and didn't want to. It was a pity, I thought, that Celia and I had never met without quarrelling after Mother died. As children we had been very close.

But Mother had left the house and furniture to me. I would rather have had the sum of money which Celia and Hughie had received but it was no use telling Celia that. She said I'd always been Mother's favourite so what could she expect? I pointed out that Hughie was Mother's favourite and she'd left me the house to ensure he'd always have a roof above his head. She'd made me promise that I'd never sell it while he was alive. Celia then said, if Hughie had been Mother's favourite why did she let him smoke the stub ends of her roll-ups from the time he was ten years old?

'Maybe she never knew,' I said.

'She knew all right. She just didn't care.'

I couldn't argue. Mother had smoked dope from the day she married, or so I gathered from an aunt who came to her funeral and said that was why Father had left us. He couldn't stand having a dope addict for a wife. This didn't stop me loving her, not even when she began taking stronger stuff than hash. I could never condemn her. She was like a child with her small delicate bones and pale skin. Sometimes, if she was in a good mood, she let me brush her long flaxen hair and tilted her head backwards and closed her eyes. In a few years her face grew as lined as an old woman's, her hair fell out and she was obliged to wear a wig.

'Her arms are all holes,' said Celia. 'I don't know how she can do that to herself.'

The word 'Hughie' sprang to mind but I didn't say it.

'Perhaps she's a diabetic,' I said. 'I'm sure she attends a clinic.'

Celia gave me a look as if to say, 'How can you be so stupid?'

When Father left us (I was never sure why in those days) we stopped going to the marigold field. Mother said she couldn't bear to go back to that place where she had once been so happy. I was surprised at this. I didn't think any of us had been all that happy with Father continually nagging at us.

'Say cheese,' he'd ordered when taking the photo. We said cheese but it didn't seem to cheer us up. 'You're the most miserable kids I've ever seen,' he told us. 'I don't know what's the matter with you. Can't any of you smile for a change?'

For years Mother maintained it was because of me Father had left.

'He couldn't stand being accused of trying to drown Hughie in the marigold field.'

'I never actually accused him,' I said. 'I only mentioned it to you and Celia.'

'Well, that's as good as being accused,' she'd said, picking up a shoe and throwing it at me. It missed. This was the beginning of her violent period. Celia and I started keeping out of her way and it was Hughie who kept her company. Of course he had his reasons. Mother always gave him money and because of that we had to live on very little. Sometimes there was only bread and margarine to eat but Mother didn't seem to mind, nor did Hughie. I sometimes listened outside her bedroom door to find out if they were talking about me, saying that I had driven Father away, things like that, but all I ever heard was an occasional shriek of laughter.

One day when he was leaving her room I said to him, 'Don't you know you're killing her with that stuff you both take?'

He shook his head and said, 'I'm keeping her alive more than any doctor would.'

'If the state she's in is being alive then perhaps she'd be better off dead.'

'Is that what you want?' he asked, staring at me blankly. At that moment I thought his resemblance to Mother was striking, perhaps because of their expressions.

'I want my mother back,' I said, 'not that stranger in there.'

'Then you shouldn't have forced Father out. That was her problem.'

'I never forced Father out. He left because he couldn't stand any of us. He tried to drown you in the burn when you were a child.'

'So you keep telling me,' he said, walking off with a jaunty swing to his hips, which meant Mother had given him money.

All that seems a long time ago, though to be honest I've lost track of time. Was it last year or the year before that Celia paid me a visit before she went on holiday? I can't remember clearly and not having heard anything, I picture her living in the Bahamas for ever with an old man at her side who resembles Father. Funnily enough I dream about Father quite a lot. I don't know why for he's not on my conscience any more. I'm beginning to believe he left because of Mother's addiction, and it was nothing to do with me or Hughie.

With everyone gone the house is so silent you could hear a pin drop, though within that silence I sometimes imagine I hear voices whispering in Mother's room. It's probably the wind. But when I go outside it's usually quite calm and this disturbs me. I can't sleep very well and jump at the least thing. Tomorrow I will put the house in the hands of an estate agent. Since Hughie died there's no need to keep a roof for him. He went quite suddenly. The certificate mentioned pneumonia but I suspect Mother's death was the cause. Without her he had no reason to live.

When cleaning out the drawers in readiness for departure I came across the photo Father took of us in the marigold field. My first thought was to have it enlarged and framed, as I had intended when Celia left it with me. But now I see the edges are curled and the surface is cracked. It's a pity because it would have looked nice on the mantelpiece of my new home. On second thoughts this may not be advisable. It would be a reminder of the past and I don't think I need that or even want it.

I was about to tear it up before putting it in the bin with the other rubbish when I suddenly remembered Mother saying that it was bad luck to destroy a photograph. Though not superstitious I dislike taking chances. There's been enough bad luck in the family. I'll keep it in the drawer until I can face it without a qualm. Otherwise I'll leave it there until it crumbles into dust.

Intruders

Nobody lived in the terrace any more apart from an old man who'd refused to leave when it had been condemned. Then one night tinkers crept in for shelter and stayed for ages. There was also a boy who hung around the crumbling doorways sniffing glue. Nobody worried about these folk. The authorities knew they'd shift when the bulldozer moved in.

Entering a room whose only furniture was a table and two chairs left by the previous owner, George the tinker asked his wife, 'Where is she then?'

'If it's Greta yer talkin' aboot,' said Flora, 'Ah dinnae ken. She was away when Ah got up.'

'Whit time was that?'

'Ah'm no' sure. Whit difference dis it make?'

'Nane.'

George lifted his tobacco-tin with an air of exhaustion. He'd drunk too much the night before and doubted if he'd feel better before he drank some more but the bottle on the table was empty. After watching him make a very thin roll-up Flora gestured to a heap of ash in the grate.

'Mibby you could see yer way to bringin' in wood for a fire afore we freeze to death.' She pointed to the child under a heap of blankets in a big pram. 'If ye don't, how wull Ah heat his milk?'

'Give it to him cauld,' said George, who had forgotten to chop up logs the night before but didn't want to admit it. He offered his wife the roll-up. She refused.

'If he takes it cauld he'll get a chill.'

'He usually takes it cauld,' said George, closing his eyes to blot out his wife's accusing face.

He opened them when she poked his arm saying, 'Mibby she's gone tae Maggie's.'

'Who's gone tae Maggie's?'

'Greta, you fool.'

He thought for a minute then said, 'Maggie's is miles away.'

'She could've got a lift.'

'And somethin' else beside,' he said darkly.

'Greta can look efter hersel'. She's nearly sixteen,' said Flora though inwardly angered as well as worried by her daughter's disappearance. Greta had been good with the child. 'Onyway,' she added, 'Ah widnae be surprised if she's got money for the fares. You know whit she's like.'

'Naw. Whit's she like?'

'You know as well as Ah dae that she's good at the cadgin', with her being so pretty and well spoken like Ah wis masel' once.'

George gave a harsh laugh. 'That must have been afore ma time.'

Flora's anger flared up as the child began to whimper. 'You'd better get that fire goin'. The bairnie's cauld.'

'He's no sae much cauld as hungry,' said George. 'Gie him somethin' tae eat.'

Flora spread some jam on a slice of bread and gave it to the child, who immediately stopped whimpering as if to prove his father's point.

'Ah telt ye he wis hungry,' said George, adding quickly when he saw the look on Flora's face, 'Ah'll fetch the logs as soon as Ah smoke this fag.'

'Ah'm no' waitin',' said Flora, blowing on her hands then rubbing them together. 'Ah'm gaun tae lie under the blankets ben the room. It's the only way Ah'll get a heat.'

'Me too,' said George. 'Ah could dae with a right cosy kip.'

'You're stayin' here tae look after him. He'll no want tae lie doon noo he's wakened and he cannae be left by hissel'.' As an afterthought she added that maybe they should take a walk later to look for Greta.

'Ah thought you said she'd likely be at Maggie's?'

'There's nae herm in lookin',' said Flora. With that she was off into a back room leaving George staring after her resentfully.

Two hours later they walked along the pavement with Flora pushing the pram. The child could easily have walked but pushing him was less trouble. When they reached the Rowantree Inn she suggested that they buy some cans of lager. George frowned as if it hadn't been his intention, then produced some silver from his pocket.

'It so happens Ah might hae enough,' he said, disappearing into the public bar. Minutes later he came out with four cans of lager, three of which he placed in the bottom of the pram. The other they drank between them before setting off. When they reached a side road leading up a hill Flora turned the pram in its direction. George asked her why as it only led to a farm.

'Ah like the smell o' dung.'

Bemused, George scratched his head then said, 'Isn't that the place where they offered me a job once?'

'Which ye didnae take.'

'Well, Ah hope you dinnae think Ah'm takin' it noo,' said George. He drew her attention to the child rolling the cans up and down the pram. 'They're gaun tae be fizzing all over the place when we open them.'

'Stop yer grumblin',' said Flora. 'Yer always grumblin'.'

George reached for a can and she told him to leave it until later.

As the top of the hill they sat on a grassy verge next to the farm-house wall with the child crushed between them. Flora was drinking from her can when George asked her why, if they were supposed to be looking for Greta, they had come up here.

'Ah'm no sure,' she said. 'Ah thought we might run intae her, but it doesnae seem likely. Mibby she's at Maggie's right enough.'

'So how can ye be sure o' that then?'

'Ah never said Ah wis sure. Ah'm only thinkin' she might be because she wis aye talkin' aboot her aunt's fine caravan and how could we no' stay wi' her instead o' that dump we're in. That's whit she wis aye sayin'.'

George swallowed some lager. 'Ah don't know how she could say that when she knows fine Ah couldnae staun bein wi' your sister for a single second, fine caravan or no'.'

'Maggie couldnae staun you either but Ah don't doubt she wid have been pleased tae see some o' her kinsfolk. It's no' fair Ah don't get tae visit her because o' you.'

'Because o' me?' said George indignantly. 'You can go and see her ony time ye want.'

At that point the child began to struggle.

'Stop that, ye devil,' said Flora, giving him a nip on the leg which made him sit still. 'Ah think Ah wull go,' she said, resuming the previous subject. 'Ah might as well enjoy masel' for a chinge.'

'Don't forget it takes money,' said George.

'Mibby Ah could get a lift.'

'Who's gaun tae gie you a lift?' said George in a derisive tone. 'Yer no whit ye'd call good-lookin'.'

Flora looked round at him dangerously. 'Whit's that ye said?'

'Ah wis just jokin',' said George hurriedly. 'Ye can be good-lookin' enough when ye want tae.'

He made them each a roll-up. Slightly mollified, Flora took hers then pointed out they could both go to Maggie's when the giro came since by then they'd have the money for fares.

'Mibby,' said George. 'But whit if Greta's no' there? Whit will we dae then?'

'We'll have tae report her missin'.'

She took a sip of lager then spat it out. 'That stuff's rotten,' she said. 'Either that or it's ma stomach.'

George then said that if they reported Greta missing the cops would find they were living in the terrace and boot them out and they'd have nowhere to go.

'So whit can we dae?' said Flora sourly. The dampness of the grass was seeping through her skirt and her stomach felt queasy. The child began struggling again and she put the can to his mouth to shut him up. He pushed it away, spilling the contents. She lost her temper and threw it over the wall, then stood up and almost flung the child into the pram.

'Ah'm gaun back,' she said. 'This place stinks.'

'Hey, wait a minute,' said George. 'There's still a can left.'

'You take it,' said Flora. 'Onyway, Ah've got this funny feelin' Greta could be in by noo and wonderin' where we are.'

'You and your funny feelin's,' said George. 'Ah widnae be surprised if you've gone clean oot yer mind.'

'Neither wid Ah,' said Flora.

In silence they walked back the way they'd come. The child was lulled to sleep with the bumping of the pram. George finished his lager and threw the empty can into a turnip field.

'Ah'll get some o' these turnips later,' he promised.

Flora didn't bother to answer. They were halfway down the terrace lane when they encountered the boy standing in a doorway with a Cellophane bag stuck to his chin.

'God, you gied me a fright,' Flora said to him. 'Whit's that thing on your jaw?'

George said, couldn't she see it was for sniffing glue, then asked the boy if he'd seen a girl hanging around the place, pretty and fair-haired. The boy, frightened at being spoken to, ran off.

'Ah dinnae like the look o' him,' said Flora. 'Ah widnae be surprised if he knows somethin'.'

'Like whit?'

'Like where Greta is. Ah'd go efter him if Ah wis you.'

George sighed. The whole business was beginning to give him a headache. He suspected Greta wasn't far away but he wished she was, for she'd been getting on his nerves lately. That last time she'd stolen his money, he'd had to keep his mouth shut about it in case she told Flora what they got up to when she was away for the messages. It would suit him better if she never turned up.

'Let's forget aboot Greta,' he said. 'There's plenty ither things on ma mind.'

'Whit kind o' things?'

'Things like me gettin' in tae the hoose so's Ah can rest ma bones in a chair. Ah dinnae ken whit's wrang wi' me this weather but Ah'm always tired.'

'So you want me tae forget ma daughter,' said Flora bitterly. 'Is that whit yer sayin'?'

'She's no' ma daughter,' said George. 'I didnae clap eyes on her until she wis ten.'

Unable to dispute the truth of this, Flora said with mounting fury, 'Ye'll be tellin' me next that bairn in the pram isnae yours either?'

'Ah widnae be surprised if he's no',' said George, taking the pram off her and pushing it along the cobble-stones in a desperate fashion. When they reached the stairs leading to their makeshift home he ordered her to give him a hand up. Sullenly she complied.

Inside the living room they both sat down on the chairs with their legs apart.

'So she never came back,' said Flora after a while.

George, who'd been about to doze off, opened one eye and said, 'She's probably at Maggie's.'

'Probably,' said Flora. She stared at the grate full of dead ash and was about to ask George to go and fetch in logs but decided against it when he began to snore. He usually got into a rage when awakened suddenly. She'd fetch them in herself. With a sigh she stood up and went outside.

From within a doorway, the boy who'd been sniffing glue saw her cross the lane and go into one of the old wash-houses and wondered if she was looking for the girl. If he hadn't taken fright when they bumped into him earlier he could have explained that he'd seen the girl go up the old man's stairs. Though they might not have believed him. They'd looked at him very suspiciously. In any case it wasn't the first time he'd seen the girl go up the old man's stairs. Maybe it was to clean his house or make him a cup of tea. He couldn't imagine what else it could be. Anyway, it was none of his business what she did and besides, tinkers were always best avoided. They didn't act like normal people. He was thinking these things when someone grabbed him by the back of his jumper.

'Got you,' said a man's voice. 'And sniffing glue as well. You're definitely for it now.'

The boy managed to twist his head round far enough to see the man from the school-board.

'Ah'll come,' said the boy, 'but leave me go.'

The man only tightened his hold on the jumper and frogmarched him down the lane. By that time the tinker girl was clean gone from the boy's mind. He'd too much else to worry about.

Léonie

This is an account of a day in the life of Léonie Fabre who lived in a village in Provence. Before the war it had been a good place to stay though the villagers sometimes referred to it as a hole in the ground, encircled as it was by a canyon of rock and overshadowed by a range of mountains. Tourists came to gaze at the mountains and the canyon and most of all the fountain of water that poured from a cleft in the base of the rock, filling a basin in the earth then spilling over to become a fast-flowing river that ran through the centre of the village. But when war broke out no one came except soldiers and foreign officials. The village had become occupied.

On the morning of this particular day Léonie opened the shutters and was dismayed to see that snow had fallen during the night. It was three years since snow had last fallen but she did not welcome it the more for that, especially when she must go to the store for bread and tobacco. Her shoes were unsuitable for walking through snow and she had nothing better to wear. She turned to her husband who sat tapping his pipe on the table.

'I suppose you have no tobacco left?' she asked.

'You have supposed correctly,' he said with a scowl on his dark, lean face. Though middle-aged he appeared much younger, perhaps because of his lithe figure, and his hair which was as black as a raven. His eyes were cold and when he smiled, which was seldom, he did so grudgingly. He was known in the village as a very proud man. Some said he was merely overbearing and conceited because of the land he owned. Most of the villagers owned land but not as much as he. His crops were the finest and even though part of them was confiscated by the foreign officials he still tended them lovingly and diligently. Léonie, though younger than her husband, had aged beyond her years. Her face, pretty at one time, was pinched and marked with lines. Her once light-brown and curling hair had become dingy and lifeless. Her expression had been serene but was now permanently anxious. Those changes had taken place after her son had been drowned on his ninth birthday many years before. They were not caused by the strain of living in an occupied village.

'I suppose you know it is snowing,' she said.

'I know.'

'You are still going to the land then?'

'Where else?'

'I thought perhaps because of the snow –'

'Whether it is snowing or not there is always something to do. Besides I would go out of my mind if I did not get to my land.' He threw her a disparaging glance. 'It is the only thing that gives me any pleasure.'

Léonie plucked at her lips nervously. 'I was thinking that perhaps I might not be able to get any more tobacco from the store. As you know it is rationed and I –'

Her husband answered loudly, 'Then I must go without.'

'On the other hand perhaps if I pay extra Madame Renet will allow me some. It is scarce, you understand, but sometimes she can get it from the black market which means I have to pay extra.'

'In the name of God,' her husband shouted, 'do not tire me with all this talk of tobacco. If you cannot get it for me someone else will and without any fuss either. You should know by this time I depend on you for very little.'

'Yes,' she said vaguely, relieved to hear that the responsibility of his tobacco did not entirely rest with her. She still knew she would have to try the store for it was not certain he would get it from someone else.

She began to speak on a subject that had been on her mind since she had heard about it from Lotz the postman.

'Do you know,' she said, 'I cannot get it out of my head about the Mayor.'

'The Mayor?'

'According to Lotz it appears he has been burned to death in some kind of place called a concentration camp. I was going to tell you last night after you finished your meal. But when you fell asleep I decided it was best not to disturb you. But isn't that terrible if it's true?'

Her husband frowned as he pondered on this. Then he said, 'I doubt that it will be true. Why should they burn a cowardly man like the Mayor who has never shown his face in the village since the occupation began?'

'Lotz said that the foreign officials took him away many months ago and only now has this terrible news been heard. If it is not true why should he tell such a story?'

'Because he is a gossip and a liar like all the others in this village who have nothing else to do than make up tales.'

'But what if it is true?'

'Then if it is true I would say the Mayor has done something to deserve it. He was always a corrupt man and easily bribed. I remember the time he got young Patrice Rouyer out of the village to stand trial in the city after he raped a servant girl and so got off with a light sentence instead of being lynched by the villagers as he deserved. Of course the Rouyer family were rich in those days so the Mayor would have been well paid.'

'I do not recall that,' said Léonie, 'but anyway, Lotz said that the Mayor was burned because his own son is one of those who lives in the mountains.'

Her husband smiled sardonically. 'Oh, well, that would be reason enough to burn the Mayor when his son is one of those who take it upon themselves to blow up a train or a bridge and let innocent people pay the price. But even if Lotz's story is true I am not concerned. I have more important matters to think of.'

He rose from his chair and picked up his jacket from their bed near the fireplace then lifted his parcel of bread and cheese from the dresser and left without saying goodbye.

The moment he had gone Léonie entered the one other room, which had been her son's, and sat on the edge of the bed where he had slept, waiting for what she thought of as his presence. This presence was nothing she could see or touch. Sometimes it was like a warm draught in her face and sometimes like a soft breathing in her ears. Once she actually thought she saw his shape at the foot of the bed but when she reached out with her hand it disappeared. She told no one of this, certainly not her husband, and she never entered this room when her husband was at home. It was her one solace.

In the afternoon she walked along the narrow pavement looking for tracks to follow in the snow. There were none. The street was deserted. Her feet quickly became cold and wet though the snow no longer fell so heavily. A keen wind had sprung up reducing it to a few scattered flakes. She came to the post office and noticed that, though the door was locked, a light shone in the upper window and the postman's bicycle leaned against the wall. She would have liked to speak to Lotz, and ask if the story of the Mayor being burned had perhaps only been a rumour, but it was not advisable to wait. If the foreign officials came by in their car they might stop and question her. Besides, it was too cold to hang about so she walked on, passing the Mayor's villa on a shelf of rock high above the other houses, stone stairs leading up to the porch. The shutters of the windows were closed. There was nothing to suggest it was occupied, not even a wisp of smoke from the chimneys. The Mayor's face came into her head, sad and inconsolable. She shook her head to be rid of it then turned a corner and crossed the bridge over the river that had taken her son, and for once wasn't aware of it. She scarcely glanced at the soldier on guard outside the town hall, though he was resplendent in black boots, long army coat and steel helmet, with rifle resting on shoulder. To the villagers he represented a situation that had become stale for everyone.

In sight of the grocery store she saw Agnès Duval approaching, as thin as a screwdriver in a long, tight-fitting, black coat, her head bare, her greasy hair flapping in the wind. Léonie would have preferred to avoid Agnès. She was known to be slightly mad but not as mad as her brother, an arsonist. Long before the occupation he had fled to the city after setting fire to the local paper-mill when the owners refused him a job. Some people said he had joined the resistance, others reported him to be in pay of the enemy. Either way he was credited with many desperate deeds.

'Good day,' said Léonie, hoping to move on quickly, but Agnès stopped immediately in front of her, saying, 'What is so good about it? There is nothing to be obtained in the store, yet the owner is as fat as a pig. What does she expect me to do – eat grass or worms? Well, I won't have it. Soon I am going to the city where everyone eats meat. This village has gone to the dogs now that the socialists have taken over.'

With that she spat on the snow and moved off rapidly down the pavement, talking to herself. Léonie entered the store shaking her arms to get rid of the snow on her coat.

'Be careful,' said Madame Renet from behind her counter. She was a stout woman with eyes as black as currants in her pale, puffy face. She pointed to a box of cauliflowers lying on the floor. 'I do not want them damaged. They are very expensive.'

Then she came round from her counter and began to brush imaginary snow from the vegetables.

'I am sorry,' said Léonie. 'The snow is everywhere. It is difficult to avoid.'

'I know,' said Madame Renet, 'but I have to keep an eye on these vegetables. They are not easy to obtain.'

'You say they are expensive?' said Léonie, eyeing the cauli-flowers wistfully. It was a long time since she had seen one. They were not grown in the village. She considered them too beautiful to eat. If she could have bought one she would have kept it in water until it rotted.

'They are,' said the shopkeeper. 'I could not even afford one for myself.'

'And who could?' said Léonie absently.

'You would be surprised who could.'

'The foreign officials, or the soldiers perhaps?'

'Not only them. The priest can afford them just as he can afford everything else that is too dear for the villagers.'

'Really?'

'But what can I do? I must sell my stock.'

'Of course,' agreed Léonie, adding, 'But what can you expect of a priest? He is used to having the best.'

'I tell you what I expect,' said Madame Renet, folding her arms over her chest. 'I expect if he was a good priest he would have spoken out against the enemy instead of sending his housekeeper round to this store to buy all the luxuries that no one else can afford.'

'It is dangerous to speak out against the enemy. He could get shot for that.'

'Then I would expect him to get shot.'

Léonie was uncomfortable with the subject. She had never attended church since her son died. She did not want to talk about the priest, though she recollected vaguely he was a young man who had come from a village far south in the region. She'd heard his sermons were more concerned with God's wrath than his forgiveness but though he was not liked on that account he was respected for his fervour.

She said, 'Since I do not go to church I do not expect anything.'

Madame Renet raised her eyebrows. 'I am surprised at that. I always go to church for I pray to God, not the priest.'

Léonie kept silent for a while then said, looking round the shop, 'Has the bread van not yet arrived?'

'I am afraid not and I doubt it will with the roads being so bad.'

Taking a deep breath Léonie asked, 'I was wondering if you have any tobacco to sell. My husband is quite desperate for some.'

With a pained expression the shopkeeper turned round and took a black book from the shelf behind her then placed it on the counter and leafed through it slowly. She stopped halfway down a page and said, 'It is marked here that your husband had two ounces a fortnight ago.'

Léonie stared at the book but could make nothing out since it was upside-down.

'A fortnight is a long time,' she said.

'I am sorry,' said Madame Renet. 'Tobacco is very scarce. I have to make sure everyone receives an equal ration.'

'I will pay you extra.'

'Extra!' said the woman as if scandalised, then, 'How much?'

'One franc.'

Madame Renet shook her head regretfully.

'All right, two,' said Léonie, judging she could afford it when there was no bread to buy.

'Very well then,' said Madame Renet with a sigh. 'I will see what I can do since your husband is so desperate.'

She brought out a packet of tobacco from under the counter then placed it on the top. Léonie took two francs from her coat pocket and handed them over. The transaction completed, she said as if it had just come into her head, 'Have you heard the news about the Mayor?'

'I have,' said Madame Renet, again folding her arms across her chest and looking grim.

'So it is true he was burned to death?'

'It is.'

'But how can you be sure? It might only be a rumour.'

'A piece of paper giving this information was smuggled into the village and passed amongst the people. Have you not seen it?'

Léonie shook her head slowly and Madame Renet said, 'Then you must be the only one.' She added, 'Mind you, if I could I would pin it to the wall of this store for all the world to see but I have my business to consider and my skin as well, come to that. If they can do this to the Mayor they can do it to any one of us.'

'Nothing like this has ever happened before,' said Léonie.

'But now it is starting.' Madame Renet lowered her voice and went on, 'Did you know that a bridge was blown up not far from this village and did you not hear that new officials are sitting in the town hall looking for names? Undoubtedly someone has named the Mayor's son and that is why they have burned his father.'

Léonie shook her head sadly. 'He was such a delicate man too. I wonder what will become of his wife?'

'I would not worry about her. She is gone from the village. Besides, she had no time for her husband. It was obvious she thought herself a cut above him because her people were wealthy. He never should have married her.'

'Well, it is all one now,' said Léonie.

The shopkeeper laughed grimly. 'It is for the Mayor.'

Léonie shifted about on the stone floor. Her feet were numb. It was as cold inside the store as it was outside. She said, 'I must be going but thank you for the tobacco. My husband will be pleased.'

As she was leaving Madame Renet called, 'Tonight they are holding a service for the Mayor. Do you think you might come to the church on this occasion?'

'Oh yes,' said Léonie, hurrying away.

At the bottom of the street she encountered Maria Defarge, a large woman with bold, protuberant eyes. She enquired about Léonie's health and without waiting for an answer began to speak excitedly.

'Do you know,' she said, 'last night I dreamed that the town hall was covered in white and from under its door ran a stream of blood. And what do I see when I awake this morning – everything covered in snow. I am positive this is a sign that blood will soon follow.'

They say dreams are only dreams – nothing more,' said Léonie.

'Not my dreams,' said Maria. 'Many times they have come true. I have the gift for seeing signs, as everybody in the village knows.'

'But of course,' said Léonie hurriedly. Maria could cure sores on the face and body as well as other minor ailments. She also cast spells, sometimes for the good and sometimes for the bad. Strangely enough she had never been able to cast spells on the foreign officials.

'It is because they have no souls,' she once explained. 'I can only deal with those who have souls.'

'I hear they are holding a service in church for the Mayor,' Léonie informed her.

'How futile,' said Maria.

'Do you not think it is fitting he should be remembered in some way?'

Maria shrugged. 'We do not need a black crow to remind us.'

'Perhaps not,' said Léonie, aware of Maria's distaste for all matters connected with the church, 'but at least it would be a token of respect.'

'Respect?' said Maria with disgust, and then walked off over the snow with long, purposeful steps as if she was being hounded.

As Léonie recrossed the bridge she saw that the river ran faster and higher than usual. She turned her eyes away from it, but the water roared loud in her ears. Although accepting that the river was a part of nature like a stone or a tree or the earth itself, she had never come to terms with it since the death of her son. It seemed to have a malevolent will of its own. Today it did not concern her so much since her head was filled with the Mayor and the manner of his death. She wished she could get him out of her mind. He was invading it with his sad, inconsolable face.

★　★　★

On arriving home she placed the packet of tobacco carefully on the table. Noticing the fire was almost dead she went outside to fetch logs from the wood-shed and saw Lotz the postman coming down the lane between the house and the shed, his postbag slung over his back.

'Good day,' he said, his face red with cold but still cheerful. Lotz always had been an affable man and the occupation had made him no less affable. He'd even been heard to joke with foreign officials.

'I suppose it could be better,' said Léonie, adding, 'I am surprised you are still delivering.'

'It has taken me much longer today since I am forced to walk.'

Léonie made the observation that it was a wonder there was any mail to deliver with all the restrictions.

'There is always enough to keep me going,' said Lotz.

Léonie told him that apart from government notices she never received any mail at all. Not that she could think of anyone who would write to her except for an aunt who lived in a mountainous region and might be dead for all she knew.

'That is too bad,' said Lotz sympathetically, 'but I do assure you some of the villagers receive mail. There are quite a few letters for the Mayor's wife.'

'So she still lives in her house?'

'I am not sure about that but I deliver them anyway.'

'Perhaps they are letters of condolence?'

'They could very well be,' said Lotz, shaking his head and for once looking serious.

'It is a bad business,' said Léonie. 'One never knows what will happen next.'

'That is true,' said Lotz, hitching his bag farther back on his shoulder. 'We can only carry on the same as usual and hope for the best.' He added, becoming cheerful again, 'I presume you are keeping well yourself?'

'I am always well enough.'

'And your husband?'

'He too is well enough.'

'He is a fine man,' said Lotz. 'He works hard, I'll say that for him.'

'He does,' said Léonie, turning away abruptly to enter the wood-shed.

She kindled the fire and made a loaf with flour and water and prepared a stew with some vegetables then placed both items inside the iron oven that was heated by the fire. After that she went into her son's room in order to feel his presence. It did not come and she was not surprised. It was unreasonable to expect it twice on the same day. In any case, her head was still filled with the Mayor. She was about to leave the room when she felt something standing behind her right shoulder as she sat upon the bed. She knew at once it was the presence of the Mayor. She could hear his breath, harsh and laboured.

'Go away,' she said. 'I have done you no harm.'

It stayed so she called out loudly, 'You cannot stay here. This is my son's room.' Then she added in a moment of inspiration, 'If you leave I will pray for your soul,' and it vanished. She went out of the room thinking she must keep this promise lest the Mayor's presence return and banish that of her son.

A while later she sat at the kitchen table, awaiting her husband's arrival. The bowls and spoons were laid out and the dish of stew simmered on the iron oven. The bread she had baked lay on the dresser, flat and solid. Flour and water alone did not make good bread but it was better than none. Her husband might not think so but at least he should be pacified with the tobacco. When another half-hour passed and he still had not returned she ate some bread and stew, washed her face under the tap in the sink, put on her coat and scarf and set off for the church. Her shoes were still damp but not as damp as they had been.

The grey stone church, diminutive and plain, stood at the highest point of the village. The bells were pealing as Léonie entered. She remembered to dip her fingers in the basin of holy water then cross herself in the direction of the altar before edging into the back pew. Apart from a couple seated near the front, the place was empty. They turned round to stare at her. She knew them slightly. Before the occupation they used to sell sweets in the market. She gave them a diffident smile and they turned their heads away, so she leaned back against the wooden partition and studied the walls. Except for a statue of the Virgin in an alcove halfway down the wall, there was nothing to admire. It had not changed since she had come years ago. Perhaps the cracks on the walls and the ceiling had deepened. There was a crack across the face of the Virgin which she did not remember but maybe it had always been there.

More people entered, filling up the empty seats. Two of them sat along from her in the back pew. Léonie waited for the service feeling less alone and more relaxed. When the priest came in from a side door and stood before the altar she leaned forward, listening. His words were indistinct. He was as she remembered him, fairly young, of medium height, his black hair combed back severely from his high forehead. From a distance his complexion looked like the tallow candles on the altar. It dawned on her he was speaking in Latin so she closed her eyes to rest them for a time. When she opened them he was speaking in a normal tongue which she also found difficult to understand as his accent was thick and guttural in the way of those who come from the South. Eventually it became clear that he was condemning certain men who had brought shame and sorrow to the village by their unlawful acts.

At first she thought he was referring to the foreign officials but as he continued it became apparent he was speaking of the men who lived in the mountains.

Now he was saying, 'Those men are lawless and without mercy. They have turned their hearts away from God and do the Devil's work in the guise of saviours. For their own ends they would destroy this village. If it were not for his son, who is one of them, the Mayor would still be alive.'

As he spoke further in this vein there was much coughing and fidgeting from the congregation. For the first time since she had entered the church Léonie noticed Madame Renet in the centre pew. She was speaking openly to her neighbour. The priest was not distracted. He continued to speak out loud and accusingly. He finished his address with the words, ' "Vengeance is mine, saith the Lord," ' then after a pause during which the congregation suddenly became silent, he added more softly, 'Now let us pray for the soul of our Mayor,' and everyone knelt on the praying stool with their hands clasped and heads bowed.

Outside the church Léonie encountered Madame Renet who said, 'It was a very bad service. I am sure the Mayor would not have been pleased with the condemnation of his son and I am certain if his son hears about it he will be even less pleased. I suspect the priest has signed his own death-warrant.'

Léonie replied, 'I am certainly surprised that he spoke out against those men. Though perhaps he thought it his duty to do so in order to prevent bloodshed.'

'He does less than his duty,' said Madame Renet. 'You notice he did not speak out against the enemy. I would not be surprised if he was the one who named the Mayor's son, causing the Mayor to be burned. In fact, after that sermon I am convinced of it. He is nothing more than a traitor.'

'I would not be so sure,' said Léonie.

'Well, I am as sure as the nose on my face.'

'But surely if he was a traitor he would be clever enough to conceal it rather than turn suspicion on himself by giving such a sermon.'

'The priest's pride is colossal. He thinks he is God himself. Apparently he has forgotten the proverb that pride goes before a fall. Mark my words, he will surely soon fall.'

'But nothing is a certainty,' said Léonie, turning away to go in the direction of her house.

* * *

On arriving home she found her husband sitting at the table with his pipe in his hand.

'You have had your meal then?' she said, glancing at the empty stew dish. He did not answer so she took off her coat and scarf and hung them on the peg behind the door then turned back to him saying, 'I waited for you as long as I could.'

But he still sat like a mussel.

She coughed and added, 'This evening I was at the service being held for the Mayor. Lotz's words were true – the Mayor was burned. It's hard to think such a thing could happen.'

'Indeed,' said her husband coldly, filling up his pipe from the packet of tobacco lying on the table.

'At least I managed to get tobacco,' said Léonie somewhat lamely.

When he had filled his pipe and puffed on it for a few seconds he said in a harsh tone, 'You had no right to leave the house at such a late hour without my permission.'

'I thought under the circumstances it was excusable.'

'Under what circumstances?'

'The circumstances of the Mayor's death.'

'So, everything must cease to function because of the Mayor's death?'

'I waited for you so long that I thought you had gone to the bar. Besides, the meal was prepared and the fire was lit. What more could I do?'

'The fire was low and the meal was cold,' said her husband. 'What kind of welcome is that when I come home tired and freezing?'

Léonie bit her lip as she confronted him. His eyes, she noticed, were slightly glazed as though he had been drinking alcohol.

'Then you must have been very late,' she said.

'But not as late as you,' he shouted. He stood up and slapped her face then said, 'Fetch some logs for this fire. It's nearly out and I feel bad enough as it is.'

Léonie touched her burning cheek then went out to fetch logs from the wood-shed, which she put on the fire after first adding some paper. She asked her husband for a match which he flung across in a vicious manner. When the logs began to burn he took his chair over to the fire and sat before it blocking out the heat while Léonie went over and sat with her elbow on the table and chin in hand. Some time passed before her husband turned to her saying, 'In any case, what was the Mayor to you?'

'Nothing,' she said, taking her hand from her chin. 'Why do you ask that?'

'Because you seem to be obsessed with him.'

'I am not obsessed with him. I simply felt sad that he had to die in such a dreadful manner. Any normal person would feel the same.'

'Why do you look so guilty then?'

'Do I?' said Léonie. 'I think it must be your imagination. You have been drinking too much Pernod.'

Her husband stared back at the fire. He appeared to be brooding on something. Léonie began to yawn, not with fatigue, but with nerves. Usually he would fall asleep after his meal but tonight it seemed unlikely. Then he turned to her again.

'I almost forgot to tell you,' he said with a twisted smile. 'The river has burst its banks and my land is covered and the crops are ruined.'

'But that is terrible!' said Léonie, taking her hand from her chin and sitting up straight. 'What will we do?'

'You mean what will I do,' said her husband smiling, or at least, baring his teeth for his eyes were cold and glassy.

Léonie whispered, 'Then what will you do?'

'Do not worry,' said her husband, 'I have my plans.' He spat into the fire with an air of satisfaction.

Léonie sat blinking with agitation. If the land was covered in water and the crops were ruined they would have no vegetables to eat, and what was worse she would not be rid of him during the day. Her life would become unbearable and although she was consumed with anxiety she felt she dare not question him further, his mood being so irrational. They sat for a good while in silence then without warning he said, 'Tell me, was it the Mayor's son that you once bore?'

Taken aback, Léonie could only stare at him. Then she pulled herself together and said, 'I do not understand you. The Mayor's son is in the mountains, or so I believe.'

'I am speaking of the son you had who was drowned in the river, or have you forgotten about him altogether?'

'What kind of talk is this?' said Léonie. 'It was your son who was drowned in the river or should I say, our son.'

'And yet,' her husband said thoughtfully, 'he never looked like me not by one single feature. I often wondered about that.'

Léonie said as if bewildered, 'If I did not know your land is under water and that you appear to have been drinking Pernod I would think you have gone out of your mind. As it is I can only feel pity that you are speaking to me like this.'

At that her husband jumped from his seat, gripped her by the shoulders and shook her so hard that when he released her she almost fell on the floor.

'Do not feel pity for me!' he shouted. 'I am a man of some pride and ambition. I will not go under like the other weaklings in this village. I have made my plans.'

Then he returned to his seat at the fire. Léonie sat, faint and trembling. After a long pause she said, 'And what are your plans?'

After a moment's deliberation he said calmly enough, 'I might as well tell you since it will let you know where you stand. My plan is to sell this house and with the money I will begin a new life in another country, where an ambitious man can succeed more easily than he would in this village of incestuous relationships where the Mayor would have any hag who crosses his path, and the priest sleeps with his housekeeper and the occupiers think of us as barbarians and I have no doubt they are right.'

'I see,' said Léonie noticing her husband's eyes were beginning to droop. 'And what of me?'

'And what of you?' he repeated in a tired voice. 'I really do not care. All I know is that I will be encumbered with you no longer. You are not only a stupid woman but an adulteress into the bargain. Even a lesser man than I would not put up with such a wife.'

'I may be stupid but there is no proof I am an adulteress.'

'Your look of guilt was proof enough for me,' he muttered, his head bowing with fatigue.

'I see,' said Léonie, clasping her hands tight within her lap. Then she spoke out firmly. 'When I think about your plan it occurs to me it is a good one. I have always had the feeling that this village was no place for a proud and ambitious man like yourself, and now that your land is covered in water and your crops ruined it would seem that the time is ripe for you to leave. In fact I will be very happy if you do so for you may be a proud man but you are a bad husband.'

He gave no sign he heard this so she spoke louder.

'And you were right about the Mayor. Indeed he was a man who would go with any willing female who crossed his path. I should know. I crossed his path quite a few times. Though I am sure the son I bore was yours but that is not important any more since they are both dead. So the sooner you go, the better.'

Still he gave no sign of hearing her and when she looked at him closely she saw he was asleep. She thought how easy it would be to push him into the fire, but the thought passed. Instead she stood up and shook him by the shoulder saying, 'I think it is time you should go to bed.' He lifted his head, stared at her blearily and said, 'Take your hand off me. I am going,' then stumbled over to the bed against the wall and lay down on it fully clothed.

Léonie took over his seat by the fire and stretched her cold hands towards the flames while her husband began to snore. She thought about his plan to leave but somehow had no faith in it. Apart from the accusation about her and the Mayor his words were similar to words she had heard before. She began to conceive a plan of her own. Rising from her seat she went over to the dresser and took from a drawer a sheet of writing paper, a pen and a bottle of ink, all of which had lain there untouched since before the occupation. Then she started to write.

Dear Aunt,

I write to you in the hope that you are keeping well despite these harsh times. In fact I was considering visiting you and perhaps staying with you for a short time or even longer if you wished. I know it cannot be easy for you to manage your small farm so I am willing to help in any way I can and I would not require any payment. As for my keep, I can give you something towards that since I have been saving money in a stocking for this purpose. You see my husband intends to leave the village in order to begin a new life in another place where his ambitions will be better realised. He is a proud man and a hard worker so he is bound to succeed. But since I am not so proud and ambitious I have refused to go with him. On the other hand if you do not find this arrangement suitable please do not hesitate to write and let me know. In any case I will be glad to hear from you since it is a long time since I have had a letter from anyone.

Your affectionate niece,

Léonie.

After addressing the envelope and putting the letter inside it, she entered her son's room and put it under the pillow on his bed. In the dark she undressed then lay between the sheets that were cold but she scarcely noticed this, her mind being so fixed on the letter and the look of surprise which would appear on Lotz's face when she asked him if he would be good enough to post it for her if she gave him money for the stamp. She was so excited by her plan that she forgot to wait for the presence of her son, which did not enter the room at any time during that night.

The Hut

The hut was so dark and dreary that I wished we had never come. Hardboard covered the window to keep intruders out, though there was nothing to steal but the spade behind the boiler where we used to light fires. I asked my husband if we should light a fire and he said it wasn't worth it as we wouldn't be stopping long.

'It's all right for you. My feet are freezing.'

'You should have put on something warmer,' he said, which was true, but I hadn't bargained on coming to the hut when we first set out. If I'd known, I would have brought a bottle of sherry like I used to do. On summer evenings we sipped it out of cracked cups while watching the sun go down. That was before he'd had the heart attack.

Everything had been cheerier then. Nowadays we didn't do anything except take the odd short walk if the weather was dry. This was the first time we'd been back for months.

'I wonder what happened to the boy,' I said.

'What boy?'

'The boy who shared the hut with us. He was going to build a pigeon loft and you were supposed to be giving him a hand, remember?'

'Yes, but I don't think he intended building anything. He was too damned lazy. Went about like a half-shut knife, he did.'

'That's not true,' I said indignantly. 'He helped you fix the fence.'

'Only because it suited him.' He lit his pipe for the umpteenth time. I went to the door and gazed out at what had been his vegetable plot. It was covered in grass and weeds and apart from the potato shaws there was no sign of vegetables. Likely they'd been eaten by slugs and rabbits. I turned and asked him if the potatoes were ready for picking.

'They should be. I'll dig them up once I've had a draw.'

I thought he was always having a draw. He said the pipe was less harmful than cigarettes. I suspected he was fooling himself. After a while he lifted the spade and headed for the plot. From the doorway I watched him dig with surprising strength, praying he wouldn't ask me to help him for I couldn't stand the sight of all those beetles crawling over my feet. Then he called on me to bring out some plastic bags. I went inside and looked around the shelves but could see nothing but newspapers.

'Will these do?' I said, stumbling towards him, my shoes covered in mud.

'They'll have to,' he said, then stopped digging to watch me wrap the potatoes. It wasn't easy. They kept falling out.

'Hurry up,' he said, then threw down the spade and said he would have to come back another day because his back was sore.

I arose stiffly, clutching the bundles. When I reached the hut he'd found the plastic bags.

'You couldn't have looked properly,' he said, handing them over. Without a word I transferred the potatoes into the bags then wiped my hands on my coat, noticing that his hands were clean.

'I hope the boy doesn't come back for the spade,' he said, as he was putting it away.

'He's probably got better things to do.'

'Like what?'

'Like enjoying himself.'

'Ah,' he said, as though I'd touched him on a sore point.

It was then I took out a half-smoked cigarette which had been in my coat pocket for ages.

'I thought you'd given them up,' he said. 'You told me you had.'

'So I have. This is the last.'

'Cigarette smoke is bad for my health.'

'Pipe smoke is bad for everybody's health.'

'Nonsense. It's a different type of smoke altogether.' There was no point in arguing. The cigarette tasted foul but gave me the courage to tell him that if he didn't light a fire I was going home.

'All right,' he said, 'but don't blame me if the wood is too damp.'

I thought, he must be cold himself, when he did as I suggested. The wood caught fire and soon flames were licking the edge of the boiler. In a better mood I said I'd like to do a sketch of the hut one day. It would be something to look back on if it was ever dismantled. He studied me narrowly.

'I recollect you saying that once before.'

'When was that?'

'One evening last summer when the boy was here. It seemed to amuse him. He laughed at you.'

'I don't remember,' I said hotly.

'Likely because you'd drunk too much sherry. I know I had a few myself but it was no excuse for his attitude.'

'What attitude?'

'He was forever interrupting me when I spoke and I caught him staring at you when he thought I wasn't looking. I don't know what would have happened if I hadn't been there.'

'For God's sake, he was only a boy –' I began, then broke off. My husband was a sick man. I'd better not say anything to put his blood-pressure up.

'I believe that's the rain on,' I said, hearing it patter on the roof. 'It's a good job you got the potatoes in when you did.'

'Yes,' he said vaguely, as though his mind was elsewhere.

A gust of wind blew the door open. As I closed it I saw the sky had turned black. When it was closed we could hardly see a thing.

'We'll have to make a run for it before the rain gets any heavier,' I said.

'I'm in no shape to run. Look on the shelf. There should be a candle in that empty sherry bottle.'

I felt along the shelf and found the bottle. There was hardly any candle left but I put a match to it while my husband puffed on his pipe. The smoke made me cough.

'I'll have to get out of here,' I said. 'I feel as though I'm choking.'

'Do what you like.'

Angered by the way he spoke and now not giving a damn about his blood-pressure, I asked what he thought the boy would have done if he hadn't been there. He stroked his chin then finally said, 'Something diabolic no doubt.'

When I told him to be more precise he said, 'The state you were in he could have stolen your purse.'

'I didn't have a purse with me.'

'Oh well,' he shrugged, 'I'm sure he would have done something objectionable. He was that type of boy.'

'You know what I think?' I said. 'I think you were jealous of him. That's why you're running him down.'

'Me, jealous of him?' he sneered. 'Don't make me laugh.'

'All right, I won't,' I said, 'but it seems strange to me when I've always found the boy helpful and obliging. His only fault, if you could call it that, was a tendency to blush, which I suppose would irritate someone like you whose skin is as thick as putty.'

As a final thrust I said the boy reminded me of my son.

'What son?'

'The son I would have had but for the miscarriage.'

He stared at me wildly. 'You're not going to bring that up, are you?'

'Why shouldn't I?' I said, staring defiantly back. Then the candle went out and we were in the dark.

'Aren't you going to say something?' I said, after a long pause.

'About what?'

'About the boy.'

'Certainly not.'

I wasn't surprised. He would be offended now. I was never allowed to mention the miscarriage. It was like a crime that had to be kept hidden. Driven by this bitter reflection, I added daringly, 'Come to think of it, our son might have turned out like the boy, both in nature and looks. Did you ever think of that?'

He groaned. 'I'll try my best not to.'

'Especially when you've got your blood-pressure to think of.'

I wondered if I'd gone too far when I saw him lift the spade from behind the boiler.

'What are you doing?' I asked.

'I'm taking this home in case it gets stolen. I'll need it for the rest of the potatoes.'

'I suppose you could,' I said, relieved but thinking him an idiot to attach so much importance to a spade. 'I won't be coming back with you. It's depressing enough without having to sit around a dark, freezing hut.'

'Suit yourself,' he said in his usual irritable tone. Then he stood up and opened the door. 'The rain's off.' Sure enough when I looked out the sky had cleared and the sun was shining brightly on the puddles.

'Right, let's go,' he said. 'You bring the potatoes and I'll take the spade.'

'Aren't you going to lock the door?' I asked him as he was walking away.

He thought for a minute then said, 'I might as well leave it open for that dratted boy. Knowing him, he's likely lost his own key. That's probably why he hasn't been back.'

'Yes, you'd better,' I said, 'since you've just stolen his spade.'

'I'm not stealing it. He'll get it back when I see him.'

I thought that could be never, but I merely answered, 'We might even have managed to buy one of our own by then.'

The Castle

It had been a long journey. Twenty-four hours it had taken because we had come the cheapest way possible: first by train and boat, then train again and finally a tedious two hours by bus. The hotel room, booked for us by the Continental Travel Agency, was small and cramped but otherwise clean. Somewhat dazed I stared over the balcony outside the window. My sister Mary Jane squeezed into the rail beside me.

'This isn't bad at all,' she said. 'What do you think?'

'Where's the sea?' I asked. The holiday brochure had said that the village was close to the Mediterranean but we appeared to be in a valley – white cliffs on one side, rolling hills on the other and, facing us in the distance, a range of shadowy mountains.

'It can't be far,' said Mary Jane, swivelling her head. 'Isn't that a castle on top of the cliff?'

'Where?' I asked, but now she was pointing to the courtyard.

'Look at that fountain, all gushing with water! And those apartments over by the river with their balconies and shutters. It's just how I imagined a French village would be – and all this lovely heat too. That's what I miss most about India – the heat.'

'It is warm,' I said, wiping my clammy forehead, 'but you'd have thought there would be more people about.' Down below, the square was deserted apart from one old woman in dark clothes shuffling along the pavement with a bundle of sticks under her arm. 'Isn't this place supposed to a popular tourist attraction?'

'The tourist season will be over by now. And I think it's perfect the way it is, slow-moving and tranquil and all this sun. What more could one ask for?'

When I looked back at the small bedroom, barely big enough for one, I wished we'd asked for separate rooms, but the booking had been done at the last minute, and it was probably too late now. I supposed it was all very nice but I was too hot and tired to appreciate it. Mary Jane suggested that after lunch we take a stroll by the river.

'Actually I was thinking of having a rest afterwards,' I said.

'A rest?' she said incredulously. 'On the first day of our holiday?'

'But I'm tired. It would only be an hour at the most.'

'Honest to God, Dorothy – didn't you have enough sleep on the bus?' She went on to say that she hoped I wasn't going to spoil everything by being tired all the time for in that case I should have stayed at home. I thought that was a good one. She knew I hadn't wanted to come – but she'd harped on so much about it that I'd finally given in. 'We might never get another chance at our age,' she'd said at the time, mentioning Father as a example of how easily one could go into a decline.

It never seemed to occur to Mary Jane to worry about money. Ever since she came home from abroad after Father died – only for a visit, she said, but that was two years ago – she'd been spending it like water. Nor did it occur to her that half-shares might be a bit unfair when I was the one who stayed at home to care for him while she went gallivanting all over the world 'having a wonderful time', as she said on her postcards. It was hard not to be bitter at times, but I tried to put the past out of my mind. There was the future to consider. She was saying, 'After all, you're only fifty-six, just two years older than me, and look at you – fat as a pudding. It's exercise you need, not a rest.'

'I'll see how I feel later,' I said, thinking I'd rather be fat as a pudding than thin as a rake like her.

Lunch was served in the restaurant downstairs by the proprietor – a Monsieur Savlon whom we'd met briefly when we arrived. Though weary I had been struck by his singular appearance.

He was almost as short as he was broad and without a single hair on his head. As if to make up for this his beard grew very thick and black. The meal he laid before us was heavy with sauce and the predominant flavour was garlic, which I cannot stand. I left half of it on my plate and drank almost a jugful of water to get rid of the taste. When Monsieur Savlon came back to clear the table he asked me in perfectly good English, 'You do not like snails?' I shook my head and hurried off to the toilet where I was violently sick. Fifteen minutes later Mary Jane came up to the room and found me lying on top of the bed.

'You really are the limit,' she said. 'Don't you know snails are a delicacy?'

'I don't want to know anything,' I said, turning on my side and closing my eyes.

The next thing I knew she was towering above me in a long white cotton night-dress. 'What time is it?' I asked, for one horrible moment thinking it was Father. For the last few years before he died he had worn a night-shirt that looked much the same.

'You may well ask,' she said, the freckles on her face standing out like halfpence pieces. 'You've been asleep for almost a day. I don't know how often I tried to wake you but you simply refused. I was really fed up. And on top of that Monsieur Savlon kept asking about you. I didn't know what to say.'

'I'm sorry,' I said, forcing myself off the bed. I went out onto the balcony where the air was pleasantly cool. A mist hung over the river. The streets and the apartments looked fresh and sparkling. There was that air of quiet expectancy about the place you get first thing on a fine morning. I began to feel remarkably well.

'Let's go out as soon as we've had breakfast,' I suggested, 'and see as much as we can before it gets too hot. We could even take a picnic to save us coming back for lunch. I'm sure Monsieur Savlon wouldn't mind.'

Mary Jane frowned. 'I hope you don't expect me to run around like a mad thing just because you've had a good rest. I haven't unpacked my things yet and I'll have to think about what to wear. I hate being rushed.'

I stifled a sigh. 'All right, we won't rush.'

In the restaurant Monsieur Savlon came over with a pot of coffee and a plate piled high with toast. 'You like?' he asked, his hands wavering over jars of honey, marmalade and jam. I nodded my head earnestly to wipe out any bad impressions I had given him previously.

'You want more?'

'No thanks,' said Mary Jane.

'This looks very appetising,' I said, and flushed, for no good reason I could think of.

'What a fussy little man he is,' said Mary Jane.

'He's only doing his best to please us,' I said, biting into a slice of toast and honey. When my plate was clean I asked her if she would mind telling him when she got the chance that I couldn't stand snails or garlic, but that this was no reflection on his excellent cooking.

'Tell him yourself,' she said.

'It doesn't matter,' I said, for I didn't want to admit that I sometimes feel shy with foreigners. I knew she would only jeer.

Mary Jane took a long time unpacking. Then she couldn't decide what to wear. 'So you think I should put this on?' she said, holding up a dark-blue dress which she had brought back from India, of a material so fine that it was almost transparent.

'Why not?' I said. 'It looks cool.'

She studied it, frowning. Then she shoved it back into the wardrobe. 'It's not casual enough for walking,' she complained. 'Anyone can see that.' Finally she settled for a pair of shorts and a T-shirt, saying that she might as well be comfortable. I thought that her thin white legs would have been better covered up but there was no point in saying so, for she'd always go against anything I suggested. All the same, I began to feel overdressed in my skirt and blouse, so as a gesture of freedom I took off my tights. We were a few yards away from the hotel when I remembered that I'd forgotten to ask Monsieur Savlon for a picnic basket. I didn't mention this, however, for Mary Jane would have insisted on turning back and with the sun out in full force I was already too hot to be bothered. As we were passing the fountain Mary Jane brought a camera out of her bag and took a snapshot of water gushing from a lion's mouth into a basin floating with dead leaves.

'What's so special about that?' I asked.

'It will look splendid when it's enlarged and framed,' she said, looking at me pityingly. 'I do know what I'm talking about when it comes to photography.'

When we were walking over the bridge Mary Jane stopped to take a shot of a woman on the other side of the road who was dragging a child along by the hand. When the woman began to shout angrily I hurried ahead. 'You shouldn't do that to people,' I said, when Mary Jane caught up with me. 'If you want to take photos of people we can take each other's.' I turned down some steps which led onto the river-bank.

'It's characterisation I want, not stodgy snaps of each other. Anyway, where are we going? I never said I wanted to go this way.'

'I thought you wanted to walk by the river.'

'I wanted to go to the castle,' she said huffily, shoving the camera back into her bag as if she had no further use for it, 'but it seems I've no choice.'

When we reached a spot shaded by trees I said that I would have to sit down since my new sandals were rubbing.

'Oh no!' she groaned.

'But look,' I said, undoing the straps and showing her my heels which were blistered and bleeding.

'You should have kept on your tights,' she said. 'What do we do now – go back?' She gave a hollow laugh and lay down on the grass with her hands behind her head. I could have wept with vexation at this point but I knew it would be a mistake. Mary Jane has a cruel streak that thrives on my tears.

'What's wrong with staying here?' I said. 'It's cool and pleasant. At least we're outside.'

'I'm bored,' said Mary Jane. 'That's what's wrong. And anyway, you forgot to bring the picnic basket, didn't you?'

The lunch was good – cold salmon and salad. 'No garlic,' said Monsieur Savlon with a twinkle in his eye.

I wondered how he knew about the garlic. Perhaps Mary Jane had told him after all. She was in a good mood now, smiling broadly as she clutched her glass of wine. She had ordered a bottle which I thought was far too much for so early in the day. By the time we had finished the meal more diners had arrived. I was glad for Monsieur Savlon's sake because until now trade had been poor. After lunch Mary Jane offered to go into the village to buy some Elastoplast for my heels. I told her I'd be very grateful; at the same time I wondered how she was going to manage this, for she must have put away four or five glasses of wine by now.

As I watched her leave I noticed that she was walking very straight. Too straight, I thought. An hour later she came back and told me that she'd been wandering round the village and had seen some wonderful sights. There was one street in particular, she said enthusiastically, that had the most amazing houses – all different shapes and sizes with cute little courtyards filled with the most amazing flowers and plants. What a pity I hadn't been with her. Then she gave a large yawn and slumped into the chair.

'Did you remember the Elastoplast?' I asked.

'Goodness,' she said, 'I completely forgot.'

Dinner that evening was an excellent steak followed by a soufflé so light that it melted on the tongue. Mary Jane, however, sat drowsily throughout the meal and eventually said she'd have to have an early night since the heat had completely worn her out. Much later I sat out on the balcony in the dark. There was nothing to see except the reflections of the bridge and the apartments cast upon the river by the street lamps. Behind me Mary Jane lay snoring.

I looked at my watch. It was only half-past nine.

The next morning when we were up and dressed Mary Jane said, 'Let's do something exciting. This is our third day and we've done nothing at all.'

'What do you suggest?'

'I was thinking about the castle.'

I pulled open the shutters. There was no cool morning mist – only the sun blinding my eyes. 'It's too hot for climbing,' I said.

'It won't get any cooler. This is the South of France, you know.'

'I'd never get up that cliff,' I protested.

'Don't be stupid. You don't go straight up the cliff. There's a path at the side. Monsieur Savlon told me.'

'Can't we leave it for another day? We've got plenty of time. We don't have to do everything all at once, surely?'

This threw her into a rage. 'We've done hardly anything,' she shouted. 'Honest to God, I wish I'd never come on this holiday. I can see it's going to be a right disaster.'

Suddenly I was infuriated by everything: the heat, this sombre village and most of all by Mary Jane. Things always had to go her way and that's what it had been like ever since she'd moved in. 'And I wish you'd never come to live with me in the first place,' I shouted back. Mary Jane's eyes narrowed and her mouth tightened ominously. I began to regret my words. I was afraid that she might start throwing things around the room and I didn't want Monsieur Savlon at the door.

'I'm sorry,' I said quickly. 'I didn't mean it. The words just slipped out.'

'You meant it, all right,' she said, storming out of the bedroom and banging the door behind her.

I followed her into the toilet and said that I was sorry, I'd spoken in a temper because I'd had a bad headache all morning, but if she was really set on going to the castle I would go with her. The main thing was for us not to fall out over trifles.

'Trifles?' she repeated, staring at me oddly in the mirror above the wash basin. 'So Father was right about you after all.'

'What do you mean?' I demanded.

'As a matter of fact, Father wrote to me not long before he died, saying that you had terrible bouts of temper. He complained that you weren't the loving, patient Dorothy he used to know. In fact, the poor thing even suspected that you were trying to poison him. He said he caught you putting something in his tea one night.'

'But he always drank cocoa,' I said, bemused.

'Anyway, by the time I arrived home he was already dead. So I decided it was best to let sleeping dogs lie, if you'll pardon the expression.'

I stared at her, outraged. Mary Jane would say anything to spite me, but to more or less accuse me of trying to poison Father was going a bit far even for her.

'I gave him a tranquilliser every night to make him sleep. He died of a heart attack. It was on the certificate.'

'I don't doubt it was, but doctors can be careless.' She paused for a minute then added defensively, 'I'm only saying what he wrote.'

Mary Jane was an atrocious liar, I knew that. I wondered if there had ever been a letter at all. Before Father died he had still been able to totter around, but I could hardly imagine him going out to buy a stamp.

'So if he thought I was poisoning him why didn't he cut me out of his will?'

Mary Jane gave a shrug. 'I'd never have mentioned it in the first place if you hadn't been so hurtful,' she said sulkily.

We were about to leave the hotel and head for the castle when Monsieur Savlon came running after us to tell us it was going to rain. Overhead the sky was monotonously blue as ever.

'It can't,' said Mary Jane.

'It says on forecast it will rain.'

'Forecasts aren't always right,' Mary Jane snapped, and left him on the doorstep shaking his head.

We crossed the bridge and had just turned right into a narrow street which Mary Jane said should take us to the bottom of the cliff, when the sky darkened. A minute later it began to pour. In two seconds we were soaked through as we ran back to the café on the corner.

Men were playing cards around a table in the centre of the room, and behind the counter a very fat woman stood regarding us with a mixture of hostility and surprise.

'This doesn't look much like a café,' I said.

'I'll see what they've got,' said Mary Jane, going to the bar, while I dumped our bags on a table beside a window which was covered with wire mesh.

Mary Jane came back to the table with two glasses of milky-looking stuff which according to her was all they sold, unless I preferred beer, of course.

'What is it?' I asked. 'Are you sure they don't have coffee?'

'Pernod,' she said. 'I was told they haven't.' She took a sip from the glass. 'It's not bad. Why don't you try it? It might take the miserable look off your face.'

'I'm not drinking that,' I said, feeling very agitated, because the card players were staring across at us intently. When one of them winked and jerked his head over his shoulder as if to suggest that we join them I said to Mary Jane that we had better leave.

'Can't you take a joke?' Mary Jane began, but I was already on my feet and heading for the door with my bag in hand. Outside it was still raining but not so heavily. I made my way as fast as I could back to the hotel, and although I turned round once or twice to see if Mary Jane was following me, there was no sign of her.

Up in the room I took off my wet clothes and lay down under the bedcovers in my underslip, wondering whether to pack my bags straightaway or wait until tomorrow. The holiday was turning out much worse than I had anticipated. If the past three days were anything to go by there was no likelihood of it getting any better. In the end I gave up trying to work out what to do and fell asleep through sheer inertia.

'Madame, are you there?' Monsieur Savlon was shouting through the keyhole.

I sat up, startled. 'Yes. What is it?'

'Your sister is in the bar. I think she has too much to drink. She is lying on the floor.'

'I'll be down in a minute,' I called, but as soon as I heard his footsteps receding down the stairs I jumped out of bed and locked the door. As far as I was concerned Mary Jane could stay where she was. Right at this moment it was quite beyond me to cope with her.

Prompt on six o'clock I went into the restaurant, for the sandwiches in my bag were damp and soggy and I hadn't eaten since breakfast. There were a few other diners in the room but Mary Jane wasn't among them. I sat down at our usual table anticipating some sharp words from Monsieur Savlon; if he ordered us out it would solve the problem of whether to leave or not, but I dreaded having to face him all the same. However, he laid a bowl of soup in front of me and said quickly, 'Your sister, she is sleeping in my mother's room. Do not worry. She will be fine.' Before I could thank him for his trouble he went on, 'Tonight I plan something special for you. I think you will like.' I looked up at him blankly. Hesitating, he added, 'Perhaps if Madame wears the nice dress she has on when she arrive it would be suitable for this plan.' Then without waiting for an answer, he disappeared into the kitchen.

Upstairs I searched for the dress he had mentioned and found it lying creased on the wardrobe floor. Anyway, what did it matter, I thought, since I wasn't going anywhere. If it was a surprise-party he was talking about, I didn't want any surprises. I would only feel awkward. I wouldn't be able to speak to anyone and I could envisage Mary Jane showing up drunk and making a spectacle of herself. I sat out on the balcony staring at the reflections on the river, wondering angrily if this was what I had come to France for. When I went back into the room, the wardrobe door was still open, and my eye fell on the dark-blue dress that Mary Jane had brought back from India. I tried it on and it fitted me rather well. The cloth had been cut in such a way that it flared out under the high bodice, flattering my full figure. As I studied myself in the wardrobe mirror I decided that I'd never looked so elegant, and that I would go to this affair after all, if only to show my face.

There was no one in the bar except Monsieur Savlon and the tiny old woman who collected the tumblers from the tables on the terrace.

'Am I too early?' I asked. It was nine o'clock. I'd imagined everything would have been in full swing by now.

'*Non, non* – you sit here,' said Monsieur Savlon, pointing to a table in the centre of the room. All the others had been stacked against the wall to clear a space on the floor. 'You will take some?' he said, opening a bottle of wine. 'Very good. Very old.' I sipped the wine, scarcely tasting it, as he sat down opposite me. 'I drink this only on my birthday,' he said.

'I see,' I said. 'You're having a birthday party?'

He frowned as if he did not quite understand. 'I celebrate with you.'

'How thoughtful,' I said faintly, as I caught the eye of the old woman, who stood watching behind the bar counter, nodding her head slightly as if in approval.

'You like music?' asked Monsieur Savlon.

'Yes, I do.'

'Then my mother will play.' He snapped his fingers at the counter, and as if a switch had been pressed the sound of violins filled the room. It struck me as all rather weird – the music, the absence of guests and in particular the fact that this small shabby woman was Monsieur Savlon's mother. I must say I would have expected someone more grand.

'You want to dance now?' he asked.

It was the last thing I wanted to do. I hadn't danced since my school-days, when we had all been forced to take lessons, but I couldn't very well refuse him. As it happened, Monsieur was an excellent dancer, which made it easy for me to follow his lead, and I began to enjoy myself exceedingly.

'The music is called "La Vie en Rose",' he said when he led me back to the table. Time passed quickly after that. We danced, then stopped to rest and sip our wine, savouring it slowly as befits a good one. After we had danced for about the sixth time – although I had lost count, really – Monsieur Savlon looked at his watch and said, 'We will now finish. It is late.' He called out to his mother, who had not moved an inch from her position behind the counter, and the violins played no more. I thanked Monsieur Savlon for a pleasant evening, but when I turned to thank his mother she had gone, and it was with a pang of sadness that I climbed the stairs, for it seemed unlikely that such an evening would ever come my way again.

Mary Jane was sitting up in bed when I entered the room.

'Where the hell have you been?' she asked, in a voice sharp as tempered steel. 'And what are you doing with my dress on?'

I explained that I had only been trying on the dress to see how it looked, and had forgotten to take it off when I went downstairs to the bar to look for her.

'You're lying,' she said. 'When I went down to the bar the door was locked. What's more, I could hear music.' I felt my face flushing as she squinted at me curiously. Then her eyes went wide with dawning realisation. 'Don't tell me you were having it off with that old dwarf! My God, you must be desperate.'

*   *   *

Next morning Mary Jane told me that she was going to have another try at the castle. 'Do you want to come along?' she asked, pointing out that it wasn't as hot as before.

'I might as well,' I muttered, finding it difficult to look her in the face – particularly since at that very moment Monsieur Savlon put the coffee pot on the table with his usual brisk 'Good morning'. After he had gone Mary Jane leaned across the table and whispered, 'Mind you, he might not be such a bad catch when you think about it. Must be worth a mint.'

An hour later we were out in the middle of a field which had more stones than grass in it. Mary Jane was walking on ahead while I lagged behind, trying to keep a good distance between us.

'I've found the path,' she shouted. 'Do hurry up.' When I caught up with her she was sitting on a flat stone, looking up at a rough track which led over baked earth and rock to the castle above.

'What do you think?' she asked.

'I think I'll manage,' I replied.

We began to climb. The path itself wasn't so terribly steep, but the effort of side-stepping over loose boulders tired me out. Mary Jane was always ahead, but not by much, and I was only minutes behind her when I reached the top.

'So you finally made it,' she said, as I stood there breathless, looking around for somewhere to rest my aching legs. 'There it is.' She pointed towards a heap of ruins at the edge of the cliff. She set off towards it, camera in hand, while I followed reluctantly. From close up, all that remained of the castle was a long, narrow enclosure of stonework. Grass and flowers grew through the smashed flagstones, and the rampart wall on the edge of the cliff was broken in parts.

'That looks dangerous,' I said, but Mary Jane wasn't listening. She was too busy focusing the camera on the scene, aiming it this way and that, as if what she was doing was all so terribly important. I might have been amused at her antics if I hadn't been so busy watching where she put her feet.

'How about one of you?' she said, pointing the camera in my direction.

'Some other time. I'm not in the mood.'

'You never are in the mood,' she said. She gave an ugly laugh. 'Except if it's Monsieur Savlon, of course.'

'Don't start that again,' I said. I walked away from her and looked over the parapet wall. It was a sheer drop down to the river below. Mary Jane came to stand beside me.

'Magnificent, isn't it? You can see everything for miles around.'

I stepped back. My head was beginning to spin. 'I must have a drink of water,' I said, turning back into the enclosure. We sat on two flat stones and drank from our flasks without looking at each other.

'I've been thinking things over,' Mary Jane said, 'and I might as well tell you I've decided to go back to India. I had a letter from Lady Bonham Fletcher and apparently she misses me terribly and is desperate to have me back. I wasn't going to go because I didn't want to leave you on your own, but the way things are going . . .' She let her voice tail off, as if there were no need for further explanation.

'Why don't you?' I said. Knowing what a liar she was, I was positive she had no intention of going to India. 'I'm sure it's the best thing you could do.'

'So we'll have to sell the house,' she added.

'What do you mean – sell the house?'

'It's plain enough. I'm entitled to half of Father's estate and if I'm leaving the country the only way I can get it is for us to sell the house.'

'Mary Jane,' I said, 'please stop all this nonsense. I know you don't mean a word of it.'

'Oh, but I do,' she broke in. 'I want the house sold. It's as simple as that. And anyway,' she went on, 'you've got to admit it's in a terrible state – all that old piping and the place is rotten with damp. Just think, with your share you could buy yourself a nice little flat. It would be so much cheaper to run and easier to clean.'

My throat had gone dry. I began to trace circles in the dust with my finger. Mary Jane stared at me stonily. 'Aren't you going to say anything? You've got to face facts, you know. You've really no option.'

'Perhaps you're right,' I said at last. 'I might be better off in a small flat. I can't say I'd considered it before, but if you say you're going back to India . . .'

'Of course I'm right,' she said with such obvious relief that I didn't know whether to laugh or cry. 'Well now,' she went on cheerfully, 'I must take a photo of you in front of the castle. Something to look back on.'

It turned out that there was too much shade there for the camera, and Mary Jane moved me on. 'I'll take it over by the wall,' she said. 'It's brighter there.' After a bit of manoeuvring to get the exact focus, she clicked the shutter. 'That's it,' she said. 'Now you can take one of me.'

'By the wall?'

'Of course, by the wall.' Mary Jane took up a pose with one arm arranged on top of the wall.

'Move over a bit,' I said. 'You're too far to the left.'

'For goodness sake,' she said irritably. Fixing her smile on the camera, she took a step sideways. Then her arm flailed in empty space and she went backwards through the gap without uttering a word of protest.

Mary Jane was buried in the village cemetery. The coroner's verdict was accidental death. Monsieur Savlon came to the funeral along with a few of the old village women, including his mother. It was a simple affair. The coffin was placed inside a marble tombstone and a priest said a few brief words. As I was leaving the cemetery Monsieur Savlon came up to offer his condolences. 'Be patient, Madame,' he said. 'Time will heal your pain.'

Personally I thought I'd been patient long enough. Through my tears I told him that it would have been some consolation to visit my sister's grave at least once a week, but alas, I couldn't even do that. Monsieur Savlon stopped and confronted me. 'But why not? You can stay for as long as you want – for ever, if you wish.'

'For ever?' I said with astonishment.

'Forgive me,' he said. 'I have offended you perhaps. It is not the right time to say this.'

'I'll think about it,' I said, turning away and wiping my eyes.

I am taking up Monsieur Savlon's offer. It's the best thing that could have happened. He has told me that there's an empty apartment across the river. He knows the owner very well and he's sure that I can get it. He assures me that the rent won't be too dear, since it's a poor village and no one is expected to pay more than they can afford. I can scarcely get over my good luck. After all those years of stagnating in Father's old house, I'm about to live in an apartment in a French village with a balcony overlooking the river. Of course I'm sad about Mary Jane, in a way. But she was her own worst enemy. Which reminds me – I must get rid of her writing bureau before I sell the house. That's where she kept all her correspondence, and as she said herself, it's better to let sleeping dogs lie. I still can't help feeling angry, though, when I think of her calling Monsieur Savlon a dwarf. How dare she say that about such a nice little man.

Marching to the Highlands
and into the Unknown

In June 1949 my first husband, baby daughter of two months, and myself set forth for the North of Scotland. This venture was prompted by an article in a paper saying that people were wanted to work land in the Highlands, with accommodation provided. I was not keen on marching into the unknown, but it was a case of squaw follows Indian brave and asks no questions. So with £11, our baby, our clothing, a two-man tent and pram we took the train from Glasgow to a station beyond Inverness called Garve. It dawned on me then that we had no idea where we were going, apart from a vague intention to reach a place called Scoraig situated on the Little Minch.

I remember we obtained a lift from a tradesman going in the direction of Scoraig, but he had heard nothing about work and accommodation. We arrived at Scoraig and the only sign of habitation was a single house staring from a high point towards the Atlantic Sea. We might as well have been in the Sahara. We spied a small brick building, possibly a shelter for animals, and inside this we huddled, hating each other, while I attempted to feed the baby. However, a woman came down from the house and took us in and gave us a room to sleep in. She must have thought us mad, but accepted our story and for a week we camped in her garden. Her husband, who worked on the road, told us it was the only work available. The only payment we could give her, though she wanted none, was a carton of Epsom salts. She was as grateful as if we had given her a magnificent gift. We promised to write when we were in better circumstances. Sadly, we never did.

We set off back through this mountainous region, possibly beautiful if you were a tourist, but to me desolate and harsh, gushing rivers and jagged rocks.

We came to an inn stuck in the middle of nowhere and, over-joyed at this bit of civilization, set up our tent beside it. The buxom woman who owned the place sold us food, even offering my husband a job. She took a fancy to him but not to me.

After two days of camping and happiness for my husband, mainly because of his access to beer, I took the initiative and unpegged the tent, wrapped it up, and we set off again in silence. I can't remember how long it took us to reach the town of Beauly but by the end of the journey we were both covered in cleg bites. The baby in her pram was protected by wet nappies hanging over the hood. The money was nearly gone. In Beauly I located what nowadays would be called a social security office and managed to obtain 14s by genuinely sobbing my heart out and holding the baby who cried too. This allowed us to buy food and walk to Inverness.

We reached Inverness and put up the tent in a place called, I think, The Black Park Camping Site, for a few shillings weekly. We stayed here for quite a while, since my husband got a job to do with erecting pylons. It couldn't have been much fun for him going to work from a tent but I had problems too, walking every day from the site to the town for a few herrings or whatever was cheap, and making food on the Primus stove which was difficult to light. I remember one occasion when my husband complained about his meal and I threw the semolina for the baby round the tent in a fit of temper. On another I nearly set the tent on fire in the night while heating milk for the baby.

And yet there were occasions when I was happy pushing the pram along the canal bank or sitting by the river. It was summer and the place was lovely. This situation continued until late September when the weather became colder and the days shorter.

About this time I decided I could not carry on living in a tent with an infant a few months old and the winter approaching. One Saturday evening I packed and, pushing the pram, headed for Inverness railway station to return home to my mother. I left my husband in the tent drinking whisky.

I had to wait some time for the Glasgow train and, before it came, I turned about and pushed the pram back to the tent and that was that. We both decided to leave. We now had some money from my husband's work so a few days later we assembled our belongings and we left Inverness on a train for Keith, another destination unknown to us. Anywhere, we thought then, was better than returning to Glasgow.

We arrived in Keith in the dark, came to a field and pulled our tent round about us. We marched through the town the next morning, not a big place then as I remember it. We purchased some groceries from a shop in the town square owned by a man called McGillviray who asked us questions – why and where and what were we doing. We answered shamefacedly. 'There's a man lives here, originally from Glasgow,' he said. 'I'm sure he'll let you put your tent up in his back garden, it's a good size.'

This man called Alec Simpson did just that and his wife washed our grimy clothes and the baby's nappies. Alec was pleased with us because my husband came from Glasgow and I had worked there. For a fortnight we camped in his back garden, burning fires at night, hanging our clothes to dry over the fence. The townsfolk called us the squatters. Before October ended we moved to a broken-down old building.

We lived there for a year. We were comfortable. We had coal, paraffin light, and my husband got a job with the English Electric Company. My second child, a boy, was born in Keith hospital. We might have lived in Keith for ever but the woman who owned the condemned building told us regretfully that it was being knocked down and we must leave. It was then my husband and I parted for a time. I returned to my home town and he went on working with English Electric. I've often wished to go back to Keith and see it all again, but no doubt everything would be unrecognisable now.

This adventure was judged by a councillor in my home town as 'irresponsible' – I was desperately applying to him for one of the available prefabricated houses. We got the prefab after waiting another year and a half and my husband and I, plus another son and daughter making four children in all, lived not particularly happily ever after until he died at the age of forty-three.

I suppose you could say my life was a struggle, as it is with most men and women of the working class even in years of good employment. I always worked when possible at anything I could find, i.e., in shop, office and factory. That was in the good old days when work brought satisfaction even if it was a hassle. Work was money and security and if I was not exactly happy with my lot I could relax with a drink at the weekend while watching the telly. Any disagreement which arose under the influence was forgotten when facing work on Monday. Yet I suppose there was always a hankering to do something better.

Twelve years ago I began writing fiction, prompted by the fact that I had joined a writing class in Alexandria. Glasgow University sent tutors, who were enthusiastic about what I wrote. When they stopped attending the class I simply carried on writing and periodically some of them got in touch as if to prod me on with that lonely business. Sometimes it was the last thing I wanted to do, especially after cleaning somebody's house, which was now the only job I could get. The years of unemployment had set in.

Then my novel *Gentlemen of the West* was published and some short stories in a book, shared with two other authors, called *Lean Tales*. This was great but didn't pay the rent, so I continued to clean houses and, with the assistance of a grant from the Scottish Arts Council, wrote another short novel called *Like Birds in the Wilderness*. It wasn't a success though some people liked it.

Eight years later, Bloomsbury published *A Working Mother* and now I have completed this collection of stories. Since the depression of the past decade took the security of steady work away from my present husband Patrick, from myself and from countless others, I am thankful to be still in the business of writing. At least I can tell my grandchildren (if they are interested) that not only did I publish a few books in my time but I once was 'irresponsible' enough to set off with my first husband and child into the unknown wilds of the Scottish Highlands where we wandered about with scarcely a penny in our pockets.

THE DARK SIDE

Hannah Sweeny

Hannah Sweeny was three years old with red hair and freckles. She seldom spoke except to say in a menacing tone, 'Ah'll throw you in a bing o' watter.' Despite this we allowed her to play skipping ropes with us. 'Ca' the rope' it was called, which meant she took one end of the rope with the other tied to a railing, then she twirled it in the air and we all skipped through. If we touched it we were out. Hannah would have 'ca'd it' all day if we hadn't been called in for our tea, though sometimes she had to watch her two-year-old brother, hurling him up and down the pavement in a push-chair to stop him screaming.

'Why don't you give her a shot of the skipping?' said my mother, though it was none of her business.

'She can't skip. She's too small.'

'Then don't make the rope so high. It's not fair she doesn't get a shot.'

'She doesn't want a shot,' I said sulkily. We kids were seven years old. She was only three and lucky we allowed her to play with us. Then a rumour went around that she was a Catholic: her mother had been seen entering the chapel. We asked Hannah if this was true but as usual she remained tight-lipped.

'She must be if she goes to the chapel,' said one of my playmates who had already told me the Sweenys had no furniture in their house except a table.

'That proves nothing,' I said. 'We'll have to take turns on Sunday to see if the rest of the family go to chapel, then we'll know for a fact if Hannah is one.'

To us being a Catholic was as bad as being a vampire so we

considered it our duty to find this out by taking turns to rise early on Sunday mornings. I volunteered to be the first and my mother was astounded to see me coming out of the toilet at seven o'clock.

'What in the name of God are you doing up at this time?'

'I was needing to go to the toilet, that's why.'

'That's because you drink cocoa last thing at night.'

'It's not cocoa, I'm drinking too much water.'

'Then you'll have to see a doctor,' she said.

Happily in our house things kept distracting my mother and she forgot about the doctor. And I saw none of the Sweenys going to chapel that morning. By the time it was somebody else's turn to watch the Sweeny's Hannah had died.

I couldn't believe it. I suppose we were too shocked to cry. Her death was less upsetting than the suddenness of it. One day she was 'ca'ing' the rope, next day she was dead. 'We shouldn't have spied on them to see if they were Catholics,' someone said, 'Especially when there was no proof.'

'What did she die of?' I asked my mother.

'Could have been she swallowed an orange pip.'

I didn't believe her. We had all swallowed orange pips at one time or another.

I went to the funeral because I didn't want left out of things. A priest was there so she had been a Catholic after all. Hannah's death had a profound effect for we never got over her absence, which hung above us like a black cloud whenever we played skipping ropes. The rope kept winding round our ankles. We stopped that game, changed to peever or catch-the-ball, but it wasn't the same. Ca'ing the rope had been more exciting for you had to be quick on your feet to play it. On dark nights I stared out of the window, hoping to see Hannah's ghost ca'ing the rope, yet I thought I was going crazy when I spied a small figure ca'ing a rope in the moonlight.

'Come quick,' I shouted, 'See Hannah's ghost come back to haunt us!'

'Don't be stupid,' shouted my mother, 'It's her young brother. He's only got taller.'

She was right – taller and thin as a matchstick in a red jumper. By the time the clear nights arrived we were all out again skipping like mad.

Then Hannah's mother asked us if we'd like to take a bunch of flowers up to her grave. We had a guilty feeling about not letting her skip when she was alive so I said we would, and grudgingly we all traipsed up to the cemetery with a bunch of dandelions which I thought looked out of place on the tiny flat stone. For some reason I began to laugh at the sight of it and could not stop. Hannah's young brother ran over and kicked me on the leg.

'Don't laugh at Hannah,' he said and ran out of the cemetery before I could kick him back. After that my mother kept me indoors. She said there had been complaints about me from the Sweenys. 'Mind you,' she added, 'They're not a nice lot and I do believe they are Catholics.'

Eventually we moved away from the district and I made a new set of friends who never played at skipping ropes or anything else. We were too busy talking about boys or a male teacher who we fancied, or else swatting for exams. If I saw anyone from the old days I'd run across the road or pretend to be engrossed in a shop window. Time passed and I left school without great qualifications. The truth was I wanted to be a film star and had no interest in ordinary jobs. Then an inexplicable fear came over me that stopped me leaving the house. The doctor said it wasn't unusual for girls of my age and would pass. It did and I managed to get a job as a filing clerk in an office. My mother was very proud of me, telling everyone how clever I was. The first day I was heading to this office, swinging my bag carelessly as if I hadn't a worry in the world, when I bumped into Hannah's young brother. I recognised the red hair and freckles. He'd turned out rather good-looking.

'Hallo,' I said, 'remember me?'

He looked at me blankly then his eyes narrowed.

'You're the one who laughed at my sister,' he said, then spat in my face. I turned round and headed for home. I told my mother I couldn't face work, not yet anyway, maybe another day.

The Writing Group

Danielle joined a writing group and was dismayed to find only five other members, very well dressed and seated at old school desks – four women and one stout gent she at once privately nicknamed Mr Portly. She knew her duffle coat, bought last winter for her fourteenth birthday, was definitely shabby. She thought of taking it off but decided her terrylene jumper and scuffed denims were in a worse condition, and wished she'd taken more trouble with her clothes before coming.

'Take off your coat dear,' said a thin, dark-haired woman who had introduced herself as Madge. 'It gets very hot in here.'

She looked at the others for confirmation and all nodded except an elderly woman called Daisy who said, in a refined accent and aggrieved tone, 'I always find it cold in here. May I be introduced to the new member?'

Danielle was glad someone else was interested in her, but wished the social worker had not told her to come, saying a writing group would build up her confidence. She began to cough, a sure sign of nerves.

'Danielle is joining us because she has been recommended by the St John's Ambulance Club,' said Madge, 'I hope the class will benefit her as I am sure it has benefited so many.'

She stifled what seemed a chuckle, making Danielle wonder what she really meant.

'What's more to the point,' said Mr Portly, 'did anyone remember to bring the wine?'

'Don't panic,' said another woman, 'I've brought it *and* plastic cups.'

'Oh, Lordy, I'm glad you remembered the cups,' said Mr Portly. With a screw attachment on his penknife he wrestled with the bottle until the cork came out with a pop. Filling the cups he said, 'But there's no cup for Danielle.'

The others looked at her with something like disapproval until she said it was alright, she didn't drink.

'That's beside the point,' said Mr Portly irritably. 'We didn't used to drink either.'

This raised a general laugh. They all lifted their glasses to Danielle who began to think them friendly enough, if a bit mad. Someone asked her if she had brought a sample of her work to read. She said, 'No, I didn't know I should. Nobody told me.'

'That's alright,' said Madge. 'Bring it next time. We want to see what you're capable of, be it prose or poetry.'

'I don't know if I'll be here next time,' said Danielle. 'I don't think I'm capable of writing anything.'

'Nonsense,' said one of the women, 'none of us is very capable. We learn as we go. Being capable is something you work at.'

'Speak for yourself,' said Mr Portly. He turned to Danielle and said, 'We don't expect miracles. Just keep quiet and listen to the rest of us.'

'Oh, do shut up,' said Madge. 'If nobody objects I'll read my poem, someone has to get us started. It's in Gaelic. Does anybody mind? Will that be alright?'

'I just love your Gaelic poems,' said one of the other women, clapping her hands in delight. 'They're so atmospheric, don't you think?'

'Definitely,' said Mr Portly. Madge's voice rose and fell like a storm at sea. Danielle felt a headache coming on, wanted to leave and go to bed, but didn't want to disappoint the social worker who had apparently taken some trouble to place her in this group.

'What did you think of that?' Mr Portly asked Danielle when Madge stopped reciting.

'I really enjoyed it,' she answered in a sincere voice, 'But I didn't know what the words meant.'

'You're not supposed to,' said Madge. 'My intonation should give the clue.'

'I see,' said Danielle. 'I didn't know.'

'You have a lot to learn,' said Madge, turning her head away, and Danielle felt like crying.

'Right, young Miss,' said one of the women, 'Are you sure you brought nothing to read? It would be so much better for us if you had.'

'I've just remembered I've got this,' said Danielle. She took a crumpled paper from her pocket and proceeded to read a story about a baby abandoned on a doorstep, one she had copied from a women's magazine found in her doctor's waiting room. She read in a low, monotonous voice, very fast, to get the story over and done with. When she stopped there was a long silence until Madge asked if this sort of thing happened nowadays, when women had the right to have abortions on demand.

'I believe you get the odd case,' said Daisy, 'But I don't think . . .'

She broke off when Madge told her to be quiet, then Mr Portly said it didn't matter if a story was true to life, what counted was ability to write.

'Surely not,' said one of the other women.

'I obviously have no talent for writing,' said Danielle and burst into tears. Mr Portly gave her a clean handkerchief to dry her face and blow her nose, while most of the others said they thought her story very good and she should definitely come back next week. Then Madge butted in, asking if she could read another of her poems to them before the lesson ended.

'Oh, yes, do! We're all simply dying to hear it!' said Daisy on a note of bitter sarcasm, obviously still smarting from being told to be quiet.

'I only wish I understood Gaelic,' said Danielle.

'This new poem of mine is in ordinary English,' said Madge.

'Even in English we probably won't understand it,' said Daisy, 'We'll just have to sit and listen.'

At that Madge stormed out of the room. Gradually others followed. At last only Mr Portly and Danielle remained.

'Aren't you leaving?' she asked him.

'It's early yet,' he said, moving over and sitting close by her side. 'Did you really leave your baby on a doorstep?'

'No, but I know somebody who did.'

He seemed to ponder this, then said, 'Were you sent here from an institution? We get these people sometimes. They swell the numbers, and our class is supposed to have at least eight.'

'My teacher sent me,' she told him. 'She said I had talent.'

'I'm sure you do.' He put his hand on her knee. She struck it off, stood up and said, 'I'm going home.'

He too stood up, fumbling with the zip of his trousers, and saying, 'Do you want to see what you've done to me?'

But before he could show her that Danielle was running out of the room and down the corridor outside with Mr Portly close behind. Before they reached the door at the end Madge entered through it saying crossly, 'I left my umbrella,' then she looked at them both intently and asked, 'Is anything wrong?'

Danielle was silent. The truth sounded improbable and from experience she knew she was unlikely to be believed. Mr Portly's lips were quivering. He told Madge, 'She tried to proposition me. I don't know what would have happened if you hadn't come back! It would have been her word against mine.'

'I knew it,' said Madge. 'We should never take on any of that lot. They do anything to get attention.' Looking scornfully at Danielle she added, 'I hesitate to think what kind of attention *you* wanted.'

'But the group needs more members,' said Mr Portly. 'If we apply again the next one might be better. I still have faith in human nature.'

He spoke as if Danielle was not there.

'Maybe so, but I'm not chancing it,' said Madge. She turned to Danielle. 'You'd better get going before I call the police. I'm sick and tired of decent folk like us being taken advantage of.'

Danielle sighed. She had liked the idea of becoming a writer but had to admit she had no talent, and obviously the people who ran the class were not worth bothering about. She was only sorry she would not see Mr Portly's face when he missed the wallet that was now safe inside her duffle coat. She didn't think he would complain to the police because several girls where she lived knew what he was like, but she was not going to point the finger. In a way she was sorry for him. They say these kind of men can't help themselves. Maybe it's not their fault.

Roses

As a child of five Carol loved to read magazines, progressing to novels when she was ten, first the foreign legion tales by P. C. Wren, then Thackery and Dickens. She even attempted Tolstoy's *War and Peace*, but could not grasp the Russian names. Her favourite book was *Oliver Twist*. Soon she had read every book in the local library and accumulated a pile of reminder notices to return them that she tried to forget. In the end her infuriated mother was forced to pay dozens of fines.

'Carrie!' she shouted one day, 'Come and help hang out the washing.'

Her daughter, lounging book in hand on a sofa, said, 'Just let me read to the end of this. I'll only be an hour or two.'

Her mother marched into the living room, seized the book from Carol's hand, returned to the kitchen and threw it into the washing tub where it disintegrated into a soggy mass. Carol did not complain, said nothing, but never forgave that, deciding to wait until revenge was possible.

Soon after that a legacy made them rich and Carol was sent to an expensive private school from which she was expelled for completely ignoring her teachers and reading *Frankenstein* when she should have been writing an essay about the countryside in spring.

'That child has perverse tendencies,' the headmistress told her mother who agreed wholeheartedly. When seventeen she pushed her mother off a cliff top as they walked by the seaside. This was not premeditated but done on impulse because the opportunity had arisen. Luckily this was regarded as an accident. Carol regretted it when forced to make her own meals but shed no tears. It was her mother's fault for destroying a good book. From now on Carol vowed she would only wash and clean up when it suited her, but she never put cleaning before reading so the house became a terrible mess. It was only put in order when a maiden aunt visited and forced Carol to pay cleaners who came every day for a fortnight. Even then the result was far from perfect.

'Now promise me you will never let the place get into that state again,' said the aunt.

Carol promised then let the house become much, much worse. When her aunt next came visiting Carol, rather than face her terrible wrath, waited for her behind the front door, hatchet in hand, later disposing of the body in the earth beneath the kitchen windows where in summertime one or two roses flourished. The police made no headway with the mysterious disappearance, finally deciding the aunt had fled the country because she had been charged with shoplifting.

Everything went well with Carol after that. She read Émile Zola from end to end and was going to start on Jane Austen when a young gardener appeared on her back doorstep, asking for work. He was handsome but not too handsome, lean and brown with the right size of bare muscular arms. She decided she would marry him if he asked her.

'How did you know I needed a gardener?' she asked in a winsome tone while boldly making eye contact.

'Aha,' he replied, wagging his finger, 'A little bird told me.'

'As you see,' she said, 'I have a big garden that I cannot possibly manage on my own. I would like new plants growing all over it, but the plot under the kitchen window must not be disturbed. I have a special reason for insisting on that.'

'What might that be?' he asked, mildly curious.

'I'll let you know when I decide to.'

He shrugged. 'Well, it's your garden, but I have a suggestion.'

In glowing terms he described a lovely bed of roses he would like to plant, roses whose scent would waft into her nostrils whenever she entered the kitchen. Harshly she interrupted him.

'Don't talk about what you want. A dead dog is buried in that plot whom I loved dearly. His remains must not be tampered with. Is that clear?'

He gave a slight bow, said her wishes would be respected, and they agreed on his weekly wage.

After that she often watched him from the kitchen window, digging, planting or trimming the hedge. She liked to see his muscles ripple under his shirt or better still, if the weather was warm, his body when he wore no shirt. Sometimes he asked for a drink of water and when invited entered the kitchen. He appeared to know his place in society, seeming ill at ease indoors but flirtatious when they met outside, as if he was two different people. She did not think she trusted either, yet panicked one morning when he did not come.

He arrived as usual next day saying, 'I had a sore throat,' but with no sign of a cold or cough so she knew he was lying. On warm days after that she sometimes went outside, lifted a rake or hoe or spade and helped him a little.

'What happened to your mother?' he once asked as they stood outside looking at the plot beneath the window.

'She fell off a cliff and died.'

'How tragic,' he said. 'You must be very lonely.'

'I have my books,' she said.

'Books?' he said, as if baffled. 'I can't even read.'

'How awful,' she murmured.

'I don't mind,' he said. 'Reading is not for the likes of me.'

'You don't know what you're missing.' She began to tell him about one of her favourite novels, but she sensed he was bored. 'I like doing things,' he said, 'not reading or hearing about them.'

Carol, greatly angered, said, 'In that case I am paying you off. At the end of the week you can collect any more due to you and go.'

He laughed as if highly amused and asked if he could first dig

316

up the earth beneath the kitchen window; he was curious to know why the roses bloomed so well in such poor soil, for there must be more than a dead dog enriching it. Carol, panic-stricken, hit him on the head with a spade she had been leaning on. He lay in a coma for a week before recovering, but was never the same again. He smiled at her like an angel and made snuffling noises like a farm animal.

'Why don't you speak properly?' she would say, shaking him by the shoulders. He would open his mouth wide but only piggish grunts came out. She began to detest him, especially when she had to wash him like a baby and change his clothes. He joined her aunt in the plot under the window and after that the roses grew better than ever, though she longed for winter when no flowers grew and she could forget them and relax with a book.

Then a man came to fix her roof that had been leaking in the heavy October rain. He seemed honest until he tiptoed into her kitchen and asked for a drink of water. As she filled a tumbler from the tap he grabbed her from behind, threw her down on a chair and gagged her with a dishcloth after tying her hands with a rope from his pocket. She had visions of being raped but he merely ransacked drawers looking for money, finally leaving with pearls she had concealed in a tea caddy. They were fake. Carol never reported the incident in case it brought police to search the house and garden, where the plot under the window was overgrown with roses that now even bloomed in winter. People passing by would stop and remark on them, and if she was in the garden ask what she fed them on. 'Tea leaves,' she would say, and they would walk on happily.

Time passed until one day she realised she was old and had done nothing much with her life but read books, most of them stolen from shops or the library, and many lying unread and covered with cobwebs. Her eyesight was now so bad she could hardly read a page. She made a bonfire of books in the garden and when they had well and truly burned she danced around the ashes with a feeling of freedom. Next day she bought herself new clothes, a suitcase and umbrella. She was going abroad to see the world and would undoubtedly meet with rain. She booked a cabin on a newly built ocean liner called the Titanic because she liked the name. It sounded lucky and she was excited and happy to be leaving home. No one heard of her after that but the roses bloomed, and people passing sniffed the air and said whoever had planted them must have had green fingers and a great love of roses, for such a colour of red had never before been seen.

Meet the Author

I'd scarcely sat down on her shabby sofa when she brought out a bottle of vodka from an equally shabby wall unit.

'I think we drink more of this than the Russians,' she said with a twisted smile.

'But theirs is much cheaper,' I said, noticing the glass she had given me had many finger marks, but why should that spoil the pleasure of drinking with a famous author? I might once have thought that, but not now.

'How's the book going?' I asked, trying to remember if she'd written more than one.

'Not very well, but I'm not the kind of author who tries to write best sellers. If I bring some pleasure to a handful of readers my work will not have been in vain. And I can only write about failures, so with most readers that doesn't go down very well.'

She gave a self-conscious laugh. I wasn't surprised she wrote about failures. She looked like one and rubbed it in by adding, 'I know what if feels like to be shunned.'

I lifted one of her paperbacks from the coffee table, suspecting she had put it there when she knew I was coming. The title was *The Wages of Fear*. The picture on the cover showed a doleful woman holding a baby.

'I don't know if you've read it,' she said, 'but you can have that copy if you like.'

'No thanks, I have one,' I said hurriedly. I didn't want to hurt her feelings, but there's a limit to being obliging.

'How is it selling?' I asked. 'You should be well off by now with money from your royalties.'

'What royalties?' she said bitterly. 'I could have made more money cleaning houses.'

'Still,' I said, 'being known as a writer gives you prestige. The publishers invite you to cocktail parties and to signing your books in shops. Aren't you proud of what you've accomplished?'

'Not really. I wasn't popular. Drink up, there's more where that came from.'

I held out my glass, feeling sucked into a drinking session I didn't want. I had come because on the phone she sounded desperate. I said, 'One more drink then I'll have to go home. Matthew will be wondering where I've got to.'

'Surely you don't have to worry about Matthew?'

I was annoyed by this but before I could reply she leaned forward and took my hand saying, 'Don't go yet, you're the only friend I have nowadays.'

She sounded tearful. I could hardly tell her I wasn't a friend so said, 'I'll stay for ten minutes.'

The bottle on the table was now half empty.

I had come to know Isabel by accident. A crowd where I worked was going to a book launch and invited me along so I went, though it was not my idea of a good time. But we were given a glass of wine and treated to a reading by the famous author Isobel Anderson, who I had never heard of. Someone said she was very entertaining. I don't like being read to and found her boring, but we all cheered up when offered a second glass of wine, and I felt better when introduced to her. Later she came with us to a pub round the corner and we stayed there late, laughing, joking and acting in the foolish way women act when drunk. Isobel fitted in well with our company and promised to come out with us on the next literary occasion. We met her once or twice again but when these meetings petered out I was not sorry. All Isobel spoke of was herself and other writers she knew, and here I now was in her shabby room and not happy about it.

She filled my glass again and I decided I would certainly leave after finishing this one. She said, 'You don't know what it feels like, being ostracised.'

'I don't know what you mean.'

'Nowadays you and your friends never get in touch with me. What have I done? I often wonder about that.'

'Nothing!' I said, trying not to show embarrassment, 'We thought you had better things to do than come out with us.'

'Not really. Nobody wants to know me and I can't write any more. I don't know what's wrong with me. I've no energy nowadays.'

'Why not cut down on your drinking? Maybe that's what's wrong.'

I was only guessing that she drank too much but had stopped caring about her. I had told Matthew I wouldn't be long and had now been away for more than an hour. She said, 'Why do you think I drink too much? You don't know a thing about me.'

'True,' I said, and stood up, and she burst into tears. It was hard for me not to leave at once. I said, 'Oh, come on now, it's not that bad. You've just got to apply yourself like Hemmingway did, three hours of writing every morning, leaning with one elbow on a dresser.'

'No wonder he killed himself,' she said with a rueful smile, drying her eyes with the back of her hand. 'Unluckily my writing was based on my family.'

'What do you mean?'

'I put all the drastic things that happened to the family in that novel. When my mother found out she said I was a disgrace, writing about events that were nobody else's business. She's stopped talking to me.'

'Is that why you stopped writing?'

'Not altogether. But I dried up, and with the family not talking to me I began hitting the bottle. So you are looking at a ruined woman. Let's drink to that.'

I was now getting sozzled and forgot to say I didn't want any more.

We didn't speak for a while. The vodka was making me tired. I had difficulty keeping my eyes open. Though desperate to get home I felt sorry for her and it came as a shock when she asked for a loan of twenty pounds, saying I would be paid back first thing when she got her giro. I gave her it, just to get away, then looked at my watch and said, 'Time to go.'

She said, 'But you've hardly been here – it's still early.'

'But Matthew worries if I'm away for long.'

'Is he still in a wheelchair?'

'Yes, and always will be.'

'I'm sorry. What happened to him anyway?'

I knew she wasn't interested in Matthew and was just asking to keep me there.

'He was knocked down by a motorbike. I thought you knew.'

'I forgot. I don't remember things half the time. I suppose it's because –'

'Because what?'

She hesitated then said, 'I have cancer.'

I was shocked into silence. Saying sorry didn't seem appropriate, and I didn't know whether to believe her. She had already said she didn't know what was wrong with her. At last I said, 'Are you sure?'

'The doctor says I've got roughly six months. Don't look so serious!' she laughed. 'I'm used to the idea.'

'Is there anything I can do?' I asked stupidly, wishing more than ever to be out of this stuffy apartment smelling of vodka, then I remembered vodka has no smell.

'No, there's nothing, but thanks all the same. Yes there is. Please get me another bottle.'

My sympathy vanished as she handed me back the note I'd given her.

'Alright,' I said, 'I won't be long.'

Outside I hurried past the licensed grocer and reached the bus stop before turning back again. I couldn't leave her waiting for what seemed the only medicine that helped.

'I'm back,' I shouted, hurrying up the stairs. 'I'm sorry I took so long.'

The front door was unlocked but the living room empty. An empty glass lay on the floor. Her book was still on the table. I called her name but she was gone. Before leaving I took the book, though I don't know why. I might never read it, on the other hand I might, so the next time I called I could discuss it with her instead of feeling guilty. But in my heart I knew I wouldn't call on her again.

At home Matthew noticed the glum look on my face and asked what was wrong. In bed that night I told him about Isobel having only six months to live. He said, 'Don't take it to heart, there's always people worse off than us. Besides, you've got me.'

He shut my mouth with a kiss. I began to feel better and fell asleep in his arms. He hardly ever sleeps but never complains, which is what I like about him. Five months later I saw Isobel's obituary in the paper and wondered if she had been alone when she died.

Confessions of a Serial Killer

M y life, as I remember it, began when I started school at the age of five years. A boy of the same age broke the zip of my new jumper so I punched and kicked him until he lay on the ground sobbing, then I ran home and told my mother that I wasn't ever going to school again. But she was adamant. I had to return and take my punishment. At that moment I stopped loving her, for it was the first time I did not get my own way.

For the next ten years I was a sullen pupil with no aptitude for learning. I scribbled on my jotter and drew skeletons sticking out of chimney tops. The teacher said I must be attracted to evil and put me at the bottom of the class. When fifteen I fell in love with an older girl who was beautiful and proud and never looked at me. I wrote her a letter declaring my love, then immediately tore it up. It was a relief when she and her parents moved away from the district.

After school I got a job in an office where I stamped envelopes and made tea for the staff who hardly spoke to me, though I felt their glances on my back. I left that job and lay all day in my bed for as long as I could.

'Whatever will we do with you?' said my mother.

'Send him to work on a pig farm,' said my father.

They did, and I liked it. There was no one to criticise me and the pigs ignored me, making gentle piggy noises with their soft brown snouts. That went on until my father died and I was again under my mother's thumb. She made rules that I had to follow without question. I was not allowed out to play on Sundays and on fine evenings had to walk with her along the river bank. This was humiliating, especially if we met former school mates who jeered and called me a Mummy's Boy. But my mother said now that I was fatherless I must stay by her side or I'd be tempted to commit all sorts of crimes. But the pigs were my main preoccupation. I would sit on the fence round their pens, watching their fat bodies roll in the mud. The farmer told me, 'Be careful – if you fall in beside them they'll eat you as soon as look at you.'

This made me think of a perfect way to make Mother disappear, but it happened another way. She died after tripping over a crack in the pavement while taking me down to the river.

Then the war came and people started dying in air raids. That's when I discovered my talent for killing. While pretending to save those buried in rubble I would partly dig them out with my bare hands then finish them off. I had to be careful when other rescuers were around but they said, 'Look at that boy! He never stops trying to save those poor souls.'

Then I was called up by the army and sent abroad where I sometimes killed our own men as well as the enemy. It was an exciting time, but I was almost caught out. A fellow soldier followed me into ruins where I was pretending to help an old man find what had once been his home. I caught sight of this soldier from the corner of my eye and at once shot him dead, but was left with a bad feeling. Perhaps my luck was running out. I told the old man to go and he hobbled away without a backward glance.

After that I decided to lie low, but I was wounded and hospitalised. I never fully recovered from the shrapnel in my head but was fit enough to join the A.R.P. who were still picking up the living and the dead after raids in Britain. With so much temptation around I resumed my malpractices, sometimes killing prostitutes, not for sexual reasons but for the thrill of the chase. But at last I couldn't cope any more. Death was no novelty. I lost my appetite for it, being unable to compete with a war that was killing people in thousands. I decided to end my own life while I was still intact.

I took a dose of something lethal that should have killed an ox, and woke later with a nurse bending over me. She said, 'You'll be alright,' and for the second time in my life I fell in love. So we married and might have lived happily ever after, if I hadn't become restless for something more exciting. I didn't know exactly what at the time, but had the taste of blood in my mouth.

'Perhaps we should go a holiday,' said my wife.

'Where to?' I asked, thinking of the beaches in Normandy.

'Saltcoats,' she said, 'Or maybe Largs.'

'Why not Helensburgh or Dunoon?' I sneered. After years of disagreeing about it we finally went to Thailand and met the tsunami full in the face. I survived but my wife did not, which was unfair. But who am I to say what is unfair and what isn't?

When seventy-five, the doctor told me I had terminal cancer. 'Wonderful!' I thought. At last I was going to leave this world of misery behind, but first I would put my house in order and make a list of people I would take with me, and I could be as careless as I liked about doing that since there's no punishment when you're dead. But a week later the doctor told me he'd read the wrong report, I had years left to live being as healthy as the next man. I got so angry that I choked him on the spot and to this day don't remember how I disposed of the body. I think most murderers who get caught are those who have ulterior motives and plan to do it. I have always acted on impulse.

The years dragged on. I became the leader of a writers' group and wrote a short novel about a man who murders a doctor for no apparent reason. It wasn't a great success but sold well enough to make me know I'm made my mark on the world, which was all I ever really wanted. The group and I parted company when a member accused me of copying a well-known novel I hadn't heard of. I was so upset that I went home and hardly ever left the house except to buy food and other necessities. After living like that for a year I decided enough was enough and again made preparations for my death, this time making sure there were no hitches. I had the plastic bag ready, the aspirins, the bottle of whisky, the rope, and then the doorbell rang.

A young woman stood on the doorstep. She said, 'I'm from Care in the Community and I was wondering . . .'

My heart sank but I heard myself say, 'Do come in,' and resigned myself to the inevitable.

The Moneylender

Before giros came by post I remember my Da saying we should all start walking to the broo to save on bus fares, since now we were in the hands of that heartless Tory Thatcher woman. Marlene, my older sister, said he could go and take a fuck to himself, she wasn't going to walk. My brother Danny said he didn't mind walking as long as he had enough fags to last all day without having to borrow from our mother. I was still at school so didn't have to say anything. Danny was a dab hand at borrowing money from Mother, always promising to pay her back with an extra pound. I don't think she ever got that extra pound, but he always wore her down by begging until she went to fetch her purse from the freezer where we all knew she kept it. Danny told me he was training to be a moneylender, since it was the only occupation that paid well. My sister was training to be a hairdresser, but I wasn't training to be anything. I'd sit in my room with lipstick on, staring at myself in the mirror and trying to convince myself that I wasn't bad-looking, but when I went outside I could only recollect a tall skinny girl with long straggly hair.

My main entertainment in those days was waiting up for Danny to come back late and give me the low-down on what he'd been doing. Some of it was a laugh and some of it, from my point of view, very worrying, but I never criticised him. He was the only company I had.

'Can I come with you?' I once asked, knowing the answer would be no. He said, 'Who ever heard of a girl in a gang?' and I suspected he didn't want me to know everything he did. Then he brought a girlfriend home and I was really cheesed off.

'I don't like her,' I told him afterwards. 'You don't have to like her,' he said, 'and don't go waiting up for me any more.'

I was so shattered I cried myself to sleep, and next morning told him he needn't worry, I wouldn't ever wait up for him again.

'What's the matter with you two?' said my mother, who was usually blissfully unaware of anything outside our livingroom where she reigned like the Queen of Sheba.

'Nothing. He just makes me sick.'

'It's because she wants to know everything I do,' said Danny.

'Like what?' said my mother, suddenly becoming alert.

'Who I go around with and that.'

'He goes around with a slagheap,' I said. 'You should see her.'

'I don't suppose I'll ever see her.'

'I don't see why not,' I said. 'She's already in Danny's bed.'

'What?' she shrieked, and turned to Danny. 'If your father finds out he'll have a stroke. He's a very moral man and he won't put up with people having sex under his roof.'

'Then he should look the other way,' said Danny. Mother swiped him with a dishtowel then said, 'Watch your step, boy. What's her name?'

'Pearl Hunter.'

'Send her through.'

When Pearl entered the kitchen we all looked at her critically except Danny, who I supposed was used to looking at her. She wasn't all that good-looking and had a sharp, cheeky manner that no doubt got her places if you counted Danny's bed as one.

'They tell me you're hanging about with our Danny,' said Mother, tactless as usual.

'I'm going out with Danny if that's what you mean,' said Pearl, casting me a sideways glance. I knew her from school. She'd been one of the older ones.

'So when are you getting married?' said my big sister, staring at Pearl's stomach which was flat as a pancake.

'Don't be daft,' said Danny. 'We're nowhere near getting married.'

'We're too young,' said Pearl.

'One is never too young,' said Mother. I noticed Pearl spoke through her nose in a way that might eventually annoy most people, including Danny, I hoped.

'Go and get Pearl a cup of tea,' Mother told him. 'There should be one left in the pot.'

'I don't drink tea,' said Pearl primly, 'nor smoke either.'

'What do you do then?' said my big sister.

'She fucks,' said Danny. 'That's the main thing.'

The rest of us were shocked but Pearl didn't turn a hair.

'Mind your manners,' said Mother angrily, 'and while we're on the subject, I don't want any bastard child in this house.'

'Where do you want it then?' said Danny but his jokes had worn thin.

'And you don't go to bed with Danny in our house either,' said Mother, 'or I'll put his Da onto you and he'll soon sort you out.'

'And he's got a beard down to his kneecaps,' said Danny, 'so you wouldn't want that.'

'I wouldn't,' said Pearl with a sickly smile and walked out the door.

Our Da wasn't bad-looking when he shaved, which was seldom, but I liked him.

'Do something with yourself,' he'd say. 'Don't be like the rest of this family, all mouth and no go. Get a job.'

'Where will I get one?' I'd ask, but he'd have fallen asleep, having a habit of falling asleep halfway through conversations.

'It's all the drinking he does,' said Mother. 'It's rotted his brain.'

I asked her if I should put my name down to train as a hairdresser but she said, 'No way. You get lice off other people's hair,' so after school I stayed at home and helped with the housework. Pearl never came back so I got pally with Danny again. He said, 'She was always moaning about something and I've got better things to do.'

'Like what?' I asked.

'Like minding my own business.'

But he couldn't resist telling me he was becoming a moneylender in a big way.

'Look what I've got so far!' he said, showing me a ten pound note and some silver. I didn't think that was much, but he seemed pleased so I asked him about the bigger moneylenders we had already. They might not be happy with another, and might do him in. He laughed and said I had seen too many films. This did not cheer me up but I was glad we were talking again. One day I asked him, 'Why don't you settle down?'

'What, at my age?'

'Settle down in bed with a hot water bottle.'

This was my idea of a joke. Danny laughed and said he would have to remember that one. It is one of the good memories I have.

The next thing that happened was four young guys in Danny's room, half of which was mine. They sat with glazed eyes on the edge of his bed. I asked what was wrong with them.

'Stoned,' he said. 'Don't worry, they're alright,' then he fell across my bed as if he was stoned too. The youths slept all night on the floor and I never slept a wink. Danny was in my bed and I didn't want to disturb him. A few days later I told him I wished I had a boyfriend, and did he think I could go out with one of his mates?

'Don't you dare,' he said. 'Anyway you're too young to have a boyfriend.'

'Well, I didn't intend to have sex,' I said in a lofty tone, trying to appear grown up, but Danny got angry and said, 'Don't let me hear you say that word again.'

'What word?'

'Sex!' he very nearly shouted. At that my Ma came in and asked what the devil we were talking about.

'She says she wants a boyfriend,' said Danny, 'that's what we were talking about. I told her she's not getting one. She's too young.'

Ma hugged me as if I had an illness: 'You'll get one soon enough. When I was your age I was going out with your Da. And look where it's got me.'

I said, 'I don't want anybody like my Da,' and Ma took the huff and said, 'What a bloody little snob you've turned out to be.'

Danny and I made faces at each other, then we burst out laughing, and maybe that was the last time I saw him properly, because of the money lending.

He had once explained to me, 'If I lend out ten pounds I get two pound interest on it, and if I lend out five I get one pound.'

'What if you only lend a pound?'

'I don't lend anything less than a fiver. Less is more bother than it's worth.'

We stopped seeing him. He had always stayed out late but now he never came home. I began to worry and so did Mother. She said, 'I don't like when he disappears. I don't know where he is. He could be anywhere.'

Sometimes I got up at night in the dark to feel for him under the sheets but there was only the damp coldness of an empty bed, and I couldn't get back to sleep again.

'I hope he never comes back,' said my sister. 'He's the talk of the place.'

'What do they say?' asked my mother.

'They say he's a moneylender and carries a knife.'

'That's only to make folk who owe money pay up,' I said.

'Honest to God,' said my sister. 'With that attitude you'll likely become a moneylender yourself.'

But on one occasion Danny did show up in our bedroom. He woke me and put a finger to his lips, whispering, 'Don't tell Ma I'm here. I need to sleep first before I can face her.'

Then he fell into a deep sleep and I climbed in bed beside him to keep him warm for he was as cold as the bricks on our outside toilet. When I woke up he had gone and I would have cried and cried but I had to keep it secret. It would have upset Mother to think he'd been in the house without letting her know. Days after that she burst into the living room and told Da to get up off his arse since his son was fighting a gang of scumbags outside the shops and looked as though he was getting the worst of it.

'No fucking way,' said my Da huddling close to the electric fire. 'He likely had it coming.'

In the end my sister, myself and my mother marched to the shops, Marlene holding a sweeping brush that was hardly a dangerous weapon. Surprisingly the gang ran off when they saw us but Danny lay on the road near the morning traffic. We managed to get him onto the pavement then dragged him back to our house. Nobody helped except an old guy who said he'd been in the war, but he wasn't much use. We finally got Danny laid out carefully in bed but he didn't become conscious so we sent for an ambulance. When it left Mother said, 'He's in safe hands now,' but I wasn't sure because of blood on the pillow. I got a taxi and we all went to the hospital except Da, who stayed huddled over the fire, crying and too drunk to be useful. At the hospital one of the doctors told us Danny was dead.

It's been six months since he was buried and I hardly ever leave my room that was half Danny's. Mother keeps looking in to see if I'm alright. I'm supposed to be a suicide risk because I tried slashing my wrist, but though I'm alright now she thinks I can't be trusted. I saw a shrink once a fortnight until he said I didn't need to come back because it's up to me now. Honestly, I don't know what he got paid for if it's up to me. Still, I shouldn't complain. The social paid for the visits as well as the funeral.

'They're not bad that way at times,' says Mother.

The Phantom Rapist

My stepfather Joe McAndless was a terrible drunk. No one guessed it who didn't know him well. He had a stern handsome face that seldom smiled but gave an appearance of knowledge and kindliness. In the pub he was the most generous of men, buying drinks all round for acquaintances but giving my mother the smallest possible part of his wages, and nothing at all to me. After my father died he had visited our house without being invited. My mother told me later she was so lonely in those days she would have welcomed anyone. I was with them at the Registrar Office when they married and afterwards accompanied them for high tea at the City Bakers. I was only eight then and thought my stepfather a decent enough man. By the time I was ten I hated him. There were occasions when he tried to keep in with me by offering a drink from his bottle. I sometimes took it to shut up his slushy voice while my mother sat by the fire moaning and shaking her head. As soon as he went out she would rush to the licensed grocers for something to calm her nerves and I'd go out on the rampage with my pals, which meant running through hedges and banging on doors. Despite McAndless I believe I was happy in those days. As I grew older I became less happy. I was always sore from the beatings he gave me for stealing from the Pakki shop, though everybody stole from the Pakki shop. Even the Pakkis did it. Then came events that put everything else in the shade. A phantom rapist appeared among us.

One dark evening old Mrs Leadbetter was pushed to the ground on her way to the library and raped, but refused a medical examination: 'Not at my age!' she said. Then Rita Johnstone, a loose type of woman aged about thirty, was apparently dragged into a close and raped before the eyes of a guy from the pub next door – he had gone there for a quick piss because there was a big queue at the pub toilet. At different intervals after that three elderly women were raped but refused to be interviewed by the local newspaper, though they all agreed that the assailant wore a long black coat and smelled of peppermint. This information was no use to the local police. Women of any age became afraid to go out alone and membership of the bingo hall went down at an alarming rate. My stepfather said this was a punishment for those who indulged in carnal sin, a remark that seemed aimed at my mother who hardly ever left her seat by the fire. One night when he put on his long black coat to go to the pub it struck me that he could be the rapist, especially when he asked me if I would like a mint imperial. I refused, saying I did not know he liked mint imperials. He said he got them for his throat as he was always coughing. I said, 'I never heard you coughing.'

We looked at each other for a moment and I was sure his eyes flickered away first.

From her seat by the fire my mother said, 'Don't be drinking too much.'

'Do I ever?' he asked.

When he left I decided to follow him. This was not easy. I stood for ages outside his usual drinking den until at last he came out surrounded by cronies and well-wishers shaking his hand, but I saw no females and trailed homeward behind him. We never passed a soul so my mission had been pointless. I was in a bad mood when I entered the house and saw Joe in a chair apparently asleep with his black coat still on. But he opened one eye and said, 'Where have you been?'

'None of your business,' I said, at which he sprang up and kicked my leg. This was not unexpected and even welcomed. It increased my hatred of him and added strength to my convictions.

'Get to bed,' he said, 'and watch your step in future for I've got my eye on you.'

Next morning my mother excitedly told us there had been another rape. Joe said he knew all about it. How could he know? I wondered. We had not read the morning paper yet and I had left him the night before settling down in his chair again. As if reading my thoughts he said, 'It was on the radio.'

'Did they catch him?' asked my mother, clutching the tea cosy to her chest as though protecting herself.

'Of course not,' said my stepfather, 'and I bet they never catch him.'

I looked at him intently. He seemed to enjoy the fact that they'd never catch the rapist, but I supposed that proved nothing.

'By the way,' he added to my mother, 'your son was in later than me last night. I think he needs to be taught a lesson.'

'Is that true?' she asked in a quavering voice, and I wished she would stand up for me sometimes. He made to unfasten his trouser belt and suddenly I couldn't take that any more and said, 'Touch me and I'll kill you.'

That made no impression on him. He knocked over a cup of tea lying on the arm of the sofa and said, 'Outside boy.'

'Outside yourself!' I said, 'And don't think I don't know what you're up to.'

I don't know why I said that. Perhaps it was desperation because I had no chance of resisting a man like my stepfather who was all pure muscle, but he let the belt dangle and his face went pale.

'What do you mean?' he asked.

'Never you mind,' I said, unsure of what I meant. Maybe I was right about him but I had nothing to prove it. But I must have knocked the fire out of him because all he said was, 'I'm going out and you'd better not be here when I get back.'

'I'm going out too,' I said reaching for my jacket with a bravado I did not feel.

I spent another wearisome time hanging around the pub in the cold. I noticed a woman on the pavement opposite, thought she might be waiting to be picked up by someone and considered telling her to go home and not put herself at risk. I didn't because I was too shy. I began pacing up and down to keep warm, and to pass the time even walked round the block. Noticing that the woman had gone I decided to leave too because the chances that my stepfather was the rapist were becoming less and less and I was beginning to feel the biggest fool on earth. Then the pub door opened and a crowd of men crushed out because it was closing time and I hadn't even noticed. I was about to leave before McAndless saw me, but a hurried glance showed he wasn't in that crowd. I waited instead, and when the street was empty went to the pub door and looked through a chink at the side of the blind in the side of the glass panel.

I saw a barman serving a woman seated at the counter, which surprised me since the pub was supposed to be closed. Two men I had not seen before came over and sat beside her with glasses in their hands, drinking and laughing and smoking in a totally relaxed manner. What's this? I wondered. Did it happen every night after the pub closed? And where was my stepfather? The woman turned and I saw she was my stepfather wearing a head-scarf, a long pleated skirt and a tweed jacket. Before I could make sense of this the man beside him planted a kiss on his cheek and I would have fallen in through the door with the shock, if it hadn't been locked. At first I thought it was some kind of joke, but some-thing else told me it wasn't and I didn't wait to see more.

That night it was I who waited up for Joe. 'Why aren't you in bed?' he said. 'Do you want a belt in the mouth?'

'No. Do you?' I said, adding the word, 'Poofter.'

Joe dropped on the floor the belt he had been unwinding.

'What do you mean?'

'I thought you were a rapist but you're only a poofter. Wait till mother hears about this. And the neighbours. And all those folk who think you're so great.'

'I'll deny everything,' he said, but his voice was shaking.

'The chances are they'll want to believe it.'

Looking at me with eyes that were as tight as gimlets he said, 'Keep your mouth shut and I'll make it worth your while, otherwise I'll beat you to within an inch of your life.'

I thought about that and decided it wasn't worth getting more scars for.

'How about twenty quid for a start?'

He gave me the twenty quid, then had the temerity to shake my hand as if we'd come to some business agreement, but before the week was up he had gone.

My mother couldn't understand what made him leave without a word but on the whole she was pleased.

'Probably found another woman,' she said, 'but I don't mind, as long as he doesn't come back.'

'Believe me, he won't.' I said, 'I hear he's left town.'

It's a funny thing but the phantom rapist never struck again. Some folk said it had all been a pack of lies told by women well past their prime who'd do anything for a bit of attention. That's what my mother says and she is now an authority on the subject of men. But I have warned her not to go visiting pubs on her own, because if my stepfather wasn't the phantom rapist, who was?

Annie Rogerson

When I was a child my mother sent me to Sunday School hoping it would make me a happy, spirited youngster instead of the sullen one I'd become.

'Why can't you be more like Annie Rogerson?' she would say. 'Look how she goes walks with her mother, and sweeps the stairs and hangs out the washing without any arguments, unlike you who wouldn't do a hand's turn of work, not even if you were paid for it.'

'Yeah, and everybody laughs at her for being such a goody-two-shoes,' I said. 'No way do I want to be like her.'

'I wouldn't want my daughter laughed at,' said my mother, 'on the other hand –'

I walked out before she finished the sentence but had to smile. First she wanted me to go walking with her, then to sweep the stairs and hang out washing. Next thing she'd be wanting me to take piano lessons, yet she didn't want me to be laughed at, which would surely happen if the big shots at school got to hear of it. But it's a fact that my mother is a snob. I had annoyed her by stopping going to Sunday School long ago, though she's told me umpteen times that she doesn't believe in God. She'd say, 'I'm what they call a Humanist. I go to church if I feel like it, and if not –'

Then she'd snap her fingers in the air like a Spanish dancer. I thought her a real pain in the neck, chopping and changing her mind about nearly everything. I was ashamed of her twittery laugh and how she couldn't pass a shop window without admiring herself in it.

'Yes Mum, you are beautiful,' I would say, then she'd tell me it was only because she was unsure of herself, not because she was conceited. I didn't like the subject because I was always looking in mirrors too, hoping to see a better version of my long skinny body and head that was far too small.

'I wish you wouldn't slouch,' she'd say when we went out together, so I added slouching to my list of bad points. I was the ugliest person in the street except for my mother, who was small and dumpy with legs like a boxer's. When we were out one day I spied some school acquaintances on the far side of the road and said, 'I must go now.'

'Where?' she asked.

'Into that shop – I see someone I know.'

Before she could open her mouth I sped along the street and joined another gang of acquaintances, hoping anybody watching would think I was part of it. As if anybody cared, but that's how I was in those days.

'I suppose you're going to the annual school dance?' said my mother.

'Not if I can help it.'

'Oh, but you must. I don't want anyone thinking I can't afford to buy you a dress. I'll sew you one, and don't worry. It will be in a modern style.'

'Then I'm definitely not going.'

'Annie Rogerson is going. Her mother told me.'

'Then that makes it a certainty I won't be.'

My mother nagged so much that I ended by going and bumped into Annie also heading for the school hall. Of course from our point of view the dance was a failure. I stood at one end of the orange-juice counter and Annie at the other. The only ones who came near us were some who ordered orange juice because they thought we were serving it. I wasn't pleased when Annie Rogerson approached and whispered something in my ear. I was about to push her away when I saw she was pointing to the opening in her cheap-looking handbag, and inside was a half-bottle of vodka that seemed to be full. 'Are you offering me some?' I said in a hushed voice.

'If you want,' she said. 'You can take it with orange juice.'

I was surprised to see how quick and expert she was at pouring some vodka into a paper cup then filling it up with the juice.

'Do you always take vodka with you wherever you go?' I asked.

'Nearly always. Sometimes it's other stuff.'

My admiration for her knew no bounds. We finished the vodka before a teacher appeared, said, 'What's going on here?' and fished out the empty bottle.

'Somebody must have put it in my bag,' said Annie, all innocence. The teacher looked at both of us intently, then said, 'Come with me. I believe you are both drunk.'

Our parents were sent for and my mother went mad when we got home.

'To think of the showing up!' she moaned. 'We'll have to leave the district.'

'I don't see why,' I said. 'It was Annie who brought in the vodka. She must have slipped some into my orange juice when I wasn't looking.'

'Are you telling the truth?'

'Of course I am. I wouldn't lie about a thing like that.'

'Then I'll have to see her parents about it,' said my mother. 'I'm beginning to think they're a funny lot. Her father's a strange man to say the least. I heard he steals women's knickers off clothes lines.'

'At least she's got a father,' I said, 'which is more than I have.'

'Your father died in a coal mining accident, which is nothing to be ashamed of.'

'Of course not, but I thought he died in a train disaster. That's what you told me last time.'

'I don't remember telling you any such thing. You must be mistaken.'

There was no point in arguing because she always won. She kept me indoors next day. I could easily have climbed out the bedroom window but why bother? There was nowhere to go. So I looked out of that window like a dumb dog waiting for its master, not seeing much beyond a line of green council bins and wishing I was dead. Then I stiffened. I saw Annie Rogerson leave the back end of the close. I expected her to start sweeping the path, which my mother said she was always doing, but instead she put a big black bottle into the bin. And it wasn't a sauce bottle.

'How much vodka does she drink in a day?' I wondered, then heard a man's voice calling. Annie ran back into the close.

Next day I was let out. It was Sunday and I decided to ask Annie if she'd like to come out and play with me – 'Only if you want to,' I would add, in case she thought I'd become desperate. I knocked on her door but there was no answer, so I tiptoed away feeling thoroughly fed up. When Monday came I was almost glad to be going to school. I met Annie on the road and by way of conversation said, 'I haven't seen you around lately.'

'I don't go out much.'

'They tell me I was drunk at the school dance,' I said, deciding to take the bull by the horns.

'I never noticed,' she said.

'With all that vodka,' I added.

'What vodka?'

I was astonished by the cool way she denied all knowledge of it. She frowned for a moment, then her brow cleared. She said, 'I remember taking medicine in the hall. I have an infection and have to take it every four hours or it will only get worse.'

I thought she was either mad or a very cunning liar.

'You must think I'm stupid,' I said, and slapped her face.

She ran off crying. I never saw her at school again or even around the back green. I blamed myself for this but thought it didn't make her less of a liar.

Then it was Sunday again, a rotten day for me at the best of times. Suddenly my mother burst into the room and said, 'Annie Rogerson's father is in all the papers, accused of interfering with his daughter after giving her vodka and other stuff to knock her out.'

I digested this information for a minute then was sick on the carpet.

'My good carpet!' moaned my mother. 'What have you been eating?'

I pushed past her and took a bath, trying not to think of Annie crying when I slapped her. Afterwards I sat looking out the window down toward the bins, wishing Annie would come out so that I could talk to her, maybe have a laugh with her at the idea of vodka being medicine. But I couldn't have done that, it was too serious. The back green had a desolate look. Likely Annie's house was empty.

'Come and get your breakfast,' I heard my mother shout.

'I'm not hungry,' I told her in the kitchen. 'But I might as well go to Sunday School this afternoon. There's nothing else to do.'

My mother clapped her hands.

'Oh, I am so glad! Sunday School could be the making of you, for no matter what we say it's always better to believe in God, don't you think?'

Visiting the Elderly

Every Wednesday my friend Maisie and I visited Mary Mountbank who was one hundred and one years old. Maisie and I were in our eighties so felt comparatively young. We mainly visited her because we knew nobody else older than us. Mary always put out a nice pot of tea with some Campbell's shortbread fingers, but she never washed and always went back to bed after letting us in so we usually avoided the shortbread. She did not add much to our conversation and mostly lay silent and brooding. When it became too obvious that she was being ignored we would ask how she was keeping and with a hostile stare she always answered, 'Fine.'

'Do you still take a wee dram of whisky, now and again?' I would ask and she'd say 'yes' and nothing else. This annoyed me as I was only trying to be friendly to an old woman nobody else could bother with. Maisie was better with questions, saying things like, 'Does your daughter still come in to do your washing?' though Mary would reply unpleasantly, 'Not a bit of it.'

Once I asked if she had thought of going into an old folk's home?

'Indeed no,' said Mary. 'I'm not thinking of going anywhere.'

'You're quite right,' I said, 'I hear the inmates get beaten up a lot and the food leaves a lot to be desired.'

Maisie gave me a dunt with her elbow to make me shut up.

'Anyway I'm not going,' said Mary. 'And you can tell my daughter that.'

Little did she know her daughter had already told us, 'She's going in next September, if we're lucky.'

344

'She won't like it,' Maisie had said.

'She's got no choice,' said the daughter. 'She can't be left alone or she'll set the house on fire.'

'It'll come to us all,' I had said, hoping it would never come to me. 'But I'd rather fall under a bus.'

The daughter walked away and we had stared after her, Maisie saying, 'That woman has a callous streak.'

I had agreed and said the family should roast in hell for their miserable attitude toward an old woman. And here we were again, visiting Mary who did not know she would get put away in September.

'Mind you,' I told her, 'there's a lot of fine old folks' homes where you could be happy as Larry watching the television and eating good quality meals three times a day and having a game of bingo if you like it. Do you not fancy that?'

She said, 'I told you already I won't be going. So shut your gob and have one of those Campbell's shortbreads.'

Gamely we took one each and I shoved mine into a pocket so hard it burst the lining.

'And anyway,' said Mary, 'they say the doctor in some types of home gets up early and rapes the old while they're doped up with their happy pills.'

Maisie and I howled with laughter at the idea.

'If that's so,' I said, 'I'll sign myself into one of those homes tomorrow.'

Next moment Mary was sound asleep and snoring.

'Should we leave while she's so peaceful?' said Maisie.

I said, 'Wait until the rain goes off.'

The room was so stuffy that I was about to doze off myself when Maisie said, 'The worst of a home is they don't let you keep the bits and pieces that prove you were once a real person.'

'They don't have room for them,' I said, 'and they don't care what you were like before.'

'I believe I was quite attractive at one time,' said Maisie.

I said, 'I never thought I was attractive at all, but I must have been because I managed to get married.'

'We hardly remember anything,' said Maisie, 'but I remember fancying the coalman, though his face and hands were so black we daren't even kiss.'

'If he was that black,' I said, 'how could you fancy him? You couldn't see what he looked like.'

'He showed me a photograph,' she said. We were silent for a while, listening to Mary's snores, then Maisie asked if I had ever fancied anyone apart from my old man.

'I never fancied my old man much. He didn't have a lot in the way of looks and had a temper like a tiger, but according to him I fancied everyone in trousers, though I don't remember why he said that.'

'Yes,' said Maisie, 'everything's a blur nowadays. Do you want another of these shortbreads?'

'Take one if you like,' I said, 'I suppose one will do you no harm if you see nothing like shit on it.'

'Do you have to say that?' said Maisie.

We noticed Mary had gone silent and stared at her as if thinking the same thing. I said, 'She's not breathing.'

Maisie put her ear close to the old woman's chest, which was more than I could have done, then said, 'She's alright.'

I said, 'Thank God. I wouldn't like to be the last one to see her alive.'

'Nor me,' said Maisie, 'though it would save her from going into a home.'

'True,' I said, 'though I'd rather she didn't die in this hole. It's dark.'

We felt for the electric switch, put it on and found the room looked better in the dark. I disliked the litter on the table next to the bed recess, where a half-empty bottle of juice lay beside a bed pan. I said, 'Let's go, now she's out for the count.'

But we looked sadly at Mary for a while. I said, 'Maybe this is the last time we'll see her.'

'Don't worry about that. She's the type that will live to be two hundred. But before we leave there's a question I'd like to ask you.'

'As long as it's not for the lend of a fiver,' I said, laughing.

'Is it true that years ago you had an affair with my old man?'

I was so shocked I could hardly speak, but managed to say, 'Who told you that?'

'Someone said that when my Alec was doing his night watchman along in Healy Street, half the time he was in your house shagging you rotten while your old man was asleep in his bed.'

For a minute I thought I was going to pass out I was so flabbergasted, but I pulled myself together and said, 'Whoever told you that is a terrible liar! That's all I can say, and why did you not ask me that question sooner instead of keeping it to yourself all these years?'

'I was always meaning to but I could never find the right words.'

'So you had to wait until Mary was at death's door?'

'It was old Mary that told me.'

'Why the dirty old bitch,' I said, angry spittles flying from my mouth. 'Let me tell you this, I wouldn't have your old man touch me with a bargepole. You'd better believe me than her lying there. Don't forget she was always a gossip and I hope she roasts in hell for all the damage she's done in her miserable life.'

In silence we crept down the outside stairs of the building. I looked back at Mary's dark window. To think of her lying there, not even dead! I'll tell you this much, I won't be visiting her again, the old gossipmonger, and may God have mercy on her soul.

Chairles Will Pay

My mother's family were a funny lot, always playing tricks and frightening each other half to death. That's what my mother told me when we were looking through old photos, some so faded I could hardly make them out.

'That's your Uncle Sanny,' she said, pointing to a snapshot of a young man wearing what looked like baggy dungarees. 'He was the worst of the lot. He pinned a poster of a big stork on the wall just before my sister Agnes came home. In those days you found posters of storks all over the place advertising Stork margarine.'

'What had that to do with your sister Agnes?' I asked.

'Well, you know a stork has long thin legs?'

'Yes.'

'So had Agnes. She wasn't bad-looking but her legs were long and thin.'

'I still don't get it,' I said.

'Sanny had said her legs were like a stork's so at the sight of that poster on the wall she chased him round the room hitting him with her handbag until he headed out the door laughing. And then there was my sister Jeanie. She liked to think she was a lady and would ask a female to tea in our shabby old parlour, and before you could say Jack Robinson Sanny would invite the guest to sit on a chair shoved against the wall for show because it had only three legs. You can imagine the outcry when it and the guest crashed to the floor. And there was my brother John who came to school barefoot, just to give me a showing up when he was sent into my class to get the belt. Mind you, I can laugh now when I look back and think of him. He never got to be a grown man. He was killed at the Somme on his first day in France.'

How rotten, I thought, that I never knew my uncles. They sounded fun, so unlike my mother who I thought a bit of a snob. She said, 'The most awful joke Sanny played was when my Granny died. Her coffin was put in the parlour, which was really our dumping ground for bits of furniture we couldn't bear to throw away. It lay on a big table covered by a red velvet cloth. The lid was slid down so we could see Granny's head rested on a white ruffled pillow that reminded me of the paper you get wrapped round a layer cake. When the coffin was closed a single red rose was tastefully displayed on the lid. I remember thinking that if Granny could see all this she would have been pleased. It only needed the bagpipes to play her off. But as we couldn't even pay for the funeral bagpipes were out of the question.'

'Then who paid for the funeral?' I asked.

'My Uncle Chairles was going to pay, but it was like getting blood out of a stone. I haven't told you the awful thing Sanny did.'

'What was it?' I asked, trying to sound interested.

'A neighbour came into the parlour to pay her respects to Granny and heard low groans from the coffin that would have made your hair stand on end. Then she seemed to hear Granny's voice screeching, 'Get that dirty brute oot ma sicht.' This was Sanny hiding under the table cover. Then a black cat dashed out miawling like mad and the neighbour fainted, though mind you I think she was putting it on a bit. Did you know your great-granny was in the Crimea War?'

'No,' I said, startled. 'Did she fight like a soldier?'

'She was a nurse, a sort of nurse. She tended to the wounded and the dying. Do you know she had to wipe their wounds with the bottom of her petticoat because there was nothing else to wipe them with?'

'Did she really?' I said, thinking it typical of this family to wipe soldiers' wounds with a dirty petticoat instead of wiping their

AGNES OWENS

fevered brows with a cold cloth like you see in the films. But perhaps there were no films in those days. I was about to ask when Mother said her granny had married a soldier called Gregor Grant who died of pneumonia, and after that married another soldier called Stewart who went back to being a ploughman when the war was over.

'She seemed to have a liking for soldiers.' I said. 'It's a wonder we're not related to Bonnie Prince Charlie.'

'I wouldn't be surprised if we were. Which reminds me I told you my Uncle Chairles said he would pay for his mother's funeral, but apparently never did.'

'Oh yes?' I said, wanting to go and play with my new skipping ropes in the cold spring sunshine.

'Well, he may have paid in the long run but for days the family were always looking out for a letter with money inside but none came. Then matters took a turn for the better. My mother and a friend attended a spiritualist meeting, which had become very popular in those days. Most families had lost someone in the Great War so everybody wanted to get a message from their dead son or brother. Mother had handed over a handkerchief belonging to Granny, one she had been clutching when she made her last gasp. Mother came home and said she got a message from the spiritualist in a voice that sounded just like Granny's, saying, 'Don't worry, Chairles will pay.'

'Did she say when?' asked my father who'd been about to pay for the funeral by taking a job as a coalman. Later he said he knew all along Chairles would pay, for he'd seen it happen in a dream. Whether this was true or not we never heard another word from Chairles, but the family's faith in spiritualism remained steadfast, because Granny had heard the piper's lament for the Stewart clan before she died, and not a single note of it was heard by anyone else . . . 'Or was it the lament for the Grants that she heard?' said my mother doubtfully. 'My memory's getting terrible nowadays.'

350

'So we don't know whether we're descended from the Stewarts or the Grants?' I asked.

She said, 'Does it matter? These clan folks are all the same when you come down to it, very superstitious, and that's a fact.'

'So who paid for the funeral?' I asked.

'I'm not sure. Maybe Chairles did eventually. He was supposed to.'

Don't Call Me

'**D**on't call me, I'll call you,' was the usual response I got on Alice's answering machine. She never phoned me until one early evening I heard her say, 'You'll have to help. I'm in deep shit.'

I am not spiteful but those words sounded like music in my ear. I asked what was wrong.

'I can't explain on the phone,' she said. 'You'll have to come round.'

Alice and I had once been married for five years. She was a born flirt, I was a heavy gambler, so it was not a perfect relationship. To prove I wasn't a complete bastard I overlooked a lot of her bad points. She overlooked none of mine until we couldn't stand each other.

'Two thousand pounds you owe me!' she flung in my face one day. 'Clear out!'

I did, and things turned out well for me. I got a Post Office job. She, on the other hand, took up with a gangster called Tony the Teeth, and her answer machine told me not to interfere with that relationship.

She answered the door of our old flat, looking furtively past me up and down the corridor. I asked her what was wrong.

'It's Tony the Teeth,' she said. 'He's here first thing in the morning, last thing at night and three times a day when I'm out, according to the neighbours.'

'I'm surprised,' I said. 'I heard Tony's not such a bad guy. Can't you tell him to beat it?'

'It's not as simple as that. I owe him a thousand pounds and he wants it back right away and he won't take no for an answer.'

I started to open my mouth but she went on, 'He says I can pay him back in kind, if you know what I mean, but he wouldn't be content with just the once. He would want me to do it all the time. Actually he wants to move in with me.'

I gave a low whistle then said, 'You are in very deep shit.'

Maybe it served her right for treating me as she had, but Tony the Teeth is the most unpleasant guy I've ever seen. His long yellow teeth stick out like rocks. His skin is so full of blackheads that you'd think his face had been dipped in coal dust. His smile is like a promise of certain death.

'So you want me to give Tony the works?' I said in an incredulous tone. 'I don't think I could manage that.'

'I know,' she said, smudging her mascara as she wiped eyes that were as dry as a bone. 'But maybe you could lend me a thousand pounds considering you already owe me two thousand.'

'But that was long ago,' I pointed out. 'And since we're divorced I now owe you nothing.'

'Tony doesn't look at it that way. He says you're responsible for my debt, and nobody can argue with him.'

Almost speechless with anger I asked how Tony knew about me in the first place.

'I've no idea. Maybe I mentioned it casually in the course of our relationship.'

'You had a *relationship* with him?'

'We were just good friends.'

'So,' I said, 'because you owe one thousand to someone else you expect me to hand over two thousand to you. Well, life isn't like that, so go fuck yourself.'

'I wish you wouldn't swear. You know how I hate it.'

'Yes, you were always a snob, but my answer is still the same. I don't have a thousand to spare, and don't get paid till Thursday, so haven't a penny on me.'

'You have a job?' She sounded surprised.

'Damn right I have. The minute I left you I got lucky.'

'I thought you didn't believe in work. That's one of the reasons we split.'

'I decided I needed exercise and fresh air so am now a postman.'

As I said this it occurred to me I should have kept my mouth shut.

'That's marvellous!' she said with a big smile and at that moment I wouldn't have minded a night in the sack with her. It was a passing thought. I didn't want to go through the hell of loving her again, but we stared at each other for much longer than was necessary until I said, 'I'm sorry I can't help you with your troubles, honey. Believe me, I would if I could.'

Her smile became fixed. She said, 'It's alright, I'll just have to give Tony what he wants.'

Then I looked at my ex-wife from her long shiny auburn hair down to her neat little feet with pearl-encrusted shoes and said impulsively, 'I won't let him near you.'

'What do you mean?'

'What I say.'

A look of annoyance crossed her face. 'You couldn't stop him. Look at you!'

I knew what she meant. I've always considered myself a sorry specimen, but I grinned and said, 'I could always get a gun.'

Then I wished I had bitten my tongue out instead. What was I letting myself in for? Her voice softened. She said, 'I know you mean well but you couldn't tackle him on your own. You don't know him like I do.'

I thought that was true. Who the hell wanted to know him anyway? In this soft husky voice she went on, 'If I could pay him off he would have no excuse to move in with me which is what I'm most afraid of. Can you imagine it?'

I couldn't, and we were both silent as if she was waiting for me to speak. I began nervously scratching my head, then heard myself say, 'Maybe I could get a bank loan.'

'You could?' she said, her eyes wide and interested.

'Well, I work in the Post Office. You can always get a loan if you're working.'

'You're right!' she said, still staring as if she saw me in a new light. By now I regretted my words but it was too late to unsay them.

'I'll pay you back,' she said, 'with interest.'

'How about a kiss to be going on with?'

She backed off, said, 'Don't complicate things, I'm in enough trouble.'

'Sorry,' I said, sheepishly, wondering why I was apologising when doing her a favour. I reminded myself that I could change my mind.

'When will you get the money?'

'Friday at the latest.' My lips were saying different things to what was happening in my head.

'No sooner?'

'I'm sorry but I don't get paid until Thursday, so Friday's the soonest,' I said, trying not to sound sarcastic.

'That's alright,' she said quickly. 'It just means I'll have to go into hiding or Tony will be on to me before you can say Jack the Ripper. Friday will be fine.'

On Thursday after I was paid I went to the bank and borrowed two thousand, one for her and one for me. It struck me I could have borrowed more, but let it go. I decided to take Alice out for a meal to celebrate the occasion. She declined the offer, saying, 'We can't be seen together, somebody might tell Tony.'

'You said you'd be alright if you gave him the money.'

'He doesn't like me being with other men, no matter what,' she said.

I gave her the cheque for one thousand and she said thanks a lot but she'd have to go now. Instead of visiting my usual pub that evening I bought a bottle and sat on the edge of my bed, talking to myself. Actually I was talking to Tony the Teeth, not that he was with me but he was there in spirit so I could say what I liked.

'Listen Tony,' I said. 'I know your game. Blackmail is a criminal offence. If you don't leave Alice alone I'll report you to the law, and then what will happen?'

'Fuck all will happen,' he said, 'I don't know anyone called Alice, only somebody who's called Myrtle who owes me one thousand pounds.'

'Is she a cute little blonde who wears pearl-encrusted shoes?'

'Maybe and maybe not,' said Tony. 'All I know is she'll be sorry if she thinks she can mess me about.'

'Don't do anything drastic,' I said. 'You'll get your money soon. She owes me as well, and by the way I'm her ex-husband.'

'Pleased to meet you,' he said, shaking my hand, and at that point I woke up and wished I hadn't.

On Saturday I rang up Alice and the dame who answered asked if I had the right number. I said I had, but maybe not the right name and she hung up. It seemed once again I had been taken for a sucker but it didn't get me down. I returned to the bank and borrowed another thousand, since it appears that banks can't give their money away quick enough nowadays, then I had a good time drinking strong liquor and betting on the gee-gees. In the evening I called at my favourite pub and bought everyone a round, and when the money ran down I left my Post Office job and got another with Headley's Security Ltd so I could pay off my debt with the Post Office. It was now three thousand pounds, two of which I don't remember spending.

I never saw Alice again. I think she left town, not surprisingly if Tony the Teeth is after her. Tony's looking great these days. He has new teeth, white, gleaming and straight as a dye. I often wonder if my money paid for them.

Mayflies

It was summer when Alec and I took the kids up to the Rifle Range, coming close to it but still well back from the targets. No one had fired a rifle there for ages, certainly not us. We headed past it for the burn where Alec had made a dam the kids could splash about in. He and I drank the South African wine I brought in my shopping bag.

'Isn't it lovely here,' I murmured through an alcoholic stupor, staring up at the clear blue sky where large birds circled above us as if waiting for the kill.

'Not bad,' he said, 'not bad at all.'

'Right,' I said, aggrieved at the way he was always so laid back about everything and reluctant to praise anything I admired. I often thought I'd married the wrong man, but there had never been a right one, and I couldn't count Jackson, even if I wanted to. I tried not to think about Jackson because it made me feel too wide awake.

'Daddy, what are these flies called?' said my eldest daughter of ten. 'They're everywhere.'

'Mayflies,' I said before he could answer. 'They always come in May.'

'What for?' said the youngest one of five. 'Why do they always come in May?'

'I don't know,' I said. 'I don't know everything. Why does anything happen anyway?'

'You should try and answer them sensibly,' said Alec. 'It's only natural they want to know why things happen.'

'If they ever do happen,' I said in a snappy tone. I hate being

357

corrected. I took another swig of the South African and closed my eyes in an effort to recapture the drugged effect I'd enjoyed a minute ago, but now something whirred around inside my head and kept me awake.

I had met Jackson at a party. I wasn't sure what the party was for or if it even was a party, but I was inside a friend's house. I wondered what the catch was, then discovered it: a good-looking guy I'd never seen before who was offering me a drink. He was maybe more attractive than good-looking, with brown eyes, black hair and a wide smile.

'Do you come here often?' he asked in an arch manner and we both had to laugh at the banal question.

'Not on your nelly,' I said. We laughed again.

My friend Ella butted in at this point. In a suspicious manner she asked, 'Have you two been introduced?' then walked away before we could answer.

'I'm Tom Jackson, by the way,' he said to me. 'But just call me Jackson, everybody does.'

He explained he was only here for the weekend and staying with his sister. I thought I'd never get to know him at such short notice.

'Are you a friend of Ella's?' I asked him politely.

'Actually I've only known her since yesterday,' he said. 'She was carrying some heavy bags, and I –'

'It's just that I've never met you before,' I said, hoping this didn't sound like an accusation. Inwardly I was panicking. I could not think of anything to say. I finished my drink and put the empty glass on the table, longing to take a sandwich from a big plate in the centre, but too nervous to do so.

'You look worried,' he said. 'Shall I get you another drink?'

'No thanks,' I said. 'I'd better go home now. My husband will be wondering what's kept me.'

I could have cut my tongue out for admitting to having a husband but he said, 'I'll drive you home,' waving aside my protests.

We drove fast in the direction opposite to my home and I never said a word, as if struck dumb. We stopped near the edge of a wood, then made love as if there was no tomorrow. I'd never felt so happy and alive. Afterwards I asked if there was any wine left, having a hazy recollection of lifting a bottle from Ella's sideboard.

'Of course. Do you think I've guzzled it?' he asked laughing.

'How would I know what you'd do?' I said, equally light-hearted. We passed the bottle between us until it was finished. We made love again, then he took me home.

I was brought back to reality when Alec said, 'I wonder what happened to that chap Jackson?' in a manner suggesting he'd been practising the question.

'Oh him,' I said. 'I really don't know.'

One of the kids let out a yell, presumably because she'd been splashed. This allowed me to escape and see what was happening.

'It's her,' said my eldest daughter, pointing to her sister. 'Now I'm all wet.'

'I didn't mean it,' said her sister. 'Anyway she splashed me first.'

'Just behave yourselves,' I said wearily. Suddenly I wanted to go home and think about Jackson, who had never showed up after the first time, but sent a note saying goodbye and it was fun while it lasted.

'I thought I felt a spot of rain,' I said to Alec, staring up at the sky and searching for rain clouds. 'Maybe we should go home.'

'We don't want to go home,' the children chanted. 'We want to stay and catch mayflies.'

'What a cruel thing to do,' I said, but gave them an empty cup to keep them in. 'And put them back in the water before they die.' I added. I didn't know the life span of a mayfly, but it must be pitifully short.

There was peace for a while. I sank back against a small grassy hillock and Alec snored at my side. I thought how rotten things can be most of the time. I had fallen in love with the perfect man and he'd turned out to be a fraud. I was worse off than before, because I felt old and ugly and unsure of myself while he no doubt was having it off with some girl young enough to be his daughter. Bitter tears came to my eyes.

Alec interrupted my gloomy thoughts. 'As I was saying about Jackson, whatever happened to him?'

'I told you I don't know.' I became tense. 'Why do you keep asking?'

I became reckless enough to ask if he thought I was having an affair with him.

'Don't be childish,' said Alec. 'I only wondered because Ella was quizzing me about him, as if I was a friend of his.'

'She was?' I said, genuinely surprised. 'Did she know him that well?'

'You know what she's like. Man crazy.'

'I didn't know that. Bad-tempered maybe, but not man crazy.'

I looked at Alec. Was he trying to tell me something? Was he having an affair with Ella or even thinking about having one? I always thought he wasn't the type to have affairs, but who can tell with anyone? The girls came over and demanded sandwiches. I served them, glad to be doing something though my mind was elsewhere. I asked, 'Are you trying to tell me she is having an affair with Jackson?'

'I'm not trying to tell you anything,' said Alec, 'but if she is I'm not surprised.'

'I am.'

I mournfully imagined the bastard breaking it off to have an affair with an old dog like Ella, but maybe she has something I haven't, though I couldn't think what it was. Some kind of new tricks. And because Alec was shooting his mouth off didn't mean he knew anything for a fact. What did it matter? Jackson no longer loved me.

'Mummy come and look at all these hundreds of mayflies,' the kids were calling.

'In a minute,' I said, wishing they'd leave me alone. I gave Alec a nudge. 'Go and see what they want,' I said. 'Something to do with mayflies.'

'It's you they want,' he mumbled through his sleep.

I struggled over to the burn where it was dammed up and swarming with the beasts.

'Watch they don't bite you,' I said, then told them we were going home soon since I was going out later.

At that Alec sat up and said, 'You never told me you were going out!' and I said, 'Do I have to tell you everything?'

'Saying you're going out is not everything and anyway, who with?'

'I might be going out with Ella. We made arrangements.'

Then to my surprise he went over to the dam and kicked it down, splattering my daughters with mud. They must have thought he was being funny for they laughed, but I knew he was in a temper, the first I'd seen in a long time.

'Right,' I said, walking past them. 'I'm definitely going home now.'

At home I went straight to bed, pulling the covers over my face and sobbing uncontrollably. Then to make it worse I remembered the note Jackson had sent me, and remembered thinking I'd better destroy it before Alec got hold of it. I searched the drawer where I'd put it and it wasn't there. I searched other drawers without success. I tried to remember the words he used and could only recall something about it being fun while it lasted. So Alec must know everything. What could I say to him now?

Neighbours

Mrs Gutters couldn't find her spectacles. This often happened, and it was a nerve-wracking business concealing it from her husband, who would shake his head and tell her she was getting worse, and if it went on he would have to put her in a home. This was meant as a joke but she saw it more as a threat. She knew she was not as fit as she had been, and as for her memory, almost anything told to her more than five minutes previous was wiped clean from her head.

'What are you looking for now?' he asked in a deceptively kind voice.

'Nothing,' she said, guiltily dropping a cushion she had lifted from the settee.

'It wouldn't be your specs, would it?' he said, a smile forming at the corners of his mouth.

'As a matter of fact it is. I know they're in the house somewhere.'

'Did you know you've got them on?'

When she touched her cheek and found no spectacles there he burst out laughing. She said, 'That's not funny.'

'If you could see your face you'd think it was.'

She flounced out of the room and immediately found them in the toilet. She was relieved to put the blasted things on, though she would rather have lain down to relax. But he was bound to shout on her about something else and she'd have to get up to listen to him because she'd lost her hearing aid and didn't want him to know about it yet. She kept looking into corners for it but it was like looking for a needle in a haystack. She had never expected all the symptoms of old age to hit her so suddenly:

extreme tiredness, loss of balance, a pain in her back from one side to another, and her shopping feeling double the weight. Then losing the hearing aid made it hard to know what people were saying, and when her husband had heard what it cost he had nearly hit the roof. He cried, 'Why didn't you get it on the National Health?'

'I did, but their hearing aid didn't work for me.'

She had disliked the young man who attended her at the private clinic. He had a face full of pimples which he shoved close to hers while displaying a substantial amount of wax removed from her ear. This made her feel so sick she thought she might faint.

'Don't worry Ma,' he said, noticing her discomfort, 'I'm used to these sort of things from old people. Some of them are a disgusting lot.'

Then he stuck something inside her ear and told her to let him know if she could hear anything.

'What will I do to let you know?'

'Anything at all. Throw your knickers in the air if you like.'

Then he laughed aloud. His firm had charged four hundred pounds and she had taken out a bank loan to cover it.

'Have you not been out the messages yet?' said her husband when he saw her putting on a coat.

'Not yet. I've been busy.'

'Looking for your specs I bet.'

He was saying something else when a fresh anxiety struck her: where had she left her purse? Then she remembered she always left it under the mattress in case they were burgled through the night.

'First place they'll look,' he said.

'I keep it under my pillow.'

'Then they'll cut off your head,' he said and went into a fit of laughing that ended in a fit of coughing.

Mrs Gutters did not completely hate her husband or even intensely dislike him, but he was bad-tempered nowadays and ready to snarl at anything. He wouldn't accept that this was due to his age.

'It's you that makes me feel that way with your stupid carry-on, always forgetting things.'

Her neighbour over the fence told her, 'Better a grumpy old man than none at all. You've no idea how lonely I am, living on my own. I don't half miss my husband at night, when it gets dark.'

Mrs Gutters wondered if she was talking about having sex or about loneliness in general. Her neighbour always seemed to be having a good time, going to bingo nearly every night and to Majorca every year for a fortnight's holiday with her daughter. Mrs Gutter's only escape from monotony was watching the telly or reading a book.

'I wouldn't be seen dead with a book in my hand,' said her neighbour. 'What good does it do you? No wonder your outlook is always so dreary.'

Mrs Gutters didn't like this neighbour who either tried to make her feel guilty about still having a husband, or was full of pity for her dull life. But today the neighbour had news: a young family was moving into the flat next door, 'With four children, too!' she added significantly. Mrs Gutters said she supposed they had a right to a flat, especially with four children.

'Maybe so, but I heard they're not even married. God knows what this country is coming to. It's just like America.'

'It's the style nowadays,' Mrs Gutters observed mildly.

'Is that what you call it? Style? It's more like disgusting behaviour, if you ask me.'

This statement forced Mrs Gutters to retreat into her house and be met with a kitchenette full of smoke and an irate husband saying, 'You left the oven on and the dinner's burnt.'

'I thought I turned the oven off,' she said weakly. 'In fact I'm sure I did.'

'That only goes to show how far gone you are, when you say you're sure.'

Mrs Gutters was almost in tears. She could sense he was going to mention going into a home without joking, and looking at the mess she could hardly blame him.

'We're going to be burnt in our beds one of these days,' he said. 'That's what will happen.'

'Especially to him,' she thought, for he spent most of his day in bed, resting his bad leg.

Her husband said, 'You'll be the death of me yet,' as she went about the business of cleaning up.

She wondered if she was going demented. This was not the first time she'd set the kitchenette on fire by walking out and forgetting to turn off the cooker. It was becoming a habit. The way things were going, she would have signed herself into a home right now if she had the money to get a good one. It would be easier to throw herself under a train, but she hadn't got the guts. To think of something more cheerful she wondered about the new neighbours. How did a mother cope with four children? She couldn't imagine it, having none of her own. Her husband disliked children because they only caused trouble, he said, but she wouldn't mind keeping an eye on them if their mother had to go out. She would offer to do that when she knew the new neighbours a little better. It didn't pay to be too forward to begin with. These thoughts were interrupted by her husband asking, 'Did you get that crossword magazine I asked for?'

'It's on the sideboard.'

'Well, things are looking up!' he said, rising to his feet with what she thought surprising alacrity, for he was usually complaining about a sore back.

Being ready to enjoy his good mood while it lasted she cheerily shouted, 'Yes dear.'

Mrs Gutters was happy to see the children playing in their back garden, which converged on hers with a fence and a tree between. When they scrambled up the tree to sit on a branch she sometimes worried that they would fall off. One day the youngest boy who always climbed highest cried for help because he couldn't get down. She hurried out and stood below, stretching up hands to support his feet, but he pulled them back and stuck out his tongue at her. She almost ran back through her own house, knocked on the new neighbour's door and, when it opened, began explaining what had happened.

'You mean they're making rude gestures?' said the young woman. 'My kids are not like that.'

'I'm not complaining,' said Mrs Gutters. 'I was just trying to help in case they fell off. I can understand they were annoyed at me interfering, but I was –'

She broke off when the young woman said, 'My kids know what they're doing! They are not stupid. Besides, it's not your tree, it's on our side of the fence.'

'I'm not disputing that,' said Mrs Gutters, quietly. In the distance she could hear a man swearing, the father no doubt. It was a pity the children had to hear such language. No wonder they were rude.

'Well, I can't stand here all day,' said the young woman. 'His Lordship will be wanting his breakfast.'

As she walked off Mrs Gutters noticed a bruise on her leg and the old woman felt a stab of pity. With a man like that she was bound to be defensive regarding her children. Mrs Gutters could have wept for her, but interfering would put her in the wrong.

Then the unthinkable happened. Next day the youngest boy fell off the tree, landing on his back on her side of the fence. Mrs Gutters ran out as fast as she could, carried him into her house and laid him gently on the couch. She never knew where her strength came from because usually a bag of potatoes seemed too heavy. When she bathed the cut on the back of his head he opened his eyes and said he wanted his mammy.

'Yes darling, you'll get her as soon as I can.'

She'd almost forgotten about his mother, being so wound up about the boy. She went next door, told his mother what had happened and the young woman went hysterical.

'What do you mean he's lying on your couch? What have you done with him?'

'Nothing,' stammered Mrs Gutters. 'He fell off the tree and I took him into my house because I thought he might have hurt himself.'

She led the way into her house where the boy sat with eyes very wide open. When his mother asked grimly, 'What happened?' he said, 'She pushed me.'

'I didn't,' said Mrs Gutters, turning pale. 'But maybe he's afraid of getting into trouble for climbing the tree, which I guess is why he is making out I pushed him, like any child would.'

'You can guess what you like,' said the young woman, 'but I'm getting the police.'

Mr Gutters, who had been dozing in the bedroom, came out to ask what the commotion was about.

'Your wife's just after shoving my son off that tree so I'm sending for the police.'

'Is that right?' said the husband to his wife. 'Are you mad? I might have known you'd end up doing something like this.' He looked at the young woman and tapped the side of his head. 'She's been like that for years.'

'Maybe she should be put away,' said the young woman, softened by the old man's reasonable attitude. 'I'll let it go this time, but you should keep an eye on her.'

'I will,' said the husband. 'Don't you worry.'

Mrs Gutters put her hand to her mouth, a habit she had when confused. She opened her mouth to speak then closed it again. The boy stared up at her fearfully when she said, 'I meant you no harm.'

The boy sat up and buried his face in his mother's skirt.

'Don't tell Daddy,' he said.

'See what I mean?' said the young woman shrugging her shoulders. 'He'll be upset about this for ages. He's a very sensitive child.'

She took him by the hand and they walked back to their house.

Mrs Gutters was already lying in bed. She hardly ever left it after that. Neighbours who had been there for years often wondered if she had been put in a home, but didn't like to ask her husband. He was always surly and one never got a civil answer.

'She was a nice enough woman,' said one neighbour, 'but you could see she was getting past it.'

The Dysfunctional Family

According to a neighbour in the flat below we were a dysfunctional family, though I wasn't sure what dysfunctional meant. I sometimes thought it meant we didn't wash enough. My young brother usually had tide marks of dirt up his arms and sometimes I had them. Or perhaps it meant my mother went around all day without stockings.

'I don't like them,' she'd say, 'they make my legs itch.'

I didn't like the sight of her bare legs with ugly blue veins showing where she sat too close to the fire; otherwise they were fat and white, like lard. I told her to wear long skirts but she said bare legs gave her a feeling of freedom. Then Albie, my older brother, was doing time for holding up an old-age pensioner with a toy pistol. Was he dysfunctional? Or my Da? He got drunk every Friday so we had to walk the streets until he fell asleep in the big room chair, otherwise he became very violent. I was the in-between sister and didn't think I did much to make the family dysfunctional, but never definitely knew, not being sure of what the word meant. A social worker visited us when Albie was in jail. I and my younger brother were ushered out of the room and pressed our ears to the door to hear what was going on. My mother came out smiling.

'What do you think?' she said. 'Albie's being let out for good behaviour.'

Da said, 'How did they figure that out? He's never had a moment's good behaviour since the day he was born.'

'Just be nice to him,' said the social worker. 'Probably that's all he needs.'

Da gave her such a look of disgust that I had to laugh.

369

'None of that nonsense from you, miss!' said my mother, 'Albie has had a terrible time in jail, and don't forget he wasn't always a criminal.'

'Does that mean he's dysfunctional?' I asked. She glanced at me sharply.

'Where do you get all these fancy words? I hope you're not swearing.'

'It's a very good word,' said the social worker. 'I bet your daughter will turn out clever by the time she leaves school.'

'That'll be a surprise. She never goes there,' said my Da.

The social worker hesitated as if going to say something about that, then shook her head and said, 'Good luck with Albie. I'll be back to see how you're getting on.'

'Do that,' said my mother, and after the woman left added, 'Interfering bitch.'

It was rotten for me when Albie came home. He lay in bed all the time smoking or snorting dope. Worse still it was my bed, so I had to sleep on the big-room couch until one day he got up early, washed and shaved without saying a word, then left the house and was never seen again. At the evening meal mother started laying out a plate for him, though before that he had never come to the table. When the plate was emptied into the bin my Da said, 'A waste of good food,' though none of us would have eaten it anyway. I had never liked my older brother but became so bored that I wished he'd come home and liven things up. When he was here you never knew when the cops would come to the door because he'd done something. At school I had written a story about him for a composition, making him out to be wrongly accused of stealing money by a spiteful old-age pensioner. The teacher said this was not the kind of story she wanted and put a big cross through it. I was so angry I stayed off until the school board came to the door threatening Da with a fine. Between one thing and another we at last forgot all about Albie except my mother, who sometimes said he might have gone to Australia to live with a cousin of hers who had a sheep farm. Da said that was unlikely, since Australia would not let in a boy who could hardly write his own name.

Our house was in a long terrace built a century ago and owned by the council because the landlord had abandoned it. The roof leaked into the big room, as we called it, and the toilet needed fixing, but we couldn't get the council to do repairs as my mother hardly ever paid the rent. But I liked living here because the terrace had big green fields behind where cows roamed at leisure and we had tons of room to play. My young brother would lie flat on his stomach and pretend to shoot at the animals with a toy gun he got for Christmas, while I played at peever on the cobblestone side lane with my trashy friends who seldom washed or went to school either. But gradually they all left for the new council flats and we were the last to go. After Albie left, the big snag in our lives was our Da. When drunk on Fridays he became increasingly violent so we took to hiding in the old washhouses. This was fine in summer after we dragged in mattresses to sleep on but we dreaded the coming of winter when it would be too cold to do that. But by a great stroke of luck Da snuffed it from drinking too much. Mind you, I cried about that. His violent nature was worsened by alcohol but still, he was our Da and not too bad to us when sober. Then next thing was mother taking to her bed with a bottle of Graham's port that she kept under the pillow. She would say, 'Your poor Da, how I miss him,' and give me and my young brother a sip of it, after which he'd be sick on the carpet and I'd have to clean it up.

'Don't hit that child,' my mother would say when I made to slap him. 'He's an orphan and the more to be pitied.'

This infuriated me for I was the only one who missed Da so I was even more to be pitied. Then one day, as if by a miracle, my mother got out of bed and poured the Graham's port down the sink, tidied herself up and said she was going to look for a job because she was fed up with living on the dole and being the talk of the street.

'That's great,' I said. 'What time will you be home at? I'll have the dinner ready.'

'I don't know,' she said, and that's when I began to worry.

'You're not leaving us?' I said. 'I wouldn't know how to take care of things.'

'You'll learn,' she said and we never heard of her again. I might have cried my eyes out if I'd known she wasn't coming back. It dawned on us gradually, though it was a terrible thing to happen. Luckily she had left the Family Allowance Book on the mantelpiece which got us food for the week if I was careful. On Saturdays me and my young brother would go for a walk round the duck pond and throw them crusts we didn't want from our bread, especially the black crusts. I believe we were quite happy then, though it's hard to imagine that now.

But things never went smoothly for us. Not long after that a social worker came to the door, the one who'd come about Albie, and asked why I was not at school. I don't think she believed me when I said mother had gone off to find work and I had to look after my younger brother.

'When was that?' she said, maybe thinking I was talking about that morning. When I said two months her face took on an ominous look.

'Two months?' she shrieked. 'I've never heard of anything so disgraceful. Get your coats on. You're coming with me.'

We both kicked and struggled and I believe I would have got the better of her if a strange man hadn't come in, got hold of us and pushed us into a van as if we were dogs being taken to the dog pound. My younger brother was yelling for my mother but I said nothing. I knew when I was beat. I never saw him again. All my family had gone and I was left on my own.

They put me in a hostel for wayward children and after a few months of that I was fostered by a very nice middle-aged couple who gave me everything I wanted. The snag was, I had to be obedient, well mannered, and speak with a proper accent which was the hardest thing to do. Also I was allowed only to befriend nice well-mannered girls, which I did without too much bother, but I swore to myself I would run away at the first opportunity to find my young brother. Once I came past our old home, half of it still standing, and it struck me it would be near impossible to find him. He could be anywhere in the wide world, maybe even dead, so I held my peace and turned my head away but not before thinking I saw his face staring at me from a cracked window pane. I knew it was my imagination, and deep in my heart by then I didn't want to find him, because I had changed so much, and the chances were he wouldn't have changed at all.

A Note on the Author

Agnes Owens was born in 1926 and has worked in a factory, as a typist and as a school cleaner among other things. She has been married twice and has seven children. She lives in Balloch.

Agnes is the author of *Gentlemen of the West*, *Lean Tales* (with Alasdair Gray and James Kelman), *Like Birds in the Wilderness*, *A Working Mother*, *For the Love of Willie*, *Bad Attitudes*, *Jen's Party* and *People Like That*.